PHILIP JOSÉ FARMER'S
THE DUNGEON

BOOK THREE

THE VALLEY
OF THUNDER

CHARLES de LINT

for
Philip José Farmer

because
I can think of no better
opportunity than my work
on this project
to thank him for
all the years of reading pleasure
that he's given me

WELCOME TO
THE DUNGEON

It is a fog where time twists minds,
and voices call out from a swallowing darkness.

It is a jungle in which finned creatures dwell
and torment all that pass through its vines.

It is a maze whose tunnels trap the daring,
and whose creatures challenge the brave.

It is a chamber in which proportions are lost,
and fortitude is one's only weapon.

From the veldt of the dinosaurs to the gates of Tawn,
this is the quest of Clive Folliot, explorer and hero.

ABOUT THE AUTHORS

Charles de Lint's fiction has been described as "fantasy for people who don't normally read fantasy." On the official and definitive Charles de Lint website (at http://www.cyberus.ca/~cdl) the author continues: "I've taken to calling my writing 'mythic fiction,' because it's basically mainstream writing that incorporates elements of myth and folktale, rather than secondary world fantasy." A full-time writer, de Lint has published over forty books—including *Moonheart*, *Yarrow*, and *The Onion Girl*—and has others on the way.

ROBIN WAYNE BAILEY is the author of numerous novels and short stories, including *Swords Against the Shadowland*, which was named one of the seven best novels of 1998 by *Science Fiction Chronicle*. In addition to his own writing projects, recent ventures include editing *Through My Glasses Darkly*, a collection of stories by Frank M. Robinson, *Architects of Dreams: The SFWA Author Emeritus Anthology*, and writing the forthcoming ibooks, inc. fantasy trilogy *Dragonkin*.

ABOUT THE ARTIST

ROBERT GOULD made his name in the 1980s with a series of groundbreaking covers for Michael Moorcock's fiction, among others, culminating in a World Fantasy Award in 1989. He founded Cygnus Press, publishing high quality prints and portfolios by such artists as Alan Lee and Barry Windsor-Smith. In the late 1980s, he started Imaginosis, devoted to "bringing magical worlds to life" through books, media and merchandising. He is also Vice President of Education First, an innovative children's charity based in Los Angeles.

PHILIP JOSÉ FARMER'S
THE DUNGEON

VOLUME TWO
THE VALLEY OF THUNDER
CHARLES de LINT

✳

THE LAKE OF FIRE
ROBIN WAYNE BAILEY

Artwork by
ROBERT GOULD

ibooks
new york
www.ibooks.net

DISTRIBUTED BY SIMON & SCHUSTER, INC.

▪ Foreword ▪

Nightmares . . .

The "nightmare" comes from the Middle English *nihtmare*, meaning *night demon*. When I was young, I thought that the word derived from female horses that galloped into your sleep with eyes flashing fire, with unhorselike teeth sharp as a tiger's, with flaring nostrils spurting poisonous gases and hooves ringed with spikes. Their monstrous whinnying was echoed in my fear-filled and desperate cries for help just as I awoke.

But even the Land of Nod has its pleasant beings, and these were the enjoyable dreams. Though I always awoke during a nightmare, I sometimes also awoke after the "good" dreams. Whether they were enjoyable or terrifying, if they were easily analyzable, I would go back to sleep soon. If the nightmares were not transparently understandable—nightmares and dreams are nocturnal semaphores—I would spend some time trying to probe their origins before going back to sleep. Most of the time, I was too tired to spend much effort on them, but would remind myself to think about them during the daytime.

Dreams and nightmares are many, but I think I've had at least one that I could remember in each week of my life. Of course, I've forgotten many of these. But, counting the period when I was an infant, at least three thousand six hundred forty dreams, interspersed with nightmares, have spurted out of my unconscious. I only logged a few, and only the most striking can be summoned up from that wild data file called the memory.

Dreams/nightmares have inspired me to write stories. One, for instance, was a short tale titled, "Sail On! Sail On!" This is about Columbus's first (and last) voyage in an alternate universe. In this, Earth is both flat and the center of the universe. And Roger Bacon, the thirteenth-century English Franciscan and proponent of experimental science, has not been persecuted by the Church as he was in our universe. Instead, he founded the Baconian order of monks. Thus, when Columbus sets out on the Atlantic to look for a new route to the Orient, his flagship has a radio shack on its poop deck and inside it is a friar operating a simple spark-gap radio.

This story was derived from a dream in which I saw a galleon sent out by Prince Henry the Navigator, of Portugal. The galleon had a shack and a friar as described above. His messages were in Latin.

The transition from the dream-Prince Henry to the otherworld Columbus was done, of course, by my conscious mind.

But the dream that inspired the short story, "The Sliced-Crosswise-Only-On-Tuesday-World," seems to have no rational connection with the story I developed from it. In the dream, I wandered through a tropical jungle (many of my dreams take place there) and came out into a clearing. This was occupied by bamboo and grass huts, in the doorways of which stood natives. Their skins were chalk white, and they had large dark rings of fatigue around their eyes. They were motionless, their faces were rigid, and their eyes seemed dead.

I've never figured out just how I went from that dream to the concept of the short story and the resulting *Dayworld* trilogy. But that came to me the next day as I was going over the dream.

In any event, I have, like some people, had serial dreams, or perhaps I should say a dream series. The adventures started in the first dream were continued in another dream, and then on to three to five dreams. There was no pattern in the time gap between the dreams. Sometimes, the sequel occurred the next day;

sometimes, a week or even two weeks later. Unfortunately, I never completed any of the series. I was like the kid who watched Saturday afternoon serials in the movie theaters of my younger days and then was prevented from seeing the final chapter. I was frustrated.

Two stick in my memory, and I may use them as the bases for stories someday. One serial dream was about a band of Vikings who had invaded the underground kingdom of dwarfs or trolls to grab the gold of these subterranean beings. (The dwarf king had some resemblance to the Gnome King of Oz. In Baum's books, not in the second Oz movie.) The Vikings had to fight their way in and out and run a gauntlet of ingenious traps.

The other dream was really fever-inspired. I was in high school when I got one of those diseases so common in the 1930s. I don't remember what it was. But I was lying in bed and hot with fever, half out of my head. The Shadow, a.k.a. Lamont Cranston, was somehow in another world and was being pursued through a jungle by a large band of beings who seemed only partly human. He was not armed with his usual pair of .45 automatic handguns. He had only a bow and a quiverful of arrows. Finally, after shooting many of his hunters, he took refuge in a cave halfway up the face of a mountain. The enemy toiled up the steep slope. Thwang! Thwang! At least six of them were struck. Six enemies of The Shadow, a vicar of The Good, bit the hard rock and tumbled down into the poisonous green jungle below.

The above took place as a serial within three days. I don't remember how many episodes there were, but there must have been at least six or seven. Their rapidity in occurring was doubtless inspired by the fever.

The above leads into the *Dungeon* series and volume III, the book at hand, *The Valley of Thunder*. This title is evocative of the spirit of my writings. As I said in previous forewords, this series springs from the spirit, or one of the spirits, of my fiction. It does not derive from, nor is it a spinoff of, any specific story of mine. It embodies the Geist, the Psyche, incorporated in my fantasy and science fiction adventure tales.

Thus, it is a nightmare. And, at times, it certainly seems fever-inspired.

But, unlike the nightmares I've had, its mysteries, and there are many, will eventually be explained. Also unlike my terrifying dreams, it will have a satisfactory and definitive conclusion. No cliff-hangings in the sixth and final book of the *Dungeon* series. Richard Lupoff, who wrote volume I, will write volume VI. He will come up with the answers and rousing climax. I am sure of that, though I have no more idea than you of how the series will end.

At the moment our hero, Clive Folliot, and his grab-bag companions are fighting in another universe for survival. They hope they will be able to solve the mystery of the forces behind this sinister world. They are half-way through their ordeal (though they do not know this), and it seems that things cannot get worse. But they do.

In this respect, the Dungeon world resembles our Earth. We Terrestrials really do not know why we were born on this planet, or who made it, or toward what goal, if any, we are struggling. We have many theories (religions and philosophies) to explain the whys and hows and toward-whats. None is truly illuminating or truly satisfying. Not, at least, to many people. It's all opinion, without any facts to back up the opinions. Even those who reject the religions and philosophies do so on the basis of opinion, which derives from the personal set of mind and the conditioning of the individual.

Opinions are just so many firecrackers. They make a light and a noise in the darkness and then are gone. However, every day on Earth is the Fourth of July of opinions, and the unceasing supply of firecrackers makes a lot of light and noise on this world.

Firecrackers are real. Opinions are real. All thoughts are real, however momentary they may be. And fiction is as real as Reality. Fiction is part of Reality.

No one can successfully deny that fiction is just as real and as event-causing as politics and religion and hem-orrhoids and headaches and stubbing your toe and slamming your car into a telephone pole. Fiction exists, and the thoughts and emotional reactions you have while reading it have an effect on you. It varies according to the story and the individual reader's reactions. Some of us are powerfully affected by a certain story, and it sticks like glue in us.

The effects are the results of electrochemical impulses, which are reactions to the fiction we read. These impulses are real because they do exist, and they bring into existence permanent things such as books, movies, buildings, paintings, music—all artifacts, in fact, and institutions and mores and changes in mores.

The thoughts you have while reading this series may result in something as real and hard as an Easter Island stone face.

The thoughts and speech of Bronze Age and Early Iron Age people were evanescent. But they made weapons and tools and buildings because of these thoughts and conversations. Some of these survive. They also, in Greece, resulted in the eventual writing down of Homer's *The Iliad* and *The Odyssey*. These have had a great impact. I know they did on me. They have influenced my writing more than my reading of pulp-magazine stories, though I am not disparaging *their* effect. As a result, my being influenced by Homer has influenced others, and they write stories which, you might say, come thousandth-hand from Homer. Who got his stuff through centuries of sieving from many others.

Then there is the Bible. I read much of that when I was a child and a juvenile, and still read it now and then. That had a powerful impact on me, yet it originally was born from a series of electrochemical impulses in the minds of a series of men of the Bronze and Iron Ages. Finally, it became "real," a book. It, though partly fiction, has been tremendously influential for both good and evil. I am a student of history and biography, and deduce from these that the Bible has been, on the whole, used more for evil than good. But then, everything has its potentiality for evil or for good. Almost everything, I hasten to say.

Dante's *Inferno* derives from the Bible and his own hatred of certain people. It has not, I believe, influenced anybody in the religious sense, but it certainly has made concrete the vision of Hell. This vision has stirred electrochemical impulses in the brains of many, chiefly preachers and writers. Many, many sermons and much written fiction have resulted from this. In several senses, the *Dungeon* series owes some of its geography and population to Dante.

In a previous foreword, I likened the *Dungeon* world to Hell. The main difference between these two worlds, however, is very significant. In Dante, Hell was the be-all and end-all for its citizens. They will suffer forever, and their characters will not change for better or worse. In the *Dungeon* world, despite all its horrors, optimism flames brightly. Our hero and his colleagues will suffer, but their characters may change for the better.

In this respect (and, of course, in many others), the *Dungeon* world resembles my Riverworld. And our own Earth.

—Philip José Farmer

▪ One ▪

The world was a flare of azure, riddled with sparks.

When Major Clive Folliot's party entered the gateway, the ground fell away underfoot as though it had never existed. A rushing sound filled their ears. Nausea struck, brought on by vertigo, but there was no sensation of falling. They simply floated in a limbo of blue, all the world a cloudless sky, so bright to view it hurt the eye. Every blink of an eyelid set up a new scattering of sparks and woke tears that burned the retina, momentarily clearing the vision until the blue glare struck again.

Have we died? Clive wondered.

His limbs flailed helplessly through the blue that felt too dense to be air. Breathing was a labored process. His stomach was in his throat. Shafts of neuralgic pain lanced through his head with each blink of his eyes.

Have we come so far only to die?

For this void seemed very much like death. Were Chambers and Darwin and those other atheist evolutionists correct? We came from nothing, climbing some damned evolutionary ladder, and we return to nothing. No God. No Heaven. Though perhaps this was Hell. Not fire and brimstone, nor the Purgatory that they had so recently quit on the last level, but a limbo of blue so painful it would drive a man insane.

Clive's hands clenched into fists, nails biting into his palms, knuckles whitening with the pressure.

Damn you, Neville. From the moment we shared the world I've been cursed to walk in your shadow. Must I now die in that same shadow?

The other members of his party were merely dark blots in his vision. He cried out to them, but the thick air wouldn't carry his voice. It rasped its way down his throat, leeching all moisture from its drying membrane. His chest ached, lungs hyperventilating as they tried to draw in sufficient oxygen, but succeeding only in creating an abnormal loss of carbon dioxide in his blood.

His vision began to cloud—not from the pain of the azure glare, but through lack of that simple substance upon which all men depend to survive.

Air.

Like a dark cloud, unconsciousness came roiling across the horizons of his pain. The glare was almost gone—pinprick sparks sprayed at the edge of the darkness.

So this is death, Clive thought.

It was not so bad. He could almost welcome the comfort it offered from the pain. It would be so easy to simply let go, to put away the responsibilities he had taken upon himself, to leave off the struggle, to let others beat their heads against the endless walls of the bloody Dungeon while he simply let go. . . .

But that wasn't his way.

Though he had to work harder than his twin at whatever he undertook, he wasn't one to quit, no matter what the odds against him were.

Not even if you were offered your heart's desire?

Clive frowned at the unfamiliar voice that interrupted his reverie—

And realized that the blue was gone.

He stood in a place devoid of color or light. He could breathe once more. There was a firm surface underfoot. A light breeze touched his cheek, tickling the hairs of his mustache. A faint scent of cloves was in the air. On his tongue lay the sharp bite of anise.

"Who spoke?" he asked.

He turned slowly, careful of his footing. Under his boots the floor was as smooth as polished marble.

The voice, he realized, had not spoken aloud. Rather, it had sounded only in his mind—a telepathic communication such as Shriek utilized. But it hadn't been Shriek's voice.

There came a whispering sound—like that of a curtain being lowered.

"Who's there?" he cried. "Where are you?"

To his right, he saw a lightening of the darkness. Where all around him was the black of a sealed tomb, there the air grayed with promise. The scent of cloves faded. The sharp taste remained in his mouth, though it too was lessening with each passing moment.

He took a step toward the grayness. Another.

Like the last gateway, the air was thick here, but he could navigate through it. It was like walking through a thin gauze, the darkness clinging to his face like cobwebs, but he made his way through it, brushing at the dark with his hands until he came at last to the gray area.

At first, he could see nothing through its wash of fog. He put a hand out and touched a membranous wall that gave outward as he pressed against it. The fog began to clear, and Clive's eyes widened with astonishment.

He was looking into a very familiar apartment. Briefly, the voice he had heard earlier echoed again in his mind.

Your heart's desire.

The room he looked into was lit by an oil lamp. Standing at the window, overlooking Plantagenet Court, was a woman. The lamplight cast her in shadow, but not so much that Clive couldn't recognize the slope of her shoulders, the coils of her hair, the neat trimness of her figure.

Your heart's desire.

By all that was holy. Somehow, he had been given a window into the London quarters of his lover, Annabella Leighton. The leagues separating London from Africa, or from wherever this damnable Dungeon lay, had been set aside to gain him this momentary view.

He called out to her, but she made no response.

He pushed harder at the membrane that held him back. It stretched, but would not give way.

He cursed the Dungeonmasters for giving him this much—but no more—and pushed harder.

One moment his hand was filmed by the pressure of the invisible barrier holding him back, then it gave through. He stepped eagerly forward, pushing his face and chest against its clinging surface, tugging at it with his other hand. Slowly—so slowly—the wall gave way.

And he was inside.

He stood, disbelieving, in Annabella's room. Looking back, he could see no sign of where he'd entered. When he studied the room, it appeared no different from how it had been the night he'd taken his leave of her—too many months ago. It was as though all his time in the Dungeon had never been.

Lord help him, had it all been a dream?

Or was he being given a second chance? If he didn't take ship this time—if he remained in London instead and, poor though they'd be, married Annabella—could he undo all the pains he had left behind him when he'd taken the *Empress* and sailed away?

Clive frowned. But if his brother was still missing, his return to London did not negate his responsibilities. He would simply have to leave again. . . .

But how could he? Knowing what he knew now, how could he leave Annabella a second time? Surely it would be a worse crime to desert her when he *knew* what his leaving would mean to her?

And then there were his companions. Had they been left behind to carry on by themselves, or had each of them been given this opportunity as well?

He regarded Annabella. He could see no trace of her pregnancy from this perspective. Perhaps she didn't show yet. Perhaps she was still unaware that she carried their child. . . .

She turned then, that familiar smile on her features. But she wore no look of surprise at his sudden appearance, Clive noted. It was as though he'd never left.

She shook her head, a teasing look in her eyes.

"Are you ready to rise now, sleepyhead?" she asked. "I . . ."

The sound of her voice tore at his heart. Her features, her smile, the cornflower blue of her eyes. . . .

He reached toward her, but she shook her head.

"Not again, my love. If you don't dress soon, we'll be late for the celebration—and that would never do. George would never forgive you."

Celebration? Clive thought. What in God's name was going on? How could she be so calm? She truly acted as though he'd never left—as though all he'd been through had been no more than some nightmarish dream.

He looked more closely at her, finally registering how she was clad. She wore an evening dress, the bodice cut low, the skirt wide. Her shoulders were powdered, her hair done up in coils that glistened in the light cast by the oil lamp on the dresser.

A celebration.

"But afterward," Annabella went on, "when we return, we will salute your new commission privately until neither of us has the strength left to move."

The promise in her eyes made Clive ache to hold her. But he concentrated on the odd things that she said. His new commission. A celebration.

Again, that echo came to him.

Your heart's desire.

Wasn't this what he had always wanted? To be able to take her for his wife, the two of them making their own life together, and to the devil with his father and twin, to the devil with her teaching?

He looked down at himself. He stood naked by her bed. Beside him, the bedclothes were rumpled.

You have just experienced a long and troubling dream, he told himself. There can be no other explanation.

He had never shipped on the *Empress* in search of Neville, never been trapped in that hellish Dungeon. . . . Of course. It made sense. The whole experience had held a nightmarish quality.

But it had seemed so real. And there was still . . .

He looked at Annabella. "My brother . . ." he began.

She laughed. "No need to worry about him—he hasn't been invited."

Clive sat down upon the bed and rubbed at his face. Immediately concerned, Annabella hurried to his side. She knelt by the bed where he sat. The hoops of her skirt made it difficult for her to embrace him, so she took his hands in hers.

"Clive—what is it?"

"I . . . I have had the strangest experience," he said slowly. "I . . ." He looked up to meet her steady gaze. "I can't remember anything about this celebration or a new commission. I dreamed I went to Africa in search of Neville and was trapped in an enormous mazelike Dungeon."

"Should we call the doctor?" Annabella asked.

Her worry was plain.

Clive shook his head. "No. Physically, I am well. I'm just . . . confused."

"We can cancel the party at the club. I'll send word to George that we won't be able to attend."

Clive gave her a rueful look. "You say he's organized the party for me?"

Annabella nodded.

"Then it's as you said a moment ago: He'd never forgive me if we didn't go."

The longer he spoke to her, the more easily he found himself slipping back into his old life. The Dungeon grew more and more like a bad dream.

"You said my brother wasn't invited," Clive said. "But, he's safe?"

Annabella blinked. "Of course he's safe! It's been over a month since his return and, by all your accounts, he's recovered enough to have returned to his old methods of dealing with you."

Anger flashed in her eyes as she spoke of his twin.

"And I never sailed to Africa?"

Her anger faded, replaced with laughter. "Oh, Clive! You're just teasing me—aren't you?"

Clive looked around the room, then settled his gaze on her. He squeezed her hands.

If the Dungeon had been a dream, then it was over and done with. He could put it from his mind. But if this was the dream, he'd be damned if he'd let it go.

"You've caught me out," he told her.

Shaking her head, Annabella rose gracefully to her feet. With quick, deft movements, she adjusted the fall of her skirt.

"Up!" she told him. "Your uniform's pressed and hanging on the door of the closet for you. I'll give you until the count of ten to be ready to leave. If you're not done by then, I'll find another escort." She gave him a broad wink. "One . . . two . . . three . . ."

Clive rose quickly from the bed. The uniform, the scarlet tunic and dark trousers of the Imperial Horse Guard—hung where Annabella had said it was, but it wasn't a major's. Rather, it was that of a leftenant-colonel.

He rose from the bed and crossed to where the uniform hung to finger the cloth of the tunic.

Lord help him. He no longer knew what was real and what wasn't.

"Seven . . . eight . . ." Annabella counted.

Shaking his head, Clive hurriedly began to dress.

▪ Two ▪

They took a cab from Plantagenet Court to du Maurier's club—a somewhat bohemian establishment, as George readily admitted, frequented by artists and writers, but at least it permitted ladies in its bar.

A London fog made the heavy traffic move even slower than was usual for this time of the evening, but Clive didn't mind it at all. He soaked in his surroundings, relishing everything he laid his gaze upon—the confusion of cabs and foot traffic, the vendors and hawkers still peddling their wares to the theater and restaurant crowds. From the squalor of the slums to the homes of the wealthy, Clive saw all the familiar sights as though through new eyes.

He had never thought to see London again, yet here he rode through her gaslit streets, Annabella at his side, a celebration in the offing.

Lord, could a man ask for more?

When they finally reached the club, Clive disembarked and handed his companion down to the cobblestoned street. He paid the cab and, offering Annabella his arm, moved toward the entranceway, which was guarded by a uniformed footman. Before they could reach the steps, however, a tattered beggar shuffled quickly from the shadows, cap in hand.

"Here!" the footman cried. "Off with you!"

"Please, gov'nor," the beggar said, keeping his attention on Clive. "Won't you help me, good sir?"

Annabella shrank against Clive's side. Ordinarily, Clive would have sent the man off as quickly as the footman was attempting to, but something in the beggar's features caught his attention. There was a certain familiarity hidden behind the grime that streaked the man's face.

"A minute," Clive said.

He left Annabella standing with the footman and stepped closer to the beggar, peering more closely at him.

"Do I know you?" he asked.

The beggar shook his head. "I'm nobody, gov'nor. Nobody a fine gent such as your own self'd be knowing."

Normally, this was true. Clive had never been one given to holding conversation with beggars and the like. But his time in the Dungeon had taught him that looks could very easily be deceiving. And there was that nagging sense of familiarity. . . .

"Just a shilling—if you can spare it, gov'nor," the beggar went on.

He held out a hand even dirtier than his face. A rank smell rose from the man—a combination of unwashed body and stale beer.

"What's your name, man?" Clive asked.

The fog was turning to a light drizzle as he spoke to the wretch.

"Clive!" Annabella called.

Clive nodded in her direction, but didn't turn.

"Your name?" he repeated.

The beggar took a step back, a frightened look crossing his features.

"I didn't mean you no harm, gov'nor," he said. "Don't be calling the law on poor Tom."

With that he turned and bolted. Clive took a step after him, then paused and let him go.

Tom. Those features. . . .

"Clive," Annabella said again.

She left the stairs and joined him on the street. When Clive turned his attention to her, he knew from the look in her eyes that she was worried about him again. He shrugged and gave her a quick smile.

"I had the oddest feeling that I knew that man," he said. "Absolute nonsense, of course."

Taking Annabella's arm, he led her up the stairs and past the footman, who kept his features carefully neutral. The footman opened the door for them and they stepped into the club.

"You're beginning to worry me," Annabella told him, once they were inside. "First, you play at losing your memory, and now, you seem set upon gallivanting about the streets with beggars."

"I thought it might be someone from the old regiment," Clive told her, "fallen upon hard times. All men aren't so fortunate as I am."

Obviously referring to her, that earned him a smile.

In the foyer a servant took her wrap and Clive's military cap, then, they went in to where George waited for them. A huge fire burned in the hearth, taking away the damp chill of the night air and fog outside. George rose from his chair with a welcoming smile and outstretched hand.

"I was about to give up on you," he said. "Our dinner reservations are for eight, but we still have time for a drink, if you like."

Clive glanced at Annabella. When she nodded, he ordered two glasses of sherry from the waiter, who stood nearby.

"George?" Clive asked.

His friend lifted his own glass, still half full, and shook his head.

"Just the two glasses, then," Clive told the waiter.

"So," George said once Clive and Annabella were seated, "have you set the date yet?"

Date?

Luckily, Clive thought the question rather than blurting it aloud as he'd been about to, for when he saw Annabella blush and lower her eyes, he realized immediately what George was referring to—their wedding. The real question now was, *had* they set a date? Annabella would think him a complete boor for not remembering, if they had.

He glanced at her, but found no answer in her features. He cleared his throat.

"Ah . . ." he began, and was rescued by the arrival of the waiter with their sherries.

"To your prosperity!" George cried, lifting his glass. "May you always be rich in health and know joy in each other's company." Before Clive and Annabella could clink their glasses against his, George added with a wink, "And a promotion certainly doesn't hurt, either, now does it?"

"To us," Clive said, touching his glass against the others, his gaze resting on Annabella.

"To us," Annabella said. She smiled warmly at him, then turned her gaze to George. "And to the best friend a young couple could have—bohemian or not!"

Laughing, they toasted each other and drank.

And then a cold thought knifed through Clive's mind.

The beggar.

Tom.

He had it now. The man bore an uncanny resemblance to the Portuguese sailor Tomàs, whom he had left behind in the Dungeon with his other companions. As a beggar here in London, he'd had a cockney accent, true enough, but the resemblance was so profound that Clive couldn't believe it mere coincidence.

Except the Dungeon was just a dream.

He was free from it now. He had awakened from the chains of sleep with the blessed relief of knowing it had all been but a dream—a nightmare, to put it mildly, but a fantasy nonetheless.

The Dungeon wasn't real. It was that simple.

But he remembered that voice again.

Your heart's desire.

If the whole thing had been but a delusion, then why did it *seem* so real?

"Clive?"

He blinked to find George and Annabella regarding him worriedly. He stood up from his chair.

"A . . . a momentary . . . dizziness," he said. "I need some air."

Before either could protest, he was walking away, back to the entrance. When he stepped outside, the footman turned to him. The man's smile took on a sudden wariness.

Clive had been about to ask after the beggar, but seeing that look on the footman's face, he realized just how foolish he was being.

"Did you . . . ah . . . happen to see a glove?" Clive asked.

The footman shook his head. "No, sir. Perhaps you left it in your cab?"

"My cab?" Clive repeated.

Get a grip on yourself, man, he told himself.

"Of course," he said with a quick smile that he was sure seemed as artificial as it felt. "The cab. Thank you."

He reentered the club before the footman had a chance to speak further. In the foyer, he smiled at the servant who came to collect his hat. The man appeared confused when he realized that he had already done so moments before.

"I just took a breath of air," Clive told him. "Lovely night."

To be sure, he thought. Fog and drizzle. Well, dammit, after months in the Dungeon—dream or not—it was a *wonderful* night.

He fled the servant's confusion to rejoin his companions. George arose immediately upon spotting him and met him halfway across the room. He took Clive by the arm and peered into his face, plainly concerned.

"Clive, are you ill?"

Clive shook his head.

"Only Annabella's been telling me you've seemed out of sorts ever since you woke from a nap earlier this evening."

"Nerves," Clive assured him. "It's not often a man gets promoted and engaged, all at once, as it were."

The reasonableness of the explanation was readily accepted. George studied him a moment longer, then gave his arm a squeeze and led him back to the hearth where Annabella waited.

"All's well, my love," Clive told her.

He was careful to control his hand as he took up his

sherry. It felt as though it would shake free from his wrist.

"So," he said as he set his glass down again, "who all have you invited to the restaurant, George? Your theater crowd, no doubt?"

George laughed. "No, no. In honor of the occasion, we'll be a respectable company, barring myself, of course."

Clive gave an appropriate smile, but he couldn't shake the sensation that he was going mad. Which was real—this, or that bloody Dungeon?

With a great effort, he put the question from his mind and threw himself into the festive mood that the evening required. Yet, he couldn't help but feel as though he were not so much present and partaking of events as watching them unfold through a dark glass. He saw again the beggar's features, remembered Tomàs and his other companions—Shriek, Finnbogg, Smythe, and his many-times great-granddaughter, Annabelle. . . .

No, he told himself. Let it go.

He was successful for the rest of that evening as they left the club and went to dinner.

A few of his fellow officers were at the restaurant, along with their ladies, as well as some of George's friends that Clive and Annabella had grown to know over time. Congratulations—both for his promotion and their upcoming nuptials—raised many a toast. There was good food and better conversation, fine drink and dancing afterward. But throughout it all, a nagging concern remained in the back of Clive's mind, discoloring all that he experienced.

With all he had already experienced—or thought he'd experienced—in the Dungeon, what was to say that this wasn't simply one more move in the inexplicable game played by the Dungeonmasters? How could he know? If this was a lie. . . .

Your heart's desire.

If this was a lie and he was given a choice—return to the struggle, or live the lie—what would he choose? *How* could he choose?

▪ Three ▪

It was late when they finally returned to Annabella's rooms. The drizzle had continued throughout the evening, fog thickening in the alleyways, making their return in the cab a damp and miserable ride—or it would have, if they had not had each other's company. Annabella's cheeks glowed from both the evening's dancing and the wine, and Clive realized yet again how empty the world would be without her.

As it had been in the Dungeon.

His dream.

Her rooms were cozy once they had the oil lamps lit and a fire burning in the grate to take away the chill. While Annabella took a bath, Clive stood at the window and stared down at the wet streets. His mind was a turmoil of confusion. He should have enjoyed himself this evening, and on most levels, he had. Everything had been perfect—the company and setting both—yet he had been unable to shake a sense of foreboding throughout it all.

Glancing at the windowsill, he noticed the tiny length of a fennel seed lying on the wood, its pale green and white stripes appearing bright against the dark mahogany. He licked a finger and touched it to the seed, snaring it with his saliva, then brought it up to his eye.

Like the errant memory he'd tried to snag when approached by the beggar outside George's club, the seed reminded him of something . . .

Absently, he put it in his mouth and bit down. The sharp tang of anise filled his mouth. A scent of cloves touched the air. When he looked out the window, the fog thickened suddenly and approached the glass panes, making it impossible to see the street.

And he remembered once again.

The gateway. Falling through the blue. That same taste; that same scent. How he'd put into words one of the basic tenets of his life: that he wouldn't quit a struggle, no matter what odds stood against him. He hadn't spoken aloud, but then, that voice had replied all the same.

Not even if you were offered your heart's desire?

God help him—was this madness?

He had listened to George and his friends discuss odd philosophies before, one of which was that this world which they all inhabited was but a dream. When the dreamer woke, all would vanish. Foolishness, of course—mere intellectual diversion. For none of them—neither those arguing for or against the conceit—truly believed it.

But what if this world *was* a dream?

Your heart's desire.

Impossible. And yet, had his time in the Dungeon seemed less real?

He pressed his forehead against the glass, closing his eyes. The glass was cool against his skin. Soothing. The scent of cloves was fading, the sharp taste on his tongue almost a memory now.

"Clive?"

He opened his eyes at the sound of Annabella's voice. Outside he could see the street once more, the gaslights reflected in wet pools on the cobblestones, the light fog haloing each lamp post.

"Clive?"

He turned to see Annabella standing near the bath, her cheeks still ruddy and glowing. She was wrapped in a towel, and wore nothing else except for her hair combs.

"Clive, tell me," she said. "What's wrong?"

He ached to look at her, hated to lie.

"Nothing."

"If it's something I've done . . ."

He shook his head emphatically. "Never."

She came to him and laid her hands on his shoulders. Looking down at her, Clive could only wonder at how the most splendid creature on God's own Earth could bear such love for him. What had he ever done to deserve her?

"You can't hide it from me," Annabella said. "I know you're troubled."

Clive led her to the bed and sat her down.

"I'm troubled by dreams," he wanted to say as he sat down beside her. "Dreams so real that they leave me questioning which is more real—this life, or the dreams."

Or, "I fear I'm going mad."

But instead of speaking, he took her in his arms and kissed her. Gently, gently. They lay back on the bed, and for a time, Clive could forget his fears and worries.

Their lovemaking was slow and languorous. It swallowed Clive's sense of desperation, balmed his troubled heart. Afterward, while Annabella slept, he leaned up on an elbow and looked at her, marveling at the slight swell of her belly. He laid his hand upon it, caressing the smooth skin, imagining he could feel their daughter move below the skin, for all that it was too early for such movement.

Did Annabella know? he wondered. Or was it still too soon for her?

Then the realization came to him that the only reason he thought her pregnant was because he'd learned of it from the lips of his descendant.

In the impossible Dungeon.

Madness.

"I would never knowingly desert you," he told his sleeping lover. "I would always return. If I didn't, it would not be through want of any effort on my part."

Annabella stirred as he spoke, but didn't wake. Sighing, Clive rose from the bed.

The wet night beyond the room called to him. He stood naked at the window for a long time, staring out at the darkness, then dressed. He closed the door to Annabella's rooms softly behind him and went out into the night streets, searching. But for what, he couldn't have told.

Clive wore a cloak against the damp chill that rode the night air, but it crept over him all the same. His boot steps echoed wetly on the cobblestones. He'd forgone a hat, so his hair was plastered, lank and dripping, against his scalp. But he paid no attention to physical discomfort. His mind was far away—sifting through memories of an impossible place that it seemed, by now, he knew better than he knew London. That he had many months' worth of these memories only bewildered him the more.

At first he had the streets to himself, but the farther he walked from Plantagenet Court, the rougher his surroundings became. Now there were doxies in the alleyways—weary women, bullied on by their fancy men to earn a last few shillings before they called it a night. Disreputable men stood leaning against the sides of buildings, watching him pass, their gazes measuring him. Beggars accosted him. Street urchins tugged at his cloak.

He ignored them all.

He ignored them with a finality that made even the cutpurses consider other options and let him pass by unmolested.

It wasn't so much the set of his shoulders, nor the military mark to his step. It was his eyes, which regarded them without seeing them. Not because they were below his station, and therefore unworthy of his attention, but because he seemed to them to walk in another world altogether, a world where even they would not tread.

Physically, he walked the London streets, but his mind walked in Bedlam.

Though the fine cut of his clothes tempted them sorely, even the criminals of Seven Dials, Spitalfields, and the like were wary of dealing with a madman. There were easier ways to turn a shilling. So they let him pass unmolested, watching him from the peekholes of their labyrinthine maze of secret apertures, manholes, tunnels, concealed passages, and hidden exits. A tall, well-dressed though hatless gent, wandering their dangerous streets without care, muttering to himself, his own gaze focused on that other world that only Bedlamites could see.

But one inmate of the criminal slums wasn't leery of him. She staggered from an alleyway to accost him under the dim light of a gas lamp. Her hair was wet and tangled, her cheap dress clinging to her body like a second skin. She gazed at him blearily, putting a hand against his chest to stop him from running her down. The impact of his weight against her arm made her weave dizzily before she caught her balance.

It took Clive a moment to escape the trap of his reveries and focus upon her. When he looked into her grimed features, he wasn't surprised at their familiarity.

She could have been Annabella.

Annabella, if fate had treated her worse than it had, reducing her to eking out a wretched existence on the streets, as this poor moll must. Her unsteadiness was due to either alcohol or opium. Plying her trade in the alleyways gave her her dirty skin and clothes.

She could have been Annabella.

Or their descendant, Annabelle.

Except Annabelle was only a part of the delusion he carried about inside himself. She wasn't real, any more than the Dungeon was.

"You look like a sporting gent," the prostitute said, slurring her words. "What say we have a bit of fun?"

She began to hike up her skirt as she spoke, exposing thighs as grimed as her hands and face.

"Get away from me," Clive told her.

But there was no force behind his words. It wasn't that he desired her. It was only the resemblance—that terribly uncanny resemblance.

"Now, don't be talking like that, sport," she said. "You don't want to send Annie back to her bully-boy empty-handed, now, do you? Wouldn't be right."

She let the hem of her skirt fall, but wet as it was, it still rode high on her thigh. Her hand lifted unsteadily to the neckline of her dress, which she pulled away from her shoulder to reveal a large, discolored bruise.

"Jack gets mean, y'see, sport. Hurts me, he does, when I don't bring home enough."

"I don't want—"

"You all want it," the woman said, cutting him off. "Or why'd you be walking these streets?"

She caught his arm and began to pull him toward the mouth of the alleyway. Clive shook her hand free.

"You say your name's Annie?" he asked.

"Didn't I say it was?"

"Annabella Leighton, I suppose?"

She blinked, momentarily confused, then grinned. "I'll be anybody you like, sport."

Again she reached for him.

"Get away," Clive said.

This time he put a hand to her shoulder and gave her a push. She staggered back, losing her balance until she was brought up against a wall. The woman's eyes went hard.

"You don't want to be treating me rough, sport."

"You disgust me," Clive told her.

Lord help him. He knew what was what now.

The Dungeon had been no dream.

Your heart's desire.

This was the dream. As sweet as he wished, with Annabella and a promotion, or as foul as seeing his lover depicted as some wretched bawdy woman, stooped to making her living as a prostitute.

Had he stayed in Annabella's rooms, would the dream have maintained itself? Was it by faring abroad, by questioning its validity, that it was unraveling?

What matter when it was all a lie? Better the torment of the Dungeon—better reality, no matter how painful—than to live his life sedated like some opium smoker, cut adrift from the world as it was by his dreams.

He sent his gaze skyward. "Do you hear me? She disgusts me! I see through your lies!"

The woman shook her head. "You're not all there, are you, sport?"

"Go away."

Clive wouldn't even look at her. He was waiting for the Dungeonmasters to reveal themselves. For the dream to end. For a gateway to open and send him plunging down to some new level, some new torment.

The woman put fingers to her lips and whistled shrilly.

"Deny me a fair wage, will you?" she said as Clive looked to her once more.

Before he could reply, there was more movement in the alleyway. A broad-shouldered man stepped out into the arc of light cast by the gas lamp. His hair was slicked to his head, from both the drizzle and grease. He wore a tattered mockery of a gentleman's suit. His feet were bare.

"Bit of trouble, is it?" he said softly.

And this will be Jack, Clive thought. Her fancy man. The bully-boy who sent her out to peddle her body on the streets, while he collected the money afterward. And if she wasn't quick enough, or didn't earn enough, he'd beat her.

"Denying my girl a living wage, are you?" the man went on.

Clive shook his head.

So this was the way it was to be. The dream played out; the game continued until it ceased to amuse the Dungeonmasters and they cleaned the board to begin anew with a new set of playing pieces. And new stakes.

"You mistake me," Clive told the man as he took a step toward him.

"No mistake, mate. There's money owed and you'll pay—one way or another."

Clive shook his head. "I meant, you mistake me for a fool and a coward. I am neither."

Two quick steps brought him face to face with Jack. As the man started to raise his hands, Clive struck aside his defenses and hit him. The smack of his fist against the man's jaw sent pain shooting up his hand. But it was a satisfying pain.

Perhaps he'd been manipulated into this situation, but he was damned if he'd fall victim to it.

He let loose with a flurry of blows, and a moment

later, the prostitute's Jack lay on the cobblestones, curled into a ball. Blood leaked from his mouth. He had at least one or two broken ribs.

"Do you see what I meant about your mistake?" Clive asked him, conversationally.

The woman threw herself at him then, but all it required was a shove to throw her off balance and she, too, fell to the cobblestones beside her fancy man.

Again he turned his attention from them and gazed skyward.

"Well?" he cried. "What have you in store for me now?"

There was no reply.

What if he was wrong? he thought. What if there was no Dungeon—if this was the real world?

What if he *were* mad?

No. He knew it to be a lie.

Your heart's desire.

The dream offered him his heart's desire—there was no denying that—but it was still a lie.

Forgive me, Annabella, he thought. But I can't live the lie.

"Answer me!" he shouted.

Ignored by him, the prostitute and her fancy man dragged themselves away, into the alleyway, where they were lost in the darkness.

"Damn you!" Clive cried. "I will not live this lie!"

And then it came to him—a wavering of his vision, the scent of cloves, the sharp taste of anise in his mouth.

The London slum surrounding him tore apart, as paper might be shredded in a storm. The fog came rolling up at his feet, swallowing him. He lost the sense of cobblestones underfoot, and once again he floated in a dark limbo.

His mind's eye filled with an image of Annabella as she had been when he'd left her, asleep in her bed—the perfection of her limbs, the angelic sweetness of her features, smooth and worry-free as she slept.

Lost again.

Stolen from him.

"Damn you!" he cried once more. "Show yourselves to me!"

• Four •

There was no way for Clive to judge how long he floated in the darkness. It might only have been a few moments, it might have been as long as an hour, but without reference points—with only the darkness that surrounded him and the confused turmoil that ruled his mind by which to gauge the passage of time—he couldn't even begin to make an educated guess.

It felt like forever.

He had cursed his unseen tormentors long and hard, and with surprising innovation, but received no reply. He had attempted to propel himself through the darkness, but while he could move his limbs, the air was thick about him, and his hands and feet could find no purchase. Finally, voice still, floating in the dark like one dead, he lay passively and waited.

And more time passed.

Interminable minutes ticked away, each lengthened far beyond any reasonable proportion. Clive felt himself begin to drift away—away from his present situation, away from the womblike dark, out of himself.

It was as though, freed of the sensory input normally provided by his body, his spirit was determined to go traveling of its own accord, like some witch's fetch riding the midnight winds when its mistress lies sleeping; as though his spirit had decided that, if its physical shell could not be shifted, it would simply leave the body behind.

So Clive drifted past his anger and frustration, past memory, away into a quiet, hidden place where peacefulness wrapped him in a dark shawl of comfort and he could simply be. Slowly, sight returned, but whether what he viewed came from external stimuli or was drawn up from his own mind, he no longer cared.

He was an invisible presence in an intricately laid out garden, flower beds and hedgerows all forming complex patterns about him. He floated like pollen, his vision encompassing a full three hundred and sixty degrees about him. As his sense of smell returned, the scents of the garden's blossoms arose about him, sweet and heady. A fruity taste came to him. The air was filled with quiet sounds—the soughing of a soft breeze and the murmur of insects.

But all was not well in his haven. He could sense, just beyond the periphery of his vision, an invisible blight. Pain lay there, and desolation.

The world he'd left behind.

The message was plain.

This acreage was his. Here he could remain in safety, freed from the madness that had taken charge of his life beyond this garden's borders. But if he strayed, if he allowed himself to explore beyond these confines, then it would all return once more.

The pain.

The madness.

No need for that warning, Clive thought dreamily. He was done with struggling. Done with it all. With the bedlamite Dungeon. With the lies that infested it like some cancerous disease. He would remain here, where he could be content.

Go back.

The voice didn't really register at first.

Clive. You must return.

He could see in all directions at once in this garden of his, but could spy no source for that voice.

It must be a ghost, he thought. Some errant presence, imperceptible to the eye.

Leave me, he told it, shaping the words in his mind, for he was only an invisible presence himself in this place. *I'm done with their games.*

You must go back, came the voice's monotonous response.

Clive recognized it now. Looking at the maze of this garden, at its patterned network of flower beds and hedges, he wondered how it could have taken him so long to do so. It was the secret voice from his childhood.

Are you a part of the conspiracy? Clive asked. *Do its roots stretch so deeply into my past?*

The tone of his voice was conversational, as though he were only mildly curious.

They have drugged you, the voice responded, *while they decide your fate. How can you allow them to treat you in this manner?*

If he'd had a body, Clive would have shrugged.

I have no choice, he replied. *They do with me as they will—whether I protest or not.*

You are a Folliot, the voice said, *and a Folliot never gives in. You've said as much yourself.*

But they change the rules each time I turn about, Clive said, beginning to show some interest in the argument, despite himself. *They wield godlike powers, while all I can do is stumble through their damned Dungeon like some bug.*

Is it really so different in the world from which they stole you? the voice asked. *Isn't it the measure of how a man struggles that marks his worth?*

Yes, but—

Shall this be your epitaph: "He tried hard, until the struggle grew too difficult, then he simply gave up"?

Easily said, but—

True worth is never easily gained.

Who are you?

There was a long pause, then once again, the voice repeated its initial command.

Go back.

The words cut through Clive's peace, echoing on and on inside him until his haven began to unravel. The garden surrounding him wavered in his sight. The hidden voice drowned out the soothing breeze and the hum of the insects. The scents of the blossoms became spoiled and the fruity taste lost its sweetness, grew tart, then bitter.

Go back.

To what? Clive demanded. *To more of the same? To the endless spin of their damned games?*

No. Return instead to be the man that they cannot bow—the man who will not give in, no matter what they do to him. Return as a Folliot.

And go mad.

Madness is relative.

It's madness or death—that's all that lies in wait for me in their damned Dungeon.

You are too strong to fall prey to madness.

And if I die? What use was it all then?

At least you'll die a man.

There was that, Clive realized. Put in such terms, it could not be denied. For he truly believed that it wasn't so much what a man accomplished, as what—in all good faith, and to the best of his abilities—he attempted.

He felt a fog lifting from his mind.

They have drugged you, the voice had said earlier. *While they decide your fate.*

A man should decide his own fate. A man should stand against monsters such as the Dungeonmasters, no matter what that which consequences were to himself. It was only that which separated him from his tormentors.

Lord help him, what was he doing *here*, when he should be with his companions, striking back at the blackguards?

Go back, the voice said once more.

I will, Clive replied.

His return was instantaneous.

One minute he hovered in the fading ruin of the garden, the next he was inhabiting his body once more, cloaked in darkness. He had a brief sense of claustrophobia, brought on by the close measure of his flesh. After the freedom of floating free, his spirit felt trapped and heavy inside his skin. But that passed quickly as he tested his limbs, one by one, growing quickly used to their familiar fit.

Are you still there? he asked the voice.

There was no response. His mysterious benefactor was gone again, as inexplicably as it had come.

Unable to thank him, Clive turned his attention to his present situation.

He could sense no real change in his surroundings. The thick air still held him in its grip and he was still unable to make any real progress through it. But turning his head, he could see two pale smudges of dim light behind him. Though he could make out nothing of their features, the two shapes were indeed recognizably human.

He swam slowly through the air, trying to reach them, pausing when he could at least hear their voices.

They decide your fate.

They belonged to two men—one with a deep, gruff voice, while that of the other was smoother—not quite effeminate, but somewhat womanly all the same.

And they were indeed discussing his fate.

They have drugged you.

He tried to call out to them, not to vent his rage this time, but merely to let them know that they had not bowed him yet. The heads turned toward him.

"You see?" said the one with the gruff voice. "He's as bad as the other. He'll never give in."

The other? Clive thought. Did the man mean his brother, Neville?

"That's precisely his value," the second man said, slightly lisping his soft C's and S's.

"And when the weapon turns in your hand?" the first asked.

The second laughed. "But that's the challenge, isn't it? Without personal risk, we become no better than the others. When we realize our victory, it will be because *we*, at least, were willing to risk all."

It was no more than he'd supposed, Clive realized. It *was* all just some damnable game to them.

"I'll show you risk!" he shouted at them.

"So, you mean to send him back?" the first asked, as though Clive had never spoken.

"There was never any question. I allowed you this experiment, precisely because I knew he would prevail."

Experiment, is it? Clive thought.

"Damn you!" he cried. "I won't rest until you're defeated—each and every one of you."

He might as well have been shouting at the wind, for all the attention they paid him.

"You were that sure of yourself?" the first said.

The second shook his head. "I was sure of him," he said, indicating Clive.

"Don't toy with me," the first said, his voice deepening with anger. "I'm not one of the bugs, to be moved about the board."

"Of course not," the second replied. "But will you listen to reason now?"

"*Your* reason."

"Plain reason," the second said. "If we bicker among ourselves, we stand to lose it all."

"The others agree with you? *All* of them?"

Others? Clive thought. Speak on. Tell me all.

"After this? Yes."

The first sighed. "Then, return him. But the suits must go—his, and those of his companions. I don't know why Green allowed them to have them in the first place."

"The suits are gone," the second agreed amiably.

"And he must remember nothing of this."

Remember nothing? Clive thought. Lord in heaven, how did they expect him to forget?

"Absolutely," the second said.

"See how he drinks in every word? If he remembers, he'll be insufferable."

"I agree."

"I will forget *nothing*!" Clive cried. "Do you hear me? I will remember every foul moment of what you've done to me."

The two heads finally turned to face him.

"Not likely," the second said. "I'll admit the process hasn't been perfected to a preciseness we'd elect—given time—but it will do the job it must. If you lose a few other memories in the procedure"—the figure shrugged—"well, so be it. I can guarantee it will be nothing you'd miss."

The first laughed at that.

Clive renewed his effort to get to them, but the dull glow that gave them shape was fading, until the darkness swallowed them and he was alone once more. Laboriously, he turned a full circle, seeking something, anything, but the black void continued on all sides.

There came a sudden sharp pain in his left upper arm—a hornet's sting, magnified a dozen times—and then an inner darkness began to swallow him, as black as that which surrounded him. He fought the loss of consciousness.

He *would* remember.

He heard voices around him. He felt hands on him, but he could not move a limb.

Then the black took him away.

• Five •

When next Clive was conscious, he was falling through the bright flaring azure once more. He could see the pinpoint specks that were his companions on all sides of him—each of them falling as helplessly as he was himself.

He sensed a gap in his memory, as though time had sped by while he stood still. It was an odd sensation—a feeling of loss—but he couldn't define what it was that he had left behind.

He must have lost consciousness for a moment, he thought, and little wonder. If he could only breathe . . .

He remembered nothing of what he had experienced in the black void.

Vertigo made his head spin. His stomach heaved with nausea. He had a raw ache in his head, as though he'd suffered a concussion. His upper left arm felt swollen, and was painful whenever he moved it. He fought for breath in the thick blue air, but the oxygen simply wasn't there to draw into his lungs.

He peered downward, then realized he was no longer certain what was up, and what was down. He had the sense of falling, it was true, but in this place they could be falling sideways for all he knew.

He needed air.

Desperately.

If he didn't breathe soon, he'd—

There was a sudden jarring underfoot as his boots came into contact with something solid. His knees buckled and he collapsed like a puppet with its strings cut. He put out his hands to break his fall, and they sank into what felt like deep grass. His eyes seemed welded shut, but he was too busy keeping down the contents of his stomach to pay any attention to his surroundings.

His arms gave way then, and his face pressed up against the grass. Before he could even try to sit up, the blackness took him away.

Clive was among the first to recover. He opened his eyes, feeling wretched, and cautiously sat up. The world did a slow spin, then settled around him.

He and his companions appeared to have landed on a grassy plateau of some sort. Higher plateaus rose up behind them to meet a craggy sweep of tors; behind them, an immense mountain range almost blocked the sky. In front and below, the land gave way to a dense jungle of forest on the left, a wide sweeping expanse of veldt dotted with trees and shrubs to the right. Cutting between the two was a broad river that meandered off into the distance to where an outstretched peninsula of jungle cut it off from view.

It still bewildered him that such vast lands could exist under the earth. Turning, he took stock of his companions and then realized that the white suit he had been wearing was gone and he was dressed once more as he had been when he had first entered the jungle.

The Dungeonmasters must have taken the suits that Green had given them while they were falling through the last gateway. But at least they had all survived the crossing from the Dungeon's previous level to this one—Lord help them, it was the fifth now.

As Clive regarded them, one by one, he realized again just what a motley assortment of companions they made.

Obviously unaffected by his transition through the gateway, the cyborg Chang Guafe stood resolutely at the edge of the plateau, staring across the landscape of this new level. The metal workings of his skull plate and visage gleamed in the sunlight. His metallic eyes glowed slightly as they fed input into his brain, which was more computer than human flesh and blood.

He reminded Clive of the clockwork toys that were so much the rage in his native London—a walking, talking simulacrum—but Clive didn't make the mistake of considering the cyborg to be any child's plaything. He'd proven himself far too dangerously capable to be underestimated in such a fashion. And at least he had the shape of a human.

Not like Shriek.

She was a four-armed, four-legged monster. Her huge body was covered with spikelike hair that she could pull out and throw as a weapon, the hair apparently carrying some sort of chemical that she could vary at will, depending on the desired effect she wished to produce on the creature she was dealing with. But she was little more than a creature herself—a humanoid spider.

Her face was the most disturbing, with its vestigial mandibles on either side of her lipless mouth, and her six multifaceted, ruby-colored eyes, scattered on the top half of her head like a child's cast-off marbles thrown hither-skither, coming to rest where they would. And, like a spider, she had a pair of spinnerets just below the base of her back.

But under that alien visage was a being that Clive had come to realize had more heart than most men he knew.

Finnbogg was easier to look upon, if only in comparison to Shriek. He was a dwarflike humanoid who seemed more closely related to the canine family than to humanity, with a volatile temperament that could have him fall in love, burst into tears, or fly into a towering rage—all at a moment's notice. Squat, shaggy, and immensely strong, he claimed to be a native of a heavy planet where the biochemistry was enough like Earth's to allow him to breathe the same air and eat the same food as humans did. But he was still a monster.

The rest of Clive's companions were human—though not necessarily fit company for a good Englishman.

The Portuguese, Tomàs, was akin to the worst magsman or garroter to be found in a London slum. He was swarthy and small, with dark, greasy hair. A wharf rat: alcoholic, dirty, and undoubtedly treacherous. His arrival in the Dungeon had rescued him as he walked the plank of the *Pinta* in the western Atlantic in 1492.

The Indian, Sidi Bombay, had joined Clive's party on the first stages of their search for his brother—before they were foolish enough to investigate the shimmering gateway in the Sudd, and plunged from it into the madness of the Dungeon. Sidi was small in stature, too, but there his similarities with Tomàs ended. His skin was a dark mocha, his hair a midnight black. Experienced and clever, there was an enigmatic mystery about the small Indian that belied his apparently unguarded and cheerful manner.

Disturbing for an entirely different reason was the presence of Annabelle Leigh. As Tomàs came from the past, she had arrived in the Dungeon from the year 1999, when her music-and-theater group, the Crackbelles, were performing in Piccadilly Circus on Halloween Eve. She was a gamine creature, brazenly showing off her feminine charms in her tight-fitting men's garb. Her black hair was shorn in jagged layers, with absolutely no consideration for fashion or style. Implanted in her forearm—giving her a disquieting kinship to the cyborg—was her Baalbec A-9, a kind of mechanical device powered by her own body heat. The controls for it lay under the bodice of her shirt.

She was also Clive's descendant—his own many-times great-granddaughter, by way of the lover Clive had left behind in England when he first left in search of his brother—Miss Annabella Leighton.

It was disturbing enough to know that this gamine was related to him—that good English morals and mores could change so drastically in merely a century and a half—but what troubled Clive more was how, day by day, she came to look ever more like his own Annabella. For she had the same startling cornflower-blue eyes, the same pale skin suffused with a healthy pink flush, the same trim figure.

It was too easy for him to look at her and see Annabella. He could imagine this descendant of theirs in a high-necked and -waisted bustle dress, with a light mantle overtop following the contours of the dress. Her hair would be long, tied up in a bun under a close-fitting hat. She would be carrying a parasol. . . .

When he let his mind travel so, ungentlemanly thoughts arose—immoral thoughts. For the love of God, she was of his own blood! he had to remind himself. And yet that resemblance . . . and to know that he would never return to his own Annabella. . . .

The only truly familiar face in the party—though by now, Clive was growing accustomed to them all, even the most alien—was that of his one-time batman, Quartermaster Sergeant Horace Hamilton Smythe.

"Batman?" Annabelle had asked when she was made aware of Smythe's earlier position. "What's that make you, Clive-o? Robin?" That was only the first of many obscure references to fall from her lips that simply could not be translated satisfactorily to a man who had left the world a hundred and ten years before her birth.

Clive and Smythe had been together for years, and Clive had reacted with great relief the morning that the *Empress Philippe* had left England's shores and Smythe had turned up aboard ship—disguised as a Mandarin.

Smythe's gift was for makeup and mimicry. He had the ability to switch from a drawling fop to a rhyming slang-spouting cockney to a country bumpkin to a fast-talking pitchman—all at a moment's notice. Odder still, when he wasn't in character, Smythe was the most nondescript of individuals, virtually disappearing into the nearest background, be it a crowd, a jungle, or a drawing room.

"Christ. Talk about your acid flashbacks."

Annabelle regained Clive's attention as he tried to puzzle out what she meant.

Guafe turned from where he stood, overlooking the view below their perch. "Yes," he said in his slightly metallic voice. "The disruption did have the hallucinogenic quality of a drug experience."

Ah, Clive thought. Opiates.

He glanced at Annabelle, looking quickly away when she stood and stretched, the unself-conscious movement accentuating every curve of her trim figure. She gazed thoughtfully around them.

"I figure it was some kinda spatial portal," she said. "Like teleportation." At the mostly blank stares that drew, she added, "You know—not really connected physically?"

"Again, I concur," the cyborg said.

The others were slowly finding their way to their feet. Smythe joined Clive, tugging thoughtfully at his new beard.

"Sir Neville appears to have eluded us again," he said.

It was true, Clive realized. He'd been so disoriented by the experience in the gateway that the reason they had come here had been driven from his mind. He looked out now across the vast panorama of forest and veldt. Somewhere out there, his older twin Neville had made his escape. It was a disheartening view. An army could be hidden below and never seen.

"Where will we begin to look?" he murmured.

"Finnbogg thinks he could be anywhere," Finnbogg said. The dwarf had followed Clive's gaze with his own, absently brushing grass from his chest hair as he did. "Gate could drop littermate anywhere."

"Look," Annabelle said. "I hate to rain on your parade, but don'tcha think it's about time we stopped running around after that asshole and just tried to get outta this place? I mean, enough's enough already. We're never gonna catch up to him. He's playing us for a bunch of no-minds."

"There is no way back," Sidi said. The Indian gave her one of his quirky smiles. "The only way out is ahead."

Annabelle shook her head. "Maybe. I say we put it to a vote." More blank looks. "You know—everybody decides what they want to do, and whatever gig gets the most hands, that's the way we go."

"*I'm* the leader of this company," Clive began when he understood what she was driving at.

"Annabelle is right," Tomàs interrupted. "*Anos.* Whenever we follow you there is only more trouble."

"At this point, I am content to follow," Guafe said.

As am I, Shriek added. Her voice rang directly to their minds.

"Finnbogg will . . ."

The dwarf glanced at Annabelle and caught her frown. It was because of Finnbogg that she had lost her chance of leaving the Dungeon with Wrecked Fred and L'Claar. If he hadn't held her back for that last moment. . . .

"I think we should just split up," Annabelle said.

"I can't leave you here alone," Clive said.

"Oh, lighten up. You think I can't take care of myself?"

How a woman of her obvious good blood could be so crass was beyond Clive's understanding.

"I am responsible for you," he tried. "So long as—"

"Screw that. I'm a big girl now, Clive-o, and the only person responsible for me's me—got that? So back off."

A flush rose up Clive's neck and he took a step toward her, but then Smythe laid a hand on his arm.

"What does your brother's journal say about this level, sah?" he asked.

Sidi nodded. "That would be the wisest course. We must see what lies around us before choosing a destination." He smiled at both Clive and Annabelle. "Who knows? Our roads might well travel together for some distance farther."

Annabelle sighed. "Okay. Check out the bloody Bible."

"It is *not* a Bible," Clive replied.

Every time he thought he was coming to turns with her brashness, she managed to shock him again.

Do you even have the journal anymore? Shriek asked.

Clive hadn't thought of that. With the switch in their clothing . . . But he patted his pocket and found the familiar outline of his brother's diary.

"C'mon," Annabelle said. "Let's get to it. Read the book already."

What I wouldn't give for some good, sturdy Englishmen who know their station, in exchange for this motley crew, Clive thought. But he took the journal from his jacket pocket and sat down with it, spreading it open on his lap. His companions gathered closer.

▪ Six ▪

Annabelle lay on her back, staring up at the sky, while Clive looked for another of the mysterious, newly appearing entries in the journal. With its salmon-colored sun, the sky here ran more toward a greenish hue than the blue of the world she'd left behind. The odd tones this lent her vision gave her a creepy feeling, but right now she wasn't much missing her own world's skies. Just thinking of their deep blues reminded her too much of the last gateway—talk about your Big Sick.

She'd thought she was going to die in that blue limbo, and was almost ready to welcome the relief from the cramps and nausea that death promised when they'd finally landed on this new level and she'd blacked out. Wouldn't that've been a laugh for the guys in the band if they could've seen her. Tough old Annie B., passing out like some front-and-center groupie swooning at the shake of Tripper's Spandexed buttocks.

It was the height—always the heights. . . .

Thinking of her lead guitarist brought on a different attack of the blues. All that was gone now. Wasn't much chance of her seeing any of them again. Not her friends, not London, not that New Year's gig where they were sharing the bill with the legendary Prince and the Revolution, partying in the next thousand years to the tune of the aging rock star's twenty-some-year-old hit, *1999*.

Instead, all she had to look forward to was dying here in the Dungeon, or growing old with this bunch of rejects from a Lucasfilm production and *still* dying here.

They were misfits all. Not to mention her many-times great-grandfather, who was suffering from a bad attack of a daddy complex.

If Finnbogg hadn't grabbed her, hanging on to her just long enough so that the bloody gate went and closed, trapping her. . . .

She was only half listening to the others talking as Clive leafed through his twin's journal.

Misfits.

She had the feeling that that was the key to this place. It gathered up the people who didn't quite fit in where they came from, and dumped them here. And what happened to them then? Who the hell knew. All she knew was that everybody here was either a misfit, or one of the hero types, like Clive and Finnbogg, who were too true blue to think about anything except chasing after previous victims.

She had to smile at the thought of someone chasing in here after her. Not bloody likely. Tripper, or her bass player, Dan the Man, or little Chrissie Nunn. . . . They'd all just think she'd pulled another one of her no-shows, and they'd be expecting her to turn up again in a week or so, like she always did. Of course, when she didn't, they might worry, but what were they gonna do? It wasn't like there were signposts or maps showing the way into this place or anything.

Maybe she should be keeping a journal herself, or a sketchbook, like Clive did, so that whoever it was that was running this place could sneak it back to the real world to lure in some more suckers, like Clive's brother had done, leading them around by the nose like the bunch of losers that they were.

She sat up suddenly. "What was that you just said?" she asked. "About that other gate on this level?"

Clive gave her one of his resigned looks. "Weren't you listening?"

"'Course I was listening. I just want to get the thrill of hearing it again, that's all. So give."

"It is in a village named Quan," Clive said after consulting the journal once more. "A place guarded by 'blue people' who should be avoided at all costs."

"And where is it?"

"It's not quite clear. Somewhere along the river."

Annabelle nodded. "That's where we should be going. If there's a gateway there, I want to see it. It'll probably just take us down to a deeper level, but maybe it could take us out. Either way, we're moving on—under our own steam."

Clive put his finger on a line of writing. "It says 'avoid at all cost.'"

"Of course it does. And that's why we should go there. Don't you see, Clive-o? When we go where your brother wants us to, all we do is get into deeper shit."

That is not entirely true, Being Annabelle, Shriek said. *We have put ourselves into as much danger as Neville's journal has led us into.*

"Okay. But I still think it's time we stopped playing the game by his rules and made some of our own."

Clive shook his head. "My brother will be heading for the lost city beyond the veldt."

Annabelle hadn't been paying much attention when he was reading that part, either. But before she could ask him to reread it as well, and earn herself another of Clive's reproving looks, Finnbogg spoke up.

"Finnbogg know story about Quan," the dwarf said. "Quanians worship a white stone that is the repository of all the souls of those who have died in their lands."

"Died how?" the cyborg asked. "At the hands of the Quanians?"

"There's also a story," Annabelle interrupted, "about how dwarves are these cute little guys who take care of princesses in trouble and whistle while they work, but that doesn't mean it's true, either."

That gave the group pause. They all knew by now that, for all his time in the Dungeon and the tales he could tell of it, Finnbogg had trouble distinguishing between reality and imagination, which made sorting out the fact from his fantasies a hopeless cause. That Annabelle had just cause to be angry with Finnbogg in no way lessened her warning. Listening to him, one needed a spoonful, rather than a grain of salt.

"Yet in his journal," Smythe said, "Sir Neville warns of danger, as well."

Annabelle nodded. "And we all know how much old Neville's looking out for us."

"He's still my brother," Clive said. "And I still have to find him." His tone was conciliatory, but firm. "I will not shirk that duty."

"I know, I know. And no one's asking you to. We just do like I said before: You go to that ruined city with whoever wants to go with you, while I go to the next gateway with whoever wants to go with me. It's simple, right?"

Clive looked as though he was ready to argue, but then he just sighed and nodded his agreement. One by one, the others made their own decisions. Smythe was going with Clive—no surprise there. Also going with him was the cyborg Guafe and Finnbogg, who had looked hopefully at Annabelle, then unhappily chosen Clive's party when all she gave him was a hard stare.

Shriek opted to join Annabelle, as did Tomàs. Annabelle was pleased with the former's decision, but not at all thrilled about having the Portuguese traveling with her. The only one who remained undecided was Sidi Bombay.

"What about you?" Clive asked the Indian.

"Well, now. I signed up to guide you, and I'm not a man who goes back on his word, but I don't know this land, so I'll be of little use as a guide."

"I release you from any obligations you feel you still owe me," Clive said.

Annabelle frowned. Like he owned Sidi. What Clive-o needed was a good shaking to loosen him up.

"Then I will go with Annabelle," Sidi said.

Well, thank Christ for that, Annabelle thought. Somebody sane to talk to and help her and Shriek keep an eye on Tomàs.

* * *

It took them most of the day to work their way down from the top of the plateau, to where they made a group camp at the base of the heights. The descent was made that much harder because of Annabelle's uncomfortable feeling with heights. After resting, they set about providing themselves with some supper.

Smythe fished in the river, using sturdy thread pulled from the bottom hem of his jacket and one of Annabelle's many earrings, bent into a hook. Grubs dug out of the mud served for bait. Finnbogg and Sidi foraged along the river bank for this world's variations on tubers and cress. By the time they returned, Smythe had caught three good-sized fish. They were bluish in color, but once they were gutted and scaled, and roasted over a fire, they proved to make good eating. They had the cress on the side, as a salad. The tubers, roasted in the coals, had a texture like sweet potatoes, and a nutty taste.

They took turns keeping watch through the night, unfamiliar constellations wheeling across the dark skies above. The stars seemed much too close—more like the special effects from the light show of one of her gigs, Annabelle thought, than real stars—and looked like winking chips of sapphire.

She and Clive shared the third watch. The air was warm and humid, so they'd let the fire die down. Annabelle had taken off her jacket and was wearing just her red leather jeans and an armless T-shirt.

"Guess you're kinda disappointed in me, aren't you?" she said as the silence between them grew too long for her.

She was a little surprised that what he thought of her made any difference at all. It was probably, she realized, that, for all her criticism of him, and his of her, he was still family. And that was more than most people seemed to get in this place. When she thought of what it'd been like when she was alone in that prison, before Clive and his party had joined her. . . .

Clive's face was just a shadow when he turned to look at her. "You carry yourself much . . . differently from the women of my own time," he said finally.

"Yeah, well, things change. The world's different."

"Too much so, I think."

"I don't know about that, Clive." She dropped the "O" that she usually tacked on just to get a rise out of him. "Seems to me freedom's a good thing."

"Freedom, yes. But when one forgets one's station . . . I find it disconcerting."

"Like a woman doing what she wants to do? C'mon. You can't tell me you really believe all that."

"Well, not exactly. But, still. Women aren't the same as men. In England—"

"Oh, gimme a break. You want to know what's happening in your merry old England right now? It's a pissant little country, up to its ass in debt, that brown-noses every major world power. Half its work force is on the dole, while the other half's running around with a pickle up its ass.

"And as for your macho attitude to women—where the hell do you come off thinking we're no better'n you?"

"Women are the weaker sex," Clive began. "It's a gentleman's duty to look after them."

"Right. The way you looked after my ancestor, Anna-bella. Knocking her up and then taking off on a little world tour for your asshole brother who doesn't even *want* to be found. Wake up, Clive."

"I had no idea that Annabella was with child."

"So tell me, was she just some tramp, as far as you were concerned?"

"I won't listen to you speak of her in such a manner."

Annabelle sighed. She reached out and added some fuel to the dying coals of the fire. Flames licked up, lighting both their faces. Shadows ran off beyond the periphery of the fire's glow.

"Look," she said. "I'm trying to make a point. You think I'm cheap—too brassy, too loose . . . a soiled woman, right? I speak my mind just like you do, I'm capable of standing up to the same shit you are, and I've slept around. I got my own kid, floating out there in the real world somewhere. What makes us so different? I'm here, aren't I—your descendant? But you never married. Are you trying to tell me that you never slept with a woman?"

"No, but—"

"Oh, yeah. I know. It's okay, because you're a man. Well, bullshit, Clive-o."

And then she grinned. By the rueful expression on his face, she knew that she had him.

"This is not fit conversation for mixed company," he tried to argue, but she knew his heart wasn't really in it.

Score one for enlightenment, she thought. Maybe there's hope for him yet.

"That's just the point I'm trying to make," she said. "We're not mixed. You're male and I'm female—right—but otherwise, we're just people. Under our skin, never mind our sex, we're the same. Do you understand what I'm trying to tell you? You're an intelligent man, for God's sake, so pay attention. Watch my lips. Under their skin, people are all the same."

Clive sat quietly, making no answer.

"That doesn't mean that every woman's gotta be hard," Annabelle went on. "There's still room for romance. People like being babied sometimes—men *and* women. Cared for, you know? But they want to be respected, too. It's a tough old world out there, Clive. We've gotta fight a lot of fights—but we shouldn't be fighting with each other."

There was another long silence.

"I . . . understand," Clive said finally.

Annabelle nodded. Yeah, she thought. At least you think you do. But it was a start. You couldn't expect miracles, but if he just stopped to think about it from time to time, it'd be worth it.

"So who do you figure for the World Series?" she asked.

"What?"

"Just a joke. Changing the subject, you know?"

"You are a very strange woman, Annabelle Leigh," he said.

She grinned. "Yeah. Real *Twilight Zone* material. What

do you say we wake up the next watch and get some sleep?"

The two companies went their separate ways in the morning. As they made their farewells, Annabelle gave Clive a solid hug and a quick kiss on the lips that made him blush. She touched the red flush on his neck with a feathery brush of her fingers.

"Never met a man who blushed before," she said. "You take good care of yourself now, okay?"

Though he looked as though he had more to say, he contented himself with a simple, "Fare you well."

Annabelle watched them set off through the tall grass of the veldt until they were lost from sight, then looked in the direction that their own trail would take them.

The jungle hung heavily over the west side of the river. Although the east bank was treed as well, the undergrowth wasn't nearly as dense. While she didn't have the best of knowledge when it came to geography, it didn't seem quite right to her that the jungle would end so abruptly at the river, and become grasslands almost immediately after leaving the water. But then, there wasn't a whole lot about this place that made much sense—not when the veldt had a mauve tint to its yellowy grass and the jungle ran more to blue-green and burgundy, with splashes of pure purple that weren't fruit. The only really green—familiar green—things she could see were the blooms on a nearby flowering vine.

She turned to look at her own companions. Shriek returned her gaze impassively, while Tomàs wouldn't meet hers at all. Only Sidi flashed her a grin, white teeth gleaming against his dark skin.

"Well, kids," she said. "Looks like it's time for us to go play Tarzan."

"Tarzan?" Tomàs asked.

"Yeah. Hit the jungle trail, and all that. Knowing our luck, we'll run into our own Opar and all get sacrificed to some monkey god or something, but what the hell. Nobody said it was gonna be a picnic, right?" Blank looks all around. "Right. Let's go."

When Shriek took the lead, Annabelle indicated to Tomàs that he should go next. No way she wanted that weasel behind her. She and Sidi took up the rear. As they entered the less dense forest of the east bank, taking a game trail that followed the river, the oddly colored foliage closed in above them.

Why do I get a bad feeling about this? Annabelle wondered as she glanced back at the sunlit field they were leaving behind.

▪ Seven ▪

The veldt was a vast, trackless sea of grass, dotted with small islands of bushes and trees. The grass swept off in endless leagues of yellowish mauve under the pale green skies, rising up to the shoulders of Clive, Smythe, and the cyborg, while swallowing the bulky but smaller Finnbogg with its height. The blades of the grass were thick and sharp at the edges, springing back up behind them after they had passed. By midmorning, the jungle was no longer visible. All they could see of their backtrail was the immense heights of the mountain range, pushing up at the cloudless sky.

It was dull trudging with so little to see in the way of landmarks. The islands of bushes and trees gave some relief, but the trees were so immense—the smallest was many times the size of the largest English oak, while the bushes were as tall as the trees the Englishmen were readily familiar with—that their presence left the company with a sense of disquiet whenever they passed through their shadows.

"She is a fine woman, is young Annabelle," Smythe remarked to Clive. "She will do you proud, sah."

The cyborg Guafe was walking well ahead of them—his tireless march was enough to make Clive weary just watching him—while Finnbogg lagged behind, so the two Englishmen were walking abreast. Clive had been relating his previous night's conversation with Annabelle to his companion—an edited version that didn't cover Clive's more personal relationship with his lover in England.

"Do you think so?" Clive asked. "She has some rather curious notions concerning class structure and a woman's place."

"If you'll pardon my candor," Smythe said, "I believe there's much to what she has to say. Take Sidi—he's more than simply clever. Give him white skin and drop him into London, and I'll wager that in a month or so, you would be hard put to pick him out from another Englishman. He's adaptable, is Sidi Bombay. A good man, no matter what color his skin."

"Oh, I'll grant you that. But he's still . . . well, common."

"And so am I. Yet we eat at the same table, you and I, and you respect me, as I do you. It isn't merely the uniform we share that allows us our friendship—at least, I would hope not."

"A man never had a truer friend than I have in you, Horace," Clive said.

"It warms my heart to hear you speak so, sah."

"But all this talk of Annabelle's . . . I must admit I find it disturbing."

Smythe nodded. "A new idea is often disturbing— warrant the furor back home over the evolutionists—but if it speaks a truth, then the wise man would do well to listen. We are in a new world now, sah—one from which we may never escape. By such reckoning, we would do well to set aside some of our beliefs and be willing to accept the strangers that we meet here on their own terms, no matter how alien or 'common' we might perceive them to be."

"But damn it, Horace, we're Englishmen. We must set an example."

"You're beginning to sound like your brother, sah," Smythe said with a smile.

"You know what I mean."

Smythe shrugged. "Perhaps it comes easier for me, sah, being common and all—"

"You know I didn't mean—"

"But you'd do well to think about what Annabelle had to say. Even if we do escape this Dungeon, who's to say in what time we would find ourselves? If the world has changed as much as Annabelle has told us it has, then we'd do well to learn to adapt to changes *now*."

"It irks me," Clive said.

"As no doubt your own reactions irked Annabelle. There's a good deal of the Folliot in her—I doubt you'd deny that."

Clive smiled. "She certainly speaks her mind."

"Headstrong—like every Folliot I've ever known."

"And not without her own charm—though, Lord knows, I don't claim that for myself."

"I wouldn't be so quick to deny it," Smythe said. "I've seen the ladies' eyes on you, sah, and it wasn't simply your uniform they were admiring."

"Yes, well . . ."

For the second time that day Clive felt his cheeks and neck burn. He cleared his throat and quickly changed the subject.

"Did we do the right thing, do you suppose—splitting the company in two as we have?"

"I worry for Annabelle, as well," Smythe replied, "but she seems a most capable young woman, and Sidi and Shriek will look after her, even if the Portuguese is of no help. Besides, I doubt we had much choice. To bring her with us would have required our binding and gagging her, I'll wager."

Clive nodded. "And as Finnbogg has pointed out, in this place there is no turning back, only faring onward. So I'll look to meet her again in the days to come. And if she promises to ease the sharpness of her tongue— why, then, I'll promise to keep a more open mind."

"No harm in practicing that now," Smythe murmured.

Clive gave him a sharp glance, then sighed. "If it's not the one of you, then it's the other."

"We're both looking out for you, sah. One can be an Englishman and still keep an open mind. It's never harmed me."

Clive smiled. "Why, then, here's my hand on it, Horace, and if you find me failing to uphold my side of this bargain, I give you permission to shape me quickly back into line—howsoever you see fit."

Smythe clasped Clive's hand and grinned back at him. "Watch what you promise, gov'nor," he said, "as there's some as'll take you at your word."

As he spoke, Smythe's features and stance shifted into that of a quick-stepping London cockney to match his thick accent, and for a moment, Clive was transported away from this bizarre world that familial loyalty had forced him into, back to the cobblestoned streets of home. A pang of loss touched him, but he kept his smile.

"I expect no less from you, Horace," he said.

Come the late afternoon, there was a new mystery for them to unravel. The grassland suddenly broke off, and they were confronted with a vast plain, pitted and scored with round indentations that measured some ten feet across. They were scattered everywhere, overlapping often. There were also indications of huge logs or something similar having been dragged about the area. The grass was reduced to stubble; the nearest copse of trees stood out like an island, and had not a leaf upon any of its branches.

"Now, this is curious," Clive said. "What are we to make of this?"

The cyborg had paused at the edge of the grassline, waiting for them to catch up to him.

"Could it have been caused by a shower of meteorites?" Smythe asked. "The heat from their descent would be enough to set fire to the grasslands—wouldn't it?"

"Unlikely," Guafe said. "The indentations left by meteorites would be explosive—these are compressive."

"Then what caused these holes?" Clive asked.

The cyborg shrugged—a very human gesture that he'd undoubtedly picked up from associating with them. "In the Dungeon? It could be anything."

Smythe was investigating one of the indentations. It was some two feet deep, and the earth was crumbly about its edges.

"Chang's right," he said as he straightened up. "If

these had been caused by meteorites, then we should be able to see some part of them at the bottom of these holes. There's no trace of them." Shading his eyes, he studied the surrounding terrain and added, "But I do see supper."

They all looked in the direction he was pointing. Near the huge trees of the nearest copse, a small group of creatures was feeding on the short, grassy stubble. They had the heads and ears of hare, elongated necks like giraffes, and the body of deer. Their coloring was dun, touched with the same mauve of the grass, dotted with white spots. Their underbellies were white. In size, they were no taller than a good-sized hound.

"What are they?" Clive asked.

"Mammals of some sort," Guafe replied.

Smythe nodded. "They appear to be a cross between a hare and a deer."

"Dares?" Clive offered with a smile.

"A dare does sound more appetizing than a heer," Smythe said. As Guafe began to move in their direction, he added quickly, "Don't frighten them."

Sitting at the edge of the indentation he'd been investigating, he took off his boots and removed the laces from one of them. He tied a stone to either end of the lace, then rose to his feet.

"A Spanish trick," he said with a smile as he whirled the bola experimentally over his head.

While the others watched, he crept forward, moving at a snail's pace, freezing every time one of the long-eared heads lifted. The wind made it easier for him, blowing toward him from his quarry, but from the prickling alertness of their ears, he was sure that they depended mostly on their sense of hearing to alert them to danger.

When he judged that he was finally close enough, he started the bola whirling again. Heads lifted among the herd at the whistling sound of the weapon, one after the other. Then one creature broke off and began to run. Smythe loosed the bola as the rest of the herd bolted, moving in a curious gait that combined a hop with a run.

They were as quick as an English hare or deer, but Smythe had been prepared for that. He gave his quarry plenty of lead before loosing his weapon. As the bulk of the herd raced away, the leather thong of the bola struck his target's neck, and the stones wrapped around it with such force that it broke.

"As I've provided supper," he said as he drew his knife and ran lightly to where his prey still kicked its feet, "I'll let someone else see to building a fire."

They had the dare meat for supper, and again for breakfast, and yet once more for supper the following night. It had a coarse texture and a slightly gamy flavor, but, considering their circumstances, they all pronounced it a rousing success.

They left the meteor field behind late on that following day, and pushed through the tall grasses of the veldt for the remainder of the afternoon before they finally made camp. The evening passed uneventfully, with Finnbogg regaling them with more improbable stories of the Dungeon and its curiosities. Smythe particularly enjoyed the dwarf's tales, matching them with ones just as preposterous from his own store whenever Finnbogg grew tired. The cyborg seemed to pay attention to neither of them—it was as though he simply shut himself off when they weren't moving or it wasn't his turn to take watch.

Clive listened with half an ear. Sometimes he sketched with bits of charcoal on the blank pages in his brother's journal, in the poor light thrown from their fire. Mostly, he worried about the other half of their company, following the river, worrying especially about Annabelle.

He had the dawn watch that morning. He was sitting with his back against a tree, the fire nothing more than dead ash, when he heard the grumble of thunder. The salmon-colored sun was already rising in the east, so the sky was clear enough that he could see it was cloudless.

Thunder without clouds? he thought.

Then the ground shook underfoot—a tremor at first,

that grew until it was impossible to stand. By now, the rest of the company was awake as well.

"Earthquake!" Clive cried.

A strange expression touched Finnbogg's features. He crawled to the nearest tree and slowly hoisted himself up its trunk, clinging like a limpet to its rough bark. He scouted the horizon, then pointed off toward the north, losing his balance as he did so. He half fell, half slid down the trunk, landing on the ground hard enough to knock the air from him.

"What was it?" Clive demanded. "Speak up."

"Give him a moment to catch his breath," Smythe said as he knelt by the dwarf and helped him sit up.

The ground shook constantly now.

Finnbogg sat up weakly. "Now . . . Finnbogg remember," he said.

"Remember what?" Clive asked.

"The danger on this veldt—the Walking Mountains."

"The walking—?"

Guafe called to them then from where he stood holding on to the trunk of the tree. He pointed north as Finnbogg had. The thunder was all around them, the ground reverberating so that it was difficult to merely sit on it.

"That was no meteor field we crossed earlier," the cyborg said. "It was the feeding ground of brontosaurs."

Clive and Smythe joined him where he stood, hanging on to the tree for support. The cyborg kept his balance now without need of similar support, riding the shock waves. In the far distance, the two Englishmen could spy an enormous herd approaching them.

"What do you mean it was a feeding ground?" Clive asked.

"Their distance makes their size deceptive," Guafe replied. "Those indentations we discovered were not made by meteorites—they were the footprints of those monsters."

"Footprints?" Smythe asked.

The disbelief in his voice was obvious to Clive. He found it difficult to believe himself, but the shaking ground and the thunder of the creatures' monstrous tread brought the truth home with a harsh resonance. He clung to the tree trunk and stared at the distant herd.

The cyborg was nodding. "They reach lengths of up to twenty-five meters and weights ranging between forty and eighty ton. It will be most interesting to observe them at close hand."

"Walking Mountains," Finnbogg muttered.

"They're coming our way?" Clive asked.

"There's no need for alarm," Guafe told him. "They are herbivores. We need only keep out from underfoot."

"What if they think we are plants?" Smythe asked.

"Unlikely. Of more concern to us will be the scavengers accompanying the herd—coelurosaurs and the like."

Clive regarded the cyborg. "And how . . . how big are they?"

"Not large—perhaps the size of an ostrich."

Clive studied the approaching herd once more, then turned his attention to their surroundings. The nearest branches above them were some seventy feet from the ground. There was no other cover. The most they could hope for was to hug the side of the tree and hope the monsters didn't notice them. But then he remembered the feeding ground they had traveled through, how all the vegetation—from grasses to the topmost leaves—had been razed.

The ground tremors were so severe now that it took all their strength to hold on to the rough bark of the trees. Of the four, only the cyborg remained standing, still riding the tremors. The rest of them knelt beside the tree, hanging on as best they could.

"What I wouldn't give for a cannon," Smythe said.

"Or a few good horses to take us out of here," Clive added.

The sky was darkening now, but there were still no clouds. It was the vast bulks of the brontosaurs, shadowing the sun.

"At least Annabelle is safe," Clive said.

▪ Eight ▪

The thing you forget, Annabelle thought, when you're watching all those old Johnny Weissmuller flicks, is that it's hot in a jungle. Hot and sticky.

She wore her jacket tied around her waist as she trudged along behind Shriek and Tomàs, her T-shirt sticking to her back. Her red leather jeans were uncomfortably heavy and chafed her legs. Her short hair hung limply against her scalp, and one hand was in constant motion, brushing mosquitoes and other bugs away from her face. The heat and humidity was draining her vitality with each drop of perspiration it sucked from her. She couldn't even spare the energy her Baalbec A-9 would need to vaporize the ever-attacking insects.

She wasn't sure how the trek was affecting Shriek, but directly ahead of her, Tomàs walked with his head bent, the heat sucking away his energy, too. His dirty shirt had sweat stains under its arms and all down its back, and his greasy hair hung even more limply than her own. Only Sidi appeared to be unaffected. He walked cheerfully at her side, not even breaking a sweat. By now, Annabelle was too hot and tired to try to imagine any more ways she could wipe that grin from his face.

What she wouldn't give for an ice-cold can of beer.

The game trail they were on continued to follow the contour of the river, under low-hanging boughs heavy with strange fruit, choked with blue and purple leaves and blossoming vines. Insects clouded around them, offering little respite. Beyond their vision, the jungle rang with odd animal cries. The few creatures they spied were uniformly bizarre.

Twice they'd seen troops of flying monkeys in the trees overhead—little wizen-faced creatures with pointed ears and white beards. They leapt from bough to bough, crossing wider expanses by utilizing the outstretched webs of skin between their fore and rear limbs. There was also a shrewlike creature, about the size of her hand, with a long, tusked snout and tiny red eyes, that she caught glimpses of in among the leaves.

They disturbed small herds of tapirlike beasts, striped like zebras, only the striping was reversed—white on black. In the river they saw swimming monkeys, with webbed feet and streamlined bodies, and a creature like a hippo that had flippers and a tail in place of limbs. It reminded Annabelle of a manatee, but was far larger. Once, they spotted what looked like a cross between a leopard and a monkey—an obviously feline creature that swung between tree boughs, its body slender to the point of anorexia. There were lizards and snakes, possumlike creatures with lupine features, and a hopping kind of rodent that appeared to be a cross between a rabbit and a squirrel.

The only things that appeared at least vaguely familiar to her were the birds. Though there was still something alien about them, they at least resembled the birds she knew from her own world, ranging from flocks of brightly colored parrots to long-legged wading birds, skimming kingfishers that fed on insects on the river's surface, and busy little hummingbirds the size of Annabelle's thumb. But they were still none of them quite right. The hummingbirds flew in flocks. The kingfishers had wide bills and a peaked fan of head feathers. The wading birds were like blue flamingos crossed with storks. The parrots chittered and scolded each other like monkeys.

"Can you believe this place?" she said, glancing at Sidi.

The Indian grinned. "We're here, aren't we? Hard not to believe what the eyes see."

"Cute. You know what I mean."

"Yes. Very strange, yet very familiar. Do you find the heat bothering you?"

"Every frigging thing is bothering me. I can't believe we've got a week of this to go through before we reach the village. Maybe we should Huck Finn it, you know? Build a raft and pole our way down the river?"

Sidi shook his head regretfully. "We've nothing to cut the trees down with, Annabelle. Nothing to lash the logs together with."

"I know. I'm just whining—don't pay any attention to me."

"Hard not to—you're the boss now."

The boss. Right. Well, the boss was beginning to regret taking the low road through the jungle. At least, out on the veldt, there'd probably be a breeze.

"Stop fighting the heat," Sidi said. "Accept it and let it flow through you—you'll feel much better."

"Easy for you to say."

"*Keh.*" He made a single, sharp clicking noise at the back of his throat that Annabelle was beginning to recognize as an indication of amusement. "Most discomforts are in the mind," he added. "Defeat them with your stronger will."

"Right now my mind's kinda turned to mush—like somebody's making a brain stew inside my head and they've got the heat turned way up."

"It will pass, Annabelle. You'll adapt."

She managed to find him a grin. "Sure. Just don't hold your breath waiting for it."

They made camp that night under a sheltering net of tree boughs that overhung the river, leaving a hut-sized space inside. When a troop of the flying monkeys passed by, high overhead, Shriek pulled loose one of her hair spikes and threw into the chattering cluster. One of the creatures came tumbling down; the rest fled.

As Shriek set about gutting and skinning the monkey, Annabelle turned away, feeling sick to her stomach. Tomàs smacked his lips.

"Did you never eat monkey?" he asked.

He added something in Portuguese that Annabelle found incomprehensible. He shrugged when she asked him to clarify.

"Muito gôsto, sim?" he said.

"Not for me, pal," she said. "It's too much like eating a relative."

While the other three feasted on the roast monkey, she settled for a vegetarian meal of tubers and cress, supplementing their blandness with a handful of greenish fruit that looked like grapes, but tasted like a blend of pear and lime, with a texture like a peach.

She planned to take the first watch—she doubted she could sleep anyway, with this heat—but before anyone turned in, a sudden silence from the jungle all around them stilled their own conversation. The hairs at the nape of Annabelle's neck prickled as she got the sudden sense that something was watching them from beyond the light cast by their small fire. Something sentient.

Chica-chic.

The sound came from their backtrail, as though someone had given a maraca a single shake. Not one of their small party even seemed to breathe. The only movement was Shriek's hand edging toward one of her hair spikes.

Chica-chic.

Now it came from the direction they'd be taking in the morning.

"What is it?" Annabelle breathed. "Some kinda animal?"

"It sounds to me," Sidi whispered back, "like the sound of a gourd rattle, filled with dry seeds."

Annabelle nodded. "Me, too. Do you think it's a person?"

The Indian shrugged, but he sat warily, his gaze roving restlessly as he studied the darkness beyond the campfire's glow.

Chica. . . .

The noise was farther away now. Muffled and incomplete. They sat in absolute silence, waiting, but it wasn't repeated. Instead, the normal sounds of the jungle arose once more. Insects. The cough of a cat-monkey. The distant cries of night birds.

Annabelle let out a breath that she hadn't been aware of holding. "That was creepy."

"This path is much too dangerous," Tomàs muttered.

Annabelle frowned at him. "Hey, nobody's keeping you. Anytime you want to take off, you got my blessing."

The Portuguese made no reply, but something ugly flickered in the back of his eyes before he gave her one of his ingratiating, thin smiles.

I smell something, Shriek said suddenly. *An odd, unpleasant smell—like a fish, but it walks on the land.*

"Like something rotting?" Annabelle asked. She lifted her head and tried to catch a sense of whatever it was that the arachnid had smelled, but her own sense of smell wasn't as highly developed.

Shriek shook her head. *No, Being Annabelle. Whatever it is, it is alive.*

"How close is it?" Annabelle asked.

I can't tell. I . . . She shook her head. *It is gone now.*

Annabelle sighed. Perfect. Now they had to watch out for some kind of walking fish that played maracas?

"I'll take the first watch," she told Shriek. "You go ahead and rest—I'll be waking you all too soon."

The arachnid nodded. As she stretched out, carefully smoothing down her hair spikes where she lay on them, Annabelle turned to the other two. Tomàs was laughing.

"Walking fish?" he said. "*Bom.* Walk them into my belly, then."

Still chuckling, he turned in, leaving Annabelle and Sidi alone by the dying fire. Annabelle fed some more wood to the coals.

"What do you think it was, Sidi?"

"I don't know, Annabelle, but we'd better keep a close watch. If Shriek thinks it's dangerous . . ." The Indian shrugged. "I trust her."

"Me, too. She's good people. You'd better turn in."

Sidi reached out and touched the back of her hand. "We'll be fine, Annabelle—you'll see."

She turned her hand to clasp his for a moment, and

gave his fingers a squeeze. His skin was dry, the palms thick with callouses.

"I hope so," she said.

She watched him curl up by the trunk of the tree, head pillowed on a root, and envied the way he immediately fell asleep. Then she sat up, feeding more wood to the fire, and listened to the jungle night. She started at every sudden noise, but the weird shaking sound wasn't repeated during her watch, nor during that of any of the others, she found out in the morning.

Tomàs had the last watch, but when Annabelle woke, she noticed that Shriek was awake as well, though still lying down, two of her six eyes focused on the Portuguese.

I shoulda thought of that, she realized. Some leader I'm turning out to be. The bloody little weasel could slit all our throats while we're sleeping.

The following day passed uneventfully. That evening, Shriek brought down one of the tapirlike creatures and this time, Annabelle ate with them. Although she was still squeamish about watching the thing be butchered, she could handle eating it. But not the monkey—that was too much like eating a cousin, or a baby. Shriek was apparently aware of that, for she'd passed up a number of monkeys in favor of the tapir, and for that, Annabelle was grateful.

Annabelle had the dawn watch that night. She built up the fire, sitting back from its heat, but wanting the comfort of its glow no matter if it made the already stifling night hotter. Light was just creeping in through the overhanging boughs when she heard the sound again.

Chica-chic.

She looked quickly around, trying to sense the place from which it was originating. To her left?

Chica-chic.

Chica-chic.

Right and left.

She nudged Sidi with her foot and picked up a length of wood that she'd been planning to add to the fire.

Chica-chic.

Shriek was awake and sitting up. She plucked hair spikes from her hide, one for each of her four hands.

Chica-chica-chica-chica . . .

The sound came from all around them. In the growing light, Annabelle could make out humanoid shapes moving toward them through the trees. Except for the strange maraca sound, the jungle was silent. Then, the first of the approaching creatures stepped into clear view.

Shriek drew back an arm, but there was a *whufting* sound and she clapped a hand to her neck where a small dart had stung her. Her arms flailed and then she toppled over.

"Ah, Jesus . . ." Annabelle murmured.

She was on her feet, Sidi and Tomàs flanking her on either side, both armed, as she was, with lengths of firewood. Another pair of the creatures joined the first one, then two more, another three, until there were a dozen or so of them surrounding the small company. Looking at them, Annabelle remembered what Clive had read from Neville's journal—"blue people"—and Shriek's warning last night.

An odd, unpleasant smell—like a fish, but it walks on the land.

No kidding, for they did reek, and they looked like fish. And they were definitely blue-skinned.

They were no taller than four feet, but broad-shouldered and stocky. Their faces had the streamlined look of fish about them, with eyes set widely apart, almost to the sides of their heads. Their noses were only vestigial, their mouths wide, lipless slits that almost cut their heads in two. Instead of ears, they had holes in the sides of their head. Their hair was black and slick on the top of their heads, but there was none on their bodies. Loincloths covered their genitals. Each had a blowgun, and a number of darts sticking up between his knuckles, obviously ready for instant use.

It was when she caught sight of the back of one of them that she realized what they reminded her of—

sharks. They had stiff fins sticking up along their spines, and when a few opened their mouths, she saw rows of sharp teeth. Mouths open wide, they tilted their heads back, and Annabelle saw their uvulas shake.

Chica-chic.

Mystery number one solved, she thought. Now, how the hell do we get out of this?

One who appeared to be a leader stepped closer to them. "Folly, folly," he said.

His voice was a wheezing rasp, and Annabelle wasn't sure what she was hearing. Was it English? Was he telling them they were stupid? No marks for brilliance there, pal. Or was it an alien word? And if so, what did it mean?

She thought of Clive and his party wandering happily across the veldt, and wished she'd been smart enough to stick with them.

"You know, kids," she told her companions, "I think the smart move now's to drop these sticks."

At the sound of her voice, blowguns lifted to the mouths of those who weren't making the weird maraca sound, each weapon fixed on Annabelle, Sidi, or Tomàs.

Chica-chica-chica.

Annabelle let her stick fall from her hand. "Take it easy," she said, in the most placating tone she could muster. "You win."

On either side, her companions let their own make-shift weapons drop.

"Did you ever get the feeling it's gonna be just one of those days?" she said to Sidi.

"Folly, folly!" the leader cried.

"You said it, pal."

A number of the creatures came up to them and forced them to lie on the ground, hands behind their backs. Their wrists were tied, and then they were forced back to their feet and pushed on down the game trail, blue hands prodding them with stiff fingers whenever they lagged. Behind, Shriek was tied to two long poles. Their captors then hoisted her bulk onto their shoulders and took up the rear.

Face it, Annie B., Annabelle told herself. You screwed up again.

▪ Nine ▪

The ground tremors grew worse as the enormous herd of brontosaurs drew nearer. It was now possible for Clive's party to see the scavenging coelurosaurs as well, though they were still dwarfed by the monstrous herbivores where they ranged in the shadow of the herd. They appeared to be a kind of lizard and were, indeed, the size of ostriches. Their rear legs were far larger than the fore, though they appeared equally comfortable running on all fours or upright like a man, their long tails thrust out straight behind them for balance.

The scavengers would be his party's principle danger, Clive realized, but it was difficult to drag his gaze away from the behemoths that made up the herd. The Walking Mountains. Finnbogg's description of them was all too apt.

It was next to impossible for Clive to calculate the sheer bulk of the creatures. It was as though the glass dome of the Great Exhibition's Crystal Palace had become flesh, sprouted enormous legs, tail, and elongated neck, and begun to march across Hyde Park. But not just one dome become monster. Hundreds of them. For as far as the eye could see.

Clinging to the tree to keep his balance, Clive could only marvel that such creatures could even exist. The cyborg's estimates of the creatures' lengths and weights seemed inadequate.

"Well," Smythe drawled at his side. "We can't complain of this being a dull sort of a place."

Clive nodded. Mopish, it certainly wasn't.

"I could do with a little boredom," he said.

"Finnbogg would settle for merely surviving to remember," the dwarf muttered.

"My circuits will preserve the memory," the cyborg said, "even if we do not survive."

Smythe rolled his eyes. "Isn't that bloody reassuring."

"We should have gone with Annabelle's party," Clive said. "As soon as we saw that feeding ground, we should have turned back. Meteorites and grass fires, indeed."

"That's it!" Smythe cried. "Finnbogg, Major—each of you take a grip of my shoulders and hold me hard."

Clive gave his comrade a puzzled glance, then braced himself as best he could and took a grip on Smythe's left shoulder. On the other side of Smythe, Finnbogg did the same. Clive glanced back at the herd. Their approach remained steady, the sound of their tread like one continuous roll of thunder. The scavengers were closer still. Any moment they would be investigating this island of trees where his small party was hiding.

He turned back to see Smythe striking flint against steel.

"What are you doing?" he cried.

"Setting a grass fire," Smythe replied. "Don't you see? We'll start a fire and fan it in their direction to chase the bloody things away."

Capital, Clive thought. And if the fire chose to burn in their direction instead? But the wind was blowing toward the behemoths, and it was obvious that no one else had a better plan.

With a bunch of dried grass between his knees, Smythe worked the flint and steel, cursing with great imagination as he attempted to set it alight. Twice he dropped the flint as the reverberations grew too severe and both Clive and Finnbogg momentarily lost their grip on him. The cyborg had turned from the view of the herd to watch them with what Clive swore was amusement in his cold features.

Then a spark flew to the grass, and the grass smoldered. Smythe blew gently until it caught fire. With his makeshift torch in hand, he closed himself from the grip of his companions and crawled unsteadily away from the tree, where he started a line of fire in the tall grass.

"Help me now!" he cried over his shoulder.

Flint and steel returned to their pouch at his belt. He removed his coat, and began to fan it at the flames. The dried grass caught fire quickly, and soon the three of them were beating the sparks that leapt back toward them while simultaneously fanning the flames in the direction of the herd.

The wind at their backs gusted, and suddenly there was a wall of fire rushing away from them. Through the smoke they could see the monstrous heads of the brontosaurs lifting on their extended necks, turning in the direction of the flames.

"That's done it!" Smythe cried as the closest of the creatures lumbered away in panic.

But now they were busy beating out the flames that threatened to engulf their hiding place. Coughing and choking, they built a fire barrier of charred ground on three sides, but they need no longer have worried. The wind drove the fire away from them, and soon there was a sea of flames bearing down on the herd; their island copse was safe.

The earth tremors increased dramatically as the herd lumbered into a panicked half-trot, the behemoths pounding the plain with their immense weight, the scavengers darting among them, quick as lizards. Dust and smoke choked the air. Clive, Smythe, and Finnbogg clung to the ground as it rocked and buckled under them. Even Guafe lost his balance and assumed a similar undignified position. The air rang with the thunder of the herd's flight.

By the time the tremors had been reduced to mere vibrations, the party was so shaken that they could barely stand. Their sense of balance was all awry, and they lurched to their feet like East End drunks, grinning at each other.

"Hurroo!" Smythe cried. "That's foxed the bastards!"

Clive clapped him on the back. "There's the man!"

The cyborg suffered none of their loss of balance.

Standing stiffly to one side of them, he brushed at his clothes.

"I see no cause for celebration," he said, his metallic voice sharper than ever. "All you have accomplished is the ruin of a perfect observational opportunity."

"Don't be such a wet goose," Smythe told him. "Would you rather be dead?"

"That is not the point. I believe it would have been far more interesting to gather data on such obscure fauna—not to stampede them."

Smythe didn't bother to reply. He spat on the ground and turned to look at where the fire was dying out as it came up against the tramped and cropped area of the behemoths' trail.

"I don't understand you," Clive said. "We might have died if Horace hadn't thought of turning the herd back with his fire."

Guafe studied the Englishman for a long moment. "Knowledge is a precious commodity," the cyborg said finally. "More important than a few lives."

"Died you would have, too," Finnbogg said. "What good's saved up *thinks* then?"

The cyborg touched his chest. "My memory circuits are stored in a casing that would survive the detonation of a nuclear bomb." At their baffled looks, he added, "By which I mean a great deal of destructive force."

"But *you* wouldn't survive," Clive said.

"That is not important."

Smythe turned to look at Guafe. "Sounds to me like a case of a wet arse and no fish."

Now it was the cyborg's turn to appear confused.

"A fruitless quest," Clive explained.

Smythe nodded. "A man's a man, for a' that," he said, quoting Burns. "For what he is, my clockwork man, for what he does. If a man's heart is true, he is more important than any cause. Better to be remembered for the good deeds you've done than for what bits of knowledge you carry around in your brain. You may have some indestructible memory chest inside you, but it'll do no one any good if you're to die here. Who's to find it?"

"My people would—"

"If your people knew where you are, they'd come looking for you, now, wouldn't they?"

"This is a pointless discussion," Guafe said, effectively ending the conversation. "We have the better part of the day ahead of us, and a long journey still to complete. I suggest we get on with it."

Without waiting for them, he set off.

It was easier traveling, following in the trail of the brontosaur herd. Without having to fight through the grass, even dodging the crater-like footprints, they made much better time, doubling the distance that they had covered the previous day.

"We're beginning to look like a pair of heavy swells," Smythe remarked to Clive as they followed the cyborg, who walked ahead of them with a stiff-backed gait.

Clive nodded, fingering his beard. A few decades ago—at least, in English years, and counting back from when they'd left London—the officers returning from the Crimea had started a new fashion of full beards, or opulent side-whiskers, that the heavy swells took as their own. They spoke in languid drawls to indicate their social superiority, turning all their r's into w's. Specimens of their kind survived well into the 1860s.

"At least we haven't descended to that wather weawisome style of speech."

"Oh, Howace. How you do go on!"

Both men broke into laughter, garnering a puzzled look from Finnbogg.

"Don't worry, Finn," Smythe assured him. "We haven't both gone knackers."

"I needed that laugh," Clive said when he'd recovered his breath.

Smythe nodded. "It's a grim world," he said. "And, speaking of grimness, are there any other dangers on this level that you haven't warned us of, Finn?"

Clive patted the pocket that held his twin's journal.

"We need all the warning we can get. Neville said nothing about those creatures."

"I wouldn't count on too much help from your brother, sah," Smythe said. "That's one thing Annabelle had right—we're more liable to run headlong into danger following his directions, than going our own way. It's what he doesn't tell us that worries me."

Clive was in complete agreement. "More surprises, we don't need."

"Finnbogg heard story of Walking Mountains and their herdsmen a long time ago," the dwarf said. "Finnbogg doesn't remember much of it. But when they came and ground shook, then Finnbogg—"

"Herdsmen?" Smythe cried. "What herdsmen?"

"Perhaps he's referring to those scavenger creatures," Clive said hopefully.

The dwarf's brow wrinkled as he searched for the memory. "Finnbogg thinks they're a kind of bird. A low-flying bird."

Clive and Smythe worriedly scanned the sky.

"Silver in color," Finnbogg went on, "and they nest in the mountains." He waved a hand in the general direction of the mountain range that, for all their traveling away from it, appeared as close today as it had two days previous.

Smythe said, "It's at least a week's march across this plain. If luck is with us, for once, perhaps we'll miss meeting up with them."

Clive frowned. "Neville wrote nothing of these herdsmen."

"He wrote nothing of the herd, either," Smythe replied.

The remainder of that day, they watched the skies, getting cricks in their necks, but there was no sign of any bird, silver or otherwise. Smythe brought down another of the curious dares in the late afternoon, so once again they had fresh meat for their supper. The dares had been congregated about a small fresh-water seep, so while Smythe cleaned his kill, Clive and Finnbogg filled their watersacks, which had been growing steadily emptier since leaving the river.

That evening, as they smoked strips of the meat for the next day's meals, the two Englishmen kept after Finnbogg, wanting more information about this level of the Dungeon. The dwarf fended off their queries, growing more upset, until he flew into a sudden, towering rage.

"Don't know, don't know!" he shouted. "Finnbogg only ever remember bits and pieces. Finnbogg would tell you if he knew more, but he doesn't! He doesn't!"

He stood over the two sitting men, glowering with rage, then suddenly burst into tears. Clive and Smythe exchanged awkward glances. They'd been through the dwarf's sudden mood swings before, but that didn't make them feel any less like heels at the moment.

"By his behavior patterns," Guafe remarked conversationally, "I don't doubt that he's a schizophrenic."

That drew blank stares from both Englishmen.

"By which I mean," the cyborg explained, "he has an abnormally high number of dopamine receptors in his brain, so these sudden shifts in mood aren't really his fault. Neurosurgery could correct the problem, though I doubt we'd find facilities advanced enough on this level for me to help him—if, in fact, that is what he is suffering from. Being unfamiliar with his physiology, I would need to do some exploratory—"

"Why don't you shut your gob for a change," Smythe told Guafe as he knelt beside the weeping dwarf. He put an arm around Finnbogg's broad shoulders.

"We're sorry," he said, giving Finnbogg a squeeze, "the Major and I. We didn't mean to have at you as we did."

"Finnbogg . . . just doesn't know any more," the dwarf said in a small voice. "It comes and goes and he can never remember sometimes."

"And we know that now, Finn—don't we, sah? You've been a great help to us many's the time already. Don't you worry now."

Finnbogg rubbed his knuckles against his eyes. Clive sat on his haunches in front of the dwarf.

"I'm truly sorry, Finn," he said.

The dwarf blinked, then suddenly appeared self-conscious under all the attention.

"Friends?" Clive asked.

He offered his hand. After a moment, Finnbogg nodded and shook. Smythe gave the dwarf's shoulders a final squeeze.

"There's the lad," he said. Then he gave Guafe a cold look. "Why don't you take first watch—seeing how you like to observe things so much and all?"

"I'll be glad to," Guafe said.

"One day," Smythe muttered, smacking his right fist into his left palm. Then he tugged Finnbogg over to where he and Clive were sitting by the fire and regaled the dwarf with a few preposterous tales, until Finnbogg was clutching his stomach with laughter.

It was on the following day, just as the salmon-colored sun was reaching its zenith, that they spied what looked to be a low hill a mile or so away on the plain before them. It was Smythe who first realized that it was a dead brontosaur, but it was Finnbogg who spotted the small silver airships that were parked around the carcass, their silver-suited drivers harvesting the behemoth's flesh. Guafe called the airships one-man hovercraft.

"The herdsmen," Finnbogg said.

Clive's throat felt suddenly dry.

"Best we don't play the jack this time," Smythe said. "Time to hide ourselves."

He jumped into the nearest brontosaur footprint, Clive and Finnbogg following suit, but it was too late. The herdsmen had already spied them. A number of the silver hovercraft left the carcass and sped across the plain toward them, riding the air a foot or so above the ground.

The flyers closed the distance between them with such speed, they realized that they had no hope of outrunning the machines.

· Ten ·

The village of the blue shark people was a half-day's march farther down the trail they'd been taking. It was a cluster of small, one-room huts, the walls and roofs constructed of reeds tied to wooden frames. Cookfires burned at the doorways. Domestic cousins of the lupine-faced possums hung by their tails from poles, heads slowly turning to watch the progress of Annabelle's party and their captors.

They were herded unceremoniously into the center of the village, where they were immediately surrounded by a crowd of the blue-skinned beings. Shark-toothed grins leered at them. Children with half-grown fins following the ridges of their spines poked at them with sticks. From all sides rose that maraca sound, as though Annabelle and her party had been dumped into the middle of a rattlesnake's nest.

Chica-chica-chica-chica . . .

Though she tried, Annabelle could discern no real variations in the sound, so she doubted it was a language. An expression of excitement, maybe? Or, how about amusement?

Prodded and pushed, they stood in a small, huddled group, with Shriek's limp body deposited at their feet. The noise of the shark people was steadily increasing, until Annabelle had to grit her teeth against the sound. It was painful—worse than feedback from her Les Paul—but it was also humiliating. She had the same feeling now as when she'd been on the receiving end of the chorusing boos her band had gotten the time they'd opened for Death Squad, whose neo-Nazi fans had eloquently expressed their impatience with the combination of music and theater that made up the Crackbelles' act.

Lookit the freaks.

When the sudden silence fell, it left a relief so profound that all Annabelle's limbs went weak. But she kept herself stiffly upright, for coming toward them through the parting crowd was an awesome figure that even the shark people seemed to hold with as much fear as they did respect.

He was a good foot taller than any of the other villagers, blue-skinned as well, but his entire body was covered with tiny white shells, which were attached by wires directly to his skin, like pierced earrings. His hair was long and braided with blue feathers. From a shell-festooned belt about his waist hung a small cluster of monkey skulls, and a flat fur pouch with a bluish tint to its pelage.

In one hand he carried a staff two feet taller than himself. From its head dangled more shells, these threaded on leather thongs, and the skeletal arms of what she assumed were monkeys, the bones wired loosely together so that the limbs swung back and forth with every movement of the staff.

He came to a stop directly in front of the captives and studied them with a considering gaze. His eyes were a cloudy white, like a blind man's, but it was obvious he could see.

"Hrak," he said suddenly, thumping his free hand against his chest.

The shells attached to his skin clattered at the impact. Annabelle winced at the pain it must have caused; but maybe these creatures didn't have nerves in their skin. When she thought about how she'd feel if her own flesh was like that, it seemed likely.

A chorus of subdued *chica-chics* arose from the crowd. The one who appeared to be the leader gazed at them expectantly, as though waiting for a response.

Great, Annabelle thought. What the hell's "hrak"

supposed to mean? His name? His title? The kind of being his is? Hello? Howyadoin'?

Impatient with the silence of his captives, the leader poked Annabelle with a stiff finger.

"Folly!" he cried.

Jesus, Annabelle thought with sudden insight. He's trying to say Folliot. Clive's brother must have passed through here, and this geek thinks anybody with skin this white's a "folly." Now, the thing to figure out was, had Neville left these guys in a good mood, or had he been shitting on them like he did in almost every other place they'd tracked him to? Only one way to find out.

Annabelle took a steady breath. "Folly," she said, thumping her chest in a manner similar to the leader's.

He glared at her from his milky eyes. There was no question about his displeasure.

Way to go, Annabelle thought. Annie B. blows it again.

Without warning, the leader batted her across the head with his free fist. Arms bound behind her back so that she couldn't maintain her balance. Annabelle hit the ground, head ringing from the blow, shoulder bruised from the impact with the dirt. The leader spat down at her.

"Folly, folly!" he cried.

The surrounding crowd took up the cry, mixed with the rattling *chica-chics*. The leader thrust a hand toward a distant hut and then eager hands were hauling Annabelle to her feet, propelling her and her two standing companions toward it. Others dragged Shriek along, hauling her by one leg and a couple of her arms. Inside the hut, they were pushed to the ground. The door swung closed on leather hinges, and grinning shark faces pressed against it to look at the captives.

They hissed and spat, uvulas rattling.

Chica-chica-chica.

As Annabelle rose blearily into a sitting position, her vision swimming, a gob hit her on the cheek, the saliva leaving a slight burning sensation on her skin. She rubbed her cheek against her knee, then back-pedaled to the farthest corner of the hut, away from the crowd of creatures at the door.

"Why were you so *estúpido*?" Tomàs demanded.

Annabelle turned to look at him. "Blow it out your face," she told him. "I didn't see you coming up with anything better."

Tomàs's lips pulled into a snarl, but he made no reply, only turned his head away. Annabelle tested her bonds. The braided grass rope still held tight. She tried to ignore the crowd of leering faces at the door, and eventually they lost interest and drew away. It was then that the captives could see the stakes being raised in the square in the middle of the village, the wood being piled around their bases.

Four stakes. Four captives. No need to guess what they had to look forward to in the very near future.

"Aw, shit," Annabelle said. "What're we gonna do now?"

"Wait," Sidi told her.

"For what? The cavalry? I hate to break this to you, Sidi, but they're not going to show."

Sidi merely nodded to where Shriek lay, still unconscious. "If she were dead, they would not have thrown her in here with us. So we wait for the effect of the dart to wear off. She is not bound as we are."

Except, what if she didn't come round in time? Annabelle wanted to know, but she didn't speak her fear aloud. Instead, she leaned back against the wall of the hut and closed her eyes.

Annabelle tried not to think of the stakes, and the pyres being erected around them. From time to time she glanced at Shriek's limp body, but the spiderlike alien still showed no sign of life. Then she'd glance away again, catching Tomàs's gaze sliding from her own. Or meeting Sidi's, which was not quite resigned, but growing steadily less confident. Or seeing the stakes again, the blue-skinned shark people milling around them.

Those damned stakes.

She closed her eyes once more and thought of the last

time she'd seen her daughter, out in front of her mother's place, where Amanda was staying with her Grannymums while the Crackbelles went on tour.

"Are you coming back, mommy?" Amanda had asked, her urchin face turned worriedly up to Annabelle's. "You won't forget me, will you?"

Amanda had a fear of being abandoned—because of all the band's touring. She thought one time that Annabelle just wouldn't come back. Like I'd ever dump her, Annabelle thought.

"No way, José," she'd told her daughter, mussing the short black curls. "I'll be back before you can say Jack Lippity Sprat."

Amanda's reply was to reach up for a tearful hug.

I'll be back, Annabelle thought, remembering. Right. She looked out at the stakes. I didn't mean to lie to you, sweetheart, but your mommy's never coming back.

"Life slips through our fingers," Annabelle's own mother had told her once. "Everyone says that—that time goes too quickly, that we never get to do everything we want to do in the time we have—but it's worse in our family, Annie. We never keep the things that are most precious to us—lovers, happiness. We never get to hold on to anything good for very long. Your grandmother used to say that there was a curse on the women of our line. 'Be happy with all your heart when you can be,' she told me, 'for it won't last. It never does. If you try to hold on, you'll only get hurt.'"

No kidding. Annabelle knew just what her mother had meant. Like saving up a lot of hard-earned cash for her first Les Paul, then getting mugged walking home with it from the store. Beautiful New York City. Like just having the Crackbelles finally start to get some decent gigs, and here she was, dusted off into Bizarro—Land of the Weird and Strange, where it looked like she was gonna end up as dinner for a bunch of monsters.

The Sharks That Walk Like Men. Now playing at a theater near you. Thrill to the chills. See the rock star and her friends become shark stew.

Aw, Jesus.

All she could see were Amanda's teary eyes. That sweet face turned up to hers.

You won't forget me, will you?

Never, sweetheart.

Are you coming back, mommy?

Tears were starting to leak from her eyes. She could feel Tomàs's disdainful gaze on her, Sidi's sympathetic one. Neither of them knew. They thought she was crying for herself, because she was scared, but it wasn't that. Not just that. It was the thought of leaving that big hole in her daughter's life. It was thinking of the poor kid growing up with first her old man, and then her old lady, dumping her.

I'm like the spell the fairies use, she thought, when they give humans gold in Fairyland and it turns out to be just dead leaves and crap when they get back to their own world. Everything I touch turns to shit.

Are you coming back, mommy?

She looked at the stakes, the wood piled up around their bases. Just waiting for her and her friends. They were probably due on that center stage at nightfall—at least, that's the way it usually worked in all the frigging movies.

You won't forget me, will you?

She looked at Shriek, still unconscious. Tomàs and Sidi watching her. The braided grass ropes around all their wrists, too tough to break. Maybe we could chew through them? Right. But then her gaze dropped down to the arms of her jacket, which was still tied around her waist.

Wake up, Annie B., she told herself.

"Sidi?"

"Yes?"

"Come help me get my jacket off, would you?"

Though he looked puzzled, the Indian slid himself over to where she was sitting and complied. When she had the jacket in her hands, she played around with it until she had a grip on one of the zippers. She held it firmly between her fingers.

"Get your hands around back here," she told him.

Sidi's eyes lit up as he understood. The metal zipper didn't have much bite, but it was going to be enough to saw through the grass ropes. It bloody well had to be.

It was tough going. The jacket kept slipping in her grip, and it was hard to work on something without being able to see what she was doing, but after a good fifteen minutes of sawing, the grass became weak enough for Sidi to break the remaining strands.

"All *right*," Annabelle said as he started to work on her own bonds.

The Indian was stronger, and he had her free in half the time, moving on to free Tomàs while she rubbed her chafed wrists and considered their next move. Shriek still wasn't moving. Should they try to make a break for it now—out the back of the hut, which faced the river, hauling Shriek as they went—or wait until the shark people came to get them, and try to take them down? There really wasn't any decision to make.

She moved to the back of the hut and explored the reed covering of the wooden frame. It'd be a piece of cake to get through that. When she looked back at the others, she saw that Tomàs was free now, as well. Sidi returned to her side, handing her back the jacket, which she retied around her waist.

"Good thinking."

"Yeah, well, I got lucky. But we're not outta here yet."

"We're going out the back?"

Annabelle nodded. "Only choice we've got, I figure. We'll hit the river and make a swim for it—it'll be easier pulling Shriek through the water than trying to haul her through the jungle. Can you swim?"

Sidi bobbed his head, white teeth flashing.

"How about you, Tomàs? A fine sailor like you—can you swim?" Considering his aversion to bathing, it was just as likely that he couldn't.

"*Sim.*"

"Great." Annabelle glanced out the door, but no one seemed to be paying undue attention to them. "Let's get going, then. Sidi, you break down the wall—and quietly, please—while Tomàs gives me a hand with Shriek."

Tomàs shook his head. "Leave her."

"No way, pal."

"She is a monster."

"She's a friend. Now, either you give me a hand with her, or we'll knock you silly and leave you behind to be fish food—got it?"

"It is a waste of time," Tomàs argued. He gave Shriek's body a nudge with his toe that got no response. "She is already dead."

Sidi had broken a peephole through the reeds in the back of the hut. "All clear," he called softly over his shoulder.

"We've got a problem with the weasel here," Annabelle told him. "He won't help me with Shriek."

Sidi frowned and left the wall, brown fingers of either hand clenched into fists.

Tomàs quickly raised his hands protectively in front of him. "*Ja nao,*" he said. "I was only joking. I'm happy to help. *Verdade.*"

Annabelle gave him a hard stare. Yeah. Sure you are. Until someone offers you a better deal. But she motioned Sidi to return to the wall. While he continued to widen the small hole he'd made, she and Tomàs dragged Shriek's heavy body toward the back of the hut. When the hole was big enough, Sidi cautiously stuck his head outside.

"Still clear," he said.

He stepped through the opening, then helped the other two manhandle Shriek's body through. In moments they were all outside. The river bank was no more than fifteen feet directly behind the hut, hidden from the village's central square by a number of other huts.

Thank you, God, Annabelle said in silent prayer, eschewing her devout atheism. But then she heard the rattlesnake *chica-chic* of one of the shark people's uvulas. She turned, looking up from her half-crouch, to find a blue-skinned creature looming up directly behind her, obviously having just come around the hut to stumble upon them.

Shit, Annabelle thought. Everything I touch . . .

• Eleven •

Unarmed, and with nowhere to run, Clive's party awaited the approach of the herdsmen in their hover-craft—Clive, Smythe, and Finnbogg bunched together in a group, the cyborg standing off to one side on his own. Their helplessness chafed at them all, but considering their situation, the only reasonable course of action left open to them was to wait to see how events would unfold. For men who preferred to control their own destinies, it was not an easy course of action. But then, since entering the Dungeon, nothing had been simple or easy.

The hovercraft made next to no sound as they darted toward the party. Their riders gave the Englishmen the uneasy sense that they were defying the laws of science—a feeling that Finnbogg shared. The cyborg appeared unaffected by their fears.

Happily content to take advantage of another "observational opportunity," Clive thought with some bitterness, with no consideration of the possible danger it presented to them. The cyborg's next comments served only to confirm Clive's feelings.

"Fascinating," Guafe remarked, almost to himself. "The craft appear to be a form of scooter, utilizing an air cushion to keep them aloft, but still capable of great speed. I wonder what their method of propulsion would be."

The machines settled slowly to the ground in a half-circle facing the party, the low hum of their engines dying as their silver-suited riders switched off the ignitions and stepped down from the machines. Settled upon the ground, the flyers no longer appeared quite so marvelous. They were merely machines now—gleaming steel, and far beyond the technological capabilities of Clive's own England—but still machines.

It seemed, he realized at the present turn of his thoughts, that their continued tenure in this odd land was leaving him somewhat inured to its wonders.

He studied the approaching riders. At least they were humanoid—very much like Europeans, really—though it was hard to make much of their features behind the goggles and helmets they wore. The shimmery material of their suits clung to their bodies like a second skin, acquiring particularly intriguing shapes on the two women in the group.

One of the women was obviously the leader.

She took a few steps ahead of the others and removed her helmet and goggles. Her hair was blonde, and cropped to within a half-inch of her skull. Her eyes were the green-blue of the sky, her features not quite classically beautiful—due as much to her lack of hair to frame them, Clive thought, as to their actual proportions—but handsome all the same. Clipped to her belt was a holster that obviously held a firearm, though of what sort neither Clive nor Smythe could even make a guess.

A casual glance at the others of her party revealed that they all bore similar weapons. The woman regarded them each for a moment, then returned her attention to Clive. A friendly smile touched her lips.

"You will be Major Clive Folliot?" she asked.

Clive blinked with surprise. "How do you know my name?"

She gave a casual shrug of her shoulders, which gave her breasts an enticing bounce. Clive forced his gaze to remain on her face.

"We have been keeping a watch out for your party," she said. "You have been expected. We thought to find you sooner, but when we spied the porten herd, we delayed long enough to bring one down." She nodded over her shoulder. "Others of my company are butchering it as we speak. There is enough sustenance there to feed the city for a month. A worthy delay, don't you think?"

Confusion still reigned in Clive's mind, but he managed to school his features to give none of it away. "Certainly," he said. "But tell me, how did you know we were here?"

"Your brother, the priest, asked us to look for you—Father Neville."

The priest? Clive thought. Was Neville coming down in the world? The last they'd heard of his religious inclinations, he'd called himself a bishop.

"I see," he said. "And where is Father Neville? Can you take us to him?"

"Of course. That is the reason we have been looking for you."

"Who are you?"

The woman smiled again. "So many questions. Father Neville told us you would be full of them. I am Keoti Vichlo, First Scout of the Dramaran Dynasty."

"Dramaran—that is the ruined city a few days' journey to the east?"

Keoti frowned slightly. "Ruined, yes—but not for long. Now that your brother has raised us from the Long Sleep, we have begun to restore it to its former glory. Still, you must not worry that all is hardship in Dramaran at the moment. We have pleasant lodgings that are still intact, under the city."

"Long Sleep?" Clive couldn't help but ask, for all that he didn't wish the newcomers to realize just how ignorant of advanced technologies and this world his party was.

But Guafe understood immediately. "That would be a form of suspended animation, I presume," he said. "Can I assume that there was some form of malfunction with your equipment, effectively trapping you in that state until the fortunate arrival of . . . ah . . . Father Neville?"

Clive and Smythe shot the cyborg a curious look. Neither had ever heard Guafe hesitate in speech before and it jolted them. Keoti gave the cyborg a considering look as well. She seemed about to speak, but Clive was quicker.

"How do you come to speak English so well?" he asked.

"Father Neville taught us," she replied with a shrug. "We fed his language into our computers through a bio-feed link and received the data in a similar fashion. Is this not the way with your own people?"

Clive had only the vaguest notion as to what she was referring to, but he nodded. "Of course," he said.

Keoti turned her attention back to Chang Guafe. "What a superior piece of workmanship," she said. "Your humanotron appears so lifelike. One would almost believe that it was truly alive, rather than a construct."

"I am a self-aware cyborg," Guafe told her coldly. "Not a construct."

"Pardon me," she said. "I meant no offense."

"None taken," the cyborg replied, though it was obvious to all that exactly the opposite was the case.

Don't start now, Clive thought. The Dramaranians appeared to be quite friendly, and he preferred to leave things that way—not insult or anger them, as Guafe was apt to do if he began to argue.

"Yes, well," Clive said briskly. "It will be wonderful to see my good brother again. Let me introduce you to the rest of my companions. Chang Guafe you have just met. This gentleman on my right is my good companion Quartermaster Sergeant Horace Smythe."

"Yes," Keoti said. "Father Neville has spoken of you, Horace Smythe. You have some gift with . . . theatrics, I believe."

"I'm not sure what you mean, madam," Smythe said.

She smiled. "A talent that allows you to appear to be something other than you are."

"And this is our friend Finnbogg," Clive said.

Keoti gave the dwarf a polite smile, but introduced none of her own companions. "We can take one passenger per flyer," she said. "If you are willing, we can begin the return flight to Dramaran as soon as I give my second-in-command—" she glanced back to where the greater number of Dramaranians were still at work on the porten's carcass "—his orders."

Clive glanced at Smythe and knew by the expression on his former batman's features that the same worries were troubling him. This Keoti woman was extremely friendly and forthcoming, but with Neville involved— and who knew what mischief he was up to—they might well be walking into yet another trap. Still, what choice did they have? When Smythe gave a brief shrug, Clive turned back to the woman.

"We'd be delighted to partake of your hospitality," he said.

Keoti smiled. "Will you ride with me?"

"I think we'd prefer to walk," Clive said. "At least as far as that . . . porten carcass your company is butchering. We'll join you there."

"As you wish."

She gave Clive a warm smile. Replacing her helmet and goggles, she returned to her flyer. Within moments the hovercraft were airborne once more, and speeding back to rejoin their companions.

"Well," Clive said, once they were gone. "They seem pleasant enough."

Smythe nodded. "Too pleasant, I'm thinking, sah. I don't like this—not with Sir Neville's hand in it, stirring the pot."

"At least they have some technology worth studying," Guafe offered, "even if their observational powers are somewhat limited."

They began to walk toward the dead behemoth, where the Dramaranians continued their harvesting work, busily surrounding the slain monster like a flock of flies.

"Did you know of any of this?" Clive asked Finnbogg. "Of this Long Sleep, or this second city, buried under the ruins of the first?"

"Not a whisper," the dwarf replied.

"What's Sir Neville up to?" Smythe wondered aloud.

"'Father Neville,' indeed. The man's about as holy as a fat, pursy gunner, living high on the hog of his spoils."

"At least he's waiting for us," Clive said.

Smythe nodded. "As he's waited for us before. The thought doesn't give me much comfort, sah. I'd sooner just give him a few stout blows in the head than take the chance of falling victim to another of his jigamarees."

"I doubt our present hosts would allow that," Guafe said.

The carcass was looming closer—truly, if not a mountain, then a large hill of flesh, rising up from the flat surface of the veldt. The Dramaranians were cutting the huge slabs of meat from the monster's haunches with some form of saw that appeared to be composed of a tightly focused band of light.

"Lasers," Guafe said.

None of his companions bothered to ask him to explain. It was all simply too far out of their depth.

"Well, I, for one, will be very interested in hearing what Neville has to say for himself," Clive said. There was a hard look in his eyes as he spoke. "He has a great deal of explaining to do."

Smythe nodded. "Very interested," he agreed. "Just don't blink in his presence, or we might find ourselves whisked away to Lord knows where."

Keoti walked out to join them as they finally approached. They had to crane their necks to look at the top part of the porten's carcass.

"I am finished here," she said. "If you are ready to go now . . . ?"

She led the way back to her hovercraft without waiting for Clive's reply.

"Careful now," Smythe whispered quickly to Clive as another of the Dramaranians motioned to him.

"And you," Clive replied.

Finnbogg, however, wouldn't go with the Dramaranian who would be ferrying him to the ruined city.

"Finnboggi weren't meant to go floating in the air," he said. "It's not right."

"We won't be going very high," the Dramaranian

coaxed him. "No more than a few feet above the ground."

"A few feet more than Finnbogg wants to be," the dwarf said. He stamped a foot against the ground. "Here's where Finnbogg is meant to be. With dirt in toes. Not playing bird."

Clive quickly interceded before Finnbogg shifted into one of his more belligerent moods. He put an arm around the dwarf's shoulder.

"It will be fine," he said. "We're all riding with them, Finn."

"It's not right," the dwarf repeated, though not so forcefully this time.

"Think of it as an adventure," Smythe said to him. "What a tale you'll have to tell—skimming for leagues over the veldt to a ruined city that's being rebuilt by its inhabitants." He rubbed the palms of his hands together. "Doesn't just the thought of it make you itch to get there the sooner?"

"We don't want to leave you behind," Clive added.

"Hrumph," Finnbogg said.

But though he walked stiffly, and frowned with every step, he let himself be led to the flyer. He mounted it gingerly, as though the machine would bite. Once he was seated, the others went to the flyers they would be riding.

It felt decidedly awkward, Clive thought as he sat behind Keoti, the machine straddled between his legs. It was like mounting a legless horse—and with nothing to hold on to, to keep from falling off. Keoti showed him where to put his feet—they went on small pegs, set into the side of the machine, that lifted his knees level with his buttocks—then placed his hands around her waist.

"Hold on," she said.

The material of her bodysuit had a metallic texture, but it was so supple that Clive could feel the bottom of her rib cage and the soft flesh of her waist, as though there was nothing between his hands and her skin. She looked over her shoulder at him, head like a bug with its helmet and goggles, but her lips were a woman's, and they smiled cheerfully at him.

The machine's engine set up a vibration against Clive's legs when it was turned on, then suddenly they were up in the air, hovering some three feet above the ground. He felt giddy at the sudden movement and clutched Keoti very tightly. Realizing what he was doing, he eased his grip. He looked around to see how his companions were doing. Finnbogg's face was blanched. Smythe's and Guafe's features were impassive.

Then the flyers shot off, and they were skimming across the veldt. They circled once around the brontosaur carcass, where the remainder of the Dramaranians continued their butchering work. The workers lifted bloody hands in greeting, and then the open plains were in front of Clive's party, and they settled down for the long trip to the ruined city, where Neville was waiting for them.

▪ Twelve ▪

Time took on a slow-motion quality for Annabelle. She and the shark man stared at each other as though they had just spotted each other's face in a crowd and were trying to place the half-familiar features. Annabelle knew she should be doing something—striking out at him, taking him down—but her limbs felt weighed down, heavy and dull.

She saw the shark man's mouth open wider. The first *chica-chic* of his approach had been a sound of surprise. Now he was going to call out a warning to the other villagers. She didn't feel she could do anything to stop him, but started to rise all the same, lead-heavy arms reaching toward him.

Then, one of Shriek's hair thorns sprouted suddenly from his throat. His eyes widened and his stillborn cry became a death gurgle. He toppled toward her.

Annabelle continued to reach for him, bracing herself to catch his weight as it fell. Before he landed, Sidi was there at her side, helping her. Together they lowered the dead shark man to the ground. Annabelle turned slowly to see Shriek half sitting up, her weight supported on three of her arms, the fourth just lowering from its upflung position. There was a dullness in most of her eyes, but one was already clear, the others clearing.

Whatever chemical she'd infused that particular spike with, it had done the job efficiently, and fast—very fast.

Is it dead? Shriek asked. Her voice echoed weakly in Annabelle's mind.

Annabelle nodded. "Thanks."

Shriek merely spat in the direction of the shark man's corpse. Sidi touched Annabelle's shoulder.

"We can't delay," he said.

Annabelle glanced down at the corpse, then gave a quick nod of agreement. While Sidi and Tomàs went on ahead to the river, she got her shoulder under one of Shriek's left arms and helped the alien to her feet. Together they hurried to join the others.

Just beyond the shielding wall of huts, they could hear the sound of the villagers—snatches of conversation in a language none of them could understand, the occasional, high-pitched bark of possum dogs, the nerve-grating sound of their uvulas, the hollowed ends rattling, the shaking sound magnified by their mouth cavities.

Chica-chica-chica. . . .

Without bothering to strip off his clothes, Sidi lowered himself into the water. Annabelle and Shriek quickly followed suit, leaving Tomàs hesitating on the river bank.

"Come *on*," Annabelle whispered sharply.

Plainly unhappy, the Portuguese slipped into the water with them. Sidi took the lead, walking them out at a right angle away from the village until the water was level with his neck. Then he kicked his feet free of the river bottom and began to swim, careful not to break the water with a splash that would alert their captors.

Annabelle and Shriek moved through the water closer to the river bank, as Shriek couldn't swim. Instead, with Annabelle there to help support her weight in the water, she half walked, half kicked herself along, using the river bottom as a springboard. Tomàs took up the rear.

Soon the village was out of view, and then even its sounds faded. The bugs were worse than ever this close to the river, and time and again they had to dunk their heads to get rid of the clouds of mosquitoes that were settling on their faces and neck, even in their hair.

"The sooner we get to that gate and outta this jungle," Annabelle muttered, "the happier I'm gonna be. I don't care where it takes us."

"At least we're free of our captors," Sidi remarked.

But he spoke too soon. Even with the distance that they'd put between them and the village, the sudden cries of outraged anger carried clearly toward them.

"Shit."

Sidi glanced at Annabelle and nodded. "We'd best get out of the river," he said. "Considering what they are, I don't doubt that they'll be able to track us through the water—just like the sharks of our own world."

"You're kidding. I thought water was supposed to throw off your scent."

Sidi nodded, then lifted his arm to show the tiny cuts and bruises there, like those they all had. "But a shark can track blood for miles."

They made their way to the shore, clambering up among the thick vines and vegetation. Low-hanging boughs hid them from view, but their trail led directly to where they stood.

Look, Shriek said.

She pointed with one arm to where the first of the shark people had come into view. He swam with an undulating motion of his body, arms kept close to his side, dorsal fin breaking the water, head bobbing up and down with the movement. In moments there were three more, close behind, then another pair.

Shriek plucked a hair spike from her thigh and, holding back a bough to give herself room, threw it at the foremost of their pursuers with a sharp snapping movement of her arm. The spike struck true. The creature began to thrash in the water, limbs convulsing, blood coughing up from his lungs. The others immediately attacked him, tearing at his thrashing limbs with their powerful jaws.

Annabelle turned away, a sick taste coming up her throat.

Shriek flung a second spike, and then the creatures were tearing at that victim as well, fighting among themselves in a feeding frenzy.

That should keep them, Shriek said.

"More will be coming by land," Sidi warned.

Nodding in dull agreement, Annabelle let the Indian lead them deeper into the jungle, away from the river. Some twenty paces in, they stumbled over the game trail, which appeared to have entered the village and then continued on to meet them here. With its more solid footing, and its overhang relatively clear compared to the surrounding forest, they set off at a mile-eating gait, trying to put as much distance between themselves and their pursuit as they could.

They paced themselves, trotting for a quarter of a mile, then walking, then trotting again. The distance fell away behind them, but they were all worn out now. Annabelle knew that they wouldn't be able to maintain this pace very much longer. She clutched the stitch in her side, waiting for her second wind to cut in. All she wanted to do was throw herself down and collapse where she lay. The heat and humidity made her mind dull and sapped the strength from her limbs.

Ahead of her she could see Tomàs lagging. Shriek, still recovering from the effects of the shark people's treated dart, had little of her usual resilience left either. Only Sidi seemed able to keep up the pace forever, if need be, but he held himself back, matching his speed to that of his slower companions.

There was no sign or sound of pursuit yet—neither on the trail behind them, nor in the occasional glimpses of the river they caught where the jungle's dense growth cleared for a moment. But they'd be coming. None of them doubted the tenacity of the shark people. They just had that look about them, Annabelle thought. They weren't the kind to give up.

Yeah, well, neither are we.

But a half-hour later her legs simply gave out from under her, and she went toppling to the ground, only just saving herself from a bad fall by grabbing onto a low-hanging vine. She lost her grip on it almost immediately, but it had been enough to break her fall. When she hit the ground, she didn't hit hard.

She tried to get up, but her calves and thighs were

locked with cramps. When the others turned back to help her, she tried to wave them on.

"Go on," she said. "Get outta here."

Sidi shook his head. While Tomàs and Shriek literally collapsed where they stood, he knelt by her and began to massage her legs with his quick, long fingers, kneading the muscles through her leather jeans until they began to unlock. Her eyes teared with pain, but she didn't complain. The relief was profound as Sidi worked out the cramps, even though the muscles continued to throb.

"Anybody ever tell you that you're a godsend?" Annabelle asked him.

Sidi grinned. "*Keh*. Not recently."

Annabelle smiled back at him, but her moment of good humor was short-lived. "I don't know if I can go on right away," she said. "I'm mean, I've always been in pretty good shape—you go on a tour that's lasting a few months, and you'd *better* be in shape—but the old bod's been taking too much abuse lately."

"We'll rest here for a little while—a half-hour."

"Those shark guys . . ."

"I observed them carefully when they caught us," Sidi replied. "Though they have a very liquid style of movement, they don't appear to have a great deal of speed on land. I think we're well ahead of them, for the moment."

"What about on the river?"

The Indian shrugged. "We'll face that when the time comes. Shriek's stopped them for a while, I think. Rest now, Annabelle, while I see to the others."

"I'm too wound up to rest," Annabelle told him, but she dozed off before Sidi had taken the two steps to where Shriek was lying.

By nightfall they'd put at least six more miles behind them. Exhausted, they sprawled around a small campfire set well east of the game trail—on the side opposite from the river. Twice they had thought they'd heard the grating *chica-chic* rattle of the shark people on the trail behind them. Both times they hid alongside the path, clutching the spears that Sidi had cut for each of them; both times they were false alarms. The second time they found the source of the sound—a small, scorpionlike creature about eleven inches long, with a rattlesnake rattle on the end of its tail in place of a stinger.

For supper they had baked fish that Sidi had speared in the river after he'd set up camp for the others. Now he was hardening the points of their spears in the fire. When he finished the last one, he covered the fire with dirt and they sat in the darkness.

Annabelle had gotten her second wind. Supper had helped, and she felt stronger now, but guilty that so much of the day's decisions and work had fallen on Sidi's slender shoulders. She was determined to pull her own weight the next day—*if* she could find the energy to get up in the morning, that is.

Tomàs sat by himself, away from the rest of them, muttering to himself in Portuguese for a time, then lapsing into a sullen silence. Shriek was grooming herself, carefully working at her hair spikes. The faint rustling of the spikes was the only unnatural sound to be heard against the noise of the jungle until Sidi came to sit beside Annabelle.

His footsteps were muffled, but sounded very loud to her, all wired up as she was, listening to the sounds of night, waiting for the jungle noises to cease at the *chica-chic* of the shark people. She shifted a little to give him room to lean against the tree trunk she'd claimed for a backrest. Their shoulders touched companionably.

"Tomorrow," Sidi asked, "we go on to Quan?"

"Christ, I don't know anymore. I'm tempted to backtrack and try to catch up with Clive and the rest of them."

"The veldt is wide, Annabelle—we could easily miss them."

"Yeah. And spend the rest of our lives wandering around out there. What do you think we should do, Sidi?"

"Go on."

"I suppose." She sighed. "Do you think they're still following us—the shark people?"

"I think so, yes,"

"We need some defense against their blowguns. I mean, these spears of yours are good and all that, but we gotta get in close to use them. By the time we do, they could've taken us all down."

She wondered about the spear lying there on the ground beside her. Could she stick it into somebody—even one of the shark people? She supposed she could, if she had to, but she wasn't really sure. She just wasn't really cut out for this kind of thing.

"I could make us shields," Sidi said. "If we had the skins, the wood for the framework, the time."

"Time. Yeah. Maybe heading for Quan's a big mistake, Sidi. What if the people there are no better than what we've got tracking us down right now? And didn't Finn say something about there being ghosts or something there? Maybe we're just walking into more trouble."

"Unfortunately, from our experiences in this Dungeon so far, that seems quite likely."

"I wonder how Clive's doing."

"Surviving, I hope. But the veldt will have its own dangers, Annabelle."

"I suppose. Okay. We go on to Quan. How far do you think it still is?"

"Three and a half, four days."

"I don't know if I can take another minute of this frigging jungle. I feel like one huge mosquito bite."

"You attract them to you by the tension you project—your irritation with them. Ignore them, and you will find they trouble you less."

"Easy for you to say—they're not bothering you."

"Because I—"

Annabelle laughed. "I know. Because you ignore them—like you do the heat. It's a cute trick, Sidi. Wish it could work for me, you know?"

"It works, Annabelle," he insisted. "Just try it."

"You can't teach an old dog new tricks," she said. "They say that where you come from?"

"No. We say, 'The cautious seldom err.' It's not really the same thing."

"Same things are boring," she told him. "They gotta be different if they're gonna spark."

She turned toward him and could just make out the shadow shape of his head next to hers. His closeness gave her a warm feeling, made her forget the bugs and the heat.

"I like you, Sidi," she said softly. "I like you a lot."

She started to lift a hand to his cheek, but then the sounds of the jungle night went still all around them. Annabelle and Sidi moved apart, reaching for their spears. Tomàs sat up suddenly, his own weapon clutched in sweaty palms. Shriek froze, then swiftly plucked hair thorns—one to hold in each of her four hands.

Chica-chica-chica-chica . . .

The sound seemed to come from all around them. The night was filled with it. Annabelle felt her chest go all tight, then realized she'd been holding her breath. She let it out slowly, tried to regulate her breathing to a slow rhythm, but all her lungs wanted to do was hyperventilate.

They rose to their feet, each of the four facing a different section of the jungle.

Chica-chica-chica . . .

"Been nice knowing you, kids," Annabelle said softly.

Her skin crawled with tension. Any moment she expected to feel one of the shark people's darts hitting her. She kept changing the way she held the spear, trying to find a comfortable way to hold it, settling for a Little John/Robin Hood kind of grip, where she could use the thing like a staff.

Silence fell suddenly.

"What the—" Annabelle began, but then she realized that there'd been another sound behind that of their pursuers' shaking uvulas.

A drumming. It seemed to come from the trees above them—a booming, hollow sound from all sides.

Now what? she wondered.

A shape moved in the corner of her vision. She turned

toward it, sighting on the shadowy, streamlined head that was there above the shadow of a dorsal fin. She lifted up her spear, ready to strike, when something dropped out of the trees above her, landing directly on her attacker.

▪ Thirteen ▪

Except for the wind in his face and the faint vibration of the machine between his legs, Clive could feel no sense of motion, of traveling—at least, not of a manner with which he was familiar. There wasn't the sway of a ship's deck underfoot, the jolting of a carriage seat, the rhythm of a horse's gait. Instead, he was carried along, like a leaf on the wind, or like a kite, floating just above ground that sped by so quickly it was a blur.

The entire concept was decidedly disconcerting, but while he grew used to it in time, he wasn't sure he would ever like it. In that sense he sided more with Finnbogg than with Smythe and Guafe, both of whom appeared to be enjoying the ride—the one immensely, as one does a pleasurable new experience, the other as a convenient method of locomotion, far superior to that of placing one foot before the other. For Clive, it remained too unnatural.

They darted across the veldt, following the track of the brontosaur herd until the trail of flattened grass that marked their route turned to the south, back toward the mountains. The flyers continued straight, rising above the height of the tall, mauve-yellow vegetation that was here unmarred by the behemoths' passage. The grasses whipped against each other as the flyers rushed by above them.

Their party was made up of five of the small hover-craft—one each to bear the members of Clive's company, and a fifth that scouted ahead, keeping in touch with the other flyers through something Keoti called radio contact. Clive assumed it was a variation of a telegraph system, and was startled to learn that actual words could be transmitted in this manner.

When they made camp that evening, the ground seemed to sway under Clive's feet for the first ten minutes or so, but he soon recovered his land legs. From compartments under the seats of the flyers, the Dramaranians brought out tents that appeared almost to set themselves up. Provisions followed, and small portable stoves to cook them with that had no source of heat Clive could perceive. The term *microwave* meant nothing to him.

"Explain to me," the cyborg Guafe asked of their hosts, after they had all eaten, "these flyers of yours. Why do you not use larger craft? Surely your technology is such that you could manufacture larger and quicker airships—ones that ride higher in the atmosphere?"

Keoti's lieutenant, Abro L'Hami, replied. He was a tall, black-haired man with a day's growth of beard and startling dark eyes. Like the other Dramaranians, he had become much friendlier to Clive's party as the day progressed.

"Most of what you see above," Abro said, "is not true sky. While there are patches that rise straight up to the upper levels of the world, most of what is above is actually a thin layer of some sticky substance that we have yet to identify. We have managed to force ships into that layer, but inevitably their engines become gummed up with the substance, causing the ships to crash."

Guafe looked up at the night skies, dotted with unfamiliar constellations. The sliver of a moon was rising in the east.

"Curious," he said.

"But what about the stars?" Smythe asked. "The sun we've seen each day, and the moon just rising now?"

Abro shrugged. "If we knew everything about the Dungeon, we would rule it. But we don't."

Keoti nodded. "Mostly, we believe that there are some things men were never meant to know. Travelers between the levels, such as yourself, are not merely rare—we find it difficult to understand why anyone would assume such a dangerous undertaking."

"We want to go home," Clive said. "It's that simple. We're not here by our own will, and we wish to return to our own world."

The Dramaranians regarded him curiously.

"This is a good world," Keoti said finally, "so long as one avoids the jungle."

Clive and Smythe exchanged worried glances.

"The jungle?" Clive asked, fear rising inside him. "Why would that be?"

"The jungle holds many strange and primitive tribes—they grow stranger the deeper one fares. They make constant war with each other, and against any strangers who trespass on their lands. Why do you look so worried?"

"We have . . . companions who entered the jungle."

Keoti gave him a sympathetic look. "They will not survive, Major Folliot."

"Please, call me Clive," he said absently. His worry for Annabelle and the others was intensifying. "With these flying ships of yours—could you take us into the jungle to rescue them?"

"Impossible. We do not go into the jungle . . . Clive. To do so is certain death. We leave the tribes alone, as they do us. We have no need to enter their jungle. We have our veldt and our own forests beyond Dramaran. We have the porten for meat—Walking Mountains of protein. All else we need, we raise for ourselves.

"It is not a bad life, Clive, and because of your relationship with our savior, you will be well treated there."

"Just how did Sir Neville become your savior?" Smythe asked.

"I told you earlier about our Long Sleep," Keoti replied. "Our seasons are long here, summer and winter each lasting for many— " she paused, as though searching for a word "—of what Father Neville calls centuries. When the portens migrate and the ice comes, we retire to our Long Sleep. It's a form of mechanically induced hibernation. Last spring, the mechanism that rouses us failed, and we slept on through the spring and well into summer.

"It was Father Neville who woke us once more."

"How long ago was that?" Clive asked.

It seemed odd to him that Neville could have accomplished so much in such a short time on this level. To begin with, how had he reached Dramaran so quickly?

"Almost five years ago now," Abro said.

"As you reckon time," Keoti added.

The shock of that statement struck Clive and the others of his party profoundly.

"Five years?" Clive asked slowly.

The Dramaranian lieutenant nodded.

That was impossible, Clive thought. Unless there had been some flux in time that had sent Neville here years before his own party had arrived, even though they had left the previous level within moments of each other. Was such a thing possible? In the Dungeon, who could tell?

"You've been looking for us all that time?" Smythe asked.

Keoti shook her head. "Oh, no. It's only been a few weeks now since Father Neville told us you would be coming."

Later, when Smythe and Clive lay in the tent they were sharing, they spoke of that.

"There's another possibility, sah," Smythe said after both had run out of speculations and they had lain in silence for a time. His voice floated toward Clive from the darkness, a disembodied sound. "It might not be Neville waiting for us in Dramaran. It wouldn't be the first time he's played that trick on us."

"But the Dramaranians know me—and you. It has to be my brother. How could a stranger be expecting us?"

Neither man had an answer. Eventually, they let silence fall between them again. Smythe's breathing grew more regular and he fell asleep, but Clive lay awake for a long time, staring up at the darkened roof of the tent.

He was thinking of Annabelle now, wishing he'd been more forceful in convincing her to stay with him.

She had been a small, nagging worry in his thoughts, ever since the two parties had gone their own ways, but while he'd worried, he'd held firm the knowledge that she was a resourceful woman, with—barring the Portuguese—trustworthy companions. He'd been able to hold out hope for their survival. But now, with the finality of Keoti's tone as she spoke of the certain fate of any who dared the jungle ringing in his mind, hope had fled.

The hard truth lay like a rock in his stomach. He would never see Annabelle or any of her companions again. It was a bitter realization, made worse by the sense of guilt he felt for letting them go off on their own. As leader, it had been his responsibility to keep the company together, yet he had failed to do so, sealing their fate.

I should have tried harder, he thought unhappily.

But now it was too late.

Not one of Clive's party—not even Chang Guafe—was prepared for the sheer immensity of the ruined city of Dramaran when they reached it late in the following afternoon. They flew over acre upon acre of abandoned buildings, pillars that lay fallen across roadways, collapsed walls that had scattered their enormous stone blocks willy-nilly wherever they might land, floors that had fallen through to shadowed basements. Here and there tall towers still remained, but most of the city had the look of a child's toy village, flattened by a large boot.

They saw no people until they reached the center of the city, where the work of reconstruction was being undertaken. Hundreds of Dramaranians bustled like ants about the building they were repairing. Strange mechanical devices were being used to lift the stone blocks and set them into place. Clive could have watched the curious work for hours, but then their flight took them to a docking area near a huge, upright thrust of rock, where the flyers landed, one after the other.

The party was conveyed inside what appeared to be a cave that was brightly lit by bulbous globes hanging from its ceiling. Keoti ushered them into a small room that could barely hold the nine of them. When the doors hissed shut and the room began to move downward, Clive knew a sudden moment of panic. The swiftness of their descent left him with the feeling of leaving his stomach in his throat. Beside him, Finnbogg made a low moaning sound.

Clive learned later that that had been his first introduction to an elevator, a conveyance that moved one from floor to floor in a building without the necessity for stairs. It was only the beginning of the mechanical marvels to be discovered in this wondrous city.

The elevator let them out at a junction of large hallways, many levels below where they had left the flyers, Abro told them. Three corridors led away from where they stood, with the elevator situated at the joining of the "T" where they met. The walls were smooth here, and the lighting came from the ceiling itself, rather than globes.

"Where can we find Father Neville?" Clive asked finally.

"He will see you tomorrow," Keoti replied. "First, I will show you to your rooms, where you may bathe and eat. If you'll follow me?"

They left the remainder of the Dramaranians there and followed Keoti down a bewildering series of corridors. Finally, she stopped at a door, which hissed open when she laid her palm against a metal plate set in the wall beside the frame.

"This will be your room," she told Guafe. "If you are unfamiliar with the workings of any of the devices, you have only to speak into this grille and someone will come to help you."

One by one she showed Finnbogg and Smythe to their rooms. Smythe hesitated at the door of his.

"Well, then, sah," Smythe said. "I will see you later."

As the door hissed shut behind him, Keoti led Clive on to his room. When they reached it, she came in with him. Clive stared in open-eyed wonder. The furnishings were spare, but luxurious. A large comfortable bed. Over-stuffed chairs. A false mantel with a mechanism under it that gave the impression that there was a fire burning there.

Much of what he saw now, he had no vocabulary for. He learned later that the realistic, full-color pictures hanging from the wall—with brushstrokes so tiny he could not spy them and too sharp and colorful to be daguerreotypes—were actually photographs. That the curious, windowlike affair in the corner was a video screen. That the feather-soft carpeting underfoot was not wool, but some synthetic material.

He turned at the sound of a zipper, to see Keoti stripping off her silver bodysuit. She wore nothing underneath it.

"Shall we bathe?" she asked with a smile.

"I . . . that is . . ."

Her matter-of-fact boldness left Clive speechless for a few moments. Keoti stepped out of the suit and tossed it onto a chair. Turning from him, she went into another small room that proved to be a washroom. Clive watched the movement of her buttocks as she walked, lifting his gaze when she turned her head slightly toward him.

"Are you coming?" she asked over her shoulder.

When he nodded, she disappeared from view. Clive hastily removed his own clothing. By the time he joined her, she was standing in a small stall, water showering over her from a faucet overhead. She drew him inside with her and handed him a bar of soap. It made her skin wonderfully slippery to the touch.

After a long, messy shower, which left as much water on the floor as had been on them, Keoti shaved his beard and trimmed the wild tangle of his hair. Clive felt like a new man—clean-shaven and civilized—as they retired to the bed. Keoti pressed him down upon the mattress and straddled him.

"You certainly are a hospitable people," he said, looking up at her.

She lowered her face to give him a long kiss. He closed his arms around her, drawing her close.

"Remarkably so," he added.

"Stop talking," she told him, then indicated other ways in which he could be occupied.

▪ Fourteen ▪

As Annabelle's attacker went down, something small whistled quickly by her ear. *Poisoned dart,* she thought. She ducked instinctively, though the dart had already passed her, so close she'd almost been able to feel it go by. Shaking her head, she moved closer, spear still raised.

She wanted to help, but all she could see of the two struggling figures was a confusing mix of shadows. She was just as likely to strike her benefactor as the shark man who'd been attacking her. Then someone caught her about the knees and brought her down. She fought the grip until she heard Sidi's voice.

"Stay down! Let them fight it out, Annabelle—they seem to know who's who better than we could."

She relaxed in his grip. When he loosed his hand and crawled back toward the tree they'd been leaning against earlier, she followed him, keeping her head low. Sidi was right. The best they could do right now was just stay out of the way.

Shriek was already there, hunched in a half-crouch, trying to pierce the confusion with her multifaceted eyes, but doing no better than Annabelle had, even with six extra eyes.

All around them, figures struggled. They heard the familiar, guttural voices of the shark people, raised in cries of both pain and anger. Mixed with them was the sound of drums and different voices that sounded human and almost decipherable. Shapes continued to drop from the trees. Then, suddenly, the surviving shark people broke away.

Annabelle and Sidi joined Shriek, who had already risen to her feet. As torches flared, they spied Tomàs curled up into a ball near another tree, hands wrapped over his head.

"It's over now, hero," Annabelle called to him.

God, what a weasel.

She turned away as their benefactors approached. Above them, drums continued to sound, but their rhythm was different now—no longer menacing, but joyous. The torches lit up their campsite, scaring away the shadows. And the newcomers . . .

How come I'm not surprised? she thought.

They were ape-men—a whole troop of them. More humanoid in shape than the gorillas and other great apes of her own world, but definitely simian, all the same. As though their evolution from monkeys had taken them along a different route, or wasn't quite fully advanced yet.

Their brows were high, lower parts of their faces protruding slightly in a chimplike fashion. The eyes were set close together over a broad nose. Their bodies were covered with fur, but they wore various pieces of clothing. All had loincloths, arm bracelets, and neck torcs. Some had sashes worn over their shoulders; others, scarves around their necks. Some wore strips of cloth about their brows, or tied on their upper arms or thighs. Earrings glistened in their large earlobes, some having a series that ran up the edge of their ears, as Annabelle's own did.

Some carried what looked like a kind of throwing stick—foot-long, with a knob at either end. All had knives at their belts or in their hands.

The foremost one stopped a few feet away from them and said something. Again, it sounded almost familiar, but Annabelle had to shake her head to indicate she didn't understand.

"We fren'," the ape-man said then. He gave them a

wide, toothy grin. "En-mee of—" he said something she didn't quite catch, that sounded like *chasuck* "—fren' we."

"You speak English?"

The Dungeon threw more curves at her than she was ready to catch. With everything that had already happened to them—ape-men who spoke a kind of bastard English?

He bobbed his head. "En'lish—talk good, yuh?"

"Very good."

"Yoo cum we, yuh?"

Annabelle glanced at her companions. Tomàs was shaking his head no, but the other two indicated their agreement.

"We'll come with you," she said. "Thank you for your help. What . . . ah . . . should we call you?"

"Huh?"

"Name you?"

The ape-man grinned hugely. "Me Chobba. Big cheef. Kill chasuck—yuh?"

Annabelle pointed at the dead shark man that had almost gotten her. "That chasuck?"

The ape-man nodded and spat on the corpse. Kneeling beside it, he drew a knife from his belt and began to saw off the dorsal fin. Many of the other ape-men were already carrying similar trophies. She thought of the leader of the shark people with his staff, and what hung from his belt.

"Those skulls we saw back at the shark people's village," she said to Sidi.

He nodded. "Were the shrunken skulls of these ape people, Annabelle."

When Chobba had the fin cut free, he offered it to Annabelle. She shook her head quickly, but made sure she kept smiling at him as she did so. Annie B.'s rules of etiquette for meeting ape-men in strange jungles number one: Until you figured out the customs, it never hurt to just keep grinning like a loon.

"No thank you, Chobba. You keep it."

He nodded. Puncturing it with the tip of his knife, he

tied it to his belt with a thong, then replaced the blade in its sheath.

"Cum," he said. "We go."

He leapt into the lowest branches of the tree directly above him. All around the clearing, the rest of the troop that was on the ground swung into the trees, joining those who were waiting for them above, drums quiet now, slung onto their backs.

"Chobba!" Annabelle cried.

He looked down at her, face wrinkled with a puzzled expression that was almost comical in its broadness.

"You no cum?"

Annabelle opened her hands before her in a helpless gesture. "Not good tree cheef like you," she said.

The look that came into his face then was one that Annabelle had seen before: it was the way a healthy person looked at a cripple. Chobba dropped back down to the ground and approached her slowly. She kept herself still as he reached out and squeezed her upper arm. He shook his head slowly, brows lifting in a question.

"Sick?" he asked.

She shook her head. "Just not good in tree."

"Chobba walk you," he said.

He turned and called up to his companions. A few torchbearers and one drummer dropped down to the ground. The remainder of the troop swung off into the night, their torches bobbing in among the trees, winking like fireflies as they disappeared behind branches, then reappeared again.

"We go now," Chobba told her. "Walk on legs, yuh?"

Annabelle smiled. "Yes," she said. "We'll walk on legs. You don't know a guy named Tarzan, do you?"

"He is rogha—like me?"

"No. He's a man in a story—like me. But big and strong, and he can swing through the trees like you."

Chobba looked around. "He cum soon?"

Annabelle laughed and shook her head. "It's just us, Chobba."

He scratched at his temple, then shrugged. Leading

them back to the game trail, he set off at a pace they could all keep. As they followed him, Annabelle walked at Shriek's side.

Walking on legs, Shriek said with a grin. *What does the Chobba being think of all of mine?*

Annabelle laughed. "What a place. More fun than a barrel of . . ."

"A barrel of what, Annabelle?" Sidi wanted to know when she just let her voice trail off.

Annabelle looked at Chobba's broad back in front of her. Another rogha walked right behind her, abreast of Sidi. Others ranged farther behind, one tapping a soft rhythm from his drum. Annie B.'s rule of etiquette number two: don't make fun of anyone who's just saved your ass.

"Never you mind," she told him.

Naturally, the rogha village was up in the trees—high up in the trees.

They reached it just as dawn was breaking, the salmon-colored sun waking sharp shadows in the blue-green and burgundy vegetation. Annabelle craned her neck and peered up among the gaps in the leaves to the boughs some sixty feet above to make out the reed huts on platforms. There were already cooking fires, sending their morning smoke into the sky.

"Home now," Chobba said.

Annabelle looked away from the village, lowering her gaze to his features.

"It's very private," she said.

He blinked, not understanding.

"Safe," she tried.

"Many safe," he assured her.

"And high."

Chobba squeezed her upper arms again. "Carry yoo, yuh?"

Annabelle swallowed thickly. "Ah . . . sure. Why not?"

"What's the matter, Annabelle?" Sidi asked.

"Well, you know. Heights scare the shit out of me."

She remembered the descent from the plateau where they'd first arrived on this level. It had been a little easier to ignore the crawling fear, because the rocks were solid, the grade not too steep, and there were people there to grab onto if she got to feeling too weird. This was going up, and staying there, their destination a bunch of swaying platforms near the top of some of the biggest trees she'd ever seen.

Sidi gave her a worried look. "Maybe we should make our own camp here below."

"Right. Where the shark men can come crawling all over us—or Christ knows what else."

"But if you can't go up . . ."

Annabelle drew a steadying breath. "Oh, I can go up," she said. "I just don't know how bad I'm gonna freak once I get there, that's all."

"No happy?" Chobba asked.

"I'm delirious with joy," she replied.

Again, that uncomprehending blink.

"Many happy."

Chobba grinned. "Cum," he said.

He motioned for her to wrap her arms around his neck. Annabelle took a couple more slow breaths, trying to still the sudden, rapid tattoo of her heartbeat. Chobba bent his knees, lowering himself to make it easier for her. She got her arms around his neck, surprised at the clean smell of his fur—it had none of the reek of a zoo monkey house—and the softness of its texture. He indicated that she should wrap her legs around his middle.

She tried not to let her fear force her to hold him so tightly that she'd choke him. He straightened for a moment, bouncing lightly on his heels to adjust himself to her weight, then leapt for the lowest branch. Annabelle left her heart behind her on the ground.

The ascent up through the jungle boughs was just a dizzying blur. She closed her eyes after the first couple of stomach-lurching springs, and kept them tightly shut until they had stopped moving and Chobba was trying to pry her fingers loose. She let her muscles go slack and stumbled. Another of the rogha caught her before she could fall, but not before she had a heart-spinning view of the drop to the jungle floor below.

A low moan escaped her, and she moved away from the edge of the platform, her grip now desperately tight on the arm of the second rogha. The ape-man grinned reassuringly at her. Gently disengaging her fingers, he steered her to the side of a hut and lowered her down so that she was sitting with her back to the reed wall, the edge of the platform a good ten feet from her.

Another rogha appeared at the edge then, a scowling Tomàs clinging to his back. As soon as they reached the platform, Tomàs stepped free and nonchalantly swaggered back toward the edge, where he peered down. Years of scrambling through ship's rigging had long ago rid him of any acrophobia he might have had.

Sidi was next, his brown face creased with worry when he looked in Annabelle's direction.

"Annabelle," he began as he hurried over to her.

She tried to copy Tomàs's cool and give Sidi a little careless wave of her hand, but all she could feel was the sway of the platform under her. Her chest was so tight she could hardly breathe.

"I . . . I'll be okay. No problem." She gave him what she hoped was a bright smile, but knew it had come out as a grimace. "Where's Shriek?"

"On her way."

"Right."

Of course. Being more spider than human, the arachnid would have no trouble coming up on her own.

Annabelle worked at calming herself. Breathe in, hold it there for a few counts, breathe out. She tried looking around at what she could see of the village from her perch, legs drawn in close to her chest, arms locked around her knees.

The huts were similar to those of the shark people—even to the possum dogs hanging from branches and poles by the doors. But there was nothing of the sense of menace that had been in that other village. Here, the people regarded them with friendly curiosity—furry women and little children, older men and women, their body fur grizzling and gray. She realized then that Chobba was missing.

Just as Shriek pulled herself up over the lip of the edge, Chobba reappeared at Annabelle's side. He was carrying a pouch from which he drew a small thick leaf, which he offered to her.

"Stop scare," he said, pushing the leaf into her hands when she didn't take it right way. "Yoo feel hokay. No more scare, yuh?"

Annabelle took the leaf dubiously. Oh, yeah? And just what the hell was it, anyway? If it was going to make her feel "hokay," it was probably some kind of drug—and sick though she was, she wasn't into getting freaked out on the local version of who-knew-what.

"I . . . I don't think so," she said. "Don't want too much happy."

How did she tell him that she wasn't into dope?

"Not happy," Chobba told her. His face wrinkled comically as he tried to find the right words. "Fetta cheef—she find. Stop scare is all."

The tree swayed, making her stomach lurch.

What the hell, she thought.

She lifted the leaf and put it in her mouth. It was pulpy, juice squeezing out as soon as she bit down on it. The taste was sweet and tart, all at the same time, and went down her throat with a numbing sensation. After a moment, she took the second leaf Chobba offered her.

"Glad now?" he asked.

It's a little early, don't you think? Annabelle thought, but then she realized that she did feel better already. Not high—not like taking some hallucinogenic, as she'd feared—but calm. Muscles unknotting, chest loosening, the panic fading. The leaves didn't give her any kind of a buzz at all. They just relaxed her.

"What do you call this stuff?" she asked.

"Byrr." Chobba said. "Yoo like?"

"It's all right," she said.

She was about to add to that, when a commotion at the

far end of the platform caught her attention. She was surprised to see a white man pushing his way through the crowd of rogha. He was slender and wiry, at least in his late fifties, early sixties. A snow white mane of hair and full beard gave him the look of a small, skinny Santa Claus, but he wasn't wearing red.

He stopped short when he reached Annabelle and her company, looking from one to the other.

"My God," he said finally. "Do any of you speak English?"

▪ Fifteen ▪

When Clive woke the next morning, he was alone in the bed. All that remained of Keoti's presence was the indentation left by her head on her pillow.

Looking around the room for her, he found Smythe instead, sitting at the table by the video screen, sipping tea from a white porcelain mug. He, too, was clean-shaven again, except for his bushy mustache; his hair was neatly trimmed. The remains of breakfast sat on a tray before him. At the setting across from him was another tray, covered with a metal hood.

Clive thought about the night before and guilt arose inside him. How could he have forgotten Annabella so easily? And for what? A tumble in the hay with some woman—all right, a damnably attractive woman—that he'd only just met. It was true that Annabella was out there—in the world beyond the Dungeon—and he was here, with little hope of seeing her again, but still. . . .

As he thought of Annabella, an odd sensation came over him. He seemed to remember a night with her. . . . They were in her rooms, then went out to a party with George du Maurier—a party thrown in honor of a promotion he'd received, and for his and Annabella's engagement.

Just a dream, of course.

But it had gone on. He seemed to remember walking by himself, later that same night, through the slums of London, and being confronted by Annabella again—only this time, she was in the guise of a prostitute. . . .

Impossible. It had to have been a dream.

But it seemed terribly real. And, hard on the heels of those recollections, other dreamlike memories fluttered. An odd conversation . . . overheard in the dark. . . . But, as soon as he tried to concentrate upon it, it was gone.

He sighed and sat up in the bed. Smythe looked up as he stirred and gave him a grin.

"Busy night, then, gov'nor?" he asked.

With an effort, Clive put away the strange feelings.

"It's too early for me to face your cockney imitation," he told him.

Smythe gave a quick tug at his forelock. "Sorry, gov'nor. Just trying to get along."

Clive couldn't help but laugh at Smythe's mock self-effacement.

"Incorrigible," he said. "That's the only term that properly describes you, Horace."

"Right you are, gov'nor. Shall I be throwing myself in the Thames for troubling your morning? Just say the word."

"No doubt picking my pocket as you fling yourself from the bridge?"

"Jerusalem! The thought never crossed me mind, gov'nor. How to regain your trust?"

"You could pour me some of that tea you're keeping to yourself."

Swinging his legs to the floor, Clive tugged on his trousers, surprised to find them clean.

"Washed, pressed, and mended while we slept," Smythe said, plucking at his own shirt. "Can't fault our hosts for their hospitality."

Clive joined his companion at the table. Lifting the hood from his tray, he found a breakfast of eggs, fried strips of what must have been porten meat, biscuits, and fresh fruit staring up at him. Smythe handed him a mug of tea.

"It's like the finest hotel back home," he said.

Clive nodded. He took a sip of the tea and was again surprised. It had the aromatic flavor of an Indian brew.

"Did Keoti show you how to work this?" Smythe asked, pointing at the video screen.

"No. We were . . . otherwise occupied. She did describe it to me as some form of window. . . ." He shrugged, the terminology she'd used to describe its functions escaping him at the moment.

"It's a marvelous machine. It can bring words up onto its screen—as a book—but it also has illustrations. Not static ones, but moving pictures that have somehow been recorded and stored inside it—somewhat in the way that our friend Guafe has described the workings of his memory, I assume."

"And what of our companions?" Clive asked. He set aside the tea and started at his breakfast. The porten meat had a delicate texture, for all the creature's immense bulk. It was tender, without a touch of gaminess about it, having a domesticated flavor, rather than that of a wild beast. "Have you spoken to them yet today?"

Smythe nodded. "Guafe's gone on a tour with a pair of the Dramaranins. I believe they're as interested in observing him as he is their machines. As for Finn—he won't leave his room."

Clive's eyebrows lifted. "Why not?"

"He now believes this level to be the realm of the Dungeon's dead. The Dramaranians are spirits of the dead, he told me—judges measuring our worth. He's waiting for them to take him away for judgment."

"Didn't he say something about a white stone that held dead spirits?"

Smythe nodded. "But that's in Quan—or so he said earlier."

Silence fell between them as they thought of the other half of their company, lost now in the jungles. Loyal Sidi. The arachnid, Shriek. And Annabelle.

Clive set aside his fork, appetite fled. He didn't care much what happened to the Portuguese, but the others . . . especially his descendant. . . .

"We made a bad mistake letting them go off on their own," he said.

"It wasn't our choice to make, sah. They are all thinking, rational adults with minds of their own."

"I was responsible—"

"For yourself, sah. You are only responsible for yourself."

"But Annabelle. She's. . . ."

"A capable young lady to do you proud. I'm not so ready to write any of them off as our hosts are. We've come through some other bad times in this place and survived. I'm not prepared to give up on them until I see the bodies."

An image flashed into Clive's head, of Annabelle torn apart by wild beasts. Or lying hurt somewhere in that jungle, her companions slain, danger closing in.

Smythe reached across the table and touched Clive's hand. "Don't think about them," he said softly.

"How can I help *but* think of them?"

Smythe sighed. "Here," he said, turning to the video screen. "Watch how this works."

He manipulated the controls as one of the Dramaranians had shown him and the screen suddenly flooded with images in full color. The picture on the screen gave them the impression of looking out a moving window, the view slowly panning across a windswept, frozen plain. Then, disconcertingly, as the view continued to shift, it proved to be one of the borderland between jungle and veldt, where they'd left their companions, though obviously at some other time from when they had seen it, for the veldt was a frozen waste, while the jungle retained all its tropical glory.

There was no sound, but only because Smythe had left it turned down.

"This machine brings to life the past," he said. "Anything that's been recorded upon it can be called up on that screen, at any time."

The two men watched as the camera continued to pan across the scene—jungle and ice fields, side by side.

"That doesn't seem possible," Clive said. "The vegetation should be dead—withered by that cold."

"This is the Dungeon," Smythe reminded him. "Anything seems possible here."

"Within reason," a new voice said.

So entranced were they with what was on the screen that neither man had heard the door hiss open behind them. They turned now to find Keoti standing there. Today her bodysuit was a bewildering pattern of blacks and reds, a swirling design that caught the eye and led it this way and that, but never let the full pattern emerge. Her weapon was no longer in its holster, clipped to her belt.

"But this," Clive said. "It defies the laws of nature."

Keoti smiled. "What you see was recorded by a remote scouting unit that was sent out while we were in our Long Sleep. Apparently an invisible barrier—made of a material that we have yet to identify—comes between the jungle and the plains at that time so that the two environments do not affect each other. Curious, isn't it?"

Both men nodded.

"Have you come to bring us to my brother?" Clive asked.

Keoti shook her head. "He wishes to see you this afternoon. I merely came by to see how you were doing, and to ask if you would like to see more of Dramaran."

"I don't think so," Clive replied.

He looked from her to the screen, but neither was enough to take his mind from the fate of Annabelle and the others of her party. A tour of the city would merely aggravate his sense of loss, for he'd always be thinking, If only Annabelle were here, to share this with me.

Damn him for not keeping their group together. He should have stood firm when the suggestion first arose, but somehow, it was all discussed and done before he'd really had a chance to think through all of its ramifications.

"I don't feel in a very . . . companionable mood," he added. "I'd just make for poor company. But you go ahead, Horace."

Keoti gave him a considering look. "You are worrying

about your friends," she said with quick insight. "The ones who entered the jungle."

"I can't forget them."

"And so you shouldn't. But brooding does no one any good." Her brow wrinkled for a moment, then she smiled. "Come with me anyway, Clive. I know something that will help you deal with what's troubling you."

"I'm not sure. . . ."

"Humor me."

Clive sat for a long moment, then finally nodded and started to rise. As he pushed his chair back from the table, he suddenly realized that all he was wearing was his trousers. A blush crept up the back of his neck—foolish, for she'd seen him in far more revealing circumstances—but he felt awkward all the same. Crossing the room to the bed, he gathered up the bundle of his clothes and fled for the washroom.

"Just let me get dressed," he called over his shoulder.

Behind him, Keoti and Smythe shared a smile.

"Will you look at this, sah," Smythe said. "A bloody gymnasium. Who'd of thought it?"

Keoti led them to a locker room, where she took two sets of matched fencing gear from a locker—foils, gloves, masks, and metallic plastrons.

When she presented one set to Clive, he laid everything down on a bench except for the foil. He tested its spring and balance, enjoying the feel of the handle in his hand. The tip of the blade was capped with a button.

"Do you fence?" he asked her.

Keoti shook her head. "I have a friend who will be meeting us—ah, there you are, Naree."

The man who entered the locker room was lean as a whip, with expressive, mobile features. His black hair was long and tied back in a ponytail, and there was a scar under his left eye. He smiled as Keoti introduced them, giving Smythe a quick glance, then focusing all of his attention on Clive.

"Finally, some new blood," he said as he took the other set of fencing gear from Keoti.

His full name, they learned, was Naree Terin, and he was a biological research scientist.

"The pleasure is all mine," Clive replied.

Keoti and Smythe took seats on one side of the gym as the two men donned their gear. Each went through a series of warming-up exercises. When they were ready to fence, Naree attached body wires to the rear of each of their metallic plastrons. The wires were fed out of reels that sat at either end of the fencing area.

"It's for scoring," Naree explained at Clive's puzzled look.

He touched the tip of his foil against Clive's chest and a small bell rang on the electronic scoring apparatus that was on a table near where Keoti and Smythe were sitting. Keoti rose and cleared the counter back to zero once more. When she sat down, the two men began to fence.

"This was kindly thought of you," Smythe remarked to her.

She smiled. "I know what it is like to have tension build up in you—the mind knots as much as the muscles."

"And what do you do to relax?"

"Are you familiar with gymnastics?"

Smythe nodded. "They can be very demanding."

"They have to be—or what would be the challenge?"

"Of course."

Smythe looked back to where Clive and Naree were fencing. The whip-quick clang of the foils rang in the large room, the two figures weaving a pattern as intricate as a set dance with their feet, back and forth along the marked-out fencing area. Neither man had scored yet.

"Naree is very good," he said.

"As is Clive. To be honest, I hadn't thought he would do so well. Naree is the best in Dramaran."

"But to him it's a sport, am I correct?"

"Yes."

Smythe smiled. "For Clive, it has been a matter of life and death—his skill being all that kept him alive."

Keoti regarded the fencers in a new light.

"I see," she said softly.

There was just time for Clive to have a shower after his workout, before Keoti collected them for the meeting with Neville. Clive was in much better spirits, muscles tender and sore in spots, but the pain honestly earned. He had won the match, seven to zero, leaving Naree puzzled, and not a little in awe.

"Now they judge us," Finnbogg said mournfully as he joined them in the corridor outside his room.

"We're just going to meet Sir—Father Neville," Smythe reassured him. "There'll be no judgments, Finn."

Perhaps, perhaps not, Clive thought. There was still the puzzle as to how his brother had arrived here five years before them when they had entered the gateway literally within minutes of each other. And considering the traps Neville had left in their way before—if, in fact, he *had* been responsible for them—Clive meant to be prepared for anything.

"Clive will see, Clive will see," Finnbogg muttered as they went down the hall to where Guafe was waiting for them. "All dead now—blue limbo was boundary between being alive and dying. And now they judge us."

"Nonsense," Guafe told the dwarf when they reached him. "They have made some remarkable technological advances, but they are hardly deities."

"Been having a good time, then?" Smythe asked.

The cyborg caught the thinly veiled hostility of Smythe's tone. "It's been a pleasure dealing with other than primitive minds," he replied.

"I think we're ready to meet my brother," Clive said before they went any further.

They rode the elevator once more, all the way up to the floor just below the ground level of the city. Though he was prepared for the sensation of the small room's movement this time, Clive was still uncomfortable in the elevator. He doubted that he would ever be comfortable with some of the Dramaranian mechanisms, but he schooled his features to remain impassive.

When they disembarked from the elevator, Smythe touched his arm, holding him back so that they took up the rear of the group.

"We'd best be ready for anything," he whispered.

Clive nodded. "I am."

Keoti had opened a door in the corridor ahead of them, and they hurried to catch up as she ushered them in. Clive's heartbeat sped up as he went through the door.

Now, Neville, he thought. Now, we'll find out the meaning behind all these games of yours.

But the man behind the desk was a stranger.

Not again, was all Clive could think as he stared at him.

He was a rotund man with cheery features, pate shaved like a friar's, blue eyes bright and curious as he looked up to meet his guests. He wore a Dramaranian bodysuit that was stretched too tight across his stomach, giving him a somewhat comical air.

A pleasant-enough looking fellow, but he wasn't Sir Neville Folliot, no matter how much one might attempt to stretch the imagination. If anything, he reminded Clive of that damnable Philo B. Goode. There was enough familial resemblance to make him at least Goode's brother.

Clive and Smythe exchanged worried glances.

Even though Clive had been expecting this—or something like it—from the moment that he had learned that his brother was in Dramaran, the fact that he'd been duped again still hit him with a hard jolt. He stood with his back straight and met the stranger's gaze—an increasingly puzzled frown. He could feel Smythe's tension, Keoti's confusion.

"You are not my brother," Clive said.

"Indeed, I am not," the stranger said. "But I *am* Father Neville Folliot. And who are you, sir?"

· Sixteen ·

His name was Luke Drew.

"Call me Lukey," he told Annabelle as he sat down on the platform near where she was sitting, his blue eyes glinting merrily in the torchlight.

The rogha treated him with a friendly familiarity, making room for him in the circle of furry bodies that were sitting cross-legged or slouched around Annabelle's party. The old man presented an incongruous picture among all those brown apes, his bony limbs protruding from the cloak of animal pelts he was wearing.

Tarzan in his fifties, Annabelle thought with a smile. This was probably what he'd really look like—forget all the muscles.

"Hell," the old man went on, "call me anythin' you like so long's you know some words that ain't monkey talk. Now, don't get me wrong. These monkeys are all Lukey's pals, you bet. But a soul gets tired a' listenin' to all their jabberin', you be here as long as me. I bin tryin' to teach some of 'em English, but I ain't had much luck. You get a good ol' boy like Chobba here, an' he's for learning, but most a' them can't be bothered to take the time, so mostly I'm jabberin' away in their lingo."

"Are you a native?" Annabelle asked.

"Hell, no. I'm a Newfie, born an' bred. Lived an' woulda died in Freshwater, Bell Island—little place smack dab in the middle a' Conception Bay—'cept a blue bogey light snatched me right out of my ol' boat one night an' dumped me here. I never seen anythin' so spooky before—though I bin seein' things since that'd make your toes curl."

"How long have you been here?"

"Don't rightly know. I used ta keep track, but I kind a' lost interest. Let's see. It was just after the big war when that blue light gobbled me up. . . ."

"Which war?"

Lukey blinked. "The big W.W. Two, girl. Is there any other?"

"'Fraid so," Annabelle said.

"Don't tell me about 'em—I don't want to know. Just tell me, the ol' Rock—Newfoundland—she's still in one piece?"

"So far as I know."

"Well, that's somethin'. What year was it when you got snatched?"

"Nineteen hundred ninety-nine."

For a long moment, Lukey didn't say anything. Then, he slowly shook his head.

"I can't a' bin here that long. I figured maybe twenty years. . . ."

"We've all come from different times," Annabelle told him. "Sidi here's from the nineteenth century. Tomàs goes all the way back to the fifteenth. And Shriek. . . ."

Lukey looked at the alien. "She ain't even from our world—not 'less things a' changed a helluva lot more'n I'd want ta think was possible."

"How did you come to live with the rogha?" Annabelle asked.

"Damn lucky—that's all. Just like you, girl."

"My name's Annabelle."

"Hokay—Anniebelle it is. Anyways, that blue light gobbled me up an' spat me out a ways from here. You bin in the upper levels a' this place?"

Annabelle nodded.

"Took me a half-year ta get this far, an' I guess I'd just be shark food if the monkeys hadn't been out raidin' the chasuck an' brought me back with 'em. Same deal as happened ta you. You folks were just plain lucky Chobba an' his boys was out huntin' some fins tonight."

"What does that mean—chasuck?"

Lukey grinned. "Well, pardon my French, but I guess the closest I can come in plain English is 'shit for brains.' That's what the monkeys figure the chasuck to be. They bin fightin' each other for years—least, they do 'round here. You get deeper inta rogha country, an' you could go your whole life without seein' one a' them land sharks. 'Course, you go too far, an' then you run into the gree."

He paused expectantly.

"And what are the gree?" Annabelle asked, taking her cue.

"Thought you'd never ask. The rogha call 'em 'dick-faces,' if you'll pardon—"

"Your French. Sure."

Lukey wagged a finger at her. "Let a man tell his story in his own way, Anniebelle. Anyways, they call 'em that 'cause they look like birds—you know, all full a' black feathers an' with big yellow beaks in the middle of their faces."

"Can they fly?"

"Nah. Well, not really. Though they can glide somethin' fierce. See, they got hands, sort a', but they're at the ends of these long black wings. They're a mean bunch—almost as bad as the chasuck—though they don't go in much for live meat. Feed on carrion, that kind a' thing."

"I don't believe this place," Annabelle said.

"You're tellin' me. Gets so you'd welcome anybody that was human."

"So, why do you stay?"

"Where'm I goin' ta go?"

"You could come with us," Annabelle said. "We're going to the gateway in Quan."

"Quan? Not an' keep your skin in one piece, you ain't. You got somethin' against livin'?"

"What's wrong with Quan?"

"Haunts. That's the only thing you'll find in there. Nobody goes there. Damn things'll strip the flesh from your bones like you was dipped in acid. Like those pie-ee-raner fish they got in Africa. Eat you up like there ain't no tomorra."

He made snapping motions with both hands, bringing them up close to Annabelle's face. She backed quickly away, and was suddenly aware again of the height of the platform as it swayed underneath her. Her face went pale, the forgotten fears rising up in a spinning whirl. Chobba plucked the pouch of byrr leaves from her frozen fingers and pressed one leaf between her lips.

She was too scared to even chew, but just the mixture of her saliva with the pulpy flesh of the leaf that slid down her throat was enough to unlock her jaws after a few moments. Relief came quickly again—no high, just a calmness that brought her heartbeat back down to normal and loosened the sudden tightness in her chest.

Just don't think about what's underneath you, she told herself. But then, she *was* thinking about it. She chewed another leaf.

"I used to chew a lot a' that," Lukey said, "when I first got here. But you get used ta the sway an' the height. In a couple a' months, you won't even notice it anymore."

"We don't plan to be here for longer than it takes to get ready to go on to Quan," Annabelle told him.

"Much bad place, Quan," Chobba said.

Annabelle glanced at him. She'd been wondering how much he and the other rogha had been following of their conversation, and decided now that Chobba, at least, understood English better than he spoke it.

"We gotta go," she said.

"Speak for yourself," Tomàs said.

She turned to look at him. "I've told you before, no one's making you tag along, pal."

"I am part of the company," the Portuguese said. "I should have a say in what we do, and I say is *estúpido* to go on."

"Blow it out your face," Annabelle told him, and looked back at Chobba. "We don't belong here," she said. "At this point, the gateway in Quan is our only hope of getting back home."

Chobba stroked his furry forearm and muttered something in his native tongue.

"What'd he say?" Annabelle asked Lukey.

The old man smiled as he translated. "'Brains must grow in hair because you don't have much of either.'"

"Do you see?" Tomàs said.

"Only that you're looking for a fat lip," Annabelle told him. "Won't you help us, Chobba?"

"Sleep yoo," he replied. "Dark bye-bye, we talk."

"Okay. That's fair enough."

Chobba nodded, grinning again. "Hokay," he said.

His good humor was so infectious that Annabelle couldn't help but smile back at him. He handed her his pouch of byrr leaves and indicated she should keep it. As the troop of rogha began to break up, he showed Annabelle's party to the hut they'd be sleeping in. Happily, it was on the same platform that they were already on.

Thank God they didn't have to do any more climbing, Annabelle thought. She'd been eyeing the other platforms, and had not been too thrilled to see that the only connections between them were swaying rope bridges—which appeared to be mostly for the very old or the very young—or the boughs of the trees, which the majority of rogha used.

She just couldn't have done it.

Later, in their hut, she sat up with Shriek. Holding hands, they could speak mind to mind and not disturb the others as they talked over what they'd learned from Lukey and Chobba. Tomàs sat glowering in a corner, muttering about how spiders were only good for being stepped on, and that went double for women who thought wearing pants gave them a man's wisdom, until Annabelle gave him one of her hard stares and he fell quiet. But she could tell by the glower in his eyes that his monologue was still going on inside his head.

We were lucky, Shriek said finally. *The Chobba being and his people arrived at a most opportune time.*

Tell me about it, Annabelle replied.

But still . . . we cannot remain here.

Thinking about living up on these platforms made

Annabelle's stomach go all queasy again. *We'll leave soon,* she said.

Shriek nodded. *Soon,* she agreed.

She touched Annabelle's cheek in a friendly gesture, then turned in on the mattress, stuffed with leaves, that the rogha had provided for each of them.

Annabelle pulled her own mattress in closer to where Sidi was already sleeping and gave him a chaste kiss good night—chaste only because Tomàs's gaze was fixed upon them.

No cheap thrills for you, you little weasel, she thought.

Sidi woke to catch both looks—hers and Tomàs's. "You make a good boss, Annabelle," he said quietly before he rolled over once more.

Annabelle sat up, staring at Tomàs, until he finally lay down—face pointed at the wall, away from hers—then tried to get some sleep herself.

Gotta do something about Tomàs, she thought as she was drifting off. He was only going to get worse.

Annabelle spent an uneasy few hours, her sleep disturbed by a series of dreams in which she kept falling from a great height. Sometimes she was trying to get from one platform to another, and the rope or branch she was holding on to simply broke. Other times, she tripped on the platform and just tumbled off. Once it was Tomàs pushing her.

Each time she woke, she was sweaty and wide-eyed, the start of a scream just building up in her throat. She'd lie there, trying not to feel the sway of the platform under her. If she didn't move, she told herself—if she just lay where she was—nothing could happen to her. She couldn't just fall off.

But then the platform would shift slightly underneath her again and she'd sit up, arms wrapped around her chest, shivering. She fumbled for the pouch of byrr leaves that Chobba had left with her, then remembered she'd left it where they'd been sitting on the platform outside.

She stared at the rectangle of lighter darkness that the

door made in one wall. Nope, she thought. There was no way she could face going out there to get the pouch.

Oh, Annie B. You gotta do it.

Outside, a wind moved in the trees. This high up, it wasn't impeded by the thick tangle of underbrush that was on the jungle floor. The platform moved with it, yawing only slightly, but it might as well have just tipped her right over the side, for the way her stomach felt.

Sidi stirred on his mattress beside her, turning in her direction.

"Annabelle?" he asked.

She hated to admit it—somehow it was worse that she had to admit her weakness to him because she wanted him to think of her as a strong person—but it was all she could do to keep her breathing relatively normal. She kept wanting to hyperventilate—to just run out there and throw herself over the edge of the platform and get it all over with.

Sidi realized her problem immediately. He moved like a shadow across the room, out the door. Moments later he was back, the pouch in his hand. He placed a leaf between her lips, as Chobba had done earlier.

"Chew," her ordered her.

Again she had to wait for her saliva and the leaf juice to mingle and trickle down her throat before she could unclench her jaws enough to chew. But finally, she did. Sidi sat close, an arm around her shoulder, holding her while she chewed, then giving her another leaf when she was finished with the first.

"Take your time with it," he said.

She chewed more slowly. By now, the effect had kicked in. The tension washed out of her limbs, the tightness from her chest. She could breathe again. Her stomach stopped churning.

Calmer now, she shook her head when Sidi offered her a third leaf. Ducking under his arm, she rose to her feet. The slight sway of the platform didn't even faze her.

"Annabelle?" Sidi asked, the worry plain in his voice.

"I gotta sit outside," she said. "Thanks, Sidi. You're a bloody lifesaver."

It was cooler outside—still warm by any normal standards, but not so close as in the hut, and a hundred times better than it had been down on the forest floor. There were next to no mosquitoes, for one thing. And the humidity was at least bearable.

She sat down, back against the hut, and looked out at the jungle night spread around her. A moment later, Sidi joined her. She reached out and captured his hand.

"Not doing too good, am I?" she said.

She could feel him shrug. "No one is free of fear."

"Yeah, but it gets pretty bad when the only way you can handle it's with something like this." She shook the pouch of byrr leaves.

"We could ask the rogha to bring us down to the jungle floor," Sidi said. "It's not long until morning anyway."

Annabelle shook her head. "Nah. I'm just gonna sit out here and wait for it to get light. When I start to get weirded out again, I'll just chew another of these. You go on and get some sleep."

"I'd rather sit out here with you."

Annabelle turned to look at him. "You're something else, you know that?"

"Something good, I hope."

"Real good."

He put his arm around her shoulder and she snuggled in close. It felt good to be held.

It was kinda weird, she thought, remembering Sidi as he'd been when she'd first met him—a sixty-year-old man, who'd looked his years. Dark-skinned and lean, worn by time, yet tough as nails, as the old saying went. Now he looked about her age—still tough, but the dark skin was free of wrinkles, the webwork of laugh lines around his eyes all smoothed away.

She'd liked him before the change, and liked him better now. In a different way.

Don't go getting all involved now, Annie B., she told herself.

But it was hard not to. It was lonely in the Dungeon,

cut off from everything she knew. When she thought of all the time she'd spent on her own in that prison a few levels back, before Sidi and the rest showed up. . . . She didn't want to feel that cut off from people she could relate to. Not ever again.

So Sidi was an old man in a young man's body. So what? We should all be so lucky.

She lifted her head, bringing her face close to his.

"Remember just before the chasuck attacked us earlier?" She asked.

"I remember."

"Now, exactly where were we?" she murmured.

She brought a hand up behind his head and pulled him toward her until their lips met. Sidi pulled back, gently disengaging her hand.

"What's the problem?" Annabelle asked.

"This isn't right," he replied.

"Says who?"

"I'm old enough to be your grandfather."

"You'd never know from looking at you."

Sidi shook his head. "That still doesn't make it right."

"It doesn't matter to me."

"But it matters to me," he said. "Please understand, Annabelle. It's not just the age difference, but that we come from such vastly different worlds, as well. Here and now, it might not seem of much importance, but in the long run, it would set us against one another, and I would not wish to lose such a good friend."

Annabelle wanted to rail at him, but she knew he was right. It wasn't just age or race. It was everything that they were. A rock 'n' roller, and an Indian who was more a Zen sensei than a Hindu. Friends could bridge the differences that would have to arise as time went by. But lovers?

She leaned against his shoulder again. "Okay, Sidi," she said. "But friends can comfort each other, can't they?"

He gave her shoulder a squeeze.

▪ Seventeen ▪

For Clive, it was as though he was in the middle of a bad dream—a nightmare in which everything familiar had been given a twist to set it slightly askew. Here was a man who claimed to be Neville Folliot, who was expecting his brother Clive—yet he was not Clive's twin. He was a complete stranger.

Given the man's poise and assurance, one could almost believe that he spoke the truth, and that all of their own memories were a lie.

Clive glanced at Smythe, but his former batman's face remained impassive, his stance that of a man prepared to defend himself at the drop of a glove. Keoti had taken a few steps away from them, and was now watching the party warily. The distrust with which she now regarded him pained Clive.

"Doomed," Finnbogg muttered mournfully.

So it seems, Clive thought. We are in desperate straits, perhaps, but not for the reason you think, Finn.

Their best course of action was to beat a hasty retreat, but that was, no doubt, already impossible. They were underground, at the mercy of the Dramaranians and their technological wonders. Even if they should manage to escape to the ground level, the Dramaranians undoubtedly had mechanical bloodhounds with which they could track them down.

As though reading Clive's mind, the man behind the desk smiled. Though he made no motion that Clive could see, some signal must have been given, for there was a stirring in the doorway behind them through which they had entered. When Clive turned to look, he saw a number of the silver-suited Dramaranians blocking their escape. Each of them held one of those curiously shaped pistols in their hands. He remembered the blades of light with which the Dramaranians had been carving up the carcass of the brontosaur. It seemed likely that these weapons would be equally marvelous and strange. And deadly.

"What manner of game are you playing?" he asked the man behind the desk.

"Game?" The man's amusement faded from his features. "We play no game. We haven't sought guesting under false pretenses, claiming to be who we are not. 'Fess up, now. Who are you, and what do you want from me?"

"My name is Clive Folliot. I am a major of Her Majesty Queen Victoria's Fifth Imperial Horse Guards. I am searching for my brother, Major Neville Folliot of the Royal Somerset Grenadier Guards, who is currently on an extended leave of absence for the purpose of exploring East Africa. Upon his disappearance, I applied for and received detached service for the purpose of seeking him out."

The man at the desk leaned back in his chair. "Very pretty. You have all the facts correct—learned by rote, I imagine—but it will do you no good, sir, for you remain a stranger to me while my brother, for all our differences, is decidedly not."

"This man is not your brother?" Guafe asked.

"He most certainly is not."

"I had no idea," the cyborg said. "I took him at his word that he was who he said he was—there was no way I could look into the facts, and I had no reason to disbelieve him before, but I now disown all association with him."

"Well played," the man behind the desk said, "and it certainly sheds light upon the purity of your dedication and loyalty to your companions, but you are a touch too late, don't you think? It's very easy to step forth now and disclaim any guilt that might be associated with the others of your party."

"I had no way of knowing the truth until this very moment."

"Yes, well. That is a shame, isn't it? But we can't simply set you free now, can we? Seeing as how you arrived here with them, being a potential enemy and all?"

"I tell you I had no knowledge of this man's true motives."

The man behind the desk raised his eyebrows. "And I suppose we'll just have to take your word for that?"

"I do not lie," Guafe said stiffly.

"Ah. Well, that is welcome news, isn't it? Quickly, my friends, allow the cyborg his freedom. Open the doors to all our secrets to him, for he is an honorable being—or, at least, the part of him which is not a machine—and he means us no ill."

Not one of the Dramaranians stirred. Guafe's cybernetic eyes flashed red, but he kept his own counsel now in the face of their captor's sarcasm.

Clive wasn't particularly surprised, or even hurt, by Guafe's attempt to dissociate himself from the rest of the party. What hurt more was the recrimination that lay plain in Keoti's eyes. But, who was she to believe? he asked himself reasonably. A stranger she had known for a day or so—intimately, yes, but a stranger all the same—or a man who was the savior of her people and had lived among them for the past five years?

There was no question. But he wished there was some way that she could learn the truth, could know that he hadn't come all this way on false pretenses, his life a lie.

She would not meet his gaze anymore, so he returned his attention to the man behind the desk.

"What do you mean to do with us?" he asked.

"That is the question, isn't it? What would you do in my circumstance?"

Clive shrugged, pretending a nonchalance he didn't feel. "It would depend upon how I would expect my lies to best serve me—if I were a man such as you, which I am not."

The man behind the desk smiled. "Ah. So you mean to continue to press your claim—that you are the true Folliot, and I the pretender?"

"I know who I am," Clive replied.

"Yes, of course you do. The trouble is, we do not."

"That is not my concern. You can believe me or not, but who I am will not change."

"Oh, yes. You assume Clive Folliot to be an honorable man, so you mean to play your role to the end, not giving an inch. What will you do next? Challenge me to a duel to settle our differences—the winner being he with the greater skill?"

Clive could not hide the momentary hope that leapt inside him. With sword in hand, just the two of them, he and this fat man with the look of a friar about him, how could he not prevail?

The man behind the desk laughed. "Poppycock! I saw the videotape of your workout with Naree this afternoon. You're very skilled, but it means nothing. Might does not make right. Truth does."

"You're frightened," Clive said. "The real Neville Folliot—*my* brother—never refused a challenge in his life."

"Then this 'brother' of your imagination is a fool, something Neville Folliot—myself, sir—most assuredly is not."

Clive nodded. Fine. If this was how the game was to be played, then he would play along.

"You've had your fun with us," he tried, "now, why don't you let us go peacefully on our way? We've certainly no reason to remain here to cause you any further trouble—not with our quest still unresolved."

"I can't very well have you wandering about the Dungeon besmirching my good name, now, can I?"

"What do you *want* from us?"

"Your true identities—the real reason you've come to this place."

Clive realized that there was nothing more he could say. He could argue forever, but it would do absolutely no good.

He glanced at the others in the room. Guafe still glared at the man behind the desk, the metal dome of his head gleaming under the lights, one mechanical hand twitching at his side. Finnbogg stood with his head bowed, awaiting his judgment at the hands of what he thought were the spirits of the dead. Keoti, standing stiffly beside the desk, now wore a stranger's mask on her features. Clive remembered the softness of her lips, but there was no memory of them in the thin, hard line they now formed. Behind him, he could feel the weight of the guards' gazes, prepared for any untoward move.

Smythe stirred beside him. "And what then?" he asked the man behind the desk.

"What do you mean?"

"We give you what you want to know—then, what happens to us?"

"I might simply set you free."

Clive frowned at his companion, but Smythe turned his head slightly away from the desk so that neither the man behind it nor Keoti could see him give Clive a wink.

"Well, then, gov'nor," he said. "I suppose we'd better come clean. Now, Finn and our mechanical friend here are just what they say they are—or, at least they are so far as we know, for we only met 'em on route, as it were. 'Course, Guafe's got a mind as busy as a hurry-whore—it never stops whirling—so who knows who he really is, or what he's thinking, if you follow me?"

"Yes, yes. I'm not so concerned with them, except insofar as their plans coincide with yours."

"Well, I'm getting to that now, gov'nor. I'm not a man of many morns. I speak to the point and do what needs doing straightaway—no sense in making folks wait, that's what I always say. I remember a time in Newgate, when I was sitting in for a pint with a couple of the lads, and Casey, he turns to me and he says to me, like, 'Jim, when you take on a job, you do it quick, and you do it right, or you don't do it at all.' A right good bit of advice, that. Well, I look him straight back in the eye—don't I just?—and I says back to—"

The man rapped the desk top with his fist. "Will you please get on with it."

"Easy now, gov'nor. Don't be such a surly boots. A proper tale takes time to set up, as I'm sure you know. You don't go rushing blindly in, or the tale will just lie there looking like a dying duck in a thunderstorm—all pitiful and forlornlike."

Smythe shot the man behind the desk a quick grin, then plunged on before he could be interrupted again. "So what I'm saying is, though I know who I am, and I know the Cap'n here, the long and short of it is, I don't know these other two lads at all—except for what they've told me, and as Guafe himself's already mentioned to yourself, gov'nor, it could all be a pack of lies."

"Just tell me who you are."

"Well, gov'nor, I'm getting to that, aren't I now?"

"Your names."

Smythe straightened up. "Well, I'm Jim Scarpery—and that's the truth—and this here's the cap'n of the best band that ever plagued England's roads—Jack Roper. We're highwaymen, gov'nor, and proud of it."

"Highwaymen," the man behind the desk said. His tone was dry, and he eyed the pair of them with an expression that Clive couldn't decipher.

Madness, Clive thought. Horace had taken complete leave of his senses. Too many years of dissembling and mimicry had finally made him lose touch with reality.

But then he realized just what it was that Smythe was up to, and he was hard put to hide a grin. Lord help them all, it *was* madness. But the Dungeon was a Bedlam house, where perhaps only the play-acting of madness could see one through.

"The Devil's own, and a pair of the best, gov'nor," Smythe said with a nod. "'Least, we were till that damned blue light snatched us away and brought us here. We ran into your brother in a prison on one of the upper levels and got the whole tale of his search and all from him. Then, when we escaped—leaving him and his sergeant behind, didn't we just?—we thought we'd take their names and continue their quest. The cap'n here always fancied being a major."

The man behind the desk pursed his lips. Elbows on the desk top, he cradled his chin on his hands.

"Why" he asked.

"Well, you know why, gov'nor. Old Clive told us that you knew the tricks of getting in and out of this place. We want to go back home, the cap'n and me—take us a load of booty and stand with both feet firm on England's green shores. There's not much for a good Englishman in this place, be they a highwayman or a peer of the realm—am I right?"

"He's telling more lies," Keoti broke in. "They demanded to see you. Why would they take such a chance, knowing you'd see through them as soon as they were brought before you?"

Smythe never gave anyone else a chance to reply. "Well, we had to, didn't we?" he said. "We had to play the game out. In for a penny, in for it all. There was a chance we could win you over—" he gave the man behind the desk a quick, ingratiating smile "—or maybe catch you unawares and then lean on you a bit till you delivered us up a secret or two.

"We're not greedy, gov'nor—I'll tell you that straight-away. We didn't want much. Right now, we'll settle for our lives. We never meant any real harm."

Smythe bowed his head then and looked at the floor, wringing his hands.

"You can't be taking him seriously," Keoti said. "The man obviously wouldn't know the truth if he tripped over it."

The man behind the desk shook his head. "I believe him."

"Thank you, gov'nor," Smythe told him. "Now, we'd be eternally grateful if you'd just let us go on our way, and we'd never be troubling you anymore, would we, Jack?"

"Take them away," the man behind the desk said, waving them off.

The guards marched them out of the office and down

the corridor, Keoti and the man behind the desk following them at a slower pace. Clive leaned closer to Smythe.

"Well played," he whispered, "but do you think he truly believed you?"

Smythe shrugged. "I just gave him what he wanted, sah. Think about it—our man there is the pretender. Do you think he wants the Dramaranians to know that? All he wants from us is proof that he is who he says he is—or, conversely, that we're not who we said we were."

"And now what?"

"Now we look to escape before we lose our heads, for you can count on this: he won't keep us around."

"Cap'n Jack," Clive muttered. "Jim Scarpery. Highwaymen."

"He wanted a tale, and any tale would do," Smythe said, "so I gave him the first that came to mind. I always had a hankering to be considered a bold highwayman."

Clive thought of the hate for him that was now in Keoti's eyes. "I'd rather you had put your quick thinking to considering a way that they might have believed us."

"'Father Neville' would never have allowed it," Smythe said.

"I know," Clive conceded. "Now, if we can just make an opportunity to escape this mess, rather than getting ourselves in even deeper. . . ."

But that moment never arrived. They were marched through a number of corridors, taken down many levels in an elevator, then marched down more corridors, until the way was blocked by an enormous metal door. The guards kept them all bunched together until Keoti and the man who called himself Father Neville joined them.

"I'm not an unfair man," the pretender said. "There's a way to the sixth level through the caverns that you will find behind this door."

Hope rose in Clive. Horace had been correct. The man *had* just wanted a tale, any tale, and now he was going to let them go.

"I might add, however," the pretender went on, "that there are . . . *things* in there that enjoy the taste of human flesh." He nodded to the guards. "I wish you luck."

Like hell you do, Clive thought. He looked at Keoti, but saw from her expression that so far as she was concerned, he no longer existed.

"You'll pay for this," Clive told "Father Neville" as the guards opened the door just wide enough to push their small company through.

The pretender came to stand beside the door. "I doubt that," he said.

It was dark in the cavern—dark, cold, and damp. Clive was the last to be hauled to the door and then pushed inside. Just as the door was closing, "Father Neville" leaned close to the crack.

"Your brother sends his regards," he said in a voice pitched just low enough to carry to Clive's ears, but no farther.

Clive lunged for him, but the fat man danced nimbly back, and the great metal door closed with a clang that echoed on and on through the dark cavern in which they were imprisoned.

• Eighteen •

Head pillowed against Sidi's shoulder, Annabelle managed to get in a couple of hours of dreamless sleep before she was awakened by a whooping gang of young rogha who were playing a mad game of tag in the trees around the platform she and Sidi were sitting on. As she watched their acrobatics, her stomach began a series of flips. She quickly reached for the byrr pouch. Taking out a leaf, she began to chew.

By the time her unreasonable fears had retreated enough to be bearable, Chobba arrived. He swung down from a branch, neatly balancing a tray laden with what looked like little breakfast cakes, fruit, fired-clay mugs, and a steaming pot of tea. The mugs didn't rattle against each other, and not a drop of the tea was spilled.

"Show-off," she told him as he settled on his haunches in front of them.

The big rogha grinned. "Sleep hokay?" he asked.

"I think I'd like to get back on the ground now, if I could," she said.

She winced as the shrieking troop of children suddenly swooped by again. They didn't so much seem to swing between branches as tumble. Chobba, obviously thinking they were bothering her with their nose, stood up and began to shout at them, until she tugged on his furry arm.

"No, no," she said. "It's not them—it's just the height. It makes me . . . sick."

"Yoo chew byrr?"

"Yeah, but I still want down."

"Yoo eat first. Loo-kee cum. Fetta cheef cum. We all talk. Then yoo go. Hokay?"

"Fetta chief?" Annabelle asked. She remembered him using the term last night, but she'd been too out of it to ask him what it meant.

"She make fetta," Chobba explained. "Plenty smart."

"I think he means a rootman," Sidi said. "Someone who makes fetishes and speaks with the spirits."

"Like a shaman," Annabelle said.

Sidi shrugged, but Chobba was nodding in response to what the Indian had said.

"Named Reena," he said. "Fetta cheef. Talk with dead rogha—read sign in root and leaf. Cum plenty soon."

Drawn by the sound of their conversation, Shriek and Tomàs emerged from the hut. At the sight of the four-armed alien, the younger rogha came bouncing through the tree boughs to peer more closely, scrambling away when she turned toward them, then creeping forward again once she looked away. Shriek laughed at their antics, the high chittering sound cutting across the young roghas' shrieks.

"Eat— drink!" Chobba said. He sat on his haunches again and pushed the tray forward, smacking his lips. "Plenty good, yuh?"

Lukey joined them while they were eating, his arrival sparking what appeared to be a good-natured series of teasing remarks that flew between the younger rogha and himself. The children hung from their perches with one hand, or one leg, waving their free limbs as they chattered.

"What does that mean, *bishii*?" Annabelle asked. It was the term that the younger rogha used to refer to the old man.

Lukey smiled. "Well, they say it means 'hairless ape', but Chobba here told me after I was here a while that it really means 'old fart.'"

"Bishii, bishii!" the children chorused.

Lukey stood up and shook his fists at them with mock severity as he tried to shoo them away, but he need not have bothered. The young rogha were already falling silent. In moments they had all fled quickly away.

Turning, Annabelle saw that it was the arrival of the fetish chief that had sent them scurrying. Taking off right now, she thought, looking at the strange rogha, might not be such a bad idea.

Reena had no legs, but it didn't stop her progress through the trees. She landed on the platform and propelled herself toward them on her powerful arms. She wore a short skirt of leather, which just covered her leg stumps, and a vest of woven grass, under which her furry breasts bounced. The vest was decorated with beadwork, feathers, and hundreds of tiny bird bones that rattled when she moved. Hanging from her neck was a large, beaded leather pouch. Dozens of bracelets jangled on her arms. Her fur smelled strongly of incense.

Her face was hidden behind a shockingly ugly mask. The mask itself was wooden—a grotesque exaggeration of a rogha's features—with copper, cowrie shells, and beads covering everything but its crown, which was a square of plain, dark, blue-green cloth. A thick fringe of antelope hair bearded the bottom of the mask, and rising like an elephant's trunk behind the plain crown was a beaded headpiece tufted with raffia.

She stopped in front of Annabelle and her party, the dark eyes in the eyeholes glittering as she studied the four of them.

"What does the mask signify?" Annabelle asked Lukey.

"A spirit of the darkworld that watches you through my eyes," the fetish chief replied. Her voice had a hollow sound, coming out from behind the mast as it did.

"You speak English?" Annabelle asked.

Stupid question, she thought as soon as she'd asked it, but Reena shook her head.

"She doesn't speak your language," that same hollow voice said. "But I do."

"Ah. . . ."

Annabelle glanced at Sidi, but he shook his head, understanding as little as she did of what was going on. Neither Lukey nor Chobba would meet her gaze.

"Who . . . ah . . . are you, then?" she asked the voice behind the mask.

"A spirit of the darkworld."

Right. Seance time in the jungle. Just what they needed.

"Can you be a little more specific?" Annabelle tried.

"The darkworld lies all about you—invisible, yet always present. We watch you, through the eyes of our mouthpieces."

"Like a ghost?"

"We are not dead, but yes, like a ghost."

"What's your name?"

"We don't have names."

"Then, how do you tell each other apart?" Annabelle asked.

"We know who we are—that is sufficient, don't you think?"

"I suppose. . . ."

"You wish to go to Quan," the voice continued, issuing hollowly from behind the mask, "to enter the gateway that lies there, which you believe will take you back to your own worlds. But I tell you now, Annabelly—" it said her first and surname as though it were all one word "—that if you go on from here, you will never see your child Amanda again."

"How can you know all that stuff?" Annabelle demanded.

"From the darkworld, we can see you as you truly are—your complete history as a whole, rather than just the outer face you present to the immediate world around you."

This was really weird, Annabelle thought. She'd never been one to go in for mumbo-jumbo stuff. Everything had a reasonable explanation. You might not have the right data to work it out at any given time, but you could count on it all making logical sense somewhere along the line. But this . . . this was just spooky.

"So, you're reading my mind?"

"I am reading your essence."

"Wonderful. And after having a good long poke around in there, the best you can come up with is to tell me that Quan's dangerous? I hate to break this to you, pal, but that's not exactly a hot news flash."

"I understand your desire to return to your home-world, but you must accept the impossibility of that. The deeper you go through the Dungeon's levels, the more danger you are placing yourself in, and the less chance you have of surviving. Quan is extremely dangerous, but it is nothing compared to what lies in the gateway and beyond it."

"Okay," Annabelle said. "But, why don't you humor me? Tell me what's waiting for us."

"In Quan, certain death at the hands of an illusion. In the gateway, certain death caused by your greatest fear made real. In the next level, certain death brought on by madness."

"Wait a sec," Annabelle said. "You keep saying 'certain death.' How can I find certain death in the gateway when I've already died in Quan?"

There was a long pause, then finally, the hollow voice admitted, "Should you go on, it is possible, though extremely unlikely, for you to survive one, or another, but not all of the dooms that lie in your way."

"But we could go on and have a chance?"

"The possibility is so slight that it is not worth considering."

"Still, you wouldn't try to stop us—I mean, physically?"

"Each individual is free to make his or her own choices in this world. That can never be taken away."

"Okay, so you won't stop us. Can you help us some more? Give us some more info? I mean, come on. What's it gonna hurt you?"

There was no reply.

"Spirit?" Annabelle asked.

Still silence.

Annabelle reached forward and touched Reena on the shoulder. The fetish chief started, then spoke to her in the language of the rogha. The voice, while it had a hollowness to its tone, was nothing like the one with which she'd been speaking moments before.

"What's she saying now?" Annabelle asked.

"'What do you wish of me?'" Lukey translated.

"We were talking . . ." Annabelle began. Her voice trailed off as Lukey shook his head.

"Nope. You were talkin' to the darkworld spirit that gives Reena her powers—not to Reena herself. I've seen it before. Bin through the same thing myself when I first got here."

"What the hell's going on?" Annabelle demanded.

Sidi touched her arm. "I have heard of this before—among the rootmen of the Africans. The spirits fill the rootman's body like water filling a vessel. When the spirit departs, the rootman remembers nothing."

"But that's not real," Annabelle protested. "Spirits . . . ghosts. It's just not real."

"There are too many mysteries in the world," Sidi said, "for me to be able to decide which of them are illusions and which are real. In this Dungeon we have already seen what we thought to be impossible become real. When the bizarre is commonplace, who can honestly say what is or is not possible?"

Annabelle nodded. "Okay. You got me on that one. But I'm still going on."

"I would not think to argue with you, otherwise," Sidi said.

Annabelle turned to Chobba. "And I'd like to get down to the ground now, if I could."

"Sorry yoo go," Chobba said. "Chobba take yoo down. Chobba and yoo walk on legs to Quan, yuh? Hokay?"

"Wish I could think of a way ta get you ta stay," Lukey said, "but damned if I can think o' one—not when you got your mind set on goin'."

Annabelle started to rise, but the fetish chief suddenly thrust out a strong hand and gripped Annabelle's arm. She spoke quickly in rogha, masked face close, dark eyes glittering in their slits, inches from Annabelle's own.

"What's she saying?"

Lukey translated. "That even though you ain't got nothin' ta ask her, she's goin' ta tell you somethin' all the same. She sees in your white face a . . ." The old man paused, looking for a word. "Not a destiny. More like a mess a' hard times comin', an' if you want ta make out okay, you got ta be willin' to depend on other people's strength, 'stead a' just tryin' ta pull the weight on your own. An' don't go lookin' too hard for what you think you want, 'cause you just might get it."

Tomàs, who had remained silent through all the various exchanges, spoke up now. "So, will you listen to me now? I say we go back to find others, *sim*? They are not so *estúpido* as you."

"Go back," Annabelle said. "Right. You ready to take on the chasucks, pal?"

"We will go carefully."

Annabelle shook her head. "*You* go, and anybody else who wants to go with you. Me, I'm going on. I'm getting outta this place, and the only way I see to pull that off is to keep on going."

Shriek moved to Annabelle's side, her multifaceted gaze fixed unpleasantly on the Portuguese. *And she will not go alone*, the arachnid said.

Annabelle smiled, and turned back to look at the fetish chief.

"Thank you," she said. "You and your spirits." She waited for Lukey to translate. "Though we must go on, I will remember your advice."

Reena nodded. She spoke softly.

"'You are a strong woman with much pride,'" Lukey translated, "'an' that, too, will be a great help.' An' then she gave you her blessin'."

The fetish chief walked away on her hands, then swung into the nearest branch and was gone.

"That's really something," Annabelle said. "The way she moves."

"Reena plenty strong," Chobba said, flexing his arm muscles. "Plenty smart. Big cheef. Like Chobba, yuh?"

Annabelle grinned. "You got it," she said. "Can we get down to the ground now? It's either that, or I'll be falling off in another minute."

With what passed for a smile on her alien features, Shriek swung over the side of the platform and started down. By the time Annabelle and the others of her party reached the ground, Shriek was there waiting for them. Chobba and a number of his warriors were planning to guide them to Quan. Surprisingly, Lukey joined the group as well.

"Well, I'm not sayin' I'm goin' all the way," he said, "but I wouldn't mind catchin' just a peek a' the place, an'—oh, hell, you never know. I might just find I'm ready to do some travelin' my own self. Bin livin' like a monkey for an awful lot a' years. Maybe it's time I learned ta live like a man again."

"We're happy to have you," Annabelle said.

"Oh, yes," Tomàs said. "*Muito feliz.* Very happy."

Annabelle turned to the Portuguese, then frowned when she saw the guileless look on his face. The little bugger acted like he'd had a change of heart and meant it. Well, who knows? she thought. Nobody says he's gotta stay a sullen little weasel.

"Walk on legs now, yuh?" Chobba said when they were all gathered on the game trail.

They each had a new pack to carry, filled with provisions and water sacks. Annabelle's also had the pouch of byrr leaves, which Chobba had insisted she keep.

"You guys know any walking songs?" she asked.

When Chobba shook his head, she taught him and his warriors the chorus for "Da Doo Ron Ron." Making up words to fit their present situation, with the rogha answering her back with a lusty if slightly off-key chorus, Annabelle walked beside Chobba and Sidi as they set off for Quan. Even with the warnings of danger that lay ahead, she still felt better than she had in a long time.

It's the ground under your feet, Annie B., she told herself. Don't go getting too cocky now.

Maybe, maybe not. All she knew was that it was good to be moving under her own steam, their party strengthened, and no pack of land sharks on their ass.

Things could be better, she thought. But then again, they could be a helluva lot worse.

▪ Nineteen ▪

They were trapped in utter darkness. Clive ran his hands along the metal door that had sealed them in, but could find no handle or bolt on this side to let them back out again.

"Damn the man!" he cried, and hammered a fist against the door.

A dull, hollow boom rang through the darkness.

"Need light," Finnbogg said.

"I've got the spark for a torch," Smythe said, taking flint and steel from the pocket of his jacket. "Let's see if we can find something to burn."

"What did he mean by *things*?" Clive said.

Smythe's shrug was lost in the blackness. "In this place, it could be anything," he said. "Wouldn't surprise me to trip over a band of kobolds."

"Can't find even a scrap of wood," Finnbogg said.

His voice came from farther out in the darkness, where he was carefully feeling his way about, looking for fuel to burn.

"Don't wander too far," Smythe warned him. "I caught a glimpse of the size of this place just before they shut us in, and it's big enough to get easily lost in."

"Perhaps I can help," Guafe said.

Clive and Smythe turned in the direction of the cyborg's metallic voice.

"God save us," Smythe muttered.

He'd forgotten one of the uses of having a cyborg as part of their company. Guafe's eyes began to glow red, then redder, casting a dim light wherever he turned his gaze.

"Nice of you to help," Clive said dryly, "all things considered."

But he was happy for the light, no matter how dim it was.

"We are in this together," Guafe replied.

"Funny how you forgot that a few minutes ago, when we were talking to the fat pretender."

"He was most . . . convincing."

"Do tell," Smythe said. "Pity for you that you weren't. You might have been spared our company."

"What we think of each other has no relevance to our situation," the cyborg said. "I merely wish to observe as much of this curious world as I may before I make my escape. This particular place holds little of interest."

Clive nodded to himself. He tended to forget that while the cyborg looked human enough, the workings of his mind would no doubt always remain unfathomable. In some ways, the cyborg was less human than either Finnbogg or Shriek, he reminded himself. It would serve them all well if he didn't forget that.

"Here, what's this?" Smythe said.

Guafe turned his gaze in the Englishman's direction, illuminating a heap of what appeared to be discarded mining gear. Smythe picked a lantern out of the debris. Checking inside, he found the stub of a candle. More searching found a number of other lanterns—most broken, but all with bits of candle in them that could be salvaged.

"The equipment seems rather primitive," Guafe said.

Considering the technological marvels of their captors, Clive had to agree.

"Perhaps that's why it's here," he said. "It's of no more use to them."

"Perhaps," the cyborg said.

Or perhaps, Clive added to himself, the *things* that the pretender had spoken of had made the Dramaranians abandon this mine a very long time ago. Though he wasn't given to either claustrophobia or a fear of the dark, he found himself keeping one ear constantly alert for any sound that they didn't make themselves. Whatever the Dramaranians kept down here to prey on their captives had to be extremely unpleasant if the best description of them was *things*.

"Look," Finnbogg exclaimed, holding up a box of unused candles.

"Good work, Finn," Smythe said.

With bits of shaved wood and some straw padding from the seat of an old mine cart, he now had enough of a fire going to light the first candle stub. Setting it back into place inside the lantern, he held the lantern up so that they could get a better look at their surroundings, but while it illuminated their immediate area, its light was simply not strong enough to penetrate the cavern's deeper shadows.

"There are rails here," Guafe said.

He was pointing to where narrow rails, set on wooden ties, led off into the cavern, disappearing into the darkness some ten feet from where they stood.

"We can follow them," he added.

Clive nodded, but first, he held up the lantern that he'd lit for himself, turning its light to the door. The face of the massive door was utterly blank, one solid sheet of metal fit so snugly into the stone walls of the cavern that it would be a very long job to try to attempt to chip their way out, even with the use of the tools that lay in the heap of discarded gear. And there was another good reason for not attempting such an escape, he realized. The sound of their work would surely draw the Dramaranians back to investigate. They might be able to overcome a small party, but then they would have the entire complex of the underground city to transverse.

No. They had to go on.

"Does Neville's journal say anything of this place?" Smythe asked.

Clive shook his head. "It was not mentioned in the last message." There was no point in looking for that entry again. He had almost become used to the way in which entries appeared and disappeared unexpectedly, impossibly, in the slim journal. Somehow Neville—or the Ren or the Chaffri, the rulers of the Dungeon—had found a way to write in the book while it rested in Clive's possession. Perhaps something had been added. He patted his jacket pocket and frowned. "Damn. I left it in my room. The Dramaranians have it now."

Smythe shrugged. "It caused us as much trouble as it helped us."

Thinking of Annabelle and the rest of her party, lost—more likely dead—in the jungles, Clive could only agree. If they had kept together. . . .

"We should follow the rails," Guafe said. "They must lead somewhere."

"They'll only take us to wherever they were mining," Smythe said.

"Not necessarily. In the Dungeon—"

"Any-bloody-thing's possible," Smythe finished. "Right. But these rails. . . ."

"Do you have a better idea?" the cyborg asked.

"This place our tomb," Finnbogg said suddenly. "Judgment of dead was that we be entombed alive, or eaten by creatures that live down here."

"Those were living, breathing men and women that put us in here," Clive said. "They were no more spirits of the dead than we are."

But again he tried to pierce the deeper darkness beyond the glow of their lanterns, an uncomfortable sensation of being spied upon crawling up his spine. *Things*, the pretender had said. Damn him. What manner of *things*?

"We have no water, no provisions," Smythe said, "and these candles won't last forever."

The stub he'd first lit was already guttering in its lantern. He lit a fresh one, then paused.

"Look at this," he said.

The candle's flame was being drawn away from the door where they were standing, deeper into the cavern, in the same direction that the rails led.

"An air draft," Guafe said. "Created by an opening to the outside farther in. So the rails do lead somewhere other than merely the last shaft in which they were working."

Smythe nodded. "Well, that's settled, at least. We follow the rails."

They salvaged what they could from the discarded mining gear. Candles filled their pockets. Finnbogg, Clive, and Smythe each carried a lantern. The dwarf took a small sledgehammer for a weapon, the others pry-bars. Smythe added a discarded tin container to his gear, tying it to his belt with a length of twine that he'd also discovered. He meant to use it to hold water, if they came across any. Over his shoulder, tied at each end with more of the twine, he carried a strip of sturdy canvas that he'd found bunched up in a corner.

"I'd feel better with a rope," he said.

"I'd feel better to simply be quit of this place," Clive said.

"There's that."

They set off then, following the two metal rails, their boots sending up hollow echoes as they tramped along the wooden ties.

With no way to measure time, it was difficult to tell how long they followed the rails across that immense cavern, but eventually, they came to its farther side. As the dark bulk of the walls rose before them, disappearing into a darkness that their lights could not penetrate, they saw that the rails entered a large cleft in the wall. Stepping through, they now found the rails leading them through a series of smaller galleries that began to slope gently downward.

Here, dripstone covered the rails in places, spindly stalagmites rising from the ties, forcing them to make detours from the actual path the rails took. Some of the galleries were small enough that their light reached to the walls on either side and the ceilings above, hung heavily with stalactites.

In one gallery they came upon the first branching of the rails. They went along the ones that led to the right, but these followed a sudden dip, leading the party into a gallery where the walls and floor were heavily covered with knobby calcite growths. Here the stalactites had grown all the way to the floor, forming a bewildering series of columns. The cave coral on the floor made the footing very unsteady.

In places the rails vanished under the dripstone growths, so thick had they become. The party retraced their path back to where the track had initially split, taking the left turn this time. Here, the downward incline continued at a gentler slope, though the farther they went, the damper the air grew about them.

They stopped twice to rest, once simply on the rails, the second time following the sound of water to the far side of a larger gallery where they found a pool of water, fed by an overhead drip. They drank there and rested again. Smythe filled his tin container before they pressed on.

Clive's sense of the party being under observation by hidden viewers neither increased nor decreased, but the farther they went, coming upon no sign of any living creature, the more ill at ease he felt. The darkness beyond their lantern lights, the soft echoing shuffle of their footsteps rebounding hollowly from the walls, all added to his discomfort, making him brood.

He worried about Annabelle and her party, his guilt at letting them go off on their own made worse by what Keoti had told him of the jungles and Annabelle's chance of surviving their dangers. Time and again he berated himself for not being firmer with her and keeping the two parties as one.

The fact that they had had to leave Dramaran in disgrace irked him as well, and not just because of how poorly Keoti had been made to see him. It was more the thought of that fat pretender sitting safely amid all those technological wonders, wearing Neville's name like a badge of honor, his lies being accepted as truth, while the truth was made a mockery. . . .

It made Clive grit his teeth. He wished that there had been an opportunity for him to cross swords with the pretender to his brother's name. He would have enjoyed seeing that smirking smile wiped from the man's fat-jowled features.

But thinking of the pretender brought thoughts of his twin to mind, as well. Ever since he and Horace had entered this damned Dungeon, Neville had been playing them for a pair of fools. Everything that happened to them seemed to be a part of some elaborate game, only no one had been kind enough to allow Clive and his party in on its rules. Finding that journal, mysterious voices, all that had happened to them following the advice that Neville had written in it. . . .

Perhaps Horace was right—they were better off without the damned thing. For if it was to have been of any use, why couldn't it have been more clearly written? Instead of riddles and vagaries, a few hard facts would have been far more than useful. Such as what this cavern entailed for them. Where would it take them? And what inhabited it?

It was Finnbogg who stumbled upon the bones.

The dwarf was walking on one side of the rails when he gave a cry and would have fallen, his lantern smashing on the rocks, if Guafe hadn't caught his arm and helped him to regain his balance. As it was, the lantern swung wildly, making the shadows dance like dervishes, and then they all saw what the dwarf had stumbled upon.

All along the left side of the rails in this newest gallery, bones lay scattered from the track to the far wall. Skulls and rib cages, the bones of arms and legs. Others that were not readily recognizable—perhaps not even human. And there were some—clearly the skeletons of humanlike creatures, with hands like men, or legs and torsos, only their sizes were wrong. Most of these were too small even to have been children's. One, if it had been a part of a humanoid, then it had belonged to a giant at least eleven feet tall.

"It's some kind of graveyard," Smythe said.

"More a feeding ground, I would say," Guafe remarked.

Finnbogg shuddered, and Clive could feel a shiver

travel up his own spine. As Smythe moved closer, holding his lantern high to cast more light, Clive followed suit, though he couldn't shake that sense of being spied upon by hidden watchers. It was stronger now than it had ever been since they'd entered the cavern. A crawling sensation that traveled up his spine and settled at the nape of his neck, knotting his muscles.

For a long time the party regarded the bone field, none of them speaking, each keeping his own counsel. Then, just as Guafe turned to him to make a remark, Clive held up a hand.

"Hist!" he said softly. "What was that?"

"I heard nothing," the cyborg began, but then his gaze traveled past Clive, his eyes widening.

Turning himself, Clive saw that dozens of pairs of small, slitted eyes watched them from the farther side of the gallery, retinas reflecting back at the party like a fox's or cat's would in the light of their lanterns.

Smythe pulled his pry-bar from where it had been thrust in his belt. "Now we'll see what manner of creatures haunts this place," he said.

"Wait a moment," Clive said. He held out a hand to stop Smythe's advance. "Let's see if we can pass them by."

Smythe hesitated, then nodded. Slowly, the party backed toward the narrow entryway that led into the next gallery, feeling their way with their feet as they went, unwilling to lift their gazes from those that were watching them from the darkness. Just as they reached the entrance, a blood-curdling shriek, like that torn from the throat of a man being disemboweled, shattered the darkness.

"Well, that's cut it," Smythe said.

As one, the members of the party lifted their weapons and prepared to meet the creatures' attack.

▪ Twenty ▪

With the presence of the rogha, Annabelle felt as though
their journey had turned into an outing. It was hard not
to have fun with the good-natured ape-men around.
They laughed and joked among themselves, making
Lukey translate what they thought were the particularly
good lines. They loved to sing, especially to the rhythm
of R&B, so the songs that Annabelle taught them were
all old Motown numbers and Fifties rock music with lots
of doo-wops, she-bops, and the like.

Their own music was harder for her to follow. It
involved a lot of sharp clicks that were made in the back
of the throat, and sounds that were like short coughs,
mixed in with a rhythmical chanting. But she loved
listening to it and trying to follow its odd tempos.

By the end of the first day, she found it easy to tell the
various rogha apart. Chobba had never been a problem—he hulked over the others, and there was no
mistaking his toothy grin. Through variation in fur
coloring at first, and then the facial features, as she grew
used to them, she soon learned to keep all the rest of
them straight as well.

Ghes was smaller than the rest, with a large nose and
a henna tint to his fur. He was quiet-spoken and the best
singer. Ninga had black and silver streaks in his head
fur, and large eyes set wide apart. A practical joker, he
loved to have a good trick played on him as much as
playing the trick on someone else. Tarit and Nog were
the hardest to tell apart, because they were identical
twins, but Tarit wore a brightly colored scarf along with

his neck torc, and Nog had a shrill laugh that couldn't be mistaken for anyone else's.

The only female among the rogha accompanying them was Yssi, with her light, tan-colored fur and soft, dark-brown eyes. Next to Chobba, she was the strongest of their little troop, and like Ghes, she was quiet-spoken, but she had a dry wit, so that when she did make a comment, all the rogha invariably broke up. She also wasn't averse to a little common tomfoolery, either.

She was the one who, when they camped that first night, tried to get Annabelle and her party to eat from a bowl of wriggling white worms and slugs that she'd collected on the journey, insisting that they were a delicacy that shouldn't be missed, and yes, they were supposed to be eaten while still alive. That was, in fact, half the charm of them.

Annabelle was disgusted, but since she prided herself on her willingness to try any native food, no matter where she traveled, she almost swallowed one of the squirming creatures. All that stopped her were the stifled giggles of the other rogha, who eventually let her in on the joke.

Ninga took to calling her Ilkgar after that, which Lukey translated for her as "eater of worms."

"Cute," she told both Ninga and Yssi. "Just remember, kids: I don't get mad, I just get even."

The rogha hooted with appreciative laughter when Lukey translated what she'd said.

The real dinner that night was a kind of jambalaya of vegetables, with the meat of a wading bird that Shriek had brought down just before they camped. The camp itself was well off the game trail, in a clearing on the veldt side of the path. The strip of jungle on this side of the river was so wide now that they no longer caught brief glimpses of the plains through the trees, as they had on their first day after leaving Clive's party. The undergrowth was thick off the game trail, while the trail itself was heavily overhung with drooping boughs and vines.

The one thing Annabelle missed about the rogha

village was the wind that moved through the treetops. Here, the air was still and humid again, the heat draining. Mosquitoes were a problem until Ghes pointed out the black mud that formed at the roots of a reedlike flowering plant growing in thick stands along the river bank. A thick white juice secreted from the roots of the plant made an excellent bug repellent when mixed with the mud. Although it did have a certain pungent odor that was almost, though not quite, unpleasant, it was better than constantly trying to fend off the bugs.

The silliest thing about it, Annabelle decided, was the way that it made them all look like a motley bunch of commandos in camouflage gear.

When they were finally ready to turn in that first night, the rogha and Lukey all swung into the trees, where they made nests for themselves, wedged in the crooks where branches thrust out from the main trunk. After the night she'd spent in the rogha village, nothing could convince Annabelle to follow suit. She, Sidi, and Shriek made their beds on the ground around the dying embers of their fire. Tomàs, however, climbed up into the lower branches of one of the trees and, after much twisting about and adjusting of his limbs, fell asleep as though he'd been born to life in the trees.

Wasn't much different from a ship's rigging, Annabelle thought.

It was during her watch that she heard the cough of a monkey-cat. It came from a good distance away in the jungle, but each subsequent time she heard it, it sounded closer. With her spear, she poked up into the boughs above her, where the nearest of the rogha was sleeping. Ghes stirred, then called down softly.

Though she was trying to pick up the language, Annabelle still had a long way to go with it. But while she didn't understand what Ghes had said, she did catch the rogha's questioning tone.

"Hear that?" she called back in very badly accented rogha. "Bad sound?"

The monkey-cat coughed again. This time it was no farther than a few trees away.

Ghes cocked his head. Hearing the monkey-cat, he made a low, warbling sound, like that of a night bird. Instantly, the other rogha were awake. They had a hurried conference, shadowy heads bent together, then swung off in various directions.

Annabelle blinked at their sudden disappearance. She clutched her spear, wondering if she should get the fire going again, when there came a sudden chorus of shrieks from the forest all around them, followed by an abrupt silence.

Sidi and Shriek leapt to their feet, brandishing their own weapons. In their tree perches, Lukey and Tomàs stirred. Then, before Annabelle could explain, a long, wailing cry broke the jungle night, followed by another silence.

"Annabelle?" Sidi asked. "What's happened? Where are the rogha?"

"There was one of those monkey-cats coming near the camp," Annabelle started to explain, but then the rogha were back.

They swung down from the trees, hooting with pleasure. Chobba was holding the slain monkey-cat by its tail.

"Lookit that!" Lukey cried. He started down from his perch. "Those damn things'd tear your heart out as soon as look at you. They like to sneak up on the baby rogha an' carry 'em away."

Annabelle slowly lowered her spear. "It's like killing a cousin," she said.

"It's killin' a varmint, that's all," Lukey said. "They're tough little buggers—mean as sin. Guess this one wasn't expectin' us to be ready for him."

Chobba was thumping his chest. "Big cheef, yuh!" he cried.

The rogha pounded each other's shoulders, all of them grinning. As Yssi and Nog started to skin the animal, Annabelle looked away. She couldn't shake the feeling that the monkey-cat, like the rogha and the flying monkeys, were all related in a way. To her, what they'd done was the same as if she'd killed a chimp. Up close, the monkey-cat didn't appear much bigger than that.

"Different customs," Sidi said from beside her.

Annabelle nodded. "Yeah. I know. It's just, when you think of the rogha or Shriek, or even Finnbogg, you get confused as to what's an animal and what's . . . a person."

Even though they'd just eaten, the rogha built up the fire once more. When the monkey-cat was skinned and gutted, its paws and head kept aside so that the teeth and claws could be collected later, the rogha thrust a spit through the animal's torso and set to roasting it over the fire.

"Eat heart—be strong," Chobba told her. "Stronger, yuh?"

"I guess," Annabelle said, regretting that she'd ever wakened anybody in the first place. Maybe she could just have shooed it away.

"Hell," Lukey said, forcing open the monkey-cat's jaws. "Will you lookit the teeth on this bugger." He showed them to Annabelle. "It could rip your arm off without even blinkin', an' that's God's own truth."

If the journey had seemed like an outing before, now it had gained a completely festive—if somewhat maca- bre, by Annabelle's reckoning—air. The rogha laughed and told jokes, and later, they feasted on the roasted cat. When Chobba offered a piece of the cooked heart to her, Annabelle shook her head, but she did try some of the meat. It was gamy, with a coarse texture, but sur- prisingly good. She found she couldn't eat very much, and what she had eaten left her feeling a little queasy.

It was a long time before the camp settled down again, with only a few hours left until daybreak. The rogha told tales, which Lukey translated, and the songs went on until near dawn. They all slept late that morning, not getting back to the game trail until well after noon.

* * *

The following days fell into a pattern of marching by day and camping by night that was broken only a few times. Once, when they were washing up at the river bank on the third morning out from the village, the rogha withdrew back into the jungle, quickly pulling Annabelle and her companions into the undergrowth with them. When Annabelle questioned them, Ninga pointed at the sky above the river. Peering through the bushes, Annabelle could just make out a small black dot floating there, its wings still, riding the air currents like a falcon.

"Gree," Ninga explained.

"They spot us," Lukey added, "an' there'll be hell ta pay."

"I thought you said they were scavengers," Annabelle said.

"Well, they are. Thing is, they don't mind killin' somethin' an' waitin' for it ta rot properly, an' they plain hate anybody wanderin' through their territory."

"This is their territory?"

"Close enough so's it don't matter."

Another time they came across the recent scent trail of a monkey-cat, and the rogha argued about whether or not they should track the animal down. Their disagreement grew so profound that Annabelle was sure that they were going to come to blows, but as suddenly as it had started, it was over, and the rogha were laughing again as they continued on their journey.

As they came closer to Quan, the rogha grew increasingly wary. Twice they had the party circumvent elaborate traps laid on the game trail. One was a pit with sharpened stakes at the bottom, covered with leaves and made to look like a part of the trail. The other was a series of nets, ready to fall on the unwary traveler when set off by a trip string. The second time they came upon a pit, it held the impaled body of one of the tapirlike creatures. The rogha descended into the pit and stole the body, and that night they had another feast.

"Who is setting these traps?" Sidi asked Lukey that night.

"Quanians, I guess. Me, I've never bin this far from the village. Just heard about what it's like, that's all."

Chobba, overhearing them, nodded solemnly. "Bad place, yuh?" he said. "Plenty trouble."

It was when they were within a day's march of the village that Annabelle spied a piece of torn cloth caught in a branch alongside the trail. It looked to be fine linen—a piece of a sleeve, torn from a shirt, with part of a frayed cuff still attached.

"I thought you said the Quanians were ghosts," she said. "But this didn't belong to any ghost, and ghosts didn't set those traps back there, either."

Lukey took the piece of cloth from her. "Guess this belonged to that other feller," he said.

"What other feller? You never said anything about somebody else coming this way."

"Didn't really think to tell you about it," Lukey replied. "It was a while ago—a couple a' weeks, maybe less? Feller came through an' we tried to stop him, but he wouldn't take no. Said he had to get to Quan, an' wasn't nothin' goin' to stop him from gettin' there."

"What was his name?" Annabelle asked.

She had a sneaking suspicion as to who it had been, even though the time frame was wrong. But then again, who knew how time worked in this place? When you considered the spread of centuries from which people were plucked, it made sense that time worked differently here as well.

"His name was Folly," Lukey said. "Neville Folly."

Annabelle remembered the chasuck, with their cries of "folly, folly." She should have remembered to ask about Clive's brother when she'd first arrived at the rogha village.

"Do you mean Folliot?" she asked.

Lukey nodded. "That's the name, all right. You know that feller?"

"We've been chasing him forever, it seems."

"Well, you can stop lookin' for him now," Lukey said. "Ain't no way he'd've survived in Quan. No way anybody can."

"Yet, you're coming with us."

"Well, now, I'm goin' to have me a look-see; that's all I'll swear to right now."

Annabelle exchanged glances with others of her party, and saw the same knowledge reflected in their eyes that she knew was in her own. Clive's party was completely off track.

"What did this feller do, anyway?" Lukey asked.

"He's supposed to know how to get out of this place," Annabelle replied, "so you can bet that if anyone gets through Quan and its ghosts, it'll be him."

"He knows for sure?"

"To the best of our knowledge," Sidi said, "he's been all the way through and back once already."

"An' now he's goin' back through a second time? Feller needs his head examined, I'm thinkin'."

"And we'll be happy to do it for him," Annabelle said.

She wondered if she'd ever see Clive and Finnbogg and the rest of them again. She'd half expected their trails to cross once more, but now she knew that the other party was so far off base that they might as well be on another planet. She even missed Finnbogg, for all that it was his fault that she was still stuck in this place.

"Bad place now," Chobba called back from where he walked ahead.

"Quan?" Annabelle asked.

The rogha shook his head. "Big trap. Go by tree now, yuh?"

Annabelle pushed ahead to where Chobba had stopped and looked ahead. She couldn't see anything on the trail at all.

"What is it?" she asked, carefully poking her foot forward in the dirt.

"No!" Chobba cried.

But he was too late. The touch of Annabelle's foot had tripped the trap. A cord whipped out of the ground, snagging her foot. Before anyone could grab her, she was jerked off her feet and pulled high into the air. The abruptness of the trap as it whipped her into the air just about dislocated her hip joint.

"Get me down!" she cried.

But then, from somewhere high above them in the trees, a bell sounded to let whoever had set the trap know that it had been sprung.

Swinging upside down, with the world swirling and spinning below her, Annabelle's fear of heights filled her with a panicking rush that left her absolutely numb.

▪ Twenty-one ▪

As the creatures charged them, Clive and his party had time to set their lanterns down and bring out their makeshift weapons, but that was all. Finnbogg raised his sledgehammer, the others their pry-bars, and then the swarm was upon them.

The light of the lanterns cast an uneven glow on the creatures as they came at the party in a skittering wave. They were barely three feet tall, spindly limbed, and with no color to them at all, except for the red flash of their eyes. Corpse-pale flesh covered torsos and limbs. Their hair hung in greasy, pale strands, tangled and knotted like snakes. The faces were flat, features more vestigial than pronounced: flat noses, lipless slits for mouths, eyes set against the slope of their brows.

They were unclad and weaponless, though they made up for the latter with rows of sharp teeth and knife-sharp claws on fingers and toes. After that first blood-curdling scream, their advance was a silent rush. The only sound they made was the soft padding of their feet on the cavern floor, the click of claws against stone.

Clive braced himself for their attack, then swung his pry-bar as the nearest creature leapt at him. His weapon caught it across the side of its head, splitting the skull with an unpleasant, wet cracking sound. The creature dropped, but there was no opportunity for Clive to regard his handiwork, for a pair of the creatures immediately took the place of the one he'd just slain.

In moments, all four of them were fighting for their lives against the swarming horde.

Because of their position in the entryway to the next gallery, the creatures could only attack them from the front and sides, so the party ranged itself, with Finnbogg and Smythe on either flank, Clive and Guafe in the center. They presented a solid face to their enemy, weapons rising and falling as they met the wave of horrid creatures. It took no time at all before each member of the party bore numerous claw cuts on their arms, while the sleeves of their jackets and shirts were torn into shredded strips that flapped when they swung their weapons.

It was steady, unpleasant work. The creatures died quickly—there was soon a mound of bodies under-foot—but their numbers were such that for long, wea-rying minutes, Clive and his party had no moment to even catch their breath, they were kept so busy. Then, finally, as some twenty or so of the small bodies lay strewn about them, the remaining attackers withdrew. Their wounded attempted to retreat as well, but Guafe immediately stepped forward and killed them as they tried to crawl away.

The creatures were vocal now. They hissed and spat at the party as they gathered themselves for another charge, jabbering to each other in high-pitched voices that grated on the ear. One or another would charge forward, almost within range of the party's weapons, then dart back as quickly.

"This isn't a battle," Clive said. "It's simple butchery."

"Better them than us," Smythe said.

Clive nodded. "But it's distasteful all the same."

He wiped his palms on his trousers. The blood of the creatures had sprayed all over the party, and they had the look of messy butchers about them.

"At least now we know what the pretender was speak-ing of," Clive added.

"They'll have to do a better job than this to stop us," Smythe said. "They have the numbers, but even with the numbers, they don't have the strength to stop us."

True, Clive thought, but the creatures could wear them out.

At the other end of the line they made, Finnbogg brandished his bloodied sledgehammer at the creatures.

"Come *on!*" he shouted at them. "Spineless worms!"

Clive toed one of the nearby corpses with his boot, starting when the creature stirred and made a feeble grab for his foot. Smythe brought down his pry-bar, splitting the creature's skull. Clive started to nod his thanks, but the horde chose that moment to renew their frantic attack.

They swarmed forward in a living wave of pale flesh, hissing and jabbering, claws flashing, jaws snapping. Clive killed two, three, then one slipped through and fastened its jaws on his shoulder. Mostly it got just a mouthful of jacket, but the teeth nipped into Clive's flesh, and the force of the creature's lunge, and its impact on his shoulder, was enough to turn Clive around.

He tore the creature off and heaved it to the ground. The thing scrambled toward his legs. As he brought up his pry-bar to kill it, he lost his footing on the blood-slick stones, and his feet went out from under him. He managed to bring down his weapon with enough force to stun the creature, but as soon as he fell, there were suddenly two more of them leaping for him, claws ripping at his chest, catching in the fabric of his jacket, jaws snapping inches from his face.

He kept them from his throat by holding the pry-bar in a two-handed grip and pushing it up against their torsos. Spittle sprayed his face as the creatures fought to get at him, but then Guafe was there. Two quick blows killed them. The cyborg took a stance that covered Clive long enough for him to regain his feet.

He glanced in Finnbogg's direction and saw the dwarf go down under four or five of the creatures. He started forward to help, but Finnbogg shrugged them off, his sledgehammer rising, killing a pair for each blow. The fifth he kicked in its stomach, then brought his weapon down on the top of its skull. Brain matter and blood sprayed from the force of the blow.

Clive turned to renew his own attack against the

creatures then, fighting beside the dwarf now, as Guafe had taken his own position beside Smythe. His arms were wearying under the work, but still the creatures kept coming, snarling and spitting, dying quickly enough, but for each that fell, there was another there immediately to take its place.

The air reeked of blood. Sweat dripped from Clive's brow, stinging his eyes. He found it more and more difficult to swing the pry-bar. Once a comfortable weight, it grew more leaden with each passing moment. Glancing at Smythe, Clive saw that he, too, was wearying. His blows had less force to them, and his responses to each attack were slowing.

But Finnbogg maintained his strength, weapon rising and falling in an untiring rhythm, while Guafe was a killing machine. The heap of corpses rose waist-high around the party, and still the creatures came. They scrambled over the wall of their dead comrades, launching themselves over the top with a ferocity that Clive had never encountered before. On and on they came, until he was sure he could lift his arms no more.

And then, suddenly, they withdrew a second time, this time vanishing into the shadows beyond the light of the party's lanterns.

"Quickly, now," Smythe said wearily. "Through to the next cave."

Guafe kept watch while the others stumbled through. There was still no sign of renewed activity in the darkness where their foes had fled.

"There!" Smythe called.

He pointed to a heap of rubble. Setting down his pry-bar and lantern, he went over and began to man-handle a rock toward the entryway through which they'd just come. Clive immediately came to help him roll the huge stone across the cavern floor.

Once they saw what he was about, Finnbogg and Guafe quickly lent their strength to the task. Taking turns watching for the creatures, they built up a wall of stone to block the narrow entryway. In the end it was only Guafe who had the strength to lift the stones up to close the final few feet of the gap. The others brought the rocks over. When the entryway was finally sealed, the party collapsed where they stood.

"God," Clive said, "I've never seen such creatures."

Smythe nodded. "If the attack had lasted much longer, they would have had us."

"Perhaps," Guafe said.

Clive felt a momentary irritation at the cyborg's calm control. Although he looked as bloody and disheveled as the rest of them, he wasn't even breathing hard. He stood, gazing off to where the rails led on across this new gallery, the battle apparently already forgotten.

But then Clive remembered who it was that had saved his life not twenty minutes ago, whose strength—along with Finn's—had been the telling point of their surviving the battle.

"Thank you," he told the cyborg.

Guafe merely shrugged. "I wish to be quit of these caverns and see what the next level holds," he said. "And I would rather travel in your company."

Why? Clive wanted to ask, but he realized that this wasn't the time to get into an argument with Guafe. Though he held no great affection for the cyborg, he was pragmatic enough to know that they would more than likely need Guafe's strength again before they were free of this place.

"Hear water dripping," Finnbogg said.

In a weary group, the party made their way across the gallery to the pool that was the source of the sound. The roof of the cavern over the pool rose in a high, dark shaft, and it was from it that the water was dripping.

They drank deeply, then stripped and cleaned the gore from their bodies and clothes. Smythe was the first to be done. Shivering in his wet clothes, he used his pry-bar to work free a couple of the wooden ties on which the rails lay. With the sledgehammer and bar, he broke one up enough to get kindling, with which he started a fire. Slowly, he fed wood to it. By the time the rest were finished cleaning themselves, he had a good blaze burning, around which they all gathered.

"We should have brought in a few of the dead creatures to roast," Guafe remarked.

Clive blanched. "We couldn't eat them—they were almost human."

The cyborg shrugged. "We have to eat."

"I think I'd prefer simply to tighten my belt for now," Smythe said.

"Suit yourselves," Guafe said. "But if we run into more of the creatures, I, at least, plan to see how they taste."

They rested by the fire long after their clothes were dry. Tearing the shredded strips from their sleeves, they bandaged the cuts on their forearms. Clive's shoulder was beginning to stiffen up where the creature had bitten him, and both Smythe and Finnbogg had wounds on their legs that were sore, but not deep.

Their greatest worry, Clive thought, was the danger of infection, but there was little they could do about it, except what they already had done—clean the wounds and bandage them.

When the fire died down, they returned to the rails and went on.

Time passed, but they had no way of telling day from night, or how long they had been traveling. They rested when they were weary, walked on when they had rested. Twice, they came upon pools in which fat, white, eyeless fish swam. The creatures were easy to catch, but they had little taste and, though they were nourishing, all were aware of a constant sense of gnawing hunger that could not be appeased. Their wounds continued to itch, but seemed to be healing. Their supply of candles was dwindling—so much, and with no end to their journey in sight, that they were using only one lantern.

They kept a firm lookout for more of the murderous creatures who had attacked them, but they suffered no further attacks after that first one. Either the cleft they had blocked had been enough to stop them, or the creatures simply didn't fare this deeply into the cavern. None of the party really wanted to dwell on why that might be, but it was something that couldn't easily be put aside. Was there something still worse waiting for them?

The rails continued on. Sometimes the track split, leading them into more than one blind alley, but mostly it took them deeper and deeper underground.

"What can we look to find on the next level?" Smythe asked Finnbogg at one point.

"A big city," the dwarf replied.

"Another ruin?"

"No. Many people there, just like us—" Which could mean just about any sort of being, Clive thought. "—ruled by the Lords of Thunder."

"And who are they?" Guafe asked.

The dwarf shrugged. "Finnbogg doesn't know."

"And what is their level of technology?"

"Finnbogg doesn't *know*."

Smythe gave Clive a quick glance. "Best leave off, sah."

Clive nodded. There was no sense in getting Finnbogg into one of his states.

"I remember hearing of these Lords of Thunder," Guafe said slowly. "From a being I traveled with on one of the upper levels. They are elected to their position, but the elections are held every seven days, so the actual lords change from week to week. Then again, the same being told me at another time that the city holds a lottery every seven days, and that the winners—or maybe I should say losers—are fed to the Lords of Thunder."

"Wonderful," Clive said.

"Sounds as though your s   rce was about as reliable as ours can be," Smythe said.

"It's not Finnbogg's fault Finnbogg doesn't know everything," the dwarf said.

"This is true," Guafe said. "With so many levels, and everything in such a confusion, a human would find it impossible to keep it all straight."

Finnbogg still looked glum—almost on the verge of tears.

"There, there, Finn," Smythe said soothingly. "We know you're doing your best."

That was the day—as they referred to their waking periods—that the rails simply stopped.

They gave out on the far side of another enormous cavern, at a cleft that dropped at a steep angle into yet another gallery. Standing at the opening of the new gallery, they discovered that this one was blocked with a wall. The light from their lantern was strong enough to show them that the wall was twelve to fifteen feet high. Beyond its height, the gallery's roof was lost in the darkness. On the left side of the cleft was a corridor that took an immediate sharp turn some ten feet down its length.

Having come this far, there was no turning back. They set off down the corridor, taking its turn, to find themselves presented with a choice of three corridors.

"Now what?" Smythe muttered.

But Clive had a sinking feeling that was soon proved all too prophetic. "It's a maze," he said.

Smythe held the lantern into each opening. From its light they could all see that each corridor opened on to others.

"Bloody hell," he said.

"There is usually some logical method of making one's way through such a thing," Guafe said.

"In this Dungeon?" Smythe asked.

The cyborg nodded. "There is that."

"Which way to go?" Finnbogg asked.

"We'll be in here forever," Smythe said.

But Clive wasn't listening to any of them. Instead, he was remembering a Midsummer's Eve when he was ten years old, and the maze that he and his brother had walked through that day. Neville, as always in such situations, had had absolutely no trouble working his way to the end, but Clive had been trapped in there for hours, eventually driven to tears of frustration by his failure to win free.

Until the voice had spoken to him.

That mysterious voice.

You may face the moon, or you can have it at your left shoulder, it had said.

Following the voice's advice, he had made his way safely through.

But something nagged at Clive as he remembered.

That voice. . . .

In a hazy fashion, he could recall another instance when it had spoken to him, in another garden. Or at least he could recall the fact that it had—not the details. Tied up that recollection was a mixture of other dream-like memories . . . of Annabella, of London, and of pain.

He rubbed at his upper left arm.

He'd been swallowed by darkness, and there had been voices bidding him to forget. . . .

He shook his head. Now wasn't the time for reverie. All it was giving him was a headache. Instead, he put his mind to the task at hand.

You may face the moon, or you can have it at your left shoulder. . . .

Clive took the lantern from Smythe's hand and lifted it above his shoulder. High above, somewhere on the roof of the cavern, he saw a glint of reflected light. It wasn't a moon, but. . . .

That voice had helped him more than once. But, he wondered, that first time . . . could that early hedge maze have been merely a preparation for the Dungeon? How could that be possible?

He was loath to put their fates on such a flimsy hope, but when he looked at his companions, and saw that none of them had anything better to offer, he squared his shoulders. Following that old advice was as likely a solution as their other options would be, which amounted to either guesswork or blind luck. So, what did they have to lose?

Realizing that it was up to him, as leader of the party, to take command of the situation—even if the source of information on which he made his decision was somewhat suspect—he faced the "moon" and started off down the left-hand corridor.

"This way," he said.

▪ Twenty-two ▪

Annabelle swung back and forth on the rope, like a weight at the end of a pendulum. She kept her eyes shut. Her face was bleached with fear. After her first startled cry, she kept quiet, trying to hold in the contents of her stomach as the rope spun her in a dizzying arc, back and forth across the trail.

The alarm bell in the trees above had stopped tolling, but its echo continued on in their minds. The Quanians, or whoever it was who had set the trap, would not be long in getting here—not with an alarm system rigged up.

The rogha came scrambling up through the branches of the trees around Annabelle. Yssi climbed to where the rope holding her was tied to the tree, and swung it until Tarit and Chobba could catch Annabelle. They quickly cut her free. Chobba put her on his back.

"Hold hard, yuh?" he told her.

Annabelle put her arms around his neck, but she didn't think she had the strength to hold on, until the first time Chobba launched himself through the air from one branch to another. Heart in her throat, Annabelle gripped his neck so tightly she had to be choking him, but Chobba didn't even seem to notice.

Warning cries came from the rest of the party still on the ground. Chobba swung onto a perch in the crook of two branches. Through her unreasoning panic, Annabelle managed to crack open her eyes and look over Chobba's shoulder, to see what the cries were about.

A small, round, metal ball the size of a softball

hovered in the air near the sprung trap. There were various small, tubelike protrusions sticking out from its surface, none of them longer than an inch. A faint whine came from the ball as it slowly spun around.

It was taking stock, Annabelle realized. A new fear cut through the haze of her panic.

"That's a mobile scouting unit," she told Chobba. "It'll have visual and audio input—probably heat sensors, as well. We've gotta get out of here. Pronto."

Chobba turned to her, his face inches from her own, the confusion in his features plain.

He didn't understand a word of what I said, Annabelle realized.

"Plenty bad," she said. "Go quick. Hide."

He nodded, but the scouting unit chose that moment to make the very real danger it presented to them apparent in a less nebulous fashion. A thin red beam issued from one of its tubelike projections. It moved in the direction where Nog was perched.

"Oh, Jesus," Annabelle cried. "It's armed!"

The laser burned through leaves and branches as it sought its target. Nog leapt away, but the scouting unit immediately tracked his sudden motion. The laser sliced a swath through the vegetation in the rogha's direction, cutting across his torso in midleap. Nog screamed, then plummeted to the ground, bouncing off branches on the way down. He was dead long before he reached the jungle floor.

The remaining rogha howled their rage. As they began to move in toward the scouting unit, Annabelle tugged on Chobba's fur.

"No!" she told him. "It will kill you all. We have to go deeper into the jungle, where the branches grow too thick for it to follow. Maybe some of the bigger animals'll screw up its heat sensors. Chobba, please."

The rogha hesitated. He started to shout out an order to the others, but when he saw Tarit launch himself at his twin's killer, Chobba leapt forward as well. All Annabelle could do was cling to his back.

The scouting unit swiveled in a quick circle, momentarily distracted by the presence of so many different targets. Shriek chose that moment to throw one of her well-aimed hair spikes at the ball-like machine.

The spike bounced harmlessly off, but it brought the party on the ground to the machine's attention. It dropped from the sky, laser burning up the floor of the game trail in a straight line that led directly for Shriek.

Sidi stepped in and threw his spear. It was a clean miss as the scouting unit spun on its axis and darted to one side to avoid the weapon, laser cutting the spear in two. Shriek threw more spikes, then plunged into the nearest undergrowth as the unit turned back to her. It dropped at a sharp angle, laser searing the brush as it looked for her. Then, suddenly, Tomàs was there.

The unit turned, sensing his presence, but the little Portuguese was too fast for it. He swung his spear like a bat. The weapon hit the unit with a sharp crack that sent it spinning out of control. It hit a tree, then dropped to the ground, laser spraying a random pattern all around it. Before it could correct itself, Tarit dropped to the game trail beside it.

The scouting unit tried to turn in the dirt to train its laser on the rogha, but Tarit simply smashed the machine with his club. He pounded it into the dirt, arm rising and falling. He wept as he continued to club the unit, crying Nog's name. The unit had split open under his blows, flashing with sparks and smoking.

Chobba dropped to the game trail and set Annabelle on the ground. She staggered, her right leg giving out from under her. Tomàs stepped quickly forward and put his shoulder under her arm.

Jesus, she remembered thinking through her pain. First he saves our asses, and now he's helping me. What's the matter with the guy?

The other rogha descended from the trees and joined Chobba and Tarit in beating what was left of the machine. They kept it up for long moments, then finally stepped away from the small ruin of wiring, circuitry, and metal. Tears streaked their facial fur. Tarit disappeared into the forest to return with Nog's body. He laid it gently on the ground.

Giving Tomàs her thanks, Annabelle hobbled forward under her own steam. "God, I'm so sorry," she said. "I never thought anybody'd get hurt. . . ."

"Nog die like cheef," Chobba said.

The other rogha all cried Nog's name again.

"We go now," Chobba told her.

Tarit clasped his twin's corpse under one arm and swung back into the trees, followed by Chobba and the other rogha. In moments they were gone.

Annabelle turned slowly to look at her companions. Lukey, who was still with them, sat down on the side of the trail and put his back up against a tree.

"What's happening now?" she asked him.

"He was a real good monkey-man," Lukey said. "Hell, I really liked him."

"Lukey, where have they gone?"

"To bury him, rogha-fashion. They'll stick him up in a treetop—the highest they can climb—an' leave him there so's his soul can rise up into the sky real easy."

"What was this thing?" Sidi asked, toeing the remains of the machine.

Annabelle glanced at him. "A kind of scouting device. A mobile unit—remote-controlled. It'd have a kind of an eye in it, so whoever sent it's gonna know we're here. We've got to get moving. When will the rogha be back, Lukey?"

The old man shrugged. "A day or two, I guess. They've got ta talk through his life up there where they leave him, so that the ancestors know who he is an' can see he's the kind a' guy that they should take up there inta the sky with 'em. Takes time."

"You say whoever sent this thing knows we are here?" Sidi asked.

Annabelle nodded.

"Then, we must go. Can you travel?"

Annabelle rubbed her leg. It ached something fierce. Her ankle, where the rope had encircled her leg, was rubbed raw. She tested her weight on it. That first moment on the ground, when it had buckled under her, had been due more to surprise at the pain than because the leg wouldn't hold her weight.

"I can manage," she said. "But what about the rogha? We can't just take off on them, after all they've done for us. And poor Nog. . . ."

"If we stay here," Sidi said, "won't the Quanians just send more of these things?"

"I guess. . . ."

We should go on, Shriek said. *Immediately.*

"Yeah," Annabelle said. "Are you coming with us, Lukey?"

"Don't have a whole lot a' choice, seems."

"We should travel quickly, *sim*?" Tomàs said. "By river, perhaps?"

Annabelle and Sidi exchanged puzzled looks. Neither of them could figure Tomàs's sudden shift in mood, from surly to friendly.

"Are you feeling okay?" Annabelle asked him.

"I feel fine," Tomàs said. "Why do you ask?"

"You're just not acting like yourself."

"I have been thinking. You—Sidi and Shriek—we are all in this place together—*comaradas, sim*? So we must be good *amigos* and help each other."

Annabelle found that she distrusted this new face of Tomàs's more than the old, but she didn't let any of that show. She simply nodded.

"Well, thanks for the vote of confidence," she said.

"Vote—*sim*," the Portuguese said, obviously remembering Annabelle calling a vote back on the cliffs to separate the two parties. It was clearly a new concept to him. "I vote we go by the river. This path is *muito perigoso*. Too dangerous."

It turned out that they were much closer to Quan than they had supposed. They waded through the water by the river bank, and after only an hour or so, they came upon a sudden drop in the land. They left the river where it turned into rapids, and made their way to a vantage point where they could look down on the clearing that lay ahead of them.

Quan.

It was a collection of mud and wattle huts, except for a white stone building at the far side of the village. Aerials and a satellite dish protruded from its roof. To one side of the building was the ghost stone of which Finnbogg had told them. It was a tall white column of rock, sticking out of the ground much like a Celtic standing stone. Figures moved about the village. They flickered strangely, winking in and out of view as the party watched.

"I can't figure this place at all," Annabelle said. "I mean, they've got the tech for a satellite dish and that mobile scouting unit, yet back on the trail they're screwing around with primitive traps and— Look at this village—mud and straw huts. What gives?"

Her companions weren't nearly so blasé.

"There really are ghosts," Sidi said.

Surprised, Annabelle looked at him. "Those aren't ghosts. They're just 3-D holograms—sort of like moving pictures, except they've got depth, as well. But whoever's running this show's working with faulty equipment, 'cause those things shouldn't be flickering like that."

"They aren't ghosts?" Sidi asked.

Well, why am I surprised? Annabelle thought. Sure, Sidi was smart and capable, but he did come from the nineteenth century—nineteenth century India, to boot. How the hell was he supposed to know about these kinds of things?

"They're projections," she explained. "Paintings that move, made by a machine—that's all. They can't hurt us."

"But something can," Lukey said. "Someone wants to hurt anyone who comes near a' this place."

"I suppose," Annabelle said. "But I've got a gut feeling that everything's just running on a program that someone set up. If there's anybody left, it's just a skeleton crew to run the place, and they're not doing such a good job."

"Tell that to Nog," Lukey said.

Annabelle's face clouded. "Yeah," she said softly. "There's that. So we gotta go careful. I wonder where the gateway is."

She returned her attention to the village. The ground sloped steeply from their vantage point in a rough rock face that ran from the jungle where they were hidden, down to the cleared fields around the village. The river was on the left. On the right and behind the village, the jungle marched on again.

Although they were high up, her acrophobia wasn't bothering her here. It only hit her bad when she was in an exposed position—like a tall bridge, or up in a tree. Here, with lots of good, solid earth around her, all she felt was a vague sense of wanting to lean out far—really far.

She pulled herself back and looked at her companions. "So, what do we do, kids? Check it out, or go back the way we came?"

Shriek pointed forward. *That is where our road lies, Being Annabelle. Not behind us.*

"One vote to go on," Annabelle said. "What about the rest of you?"

Tomàs and Sidi both nodded their agreement. Lukey said nothing.

"I feel bad about just taking off on Chobba and the others without saying goodbye," Annabelle added. "They were good people."

Lukey sighed. "Hell, I'll say your goodbyes for you."

"You're not coming?"

He shook his head. "I'm too old ta start all over somewhere else," he said.

"We should make a plan," Tomàs said.

Annabelle nodded. "I'm not big on exploring this place, myself—who knows what kinda booby traps they've got rigged. I'm for finding the gateway and getting outta here."

It will either be in that building, Shriek said, *or below us, at the bottom of this cliff. I see no other choices.*

"'Cept that stone," Annabelle said.

* * *

They waited until dark, and then, after saying their farewells to Lukey, cautiously made their way down the rock decline. Although the angle was fairly steep, there were so many handholds that it was not much different from going down a ladder. Even Annabelle had no trouble with it. When they reached the bottom, they carefully checked it for a cave or opening, foot by foot, but came up blank.

"Looks like it's the building," Annabelle whispered.

Even though she knew the figures were holographs, the idea of walking among them didn't exactly appeal to her. But she didn't see any other options. They decided to circle around by the river and approach the building from the left, but as they passed the standing stone, its surface began to glow.

"What the hell . . . ?" Annabelle murmured.

In the middle of the stone's pale white glow, a dark opening was appearing. *The gateway,* Annabelle thought. It had to be. Cautiously, they approached it. Fingers tingling with nervous anticipation, Annabelle reached out toward the dark, door-shaped opening. There was a momentary buzz of a shock—no stronger than picking up static electricity from a carpet—and then her fingers entered the rock.

"This is it—" Annabelle began.

At that same moment, the alarms went off.

Bells rang. A piercing siren sounded. Floodlights awoke from the sides of the white building, turning the night into day all around them. Figures in metallic bodysuits issued in a stream from the building. They carried laser rifles. When they fired, the air around the party crackled.

"We've got no time to pussyfoot around," Annabelle cried. "Let's go!"

She stepped inside and found herself on a small platform, the others following on her heels. She'd been expecting it to be dark inside, but a dull, phosphorescent glow lit what appeared to be a vast cavern. The roof and sides stretched impossibly huge all around them—as did the drop below. There was only the small platform on which they were standing, and a narrow band of a path that led straight across the chasm. It was no more than a foot wide, dropping immediately on either side to unguessed depths.

Platform and path. There was no other place to go.

"I can't do it," Annabelle said.

She was already trembling violently.

"We have no choice," Sidi cried.

Behind them, the sirens and alarms were still sounding. They could hear the voices of the Quanians raised in angry shouts.

"I . . . I just can't. . . ." Annabelle mumbled.

▪ Twenty-three ▪

"We are simply going in circles," Guafe said after long hours in the maze.

"I don't think so," Smythe said. "I don't sense the walls of the cavern to be that close to us anymore. I believe we've come a good way through."

Guafe shook his head. "We—"

"It's just the winding of our route," Smythe broke in, "that's giving you that impression. Besides," he added, glancing at Clive, "the major knows what he's doing."

I wish, Clive thought. But he had to be doing something right. By either facing the "moon," or keeping it to his left shoulder whenever there was a choice to be made in their route, they'd fared steadily, if tiresomely, onward. There had been no blind alleys, except for the one time Guafe had argued that they should take a different turn from the one Clive had chosen for them, and they'd wound up in a dead end.

The cyborg had kept his own counsel after that—at least, until now.

"There seems to be a kind of a spiral effect," Clive said in answer to Guafe's comment, "but I think we've come a fair distance across—even with the twisting back and forth."

Finnbogg nodded. "Who knows how big this place is?"

But Guafe had lost his patience again. "You say we turn right here," he said, "but *I* believe the other side of the cavern lies straight ahead—down this central corridor."

"The last time we followed your lead," Smythe said,

"we wasted a good half-hour backtracking our way out of that dead end."

"No maze can be as large as this one appears to be," the cyborg replied. "We are going in circles, and getting nowhere. I say we go straight now."

Finnbogg and Smythe both turned to Clive, who simply shrugged. They *had* been traveling through the maze for a very long time, and all he was using to lead them was old advice from a mysterious voice he'd heard in another maze when he was a child. While the voice's advice had been enough to free him from that hedge maze, and had helped him again since then, there really was no logical reason that it should be effective here as well. And while it was true that they hadn't run into any dead ends following his route, they didn't really seem to be getting anywhere, either.

"We might as well try it," he said.

Guafe nodded brusquely, pleased to be leading, and set off at a brisk walk down the corridor he'd chosen. It twisted and turned on them, but there were no branches running off, and they did seem to be generally heading in one direction. When they reached the first split, the party paused while Guafe studied each corridor.

At length he nodded. "Left, I say."

It was not what Clive would have chosen, but he said nothing.

Guafe gave them each a questioning look, then, satisfied that he was still in charge, led them on again. A half-dozen paces down the new corridor, it took a sharp right turn. As they entered it, one of the stone blocks shifted under their weight.

A loud grinding noise arose all around them, like sudden thunder.

"Move!" Smythe cried.

He gave Clive and Guafe a shove forward, then darted after them, Finnbogg hard on his heels. The stone that had been underfoot dropped away with a resounding, hollow crash, and one of the walls behind them groaned, then slid across the corridor, effectively blocking any retreat.

Stone dust filled the air, the motes dancing in the light of their lantern. They coughed and stared back through the dancing cloud at the new wall that filled the corridor behind them.

"Well, that's done it," Smythe said, turning to Guafe. "Well-led."

"Finnbogg want Clive-friend to lead," the dwarf said.

For once, the cyborg seemed completely taken aback. "I had no idea . . . " he began.

Though he agreed with the others, Clive saw no reason to take it out on Guafe at this point. The deed was done now, and there was nothing they could do about it.

"We've no choice now but to go on," he said.

Finnbogg turned to him. "Yes, but—"

"There's nothing we can do about that," Clive said, indicating the new wall blocking their retreat. "Lead on, Chang," he called ahead.

Guafe nodded and led the way once more, but the corridor soon ended against another blank wall.

"I fear my miscalculations have done far more harm than good," he said.

It was the closest Clive had ever heard him come to an apology.

"It wasn't your fault," he told the cyborg. "We're all going blindly in the dark here, and—"

"Hsst!" Smythe said suddenly.

They could all hear it—a whispering sound, like a great soft weight being pulled across the stone floor.

"Is it those creatures?" Clive asked softly, reaching for the pry-bar in his belt.

Smythe shook his head. "No. It doesn't sound quite right."

He took the lantern from Finnbogg, who had been holding it, and held it up at arm's length to investigate the walls above them. He moved the lantern slowly along until he saw what looked like a break in the stone, high up in one part of the wall. It was a place where the stones weren't set quite properly together, leaving an indentation between the blocks.

"Could you lift me toward that?" he asked Guafe.

The cyborg nodded. "What do you mean to do?"

"Get us out of this trap you've put us in. If I can get up on top of the wall—" he tapped the sheet of canvas that he'd been carrying all this time in a rolled-up bundle "—I could lower this to the rest of you and pull you up."

"And we could follow the maze simply by walking on top of the walls," Clive finished. "That's a capital idea, Horace."

With Clive holding the lantern and Finnbogg bracing Guafe, Smythe stepped onto the cyborg's shoulders. Guafe straightened to his full height, but the mis-set blocks Smythe was aiming for were still out of reach. Guafe slipped his hands under Smythe's feet and then straight-armed him up.

"Got it," Smythe said as he scrabbled for a hold. "Just don't let go yet. Wait a bit. All right . . . now."

Guafe gave a final upward surge, and Smythe scrambled the rest of the way, scaling the wall like a monkey.

"What do you see?" Clive called up to him.

"Nothing. I need a lantern. Pass it up to me."

He dropped the twine with which he'd rolled up the canvas, then lowered the canvas down the side of the wall. It came to just above Guafe's head. Using the twine, they tied the lantern to the canvas, and Smythe hauled it up.

"Can you see anything now?" Clive called.

"My God," Smythe said.

"What is it, man?"

Smythe shook his head. "There's no time to talk. Quick. All of you, up here!"

He lowered the canvas, bracing it on top of the wall with his weight. Clive was next, pulling himself up with handfuls of canvas. Finnbogg was next. The material of their makeshift ladder made ominous tearing sounds under the dwarf's weight. Both Clive and Smythe braced the canvas at the top of the wall until Finnbogg was in reach of Clive's hand. As the dwarf scrambled up the last few feet and took Clive's place bracing the canvas, Clive picked up the lantern to see what had alarmed his fellow soldier.

"Come on now, Guafe," Smythe was saying.

The light of the lantern wasn't strong enough to travel far. It showed the tops of the walls, running in all directions like elevated paths, but the spaces on either side of them were lost in shadow, and the paths soon disappeared into darknesses beyond the reach of the lantern. He saw nothing alarming until he turned in the direction from which they'd come.

There, he saw a huge white shape that seemed to fill the corridor.

Clive took a few steps closer, holding the lantern high. When the massive head lifted from the corridor, he almost dropped the light.

Things, the man pretending to be his brother had said. He hadn't been referring to the feral pack of creatures that had attacked them days ago. No. It had been *this*.

It was monstrous—a cross between an enormous snake and a slug. The flesh was pale and slimy, but scaled as well. It was from the latter that the heavy whispering sound came, as they rustled against the stone. The head was a good yard across in width, stubby and square in shape. It had large, milky-colored eyes, with a pair of antennae above each—one large feeler, and one smaller one. The mouth, when it opened its huge jaws, showed three series of barracudalike teeth.

As Clive watched, it began to undulate up from the corridor, the enormous weight of its body rising to the top of the wall, then straddling it with a huge coil of its pale body. The head moved toward him, but the monster's bulk was too much for it to balance easily on the wall, which was only a foot and a half wide.

As it lost its balance, it coiled its body to fill the corridor. Using those coils as a lever, it flexed suddenly. The stones on either side of it groaned under the pressure.

Fascinated despite himself, Clive watched the creature relax its muscles, then flex them again. This time, the walls of the corridor on either side of it collapsed under the pressure.

The stone blocks that fell on it seemed to give the creature no discomfort whatsoever. It merely shrugged them off. More of the wall fell in, and the creature began to rise, using the rubble as a ramp to slide up.

As it approached him, Clive remained spellbound, staring. There was a terrible beauty in its ugliness, in its sheer physical power.

"Sah!"

He set down the lantern and then stepped over it, moving toward the creature. The sudden urge to feel that slick hide, the muscles running underneath it, was too strong to ignore.

"Sah! Have you taken leave of your senses?"

The large milky eyes were blind, he was sure, but they impressed him with their hypnotic spell all the same. He could hear Smythe calling him, but his companion's voice was strangely distant, as though he heard it from under water, or in a dream.

At this moment, it was the creature that took up all of his attention.

Demanded it.

Would not be denied.

He stepped closer still, almost within the reach of those immense jaws, then suddenly, Smythe had a grip on his shoulder and was pulling him back. Clive protested, until he began to lose his balance. Then he was forced to look away, and the creature's blind eyes no longer filled his sight. Suddenly, his will was his own again.

The monster lunged forward at being denied its prey, but Smythe had already pulled Clive out of its reach. The new wall on which the creature found itself buckled under its weight, and down it plunged once more. The walls shook at the impact this time; clouds of dust rose about them like a thick London fog.

"'Ware its gaze," Clive warned as he followed Smythe back to where the others waited. "The damn thing looks blind, but it hypnotized me all the same."

"Quick," Smythe merely said. "Take the lead, sah, and get us out of here."

Behind them, the monstrous snake was rising from the rubble once more—a huge, pale shape moving in the clouds of stone dust. Rocks ground under its weight, and the wall trembled as it once again attempted to get at them.

"Sah!" Smythe cried, as Clive continued to stand in place.

"Let me get my bearings," Clive told him.

He searched the vault of the dark cavern roof above them, looking for the reflective "moon" that had guided him earlier. When he finally had it, he set off at as brisk a walk as he dared along the narrow width of the wall's top.

They heard another rumbling crash behind them. Guafe, who was in the rear, turned. The red beams of his gaze pierced a new cloud of stone dust, to show that the monstrous snake had broken from the cul-de-sac and was now slithering along a corridor toward them.

"Let's get some walls between that monster and us," Clive said.

Ignoring his guide in the ceiling of the cavern for the moment, Clive led them off at a sharp angle. Due to the way the maze was laid out, they were soon able to put a number of walls between themselves and the creature. As they paused to catch their breath, they could hear the huge snake battering at one of those walls.

"It's fiendishly clever, really," Smythe said. "The design of this place, I mean. Obviously, we were meant to be kept trapped by that sliding wall until the creature arrived. Then, I don't doubt, it would trip some mechanism that would shift the wall back into place, allowing the creature access to where its prey was trapped."

"Only this time, its prey escaped," Guafe said.

Smythe nodded. "Exactly. And it's driven the bloody thing mad. Having its prey light out on it is something that's never happened to it before, I'll wager. Have you got your bearings again, sah?"

"I think so—yes."

With the "moon" at his left shoulder, Clive led them off. They kept up a brisk pace, for they could still hear the monster following them, battering down the walls as it made its own blundering route through the maze.

There'd be little left of the place when the monster was finished with it, Clive thought. Not that it was any of his concern. It was just that the next party faring through would have an even rougher time of it than they had.

"How are we doing?" he called back to Guafe, who was still in the rear.

"Well enough," the cyborg said. "We seem to be leaving it far behind."

"Behind?" Finnbogg asked. "Then what does Finnbogg hear over there?"

He pointed to his right.

"Echoes," Smythe began.

But Guafe was already shaking his head. With his sharper senses, he was already aware of what the others were not.

"No," he said. "It's another of the creatures. Heading our way." He pointed to their left and ahead now. "And there's a third, approaching us from that direction, as well."

"Wonderful," Clive said.

• Twenty-four •

Your greatest fear made real.

That's what the darkworld spirit had told her through the medium of the rogha fetish chief. How could it have *known*? Because here that fear was, in all its dark glory.

Annabelle swayed on the ledge. The chasm that dropped suddenly on both sides and in front worked on her acrophobia, calling her down into its black depths.

Come to me, it called. *Accept your destiny. Be one with me. There is nothing to fear.*

And she wanted to. She wanted to just let herself go and fall into the blackness.

Come to me. To a better place.

She needed a better place. Where she could be with her daughter and her friends, where all of this, the Dungeon, and its incomprehensible madness, was just a bad dream.

Come to me.

She wanted to. Desperately. But just as she couldn't back away, she couldn't move forward, either. She was paralyzed with fear.

Dimly, through the ghostly outline of the gateway, she could hear the shouts of the Quanians growing closer. Around her, the voices of her companions were nothing more than a babble of unintelligible sounds as they tried to get her to set foot on the narrow pathway that led across the chasm. But she couldn't do it. And there wasn't time to get out the byrr pouch.

No time to pull out a leaf.

No time to chew it.

No time.

Only the chasm, calling out to her as she swayed at its lip.

Come to me.

"Annabelle, *please*," Sidi said.

She tried to turn her head to tell him how she just couldn't, but she was unable to tear her gaze from the chasm. She could barely hear anything except its hypnotic voice, calling out to her.

Her throat was thick and blocked, swollen with fear. Her chest was a knot of tension, lungs desperate for air. Every muscle in her body locked tight.

"Annabelle," Sidi said. "Just take my hand."

I can't move, she wanted to tell him, but she barely formed the words in her mind. Voicing them was impossible.

Get outta here . . . Sidi . . . all of you. . . . Leave me to the chasm, to its dark promise. . . .

She wondered, Is this the darkworld? Will I become a spirit in it, if I just let myself go?

But the chasm promised more. Freedom from the Dungeon. To be reunited with Amanda. Peace.

Come to me, its dark voice whispered.

I will, Annabelle told it. But just let me move. Just give me time to think.

Because there was something wrong about the chasm's promise. How could it deliver her back to the world she'd lost? To her daughter and friends? If it was that simple. . . .

It couldn't be that simple. Nothing ever was.

She swayed at the edge, the darkness swallowing her soul. She wanted to be free—not just of the Dungeon, but of the chasm's dark call, as well. To be free of the fear that paralyzed her, making her body betray her.

Just let me go, she told the darkness. Give me time to figure out what's going on. . . .

Then Shriek literally took matters into her own hands. She caught Annabelle with her lower arms, hugging her close to her chest, and set off at a run along the narrow pathway, using her upper arms for balance.

Sound finally escaped Annabelle's swollen throat—a raw, piercing scream tore from her lips—and finally, she could move. She struggled in Shriek's grip. The movement threatened to unbalance the alien, plunging them both into the chasm. Without missing a step, Shriek withdrew a hair spike with her upper right arm and thrust it into Annabelle's arm.

The thornlike spike broke her skin. As its potent chemical content entered Annabelle's body, mixing with her blood system and bringing relief in the form of unconsciousness, she went limp in the alien's arms. Shriek flicked the spike away into the chasm and continued to run.

Behind her, Sidi and Tomàs followed at a trot. They were a good hundred yards down the narrow path, the chasm dropping sharply on either side, when the first of the silver-suited Quanians stepped through the gateway. Leveling his weapon, he fired. The red laser beam crackled in the air beside Sidi's head, coming so close that it burned some of his dark hair.

He knew, without a doubt, that the next shot would hit one of them.

The skin between the blades of his back prickled in anticipation. He chanced a glance back, saw the man aiming his weapon more carefully, and braced himself for the impact. But a second man stepped through at that moment, laying his hand on the first man's arm. The first man lowered his weapon.

The two of them looked at the escaping party, arms folded now across their chests.

Why weren't they firing? Sidi thought.

Then the answer came to him. There had to be something worse awaiting the party farther down this narrow ribbon of a path. Something that so assured the Quanians of their fate that there was no need for them to chase after the trespassers or shoot them down. They would simply stand guard to see that none of the party attempted to retreat.

Giving them a last glance, he hurried on after the others. The phosphorescent glow continued to light their surroundings. For as far as he could see, the path simply bore on ahead of them, with no destination in sight.

Finally, they had to rest. They sat straddling the path, legs dangling on either side of it, the dark of the chasm licking at the soles of their feet. Shriek continued to hold Annabelle close with her lower arms, resting the human's weight on her knees now. The alien had turned so that she sat facing the other two.

Seeing Annabelle's limp form in her arms, Sidi knew a moment's panic. Had she been hit by one of the Quanians' weapons?

"What happened to her, Shriek?" he asked.

It was necessary to inject Being Annabelle with a tranquilizer, the arachnid replied. *Otherwise, she would have tumbled us both from the path.*

"But is she . . . ?"

She will be fine, Shriek assured him. *She is merely sleeping. The effect of the tranquilizer will wear off soon.*

Sidi's relief was almost physical.

They rested for a good fifteen minutes, before Shriek rose to her feet again.

Time to go on, she said.

Hefting Annabelle easily, she regarded the pair of them. Tomàs and Sidi arose to stand with her, and then the three of them began to trudge on once more, following the narrow path.

They were hours crossing the cavern. Annabelle was just beginning to stir as the path led them onto another ledge. The cavern face had another opening here, but it wasn't set off by the same shimmering glow as the one in Quan had been. The phosphorescence remained with them as they entered the tunnel. Well inside it, Shriek lowered herself into a sitting position. She propped Annabelle up, keeping a firm grip on her until Annabelle could sit up by herself.

"Oh, my head," Annabelle said.

She blinked slowly, trying to place her surroundings. The last thing she remembered had been the call of the chasm. She'd been about to step over the edge, into its darkness, when. . . .

"You saved my life," she told Shriek.

I'm sorry I could give you no warning, Shriek replied.

"Well, you're not going to hear me complaining. You did the right thing."

Annabelle looked around. They were in a tunnel. She sat beside Shriek. Close by, Tomàs and Sidi sat as well, gazes fixed on her. But it was what lay beyond them that called up a sense of vertigo in her. She could just see the end of the tunnel, the chasm beyond it.

She shivered and turned her head quickly. "Now I know what undying thanks are," she told Shriek. "All I've got—they're yours."

The alien gave Annabelle one of her odd, lopsided looks that passed for a grin on her curious features. *They are accepted, Being Annabelle,* she said.

Annabelle looked at the other two. "Any idea where we are?"

"We crossed the cavern," Sidi said simply. "Other than that, you know as much as we do."

"But the Quanians . . . ?"

"They seemed happy to just let us go."

Annabelle frowned. "As though there was something in here that would take care of us?" she asked, thinking aloud. "Or maybe they were just happy to see the back of us."

"Considering most of the people we've met down here," Sidi said, "I doubt their thoughts were charitable."

"In other words, expect the worst."

Sidi nodded. "Who knows? Maybe we'll get a pleasant surprise."

"Right. Like a bullet with our names on it."

She rose to her feet, one hand against the wall for support, and concentrated on her body. Her headache was fading, but the pain in her leg was rising up to take its place. Otherwise, she felt pretty much in one piece.

She looked at her companions. "So I guess we go on," she said.

The tunnel wasn't long. After a few turns that— thankfully, as far as Annabelle was concerned—put the cavern, with its chasm, well behind them, it opened up into a new cave. Here there was less of the phosphorescence, making the light dimmer, except in one corner, where there was a hole in the floor from which a bright, honey-gold glow issued. Other than the hole and the tunnel through which they'd just come, there was no other way in or out of the cavern.

They made a thorough search of the walls before they finally gathered around the hole. Looking down into it, the yellow glow was very bright. Sparkles floated in it, like dust motes set on fire. There was no way to tell what it was, or where it led, but there was a ladder set into the rocks leading down into it.

Annabelle stepped back from the edge.

"Chew one of Chobba's byrr leaves," Sidi said.

Strangely enough, Annabelle got no sense of real depth from the hole. Her breathing remained normal, her chest muscles loose. The trace of unreasonable fear that flickered at the back of her mind was only her memory of the chasm and its seductive voice.

"It's not that," Annabelle said. "I just don't like the way we don't have any choice about where we go. It's like, we either go down there, or we go back. If the Quanians are guarding the gateway back there, that means we can't go out. So we either head down this ladder, or. . . . "

She left the remainder of her thought unspoken, but it lay heavy inside her. Or we go back to the chasm.

She looked at her companions. Had any of them heard its voice? The promises it had made? What if she'd blown her one chance of getting home again by not listening to it? If Amanda was gone forever. . . .

"Or what?" Tomàs asked.

Annabelle shrugged. "Or nothing. We stay here, which is not a good game plan, right?"

Tomàs nodded. Beside him, Sidi regarded her thoughtfully.

"The pouch," he began.

"I really don't think I'm gonna need a chew of the old byrr," she told him.

Right now, she wanted to be attentive, not relaxed.

"But," Sidi began.

Annabelle shook her head. "Nope. C'mon, kids. Last one in's a dirty duck."

Without waiting for a response, she stepped over to the hole and lowered her feet down to the first rung. She hesitated a moment then, waiting for the fear to grab her, but everything remained normal. She was a little tense, but no more than she expected to be, heading into the unknown. Taking a couple of slow breaths, she started down.

Once her head was below the lip of the hole, she couldn't see anymore and had to go only by feel. The honey-gold glow was so bright, dancing sparkles flickering in her sight, that she ended up closing her eyes. And even then, the glow was a bright redness through her closed lids. The air began to feel thicker, although it didn't affect her breathing. It was just . . . really like honey, she thought, the sparks like speckles of crystal in an otherwise clear liquid. Moving down was like descending into water that one could breathe.

She felt for the next rung with her foot, going carefully as she put her weight on her bad leg. Settled on that rung, she lowered herself to the next.

The glow continued to get brighter, but there was no heat, and the air continued to thicken. She was aware of the others following her, by the vibration of their movement through the metal rungs of the ladder.

"Everybody okay up there?" she called. She almost expected to see bubbles form as she spoke.

"*Muito bem*," Tomàs replied. "No problems."

Sidi and Shriek called back, as well, their voices a little more distant.

Descending the ladder, Annabelle found herself

thinking of entirely inappropriate things. Like a recent gig of the Crackbelles, before the blue glow took her away, when they were interviewed backstage by a writer from *Rolling Stone*. Instead of letting the journalist interview them, they kept firing questions at him, driving him crazy. Asking him what it was like working for the *Stone*. Had he ever done a piece on The Wailing Men—Jimmy Dancer's latest band? Had he ever met Hunter S. Thompson?

Hunter S. Thompson.

I should've been taking notes, she thought. If I ever get outta here, I could sell it to the *Stone*. "Fear and Loathing in Bizarroland." Things not weird enough for you, Hunter? You should try this place.

Her foot, reaching down for the next rung, came up empty.

Wait a minute, she thought.

She lowered herself a bit more, foot carefully feeling about to see if there was merely a rung missing, but that was it. End of the line. From here on out, you're on your own.

"The ladder just ended," she called up.

"Are you on the ground?" Sidi asked.

"Nope. At least, not so's I can tell."

Tomàs sighed heavily above her. "Then, back we go," he said.

"I don't think so," Annabelle said.

"Annabelle, don't!" Sidi cried.

"Look, what've we got to lose? We go back up, we get a choice between the chasm and the Quanians. This thing's gotta go somewhere, right?"

"This is *estúpido*," Tomàs told her.

And he was right, Annabelle thought.

But when you stopped to think about it, everything was totally screwed up. This might be suicide, but at least there was no darkness down there, calling up to her with its silky voice. No way she could face the chasm again. Not a chance. Besides, the air felt so thick she figured she'd just end up floating.

Wouldn't she?

"Annabelle!" Sidi cried.

"I'm gone," Annabelle called back.

Then she let go.

▪ Twenty-five ▪

With three of the enormous snake creatures coming at them from as many directions, Clive was at a loss as to which way to lead his small party. No matter which direction he chose, it would be leading them toward one of the creatures. There was no safety for them anywhere in the maze. There wasn't any in the whole bloody Dungeon, when you came right down to it, he thought.

"Sah," Smythe said. "We have to get moving."

Clive nodded. "I agree—only, which way do we go? I'm open to suggestions."

"Away," Finnbogg said.

Clive regarded the dwarf's hopeful features and gave him a brief, vague smile. Away. Yes. Very good, Finn, he thought. But away to where? No matter which direction they chose, one of the creatures was waiting for them. And if they remained in one spot long enough, all three of the monsters would arrive, to find the party dawdling here while he tried to come to a decision.

Use your head, Folliot, he told himself.

Then, to his annoyance, he found himself trying to think of what Neville would do in a situation like this. Not that his twin was likely to ever get himself in such a situation in the first place. Oh, no. Not Neville. He was too clever by far—always in control, never without an answer to any problem.

And considering how things had been for them so far, Clive wouldn't have been surprised to find that Neville had orchestrated this little surprise for them, as well.

Your brother sends his regards, the man pretending to be Neville had said.

Yes, it was all part of some complicated game Neville was playing. What Clive couldn't decided was if Neville was playing the game with his own twin as his opponent, or if he played with someone else, making Clive and his party merely pawns in their game. Or were they higher ranked than that? One of them a king, perhaps? Protected by a bishop, a horseman and a rook?

He tried not to think of the queen, for that would be Annabelle. Her piece removed from the board. Lost or dead. . . .

An elaborate chess game.

Clive knew himself to be a better player than Neville, but it was difficult to make a move when one could only see a few squares of the board at a time. When one only had four pieces left to play, while one's opponent had an endless array of pieces to set upon the board, pieces that appeared in no sensible order, with moves far too random for logical defense.

Such as black moving giant snake to queenside rook five.

Your move, white.

"Whatever you decide," Guafe said, "it had better be decided soon."

Startled out of his reverie, Clive blinked, then nodded. Make a decision. Yes. But every time he reached for a plan of action, he came up empty-handed.

"Can you find us another of those cul-de-sacs?" Smythe asked.

"Probably."

"Then, lead on," Smythe said, "and we'll have on them yet."

It took Clive a moment to find his guiding "moon" in the lofty vault of the cavern above. When he finally spied it, he put its flicker at his right shoulder and led the party off. Their route took them directly toward the second creature that Guafe had spotted.

With a decision made, Clive found his mind clearing. He set the puzzle of Neville and his complicated designs at the back of his mind and concentrated on the task at hand. Some ten minutes after their earlier unplanned stop, he found what Smythe had been looking for. They stood above the dead end, looking down.

"Now what?" he asked.

Smythe didn't answer immediately. He glanced in the direction of the approaching monster, then moved back along the wall. Finally, he knelt down to investigate the stones where he had stopped.

"Can you move one of these?" he asked Guafe.

"Do you mean lift it?" the cyborg replied.

That, Clive thought, was beyond even Guafe's strength.

Smythe shook his head. He had Finnbogg hold the lantern out so that its light was cast on the floor below.

"I just want you to push it down onto that stone there," he said. "Hopefully, it will trip another of the maze's traps."

"What's the point in that?" Clive asked.

"The creatures are blind," Smythe replied, "and they don't appear to have a sense of hearing. By such reckoning, I believe that they're following us either by the vibration of our tread on the stones, or by what they 'hear' of our thoughts."

Remembering the pressure of the creature's mind on his own, Clive nodded slowly.

"Perhaps . . ." he said.

"I know, sah. This reading of minds doesn't rest easily with me, either, but we know it's possible."

Because they had all experienced sharing each other's mind when caught up in Shriek's neural web.

"So," Smythe continued, "I want to trip the trap and bring them run—ah, slithering here. We'll wait, filling our minds with thoughts of panic, and we'll remove our shoes. When the creature's here, we'll creep off, barefoot and silent, keeping our minds empty, until we put enough distance between it and us."

"Do you really think that will work?" Clive asked. It was hard to keep the doubt from his voice.

"All we can do is try."

"And the others?" Clive asked.

"Let's break through the circle they have us in first," Smythe said, "and worry about that later."

Before anyone else could argue, Guafe bent down and put his strength to the stone. It shifted in its setting, then slowly groaned and tipped, falling to the ground with a crash. The four of them looked down, waiting for the trap to be sprung. Dust flew in the air, and the wall shook at the impact, but nothing else happened.

The trap remained unsprung.

"When Guafe led us into that first dead end," Clive said, "we didn't spring a trap."

The nearest of the monstrous snakes was very close now, the other pair closing in.

"Maybe not all traps," Finnbogg offered.

Smythe made no reply.

"Try hitting the next stone," he said, turning to Guafe.

One thing wouldn't be difficult, Clive thought as the cyborg worked at shifting the second stone block, and that was filling his mind with panic.

The second stone hit the floor of the maze. For a long moment there was no response to it, either; then they saw the floor begin to drop. The wall under them started to shift, and they darted onto the next section.

"Shoes and boots off," Smythe said.

As Clive removed his boots, he watched the huge creature approach the sprung trap, its antennae weaving back and forth above its huge, blind eyes. One of the other snakes was only a few corridors away.

"There's more than one of them going to arrive at almost the same time," Clive said.

"Don't talk, sah," Smythe warned him. "Lie doggo and just fill your mind with thoughts of panic. You're trapped, see, and there's no way free."

All too true, Clive thought, but he did as he was told. It was easy to slip into the required sense of panic.

With their walking gear in hand, the stone blocks of the wall cold against their feet, they watched the creatures approach. As the monstrous head of the closest snake came into direct view below them, Smythe rose to his feet. Finger at his lips, he motioned for the others to follow him.

Clive tried to empty his mind, and found that it was easier to fill it with panic than to think of nothing. He tried pretending he was one of the stones that made up the wall underfoot.

He doubted that he was having even marginal success.

They heard the grind of stone as the walls shifted back to allow the creature entrance to where its prey should be trapped. Clive, last in line, glanced back and saw the snake about to enter, when the second closet of the monsters arrived on the scene. Without a moment's preamble, it shot its head forward and bit into the first creature's tail.

Clive paused in his flight. "Hist!" he called ahead.

The others stopped to look back with him.

For all the narrowness of the corridor's confines, the first creature turned with a sinuous sweep of its body, jaws wide as it struck at its attacker. But the second snake had already loosed its grip, its head rising like a cobra's, slowly weaving back and forth, ready to strike.

The first snake's jaws closed only on air. Its attacker immediately lunged forward, its pale, slimy coils wrapping around its victim, who immediately brought its own coils into play.

They began to thrash as each fought for dominance, the walls buckling on either side. Huge blocks crashed down upon them as the walls collapsed, but the creatures merely ignored the rubble, all their attention on each other. Stone dust rose to cloud the air.

"Bloody hell," Smythe said. "They've solved our problem for us."

He bent down and put his boots back on. A moment later, after the others had followed suit, the party set off at a quick trot, Clive in the lead once more.

Using the "moon" to guide him, he had little trouble with the necessary decisions, and they made good time. From far behind them they could still hear the battling snakes, knocking down the walls in their struggle. A series of high-pitched whines came from the battle—so piercing that it hurt their ears. When they paused for a breather, Clive turned to the cyborg.

"Is there any sign of the third one?" he asked.

Guafe shook his head. "I think it has joined the battle." Sudden silence fell from behind them.

"No time to rest," Smythe said. "Let's keep moving."

Wearily, the party set off again.

Was there no end to this damned maze? Clive wondered. It simply went on and on, wall after wall, corridor following twisting corridor. Their lantern cast an island of light, but what it lit up didn't really change. It was always more of the same, surrounded by the darkness. And then he saw, far ahead, a faint glow. At the same time, Guafe called up from behind him.

"There's another of the creatures on our trail."

Smythe cursed, but Clive pointed out the glow.

"How far back is the monster?" he asked.

"Far enough," Guafe replied. "For now. But it is following the same route we are, and is moving very quickly."

Clive didn't bother to look behind. Instead, he set off at a run for that distant glow. The walls here formed a snarl of corridors—the last attempt of the maze to snare those who got this close to its exit, Clive supposed—but by using his guide, he had no trouble working their way through the complex pattern.

The glow was closer now. But so, by Guafe's reports, was the creature pursuing them. Clive led the party on through a last bewildering series of turns and twists, and finally, the glow was no more than a few walls away—so close he could almost taste it.

"It's almost upon us!" Guafe called.

No, Clive thought. It won't have us—not when we've come this close to escaping it.

For now he could see the source of the light—light spilling from an open doorway. The end of the maze, at least. Perhaps the entrance to the sixth level of the Dungeon, as well? And what lay waiting for them there? Don't even bother to worry about it, he told himself. Let's try to survive the moment first.

They ran the last few yards, and then there was only an open expanse between the lit doorway and themselves. The door itself was set at the top of a short flight of stairs. Its height was just enough for them to get through, small enough to keep the creature out. But there was a twelve-foot drop between the top of the wall and the ground running over to the stairs.

Clive crouched on the wall. Holding on to the top by his hands, he lowered himself over and down, dropping the last few feet. He landed lightly on the balls of his feet. Guafe and Smythe landed on either side of him. Only Finnbogg remained above.

"Come along then, Finn!" he called up to Finnbogg.

"It's too high for Finnbogg to jump," the dwarf replied.

"Jump!" Clive cried. "We'll catch you."

As Finnbogg lowered himself nervously over the edge, the three of them positioned themselves under him to break his fall. And then the head of the monstrous snake appeared around the corner.

"For God's sake, jump!" Clive shouted.

Smythe moved away from them, bringing the rolled-up canvas from his shoulder. Moving quickly, he pulled off the twines binding either end, and shook the cloth open. The snake's enormous head wove back and forth above him, but Smythe kept his gaze firmly fixed on the creature's jaws, refusing to meet its blind gaze.

Finnbogg held on to the top of the wall, then let himself go.

The snake's head darted forward. As its jaws opened to snap at him, Smythe tossed the sheet of canvas into its mouth.

Guafe and Clive caught the dwarf, the cyborg absorbing most of his weight.

The snake snapped its jaws on the cloth, shaking it as a terrier would a rat. The canvas got snarled in its teeth.

"Run for the door!" Smythe cried.

As the other three broke for the stairs, Smythe threw his pry-bar, straight for one of the creature's milky-white eyes. The weapon embedded itself in the enormous orb, and that high-pitched whining they had heard earlier issued from the snake's huge mouth. Hands clapped over his ears, Smythe broke for the doorway as well, hard on the heels of the others.

Guafe was through, then Clive and Finnbogg. The snake whipped its head forward, straight for Smythe where he ran up the stairs, still making that piercing cry of pain. At the last possible moment, Smythe threw himself to one side, and the snake's head battered the stairs, shattering stone. Smythe rolled to his feet, darting for the doorway as it lifted its head for a second strike.

Smythe threw himself through the doorway at the same instant the snake struck at him again. This time, its massive head crashed against the sides of the door. Rocks fell as the doorway widened. Drawing back its head, the snake struck again, and the doorway widened some more, opening onto another tunnel.

The others had caught Smythe as he flung himself forward. On their feet now, they raced down this new tunnel, the bright lights set in its ceiling hurting their eyes. Behind them, the snake continued to pound at the sides of the doorway, knocking pieces of it down with each blow.

The party turned one corner, then another, and came up against a massive door, so similar to the one that the Dramaranians had thrust them through that it might have been its twin. Guafe pounded on it. Behind them, the crash of falling rocks continued.

Again and again the cyborg pounded on the metal panel, the others joining him, and finally, it opened. They almost fell through in their haste to get out of the tunnel, and found themselves in a large, empty room, facing a curious individual.

As the door closed behind them, shutting off most of the high-pitched whine of the snake and the thunder of its pummeling the doorway, they slowly rose to their feet. Their rescuer was a short, tubby individual with a broad, fat face, bald pate, and eyes that gleamed metallically, like Guafe's.

Another mechanical man, Clive thought.

The strange being spoke to them, but the words made no sense.

"I'm sorry, we don't understand," Clive said.

"You are Englishmen?" he said then, in perfect Queen's English.

Clive nodded.

"Then you will be the assassins we were told to expect." The broad face grinned. "The Lords of Thunder will feed well on you tonight."

He pulled an instrument from his belt and aimed it at them, thumbing a lever. A numbness settled over the party and, while they could still see and hear, they could no longer move a muscle.

▪ Twenty-six ▪

You've screwed up bad in your time, Annie B., Annabelle told herself as she let go, but this probably tops them all.

Letting go.

To fall down the shaft, like Alice down the rabbit hole. Except this wasn't a dream from which she was going to wake, as Alice eventually had.

All her muscles clenched into tight knots in anticipation of the coming plummet, but while she descended, floating in the thick, golden air, there was no sense of falling. The descent was as calm as riding an escalator from one floor to the next, as comforting as lying on a warm waterbed, the mattress moving gently underneath.

The sparks that specked the honey glow strobed in her eyes. Each flash burned through her retinas to carry its fire into the recesses of her mind. A Catherine Wheel of memories, sparked, seen, then gone to make room for still more. Each one, here and gone, all in an instant.

Good memories.

The kind smile of a stranger peering down at her as her mother pushed her pram down a crowded city street.

Her first kiss, courtesy of freckled Bob Hughes, in the back of the rubble-strewn lot across from the grade school.

Her second Les Paul—to replace the one stolen as she was bringing it home from the store—that Des helped her strip and paint a canary yellow.

Holding Amanda for the first time, the red, squalling

face turned up to hers, features calming as she soothed her.

Hearing about "Gotcha in my Heart," the band's third single, entering *Billboard*'s Top One Hundred—thirty-four with a bullet.

Walking a rain-slick London street with Chrissie Nunn and Tripper on their way to the sound check of the first gig of their first European headlining tour.

Lots of first times.

First times were best. Those initial moments that you never forgot.

Good memories.

When her feet touched ground and the sparks lost their hold on her mind, the memories fading, she felt a sense of abrupt loss that knifed straight to her heart.

Not yet, she wanted to tell them. Don't go yet. . . .

Her knees started to buckle, a sharp pain rising from her hurt leg, and then she was blinking in the golden glare, one hand pressed against the smooth wall of the shaft for balance. She turned in a slow circle and found the cutaway door that led to—

Where?

More dangers, more pain? She didn't want anything more to do with the Dungeon. She just wanted to float in the golden shaft, remembering the good things of her life. Times past and gone forever now. Better times than what was going to lie waiting for her through that door, of that she was sure. The shaft delivered what the chasm had only promised.

She looked up, but there was no retreat. No ladder rungs leading up into the rich honey glow. No handholds. No way up.

But there were voices. It took her a long moment to focus on them enough to make out what they were saying.

"Annabelle, Annabelle! Can you hear me?"

Slowly, she shook off her reverie. That was Sidi. At least there was something good about her present situation. Sidi and Shriek. Good friends. Maybe even Tomàs as well, seeing how he was turning over a new leaf.

"Annabelle!"

"I hear you," she called back.

"Where are you? Are you all right?"

All right? When she'd just been reminded of all that she'd lost?

"Yeah," she called back. "I guess I'm okay."

Because life just went on, didn't it? Made no difference if you wanted to slow the ride down, or get off, the old ferris wheel just kept on spinning. Up and down. You have a few laughs, some good times, and then you had to go through the times that weren't so good.

Like now.

"It's a real smooth ride," she told her companions. "So c'mon down."

She moved out of the shaft, through the portal, regrets and loss clinging to her like cobwebs.

You never used to be this moody, Annie B., she told herself as she took in their new surroundings.

The place had the feel of a waiting room in a train station or bus depot about it. Nothing was permanent here, everything's just passing through. On the far side of the dimly lit chamber, there was a door set in the wall.

Level six, Annabelle thought humorlessly. Another stopover that we just don't need. Maybe we should've grabbed an express.

Hearing a scuffling sound behind her, she turned to find Tomàs standing in the golden glow, sparks flickering around his dark head. The Portuguese's eyes were shiny with unshed tears.

"You okay?" she asked.

It took Tomàs a moment to focus on her, then he nodded slowly and joined her. He said nothing of what he'd experienced in the shaft, but his losses were written as plainly in his features and stance as Annabelle's own had been.

Well, what *could* you say? Annabelle thought.

It was the same for the others. One following the other, Shriek and Sidi stepped through the portal and crossed to where Annabelle and Tomàs were standing in the broad, empty room, waiting for them.

"Some trip, huh?" Annabelle said after a few moments.

Regrets swam in Sidi's eyes. "In some ways," he said, "that was the worst thing I've experienced in this place."

"Yeah. I know what you mean. We didn't need to be reminded."

She turned to Shriek. The alien's multiple, many-faceted eyes didn't show sorrow in the same way a human's would, but Annabelle knew Shriek had experienced the same kinds of losses that they all had.

"It was hard," Annabelle said to the arachnid, "to have the past, just for a moment, then lose it again."

Shriek nodded. *Very hard,* she agreed.

Her voice, echoing in Annabelle's head, was oddly subdued.

They stood in a quiet group, coming to terms with what they'd experienced in the shaft. Then, finally, Annabelle stirred.

"Guess we should check out what's behind Door Number One," she said, glancing at her companions. "Or do we trade it for what's behind the curtain?"

"Curtain?" Tomàs asked, looking around the empty room.

Annabelle shook her head. "Don't pay any attention to me."

She led the way to the door and tried the handle.

Locked.

Perfect, she thought.

Shall we break in? Shriek asked her.

"Let's try the polite approach first," Annabelle replied.

She raised her hand and knocked sharply on the door. Waiting a few heartbeats, she knocked again. When there was still no response after her third knock, she turned to Shriek and was about to tell her to do her stuff, when she heard the lock being disengaged. She faced the door again as it slowly opened.

A scaled-down model of Chang Guafe stood in the doorway.

Well, he wasn't exactly like Guafe, Annabelle decided,

but he was close enough. He was the size of a twelve-year-old, but obviously much older; male, slender, half his body parts made of gleaming metal, both eyes implants. His head was shaved, or he was naturally bald—it was hard to tell which. He wore red trousers and a green shirt. His feet were bare. If his ears had been pointed, she might have put him down as one of Santa's elves undergoing chemotherapy.

When he spoke, his voice had the same hollow ring as Guafe's, and she couldn't understand a word he said.

"Say what?" she asked.

She could almost hear the circuitry humming in his head as he tested her words and began to match them up with what he had stored in his memory.

"You speak English?" he asked finally.

"You bet. What's your name?"

"Binro."

"Okay. I'm Annabelle." One by one she introduced the rest of her company. "Is this the sixth level?"

Binro nodded. "Welcome to the Holy City of Tawn, pilgrims."

"Pilgrims?"

"Surely you have come to view the Oracle of the Lords of Thunder?"

Annabelle blinked, then quickly smiled. "Surely," she said. "What else?"

"Are you Haves or Havenots?"

"Ah. . . ."

Annabelle shot a glance at Sidi and the others, but they were having as much problem following the conversation as she was.

Wonderful.

C'mon, guys, she wanted to say to them. Time for somebody else to lend a hand.

But they made it obvious that she was in command.

Haves or Havenots. It sounded like a trick question. What if they came up with the wrong answer?

"Havenots," she said, deciding that they had less than they should.

Binro beamed. "Then be thrice welcomed, pilgrims."

"We're a little . . . ah . . . vague on protocol," Annabelle said. "What's the deal with this oracle? Can we ask it anything we like?"

"That depends on whether or not your names are chosen in the drawing," Binro replied. "But, you're in luck. There is a lottery tonight. The Lords be willing, you might win a chance to speak to them through the Voice of Their Light."

This was getting too weird again, Annabelle thought. Drawings. Lotteries. What the hell was he talking about?

"Ah . . . what do we do until then?" she asked. "You know, until the lottery's happening?"

"There are always rooms kept in readiness for Havenot pilgrims," Binro assured her. "Come. Follow me."

He ushered them through the door, then carefully locked it behind them. Pocketing the key, he led them down a long hall and up a stairwell. Four stories later, they stepped into another corridor. This one had doors opening from it, all along its length.

It's like a hotel, Annabelle thought. She wondered what sort of payment they'd be expecting.

"Would you like separate rooms?" Binro asked.

Annabelle's first inclination was to go for that, but then she decided that they'd be better off staying together as a group.

"Maybe not," she said. "We're all strangers here and, you know, we'd like to stick together."

"As you wish."

He took them down to the middle of the hallway and opened a door into a large, carpeted room. Bright sunlight came through the windows, making them all blink. There were two double beds, a dresser, mirror, couch, and some easy chairs by the window, and two other doors leading off on one side of the room.

Closet and washroom, Annabelle decided. God, the place was like a Holiday Inn. She wondered if they had a shower.

"Will this be suitable?" Binro asked.

"Oh, yeah. It's great."

"There are clean garments in the closet." He pursed

his lips for a moment, taking in Shriek's four arms. "I will have a custom-fitted robe prepared for you, Miss Shriek, which will be delivered in a half-hour."

That will not be necessary, Being Binro, the arachnid said.

Binro chittered in response—speaking in Shriek's native language, Annabelle realized.

Right. The Holy City of Tawn. With an Oracle, expecting pilgrims. All languages accepted here. Stay in our beautiful downtown Hilton while you wait for the results of the lottery.

"Please make yourself at home," Binro added. Then he was gone.

Annabelle slowly closed the door behind him.

"Anybody know what's going on?" she asked.

Sidi and Tomàs shook their heads. Shriek, who had crossed the room to look out the window, called out suddenly, indicating something she saw outside. The others hurried over.

Look, the arachnid said, pointing to a figure that stood on a street corner below.

It took Annabelle a moment to focus on the figure. First, she took in the vast sweep of buildings and streets—it was like being in downtown New York. Tall, gleaming buildings rose high all around them. There was traffic on the streets, both pedestrian and vehicles, though the latter weren't quite right. At least, not for the cities Annabelle was familiar with. They were all either public transports, like old tram cars, or small one- or two-person scooters and what looked like golf carts.

"Jesus," she murmured.

Shriek tugged on her arm, still pointing. Annabelle let her gaze pan down to the figure that had caught the alien's attention.

"Clive!" she cried.

But Sidi shook his head. "No. That's Neville Folliot."

Annabelle started to turn for the door. "We've gotta grab him before he takes off again."

"Too late," Sidi told her. "He's gone now—lost in the crowd. We'll never find him."

"But he's here. . . ."

And Clive wasn't. Jesus. Were they going to spend the rest of their lives careening around this place like pinballs, just catching glimpses of each other, never getting close again? The thought of it depressed her.

"I'm gonna see if they really do have a shower," she said.

Later, refreshed from long showers and the meal that Binro had brought them, they sat around their room, just taking it easy. Except for Shriek, they had all put on the robes that they had found in the closet.

We look like a bunch of acolytes from some weird monastery, Annabelle thought as she sprawled on one of the beds, hands behind her head. God, it felt good to be clean again.

The others had wanted to go exploring, but she refused to budge until her old clothes, which she'd washed when she took her shower, were dry enough to wear. No way she was gonna go running around looking like some Hare Krishna. She had a rep to think of.

In the end they all stayed; none of them wanting to separate. Shriek and Sidi sat by the window, fascinated by the endless parade of people and vehicles below. Tomàs was asleep on the other bed. Bored, Annabelle opened the drawer of the night table beside her bed.

She was used to hotel rooms—and, weird though this one was in terms of *where* it was, it still wasn't all that different from a hundred others she'd stayed in while on tour. She wasn't sure what she was expecting to find in the drawer. Not a Bible. Not here. Though maybe the Tawnian version of one?

Her fingers closed on a book and she drew it out. When she looked at what it was, a cold chill traveled up her spine.

"Oh, shit."

Sidi turned from the window. "What is it, Annabelle?"

Numbly, Annabelle held up her prize. It was Neville Folliot's journal.

▪ Twenty-Seven ▪

Clive had never felt so helpless as he did at that moment. Whatever the small box that their captor held was, it had somehow managed to freeze all their muscles, locking them into tight knots so that not one of them could move—not even Guafe, who was composed of at least a third mechanical parts. They couldn't even twitch.

Whistling to himself, their captor unclipped another small box from his belt and spoke into it. Whatever he said was totally incomprehensible.

"Won't be long now," he told them, switching to English. "We'll soon have you transported to a nice little holding cell where I'll free you from your state of stasis."

Why? Clive wanted to ask him. What was all this about?

"You didn't truly believe that you could actually succeed in assassinating the Lords of Thunder, now, did you?" their captor asked, as though reading Clive's mind.

There it was again, Clive thought. The mechanical man thought they were assassins. But all they knew of the Lords of Thunder was their name, nothing more. All they wanted to do was find his brother and leave the Dungeon. If he could only find some way to talk to the man.

"You're not the first to try, of course," their captor continued. "Nor will you be the last, I presume. But no one ever has, or will succeed. It simply isn't possible. The Lords are beyond the hand of death. Still, your kind does provide some amusement for them. I wonder, are you free agents, hoping for spoils, or did the Madonna send you?"

What had the Mother of God to do with any of this? Clive thought. But then he realized that in this place, the name could mean anything. And anybody.

"Ah, here's your transport now," their captor said as a door hissed open in what had appeared to be a blank wall.

A small horseless cart on fat wheels rolled through and came to a stop in front of them. The sound of its engine was a low hum. There were two seats in the front—one occupied by the driver, the other empty—and a cargo area in the back where, presumably, their stiff bodies would be laid.

The driver, while obviously of the same half-human, half-mechanical race as their captor, was otherwise as different from the first man as night was to day. He was thin as a rake, almost cadaverous, bones prominent against the tight fit of his skin, eyes deep-set and ringed with black circles, skin pale. Where the first man had a jolly look about him, the newcomer looked as dour as a Scots churchman.

Because the pair of them were transporting bodies, albeit living ones, Clive promptly christened them Burke and Hare. Burke was the newcomer; Hare the rotund captor who had first snared them.

"Easy now," Hare was saying as they laid Smythe in the back of the cart. "Don't want the goods damaged before the lords have their fun with them, or maybe you'll be taking their place."

Burke muttered something unintelligible in their own tongue.

"It was just a joke," Hare replied. "Of course the Lords would never feed on us. *We* never meant them any ill."

It was obvious, Clive thought, that Hare continued to speak in English just to make them feel more ill at ease. He wanted them to have to think about what lay ahead.

Clive was the last to be loaded onto the cart. He felt nauseous when it came his turn to be hoisted up and laid down beside the others. His skin crawled at the feel of their hands on him. Unable to move, unable to even speak. To be so helpless. . . . If he'd had a weapon in hand, Clive would gladly have killed the pair of them in cold blood.

"Oh, you're a hater, you are," Hare said, looking down into his face. "Hold that hate to you, assassin. The Lords feed on it."

Laughing, he got into the passenger seat. Burke sat down behind the wheel and the cart moved smoothly off on its fat wheels, through the door and down a long corridor. All Clive could see of their passage was the flicker of the ceiling lights as they went by. He tried counting them, as a means of memorizing the route, but he soon lost track of both the number of lights and the turns that they took.

Finally, after what seemed like an inordinately long journey, through corridors as bafflingly laid out as the maze that they had so recently escaped, the cart came to a halt, and Burke and Hare were hoisting them from the bed of the cart and carrying them into a jail cell. The pair stood Clive and his companions up against one wall, vacated the cell, and locked the door behind them. Not until then did Hare take that small box from his belt once more and aim it at the four.

When he depressed its control button, use of their own muscles returned to Clive and the other three. But their legs buckled under them, and it was all they could do to keep themselves from smacking their heads against the floor.

"Goodbye for now!" Hare called cheerily.

"W-wait. . . ." Clive called.

But Burke had already set the cart in motion, and the pair of them whizzed out of sight.

Slowly, Clive sat up. His muscles felt bruised and sore. His head ached. He was hungry and thirsty, and what little patience he had had completely run its course.

"Damn them all to bloody hell!" he cried.

"Keep it down, would you?"

The voice was familiar, though it didn't belong to any of his companions. Clive turned slowly to face its source, gaze taking in the double set of tiered cots—one pair to either side of the back wall—the water bucket, another for bodily wastes, until he was looking at the man who had spoken.

This was too much.

"You!" he cried. "It's your fault that we're here."

"Me? I've never seen you before in my life."

But if the man wasn't Father Neville of Dramaran— the one who'd stolen the history and name of Clive's twin and abandoned them in the cavern, with its maze and monsters—then he was an identical twin.

Clive rose to his feet and stalked over to the other side of the cell, until he stood against the bars looking into the neighboring one.

"I'm tired of your lies," Clive said.

"I tell you, I've never met you before."

Clive thrust an arm through the bars, and the man backed hastily away, even though Clive couldn't reach far enough into the other cell to hurt him anyway.

"Wait a minute, sah," Smythe said. "Let's give him a listen, first."

"What for? To hear more lies?"

Smythe shook his head. "Look at him. He thinks he's telling the truth. I'll wager that he *has* never seen us before. And besides, how could he have gotten here before us?"

He tugged at Clive's arm, moving him away from the bars as he spoke, and settling him on a lower cot in their own cell.

"The resemblance is uncanny," Guafe remarked. "All the way down to the mole at his wrist."

Smythe nodded. "What's your name?" he asked the man in the other cell.

"Edgar Howlett," he replied. "I came to the Dungeon twelve years ago, from the continent known as North America, on a planet called Earth. The year I was taken was nineteen eighty-three."

Clive, feeling a little calmer now, took in that infor- mation. But more importantly, he weighed the man's delivery. Horace was right. Whatever else might be, the man truly believed he was who he said he was.

"And do you have a brother?" Smythe asked.

Howlett shook his head. "Not one," he said. "Now it's my turn for questions. What are your names? Where are you from?"

In the same manner as Howlett had done, they gave him their names, places of origin, and the years of disappearance from their homelands. Finnbogg was the last to speak.

"Ten thousand years?" Howlett said in disbelief. "You've been here that long?"

The dwarf nodded.

"This place has got to be Hell," Howlett said.

In that they were all in agreement, except, of course, Guafe.

"But there is so much to learn here," the cyborg said.

"Screw learning," Howlett told him. "I finished high school. I'm a plumber, okay? What else do I have to know? I just want to get home again—see the wife and kid. Christ, Tommy'll be—what? Eighteen now. I missed seeing him grow up. I . . . aw, what's the point. I figure I died, you know? Back in Milwaukee. I didn't think I was that bad a guy, but this sure isn't Heaven, so it's got to be Hell."

"We are not dead," Guafe said. "I would know if I had died."

"Christ, look who's talking. The Bionic Man himself."

"I am not sure that I care for the tone of your voice," Guafe said.

Howlett shrugged. "So what're you going to do about it? Call for a guard?"

Guafe stepped up to the bars separating their cells. Getting a firm grip on two, he began to exert pressure on them. Slowly, they started to bend.

Before things got too serious, Smythe crossed to Guafe's side and laid a calming hand on his shoulder.

"There's much we could learn from Mr. Howlett," he said.

Guafe turned, metallic eyes flashing, but Howlett, his

own eyes going wide as the bars bent under the cyborg's strength, stood up and held his hands placatingly in front of him.

"Hey, easy now," he said. "You've got me all wrong. I used to love the Bionic Man. It was my favorite show— you know what I'm saying?"

Guafe let his hands fall from the bars. Howlett let out an audible sigh of relief. Then, before anyone else could speak, he turned to Clive.

"You said your last name's Folliot?" he asked.

Clive nodded.

"Any relation to a guy named Neville Folliot?"

Clive's suspicions rose to the fore once more. "He's my twin brother," he said. "How do you know his name?"

"It's also the name *your* twin was calling himself the last time we saw him," Smythe put in.

"I told you," Howlett said. "I don't have any brothers—or sisters. The guy you saw must've been a clone, but I do know Neville Folliot. He's the reason I'm in this jam."

"A clone," Guafe said. "Of course."

"What's a clone?" Smythe asked him.

"Cloning is a form of genetic manipulation whereby an entire exact replica of a being can be grown from just one cell taken from the donor."

"That kind of thing's possible?" Howlett asked.

"Very possible," Guafe replied.

Howlett shook his head. "I only saw it in the movies, you know? I didn't think it was real."

"What did my brother have to do with your present situation?" Clive asked.

"Well, I met him, must have been five or six years or so ago, up on one of the upper levels. We hung around together for a while—came down from the third level, through the fourth and fifth—did you see the dinosaurs on the fifth?—until we finally ended up here. We got snatched by the border patrol, or whatever the hell they're called, and that's when old Neville put the knife to me."

"He attacked you?" Clive asked.

"Naw. He turned rat on me. Told the authorities that I was an agent of the Madonna's—you heard of her?"

"Briefly," Smythe said. "In our time, we refer to the Madonna as the Mother of Christ."

"Yeah? Well, in mine she's a pop singer, sexy as all get-out. But here she's some kind of, I don't know—I think demagogue's the word Neville used to describe her."

"Is she of the Ren, or the Chaffri?" Clive asked.

"No way of telling," Howlett told him. "I never could keep those sides straight. I don't think anyone can. Anyway, this may be something strictly local. There's an awful lot in the Dungeon that the Chaffri and the Ren don't bother getting involved with, even if they are the big bosses."

"What about Green?" Smythe asked.

"Green what?"

"A man named Green. Did Major Folliot—Neville— ever mention him? Is he an ally or a foe? Ren or Chaffri?"

"Never heard of him."

Clive shook his head sadly. Would they never find two pieces of information that fit together?

Howlett continued his tale. "Anyway, Neville told the authorities that I was the Madonna's agent, and not only that, but that she was also sending in a bunch of assassins to kill the Lords, and the way to recognize them was that they'd be speaking English.

"They only half believed him. Kept him in that cell you're in right now up until about a half hour ago—I guess that's when they caught you and found out he was telling the truth. Or, at least, what they perceived as the truth. So they let him go. Or took him away, anyway."

"He was here?" Clive cried. "In this very cell, not half an hour ago?"

"'Fraid so."

"God damn the man. What is he playing at?"

Howlett shook his head. "Damned if I know. I thought we were buddies." He paused, thinking for a moment. "This other guy looked exactly like me?"

"Down to the mole," Smythe said.

"Christ, talk about giving you the creeps."

"What we should also consider," Guafe said, "is the possibility that the Neville Folliot we are chasing is another clone. Who knows how many of them there might be?"

"A clone?" Clive said. "As this man's twin was? This is really possible?"

"In my world it is," Guafe said. "And in this Dungeon. . . ."

He let the sentence trail off, unfinished, as Clive sat back down on the cot and bent over, face pressed into the palms of his hands.

"I feel like I'm going mad," he said.

"First things first," Smythe said. "Let's get out of this place, *then* you can go mad."

"But, Horace. When you think of it . . . two, perhaps dozens of Nevilles running about. . . ."

"I know, sah. It's not a pleasant thought, by any stretch of the imagination. But we still have to escape."

He turned slowly, then his gaze settled on the bars that Guafe had bent between Howlett's cell and their own.

"We need your strength for this," he told the cyborg. "Can you pull the bars far enough apart for Howlett to join us, and then repeat the trick on the ones facing the corridor?"

Guafe nodded. He returned to where he'd first opened a gap between the bars. Gripping them once more, he began to exert pressure on the steel. Slowly, the gap widened until it was just big enough for Howlett to squeeze through. Turning, Guafe stepped over to the bars facing the corridor and repeated the maneuver.

Moments later they were all standing out in the corridor.

"Now what?" Clive said.

"We find your brother, or we find a way out of here," Smythe said. "Whichever comes first."

"I'd like a piece of him," Howlett muttered, but then he realized who he was talking to. "Sorry. I forgot he's your brother. It's just, after the way he screwed me. . . ."

"I sympathize," Clive said. "But if you want a 'piece of him,' as you put it, I'm afraid you'll just have to wait in line."

▪ Twenty-Eight ▪

"I don't get it," Annabelle said, leafing through Neville Folliot's journal. "What's this doing here?"

Unspoken, but lying there plainly behind her words all the same, was the thought, If the journal's here, then what had happened to Clive and the others? The last time they'd set eyes on this book, it had been in Clive's possession.

Could it be a copy? Shriek asked.

Annabelle shook her head. "I don't think so." She glanced at the others. "You got any ideas, Sidi? Tomàs?"

"Something has happened to the others," Tomàs said. "*Sim?*"

"Yeah. I got a real bad feeling about this, too." She looked around the room. "I wonder how you buzz room service in this place?"

"Room service?" Sidi asked.

"To talk to Binro, or whoever's in charge. I want to know what this is doing here."

"Perhaps that wouldn't be such a good idea, Annabelle. If the journal is here and something *has* happened to the others, then it stands to reason that our hosts must be involved."

"Right. So let's get outta here."

She swung her feet off the bed and, journal in hand, headed for the door. She gave the knob a twist, but it wouldn't budge.

"Perfect. We're locked in. God, what a bunch of assholes we've turned out to be. Pilgrims, right. Guests. Let's try prisoners on for size."

She turned to Shriek to see if the alien could take down the door.

"Does the journal say anything about Tawn?" Sidi asked.

Good point, Annabelle thought.

Returning to the bed, she sat down and began to flip through the pages. She passed through sections where Clive's sketches filled the blank spaces where once there had been Neville's entries. There was enough there to tell her that Clive and his party had successfully crossed the veldt on the fifth level, and had reached a city there. She didn't want to think about what the portrait of the woman meant. At last, she found a new message.

"Here we go," she said.

As far as they could figure out from Neville's rather cryptic words, Tawn was the focus of an ancient and continuing war between factions led by the Lords of Thunder, on one side, and someone called the Madonna, on the other.

"Jesus," Annabelle said softly as she read further. She looked up at her companions. "What did you see out that window?"

"A large city, much like Calcutta," Sidi said. "Just below our window is a marketplace."

Tomàs shook his head. "No. It is a harbor, filled with ships from many nations."

When the question was put to Shriek, she described some alien cityscape.

And I saw a variation on New York, Annabelle thought.

"There's nothing out there," she said, "according to Neville."

"Nothing?" Sidi asked. He returned to the window. "But it seems so real. . . ."

"They're playing with our heads," Annabelle said. "The whole thing's a scam. Listen to this. 'Trust not in Tawn, even in what your own eyes tell you, for they fill up emptiness with what is familiar. Keep a sphinx's riddle for the Lords of Thunder, lest you be taken for fuels.'"

"The riddle of the sphinx is a question that can't be

answered," she explained. "And I don't think I wanna find out firsthand what he means by 'taken for fuels.'"

Annabelle slammed the journal closed.

"We don't need this crap," she said. "Shriek, can you get that door open?"

The arachnid flexed her multiple arms. Advancing on the door, she pressed the palms of her upper arms against it to get a sense of its density.

Bring me a chair, she said.

Annabelle brought one of them over, but before Shriek could use it as a makeshift battering ram, the door opened and Binro was standing there, a smile touching his features. He held a small device in his hand that reminded Annabelle of a remote control for a TV.

"Congratulations," he said. "I took the liberty of entering your names in the lottery as a group, and you have won the privilege of speaking with the Oracle."

"As opposed to being godfood without trying to stump the Oracle?" Annabelle asked.

Binro blinked. "Pardon?"

"Outta the way, pal. We've decided to find new lodgings."

The little man sighed as Annabelle advanced on him. Before either she or Shriek could grab him, he thumbed a button on the device in his hand.

There was nothing to see, and little to feel except for an electric tingle that ran up their nerve ends. But when Annabelle tried to move, she realized that every one of her muscles had been paralyzed. From her companions' lack of movement, she realized that they'd all been hit by an invisible stasis ray.

Oh, beautiful, she thought. The little twerp was a science fiction freak. Except this wasn't the movies. It was the real thing, and they were up the proverbial creek without a paddle.

Fuming, all she could do was watch as Binro called up what looked like a small golf cart to transport the four of them to the Oracle. Its driver was much taller than Binro—a thin, cadaverous individual who made Annabelle think of a junkie. With the driver's help, Binro loaded them onto the flat bed at the back of the cart, then they were carried down a series of long corridors to an elevator.

Binro leaned back to look at Annabelle's frozen face. "There was really no need for things to be so unpleasant," he told her. "This is a great honor for you—speaking with the Oracle, and then meeting the Lords of Thunder."

Screw you, Annabelle thought.

Binro must have read something of her feelings in her eyes for he frowned, then gave a shrug and turned in his seat, leaving her to herself once more.

When I get out of this. . . . Annabelle thought.

The elevator doors slid open, and the cart pulled out into a vast chamber with cathedral ceilings. Binro and his companion unloaded them. When all four of them were lying on the floor, staring up at the vast ceiling, the cart withdrew, back into the elevator. Though she couldn't turn her head to see what they were doing, Annabelle assumed that Binro had thumbed his stasis device again, because she started to feel a new tingle in her nerve ends, and her muscles went slack. She turned just in time to see the door of the elevator slide shut once more.

Her body had that numbed, prickly feeling of an arm or leg that had fallen asleep. It took a few moments for it to wear off enough so that she could sit up and take stock.

"Everybody okay?" she asked.

The stasis ray appeared to have had the worst effect upon Shriek—probably due to her alien musculature—and she was the last to recover. Annabelle helped her to her feet.

"What is this place?" Sidi murmured.

"Home of the gods," Annabelle said. "Can't you tell?"

But for all the lightness of her tone, the place gave her the creeps. The room was enormous—a feeling that was compounded by the immense ceiling that rose some three stories above the floor. There were glass domes set into its curved features, through which a pale, orange-yellow light issued. The floor was the size of half a football field.

Set in the walls, in a long row that ran along two sides of the chamber, were what looked all too much like gigantic sarcophagi. Although they were decorated with glyphs and designs, the motif didn't strike Annabelle as Egyptian so much as heavy metal punk. Lots of ornately detailed figures were carved on the lids of the sarcophagi, their clothing made to represent leather, chains, and studs with lots of sharp-edged objects. Razors. Knives. Swords.

Against the wall facing them was a series of steps that led up to a raised platform. A still figure lay there on a stone slab—corpse-white and huge. Annabelle thought it was another carving, until they got closer and she saw that it was the body of a dead giant. Male.

Alive and on its feet, it would have stood twice her height. The skin was smooth, hair black and fine, spread out in a fan around the head upon the gray stone. The body wore the same kind of leather gear as the carved bas-reliefs on the sarcophagi. Leather skirt, crisscrossed strips of leather across its chest like bandoleers. Lots of shiny silver studs. Small, sharp blades hung from its ears like earrings—six to each ear, running up from the lobe to the top of the ear. Two more hung from each nostril. More dangled down the length of its arms, the wires piercing the alabaster flesh.

Standing around the stone slab on which it lay, all they could do was stare at the corpse.

"What is it?" Sidi said. His voice, though hushed, seemed loud in the silence.

"The Oracle," Annabelle said.

Her hand lifted to touch the shape of Folliot's journal where it sat in the inner pocket of her jacket. They had to put a question to the Oracle that he couldn't answer— that was the only way out. Because otherwise. . . . Her gaze drifted to the sarcophagi lining the walls.

Were there more corpses in them? And what about the Lords?

Tomàs made a sudden sound. Breath sharply drawn

in. Annabelle looked back at the corpse and took a step back. The eyelids had flickered open, cold blue eyes staring up at the ceiling. Annabelle's pulse doubled its tempo.

"WHAT WOULD YOU ASK OF ME?" the corpse asked.

Me, me, me. . . .

Its voice boomed hollowly, echoes resounding through the vast chamber. Annabelle and her party all withdrew from the stone slab. Annabelle reached for Sidi's hand and gripped it tightly.

"PILGRIMS," the corpse repeated. "WHAT WOULD YOU ASK OF ME?"

Me, me, me. . . . the echoes chimed in again.

Oh, Jesus, Annabelle thought. We only get the one question.

"PILGRIMS," the corpse said once more.

Grim, grim, grim. . . .

"Give us a moment!" Annabelle blurted out.

Slowly, the enormous head turned, steely blue gaze fixing on her. Annabelle started to take another step back, but that cold gaze nailed her in place. Her insides began to churn. There was a knot in her stomach, like a hard rock sitting there. A sour taste rose in her throat.

A faint smile touched the corpse's dead lips. "THERE IS NO NEED TO HASTEN," he said.

Ten, ten, ten. . . . the echoes chorused.

"WE HAVE ALL THE TIME IN THE WORLD."

World, world, world. . . .

The voice seemed to come from all around them, the echoing words drifting across each other to become a babble of sound.

Swallowing thickly, Annabelle nodded at the corpse. "R-right," she said. "All the time."

"MYSTERIES AWAIT YOU."

You, you, you. . . .

Knees weak, Annabelle kept retreating. She would have fallen at the top of the stairs, except Sidi was there to help her keep her balance. The small group backed carefully down each step, unable to pull their gazes from the monstrous dead figure.

"PLEASURES YOU CANNOT IMAGINE."

Gin, gin, gin. . . .

I could use a drink about now, Annabelle thought, and almost giggled at the incongruity of the thought.

A drink. Right. What was happening was that she was losing it. Giddy with fright.

Pull yourself together, Annie B., she told herself.

They retreated all the way across the room until they were standing by the elevator again. The corpse's gaze followed them until they paused, then slowly, it turned its head to stare up at the ceiling once more.

Freed of the prison of its gaze, Annabelle sagged against the wall behind her.

"What if it gets up?" she said. "What if it gets up and comes after us?"

"There is no place to hide," Tomàs said.

Sidi nodded. "And no way to escape. We have to put a question to it."

"God." Annabelle rubbed her face. "What kind of question?"

But she knew. An obscure bit of schooling rose bubbling up in her mind. Question and answer time. Final exam. The teacher grinning because he knew she hadn't been studying.

It had to be a riddle. This Oracle was like the Greek sphinx in Thebes, except instead of it posing the riddle, and then devouring those unable to find solutions, it was up to them to come up with a question. And if it gave them an answer, they were godfood.

Oedipus, where are you when you're needed?

"What do we ask?" she repeated.

Her companions shook their heads.

"It's gotta be obscure—maybe something from our own experiences, something it couldn't possibly know about? Like who used to play lead guitar for the Wailing Men before Lee Sands?"

But she didn't think that would cut it.

"The journal said merely a question," Sidi said. "Any question."

"Yeah. And we all really put a lot of trust into what Neville Folliot's got to tell us, don't we?"

"Then ask it that, Annabelle. Where we can find Neville Folliot."

"And when it tells us? Then we're just godfood."

Ask it that question, Shriek said. She gave the Oracle a long, considering look. *I will stop the Oracle.*

Annabelle pointed to the sarcophagi. "Want to bet there's more dead giants in those? Dead giants that can move? I'll bet these are the Lords of Thunder."

Ask the question, Shriek repeated firmly.

Annabelle drew a deep breath. "Sure," she said. "Fine. I mean, what've we got to lose, right?"

Just everything, she thought as she led the way back to the dais on which the Oracle lay.

The immense head turned toward them as they approached. "PILGRIMS," it said. "WHAT WOULD YOU ASK OF ME?"

Me, me, me. . . .

The weight of its gaze made Annabelle's legs feel all watery again. She cleared her throat.

"Uh, we want to know where we can find Neville Folliot," she said.

"WHICH NEVILLE FOLLIOT?" the Oracle replied.

Ot, ot, ot. . . .

Annabelle and her companions exchanged puzzled looks.

"What do you mean which?" Annabelle finally asked.

"THERE IS MORE THAN ONE."

One, one, one. . . .

Wasn't that just perfect? Annabelle thought. Bad enough just trying to track down one of Clive's twins. Now they find out that the bugger's gone and cloned himself.

"The real one," she said.

▪ Twenty-Nine ▪

"Do you know how we may exit from this place?" Clive asked Howlett.

"Well, now." Howlett pointed to the left. "That's the direction that they brought you from. And that—" he pointed the opposite way "—is the direction they took your brother."

"Then that is the way we will go," Clive said.

He led off, Smythe beside him, letting the others follow as they would.

"This time we'll have him," Clive said. "He only has an hour or so lead on us. I can almost taste his presence."

"I'd be happier with a weapon in my hand," Smythe said, "for when we flush our captors."

"I'll be happy just to have a grip on Neville's throat."

Smythe nodded. "The humbugger's led us by the nose, all right."

"And do you know what?" Clive said, glancing at his companion. "What will you wager he'll have some convincing tale to make good all he's put us through?"

"If it *was* him," Smythe said. "You heard what Guafe said about these clones."

"Oh, I'll know my brother—don't you worry about that, Horace."

But then he thought about the pretender in Dramaran and Howlett, and how difficult it had been for him to accept that they were not one and the same. Could the replicas be so exact that they *couldn't* be told apart?

"These replicas," he asked Guafe, looking over his

shoulder. "Do they all carry the same memories, as well?"

"Unlikely."

"There," Clive said. "You see, Horace? All we'll need to do is put a question or two to our man when we have him, and we'll know soon enough whether or not he's a replica."

They came to a branch in the corridor and paused. Down the one that led to the right they could see more jail cells, which appeared empty from the perspective they had of them. Down the other there was a long expanse of empty hallway, but near its end they spied a number of doors leading off.

"What do you say, Edgar?" Clive asked.

Howlett shrugged. "Your guess is as good as mine."

"Then we'll take the left," Clive said.

They made a grim company as they strode down the hall. Lies and trickery had been all they had met since first entering the Dungeon, and they were all weary to death of being played the fool.

"It's like Chinese boxes," was how Smythe put it, describing the various levels. "Every time we think the end's in sight, there's another box to open, another puzzle lying in the way."

Well, no more, Clive thought. A man could brook only so much of it. It was time to stand up like a good Englishman and be counted, and by God, he meant to do just that.

When they reached the first closed door, they paused again. Smythe took hold of its knob. At a nod from Clive, he cautiously tested it, then turned it sharply and flung the door open. Clive darted in, with Guafe and Finnbogg on his heels. Howlett remained behind in the hallway.

There was another mechanical man sitting behind a desk in the room. He looked up, startled at their sudden entrance, then reached for one of the black boxes with which Hare had incapacitated them earlier. Clive didn't give him the time to use it.

He crossed the room, one hand closing on the man's

fist, the other sweeping the box to the floor. Before the man could break free, Guafe was there, lending Clive his strength. At the pressure of the cyborg's grip on his arm, all the fight went out of their captive.

He spoke rapidly in an unfamiliar language.

"Speak the Queen's English," Clive told him, "or shut your gob."

"Please," the man said quickly, switching to English. "Don't hurt me."

"Brave lot once they lose the upper hand, aren't they?" Clive said, to no one in particular.

Their captive quivered.

"Hold him, would you, Chang, while we search him for weapons."

Though how they were supposed to recognize a weapon in this place was beyond Clive at that moment. With boxes that sent out an invisible ray to steal a man's strength, who knew what else they might have?

They emptied everything out of their captive's pockets and spread it out on the desk, then bound him to his chair. Guafe fetched the black box from where it had fallen.

"Primitive," he remarked, studying it. "But effective."

"Was it damaged?" Smythe asked.

The cyborg pointed it at their captive and thumbed the control. The man went inmobile. When Guafe thumbed the control again, he slumped in his bonds.

"It appears not," Guafe said.

"Look," Finnbogg called.

From a closet he was pulling various bits of gear—things that had obviously been taken from the Tawnians' prisoners, for Smythe recognized his own knife near the top of the pile. Clive smiled when the dwarf held up a saber in a plain leather scabbard. He took it and belted it on.

"That feels better," he said.

He drew out the blade and tested its balance. It was a beautifully crafted weapon, without a blemish in the metal. The balance was perfect.

By now Howlett had entered the room and was bent

down beside Finnbogg at the door to the closet. When he stood, he held a modernistic-looking pistol in his hand.

"Now, this is more like it," he said.

"What is it?" Smythe asked.

"This, my friend, is a Smith & Wesson .44 Magnum, one of the world's most powerful handguns, as Dirty Harry'd say."

"And who is he?"

Howlett gave him an odd look. "I forgot. You guys don't know anything about my time. Harry's just a damn straight shooter—played by an actor named Eastwood."

"I . . . see," Smythe said.

Shrugging, Howlett cracked open the magnum's cylinder. He shook out its bullets into the palm of his hand.

"Damn," he muttered, discarding the empty shells. "Only three shots. Do you see any ammo in there, Finn?"

"Finnbogg find this."

He stood back from the closet with a deadly looking mace in his hands, the head spiked with steel flanges, and gave it a couple of short practice swings. As Guafe and Smythe rooted around among the gear for weapons for themselves, Clive returned his attention to their captive.

"What's your name?" he asked.

"M-merdor—if it pleases you."

"Nothing about this place pleases me. What are your duties here?"

"I keep the records of the . . . prisoners," Merdor said. His brow was beaded with sweat.

"And?"

"And catalogue the gear we take from them. That's all—I swear! I have nothing to do with deciding who fuels the lords and who does not."

"Your records," Clive asked. "Are they current?"

"Oh, yes, sir. Completely current."

"Then, show me what you have concerning one Sir Neville Folliot."

"Folliot? He was just released, not an hour ago. The records have already been transferred upstairs."

"And what has become of him?"

"I . . . I'm not really sure," Merdor replied. "I assume he's been set free to go upon his way."

"Damn you!" Clive cried. "Tell me where I can find him."

"But, I don't know—I swear I don't."

Smythe appeared at Clive's side, buckling another saber to his own belt.

"What about the next level?" he asked. "Where is the nearest gateway?"

Merdor blinked. "In the Hall of the Lords of Thunder—where the Oracle sleeps."

"What exactly are these Lords of Thunder?" Guafe asked.

Now Merdor seemed astonished. "They rule this level," he said after a few moments. "They always have, always will."

"Until this Madonna puts the blade to them," Smythe said.

"You would know that better than I," Merdor replied. He sat as straight in his chair as his bonds would let him. "You are her assassins, not I."

"We are not assassins," Clive began, but then thought, Why bother trying to explain? "What is the quickest route to this hall you spoke of?"

Merdor told them without hesitation.

"He seems very pleased with himself," Smythe said. "Perhaps we should take him with us to defuse any . . . surprises that might await us."

"Please—no."

Smythe grinned. "Ah-ha! What did I tell you?"

"It's not that," Merdor said. "I swear you'll have no trouble reaching the hall. It's only when you're inside. . . ."

"Yes?" Clive prompted him.

"Well, it's the lords. They won't be pleased. And what displeases them, they use for fuel."

"You mean eat, don't you?" Howlett said.

Merdor hesitated.

"Speak up, man," Smythe told him.

"Well, in a manner of speaking," Merdor said. "Yes. The Lords do convert the living into fuel for their bodies."

Smythe glanced at Clive, who gave him a nod. Smythe quickly cut their prisoner free, then retied his arms behind his back.

"Lead on," he said.

"Please," Merdor said. "The Lords see no difference between the prisoners we bring them and ourselves. If you want to throw your lives away, I won't stop you—obviously, I *can't* stop you—but but why drag me in with you?"

"Curiosity," Clive said. "We want to see exactly how the Lords 'convert' a man into fuel. Naturally, we're not interested enough in the experiment to use one of our own party for it."

Smythe could feel the man tremble under his hand as he shoved Merdor toward the door. They made him take the lead, Clive and Smythe walking directly behind him. Howlett came next, the magnum thrust into his belt. There had been no extra ammunition for it. Guafe and Finnbogg brought up the rear.

Clive paid attention to the route they took, matching it in his mind with what their captive had told them. So far, there had been no discrepancies. Perhaps Merdor had been telling the truth. But what about this hall where his brother had gone? Would Neville survive his encounter with the Lords? Had he already vanished once more, into the next level?

The sense of time in the Dungeon was obviously very much askew. For Neville, or even his replicas, to have spent anywhere up to five years in places, it seemed that time worked at varying rates for each being trapped in it. One could arrive at the same time as one's companions, become separated, and then a year might pass for you, while only a day or so for them before you met again.

It made no logical sense. But, then again, as they were all so fond of telling each other, nothing here made logical sense.

But there had to be some connecting thread—some reason for it all—no matter how alien it might seem to them. Clive couldn't shake the sense that they had all been specifically chosen to come here—at least all save for Horace, Sidi, and himself, who had merely blundered in while searching for Neville. What was it that connected his brother with Guafe and Shriek and a Portuguese pirate? With Clive's own descendant, Annabelle?

Thinking of her again awoke a pang of sorrow in Clive. He should never have let her—

"My God!" Smythe cried suddenly. "It's him!"

They had come to another branching of the corridors. Down the length of one that led to the left was a small group of Tawnians, with the unmistakable figure of his twin standing among them. One of the Tawnians began to level his black box at them, but Howlett was suddenly pushing between Clive and Smythe.

"Get out of the way!" he shouted.

He had the magnum in his hand, the weapon leveled, left hand gripping his right wrist to absorb the handgun's recoil. When he fired, Clive was sure that his eardrums were going to explode, the sound of the weapon was so loud in the confined space of the corridor. Long after the shot, his ears were still ringing. But down the hall, he saw the Tawnian with the black box lifted from his feet as though a puppeteer had jerked his strings. The Tawnian was flung back against a wall, where he slid to the floor, leaving a red smear on the surface of the wall behind him.

"Don't even think of it," Howlett cried as another of the Tawnians reached for his own black box. "Christ, I've always wanted to use a line like that," he told Clive out of the corner of his mouth.

His gaze never left the group. Besides Clive's brother, there were three other Tawnians, each of them like their earlier captors—part man, part machine. They stood frozen, their gazes shifting from the weapon in Howlett's hand to what it had done to their conpanion. The shock was plain in their features.

With Howlett leading, the party moved down to join
the Tawnians. Clive's gaze was riveted to his brother's
features, searching each line for its familiarity. There
could be no mistaking Neville. This was no replica. He
had the stance, the cocky set of Neville's head, the
amused look in his eye.

"Well, little brother," Neville said. "For once, you've
arrived in time to rescue *me*."

Clive's ears still rang from the handgun's blast, but not
so much as they had earlier. He could hear again—
enough to know that the man standing before him even
had Neville's sardonic manner of speech.

"Careful now," Smythe said softly at Clive's side.

Clive nodded. He would be careful.

"What?" Neville asked. "Nothing to say?"

Easy now, Clive told himself. Don't let him goad you.

Oddly enough, having finally caught up with his twin,
he felt strangely let down. The anger that had been
brewing inside him like a hot fire was gone. He felt
curiously flat—devoid of emotion.

"Disarm them," he said.

His companions approached the Tawnians, careful to
make sure that they never stepped between Howlett and
the weapon he kept leveled at the three that were still
alive. The Tawnians submitted to the search, but when
Guafe approached Neville, Clive's twin stepped back,
clapping a hand to the hilt of the saber buckled at his
belt.

"I think not," he said.

Howlett's weapon moved to cover him, but Clive
stepped in the way to face his brother.

"What was the name of Nanny's lapdog?" he asked.

"What?"

"You heard me."

"For God's sake, Clive. We don't have time for games."

"If you're truly my brother, you'll know the answer."

"Clive, *what* are you driving at?"

He doesn't know the answer, Clive thought. God help
us, he's so much like Neville he could be his identical
twin—more so than I.

"The game's up," Clive told him. "Whoever you are, or think you are, you are not Neville Folliot."

The replica took a few quick steps back, drawing his saber as he did so. But by the time he had it free of its scabbard, Clive's own blade was naked in his hand.

"Get out of the way," Howlett said.

He moved forward again, trying to get a clear shot, but Smythe pulled him back.

"All of you—keep out of this," Clive said, never taking his gaze from the replica's eyes.

▪ Thirty ▪

The Oracle gave a smile at Annabelle's question, thin-lipped and humorless.

"THE REAL NEVILLE FOLLIOT?" it asked.

Ot, ot, ot. . . .

"THAT IS CHILD'S PLAY."

Play, play, play. . . .

"I EXPECTED BETTER OF YOU."

You, you, you. . . .

As the Oracle arose slowly from its supine position, Annabelle and her companions stepped back from the stone slab once more. The babbling echoes that followed its voice rang back and forth in the room, growing in volume rather than fading. There was a ringing in their ears, and the surface of the floor seemed to tremble underfoot.

Sitting up on the slab, the Oracle towered over them. It lifted an enormous, corpse-pale arm and pointed to the nearest of the sarcophagi.

"THERE IS THE ONE YOU SEEK."

Seek, seek, seek. . . .

"A LORD'S FRESH MEAT."

Meat, meat, meat. . . .

The echoes rebounded until Annabelle had to put her hands over her ears. Lords of Thunder, she thought. They call them that because of their big mouths. But then the moment of black humor drained from her.

The lid of the sarcophagus that the Oracle had indicated was slowly opening, with a rumble of grinding stone. Standing upright inside it was a twin to the enormous shape of the Oracle—just as huge, its skin just as alabaster, its clothing a similar heavy metal punk cut. But the monster wasn't alone in its crypt. Hanging from it was a human figure, dangling from its chest like a marionette with its strings cut. From out of the Lord's mouth a number of tubes protruded that were attached to the man's back.

The Lord was feeding on him.

"N-Neville . . . ?" Annabelle asked, her voice breaking.

She wanted to throw up.

"A SMALL, MOVABLE FEAST," the Oracle said.

East, east, east. . . .

"BUT MY BROTHER FEEDS NOT NEARLY SO WELL AS I WILL."

Will, will, will. . . .

"FOUR CHOICE MORSELS."

Sels, sels, sels. . . .

The Oracle had stood up from its slab now, and was coming toward them. As she turned, staring up at its towering bulk, Annabelle realized how the game was set up. The Lords took turns playing the Oracle, feeding on the hapless victims when they couldn't come up with a decent question.

How in God's name were they supposed to deal with something this size?

Her daughter's features rose in her mind—that expectant look, hope and fear mingled in her eyes.

Are you coming back, mommy?

I promised, didn't I? I'll try, but Christ, Amanda. . . .

You won't forget me, will you?

No way. She was going to make it. They were all gonna make it. There wasn't a chance in hell that she was gonna let any of them end up godfood without going down fighting, first.

"Shriek!" she cried, and pointed toward the dais.

The arachnid pulled free a handful of hair spikes, whipping them at the Oracle in rapid succession, but they didn't slow the monster down at all. So she charged the Oracle, Sidi at her side, as Annabelle ran for the open sarcophagus. With Tomàs's help she pulled the limp form of Neville from the Lord's chest. The tubes made suckerlike popping sounds as they pulled free, leaving ugly, round red welts on Neville's pale skin. But he was still warm to the touch. Still alive.

They dragged him back, away from the sarcophagus. As they did, the Lord's eyes flickered open, the cold iron of its gaze fastening on them. For one long moment Annabelle froze in place.

"YOU DARE?" the monster roared.

Dare, dare, dare. . . .

Maybe she was crazy, Annabelle thought, but yeah, she dared.

She shook her head fiercely and fell back to dragging Neville beyond the monster's grip once more, a new strength fueling her. Tomàs hesitated at her side as the Lord swallowed its feeding tubes and then stepped forth.

On the dais, Shriek barreled into the Oracle, hitting one of its legs with her full weight and alien strength. The monster tottered, started to regain its balance, but then Sidi struck it across the back of the knee on the same leg. The leg gave out, and the two of them hopped out of the way as the creature came crashing down.

One arm batted out, striking Sidi a glancing blow that sent him skidding across the chamber's floor. Shriek lunged for its head, lower arms grabbing hold of its neck, upper ones aiming blows at its eyes. But no sooner had she grabbed hold of the monster than its huge hands gripped her, and feeding tubes came snaking out its mouth to attach themselves to Shriek's torso.

The alien cried out with shock at the pain.

Annabelle turned at the cry. She saw Shriek raining blows on the Oracle, but to no avail. It merely gripped her closer, more feeding tubes coming from its mouth to fasten onto her.

Oh, Jesus. She didn't know what to do—help Neville or Shriek?

There was really no choice. Shriek was her friend. All she knew about Neville was that he'd been leading her on a goose chase ever since she'd first joined up with his twin.

But as she started to drop Neville's arm, she saw Sidi gather himself up from where he'd fallen and charge the Oracle again. The fallen giant swept out his arm, but Sidi jumped nimbly above it and darted forward. He hammered the Oracle straight in its open eye with a fist.

The Oracle bellowed, and the floor literally shook underfoot. It made a grab for Sidi, but the little Indian slid past the Oracle's grasping fingers. He caught hold of two feeding tubes and ripped them from Shriek's back, continuing to pull on them until he had torn them from the Oracle's mouth. The Oracle's cry of pain was now a wet gurgle as blood bubbled up through its lips.

Annabelle concentrated on her own troubles then. She and Tomàs dragged Neville to the center of the room, but the Lord was out of its sarcophagus now and advancing upon them. Annabelle took a stance between Neville and the Lord.

What do I do?

Then she had it. They'd split up, she and Tomàs. Whoever the Lord went after, the other'd move in and try to take it down the way Sidi had, hitting it behind the knee.

She started to turn to Tomàs to tell him, but the Portuguese suddenly pushed her directly into the approaching giant's path and bolted for the elevator doors. Trying to regain her balance, she fell to the floor, using her arms to break her fall.

"You bastard!" Annabelle screamed at Tomàs.

She scrambled to her feet, the monster towering over her, and bolted to one side. The Lord dropped to its knees and swung a meaty fist in her direction. She tried to copy Sidi's move, but she didn't leap high enough, and the monster's arm swept her legs from under her. All that kept her from cracking her head on the floor was the fact that she fell backward, against the Lord's arm. It reached for her with its other hand.

On the dais, Sidi hauled on two more of the tubes, and by then, Shriek was recovered enough to lend her own strength to the task. The Oracle batted at them, but this time Shriek grabbed the large arm with all four hands. Muscles straining, she snapped the bones of his forearm in two.

At the elevator, Tomàs was hammering on the metal door. That sent up echoes that mixed with the general cacophony of the monsters' bellows, creating a kind of thunder that rang against the cathedral ceiling.

Annabelle dodged the Lord's hand. Using the arm she'd fallen on as though it were a pommel horse, she vaulted over it and took to her heels. But the leg she'd hurt previously buckled under her, and she wasn't quick enough to recover.

This time, the Lord's meaty fist ranged out and snagged her. It drew her toward it, the feeding tubes already snaking out of its mouth. Annabelle struggled in its grip, but it held her tight as a vise, its fingers squeezing the strength out of her.

The first tube slapped against her neck, and the end attached to her skin with a wet, sucking sound.

On the dais, Shriek had a grip on the Oracle's other arm. As it tried to bat her with its head, Sidi launched himself forward, delivering a kick directly under its unhurt eye with such strength that it popped the eye from its socket.

The Oracle screamed. It tried to reach for its eye, but Shriek had too strong a grip on its arm now. She broke that one as well. As the Oracle collapsed on the floor, she and Sidi each grabbed it by an ear and smashed its head against the corner of the stone slab that it had first been lying on.

Once, twice, they battered it against the corner, and then the skull cracked. The Oracle began to convulse, and they both jumped free from the wild jerking of its limbs, running to Annabelle's aid.

Sidi grabbed the feeding tube attached to her neck and ripped it free. As more of the tubes came at the Indian, Shriek got a grip on the Lord's leg with all four arms and toppled him over. The monster fell on its back, Annabelle's weight on its chest. Without its hands free to break its fall, the back of the Lord's head hit the floor with a sharp cracking sound. And then it lay still.

Silence fell across the vast chamber.

Shriek pulled Annabelle free from the monster's chest and helped her stand.

"Oh Jesus, oh Jesus," Annabelle was muttering.

"Everything's fine now, Annabelle," Sidi said.

He stroked her hair as Shriek lowered her to the floor.

"Th-that thing . . . was sucking on me. . . ."

"It's dead now," Sidi told her. "That's all that matters."

Slowly, Annabelle sat up.

Dead.

She looked at the Lord lying stretched out on the floor, then up to the dais, where the Oracle now lay still as well.

They were really dead.

"Christ, we did it," she said.

Sidi nodded and gave her a weary smile. Annabelle's gaze traveled to the far side of the room, where Tomàs was standing very still now, his back against the elevator doors.

"You bastard," she told him. "I'm gonna rip your lungs out and. . . ."

But she didn't finish. Her heart wasn't in it. Scared as she'd been, she found it hard not to understand the Portuguese's panic. So he was a coward. Big deal. Well, so was she. She just hadn't been lucky enough to get free, that was all. And it wasn't like they hadn't already known that he was a weasel, the weasel.

I will kill Tomàs, Shriek said matter-of-factly. Her multiple eyes flashed dangerously as they gazed at him.

Annabelle shook her head. He wasn't worth it.

"No," she said. "Leave him alone."

Slowly, with Sidi's help, she got to her feet.

"What's the story with Neville?" she asked. "Is he still alive?"

Leaning on Sidi's shoulder, she hobbled over to where Clive's twin lay. When she knelt beside him and turned him over, she flinched. There were little round welts all over his skin.

"Jesus, what were they taking outta him, anyway?"

"His life force."

Annabelle started to feel sick all over again.

"I wonder how long they had him in there?"

She reached out a hand to touch Neville's pale cheek, and started when he stirred. His eyelid flickered, and suddenly he was looking a her—right at her—but it was obvious that he wasn't seeing her.

Weakly, he tried to push her away.

"It's okay," she said. "We killed the bugger that had you."

Slowly, his gaze focused on her.

"W-who are you . . . ?"

"Friends of your brother's."

"Clive? He . . . he's here?"

Ah, shit, Annabelle thought. So what do I tell him? We split up, and your brother's probably dead?

"Sort of," she said. "We kinda went our own way a few days ago. Listen, we need some information—like, what the hell's going on around here, anyway? What's with the journal? What's with the mind games you've been playing on our heads?"

"The journal? You found that?"

"Clive did," she said. "And lost it somewhere, and now I've got it. Which gives me the bad feeling that he's dead."

Neville shook his head slowly, wincing at the pain the movement caused him.

"Hey, take it easy," Annabelle told him.

"Clive . . . can't be dead. I would know if he . . . were. . . ."

Right. The bond between twins, and all that stuff. All wired up to a human vacuum cleaner that was sucking up his blood, he was really gonna have had time for that kind of thing.

"Right now," she said, "all we want to know is, how do we get outta this place?"

Neville closed his eyes and lay still.

"Don't fade on me now, Neville." She shook him lightly. "Neville? Damn! He checked out on us."

Sidi leaned closer. "Is he dead?" he asked.

Annabelle shook her head. "He might as well be, for all the good he's gonna do us, but naw, he's just passed out again." She looked from Sidi to Shriek. "So, what are we gonna do?"

At the sound of a step on the floor, she glanced over to see Tomàs nervously approaching them.

"I have been *muito estúpido*," he said. A weak, hopeful smile touched his lips. "I am . . . there was such a fear on me. . . ."

Annabelle nodded. "You panicked," she said. "Plain and simple. It happens."

"I don't see how you can be so forgiving," Sidi said.

He glared at the Portuguese. The look in his eyes was fierce, though not so fierce as Shriek's.

"We're all in this together," Annabelle said. "Don't ask me why I'm not pissed. I mean, I'm the one he left in the lurch, right? But I don't think he was being mean-minded. He just freaked, okay? Like I did when we stepped through that last gateway, and couldn't take the bridge. So let's just drop it."

"*Madre de Dios*," Tomàs said. "I will honor you forever. . . ."

Annabelle waved him quiet. "Give it a rest, would you? I already said it's okay. What we've gotta do now is stop farting around and. . . ."

Her voice trailed off as a rumbling sound filled the vast room. Knowing what she was going to see, not wanting to look, but unable to stop herself, she turned her gaze to the sarcophagi that lined two walls of the chamber. One by one the lids were sliding open to reveal more Lords of Thunder. At least twenty of them. Stirring. Eyes opening, cold gazes fixing on them.

"Oh, shit," Annabelle said.

· Thirty-one ·

He would have satisfaction, Clive thought as he faced the replica of his twin. There had been enough—too much, by God—dilly-dallying about as they were led from one disaster into another, always following the nebulous trail of his brother Neville. He had a grudge to settle with both his twin and whoever was behind this Dungeon. And while the man who stood before him now might not be Neville, nor even one of those responsible for the rule of this damned place, he was still here, close at hand, and Clive meant to have that satisfaction from him.

The saber was a comfortable weight in his hand and he had no doubts as to his own skill with the blade—unfamiliar though this particular weapon might be to his hand. As for the replica, if he followed Neville's lead, he would be relying more on strength and daring in his swordplay than finesse. The latter had always been Clive's particular forte.

The replica looked across his blade at Clive. A sardonic smile touched the corner of his lips.

"What?" he said softly. "Taking up arms against your own brother?"

"You are not my brother," Clive said. "It's that simple."

"I say I am! You are wasting our time."

"On the contrary, it is you who wastes our time."

"You know nothing about this place."

"Exactly," Clive agreed. "Yet I do know that I want satisfaction, and I'll take it out of your hide."

"The Good Lord frowns on fratricide," the replica said.

Clive knew what he was trying to do. If the replica could keep even a bare rumor alive in Clive's mind that this was his own twin with which he would be dueling, that vague indecision would work against him. Not much, but enough to throw off his timing. And against the replica's superior strength, that could be crucial.

"I don't doubt that He also frowns on the replicas that men make of His own creations," Clive said.

"I am not a replica."

"Then answer my question."

"Your question insults me."

Clive shrugged. "Then, have at you!"

He stepped forward, left hand on his hip, blade licking out. The two sabers met with a clash of metal that rang in the hallway. Sparks leapt at the impact. Parrying and thrusting, Clive forced his opponent to back down the hall.

The replica met his every blow with the perfect parry, but such was the impetus of Clive's attack that it allowed the replica no opportunity to mount his own offensive. He was forced to retreat, continually kept on the defensive.

Clive's companions and the captive Tawnians were behind him, so that when he heard a sudden uproar to his rear, he was well-tempted to turn to see what was up, but he knew the replica was waiting for just such a foolish move. So he kept his gaze on his opponent, forcing him into the wider breadth of a joining of corridors. He flinched when he heard the thunderous boom of Howlett's handgun resounding through the hall, but he never turned.

God help them, Clive worried. Now what? But he had no time to think of it.

This crossroads of corridors had given them more room to maneuver, and now the replica took the lead, mounting his own offensive. He feinted, blade darting in toward Clive's left flank. As Clive brought his blade around to block the strike, the replica abruptly changed the line of his attack.

Clive was already committed to his defensive action. He brought his own blade up, enough to catch the main force of the replica's blow in a shower of sparks, but too late to stop his opponent's saber from nicking his shoulder.

"First blood!" the replica cried.

There was a moment's lull during which Clive conserved his energy and said not a word. The wound was nothing. It had missed the muscle, but it was bleeding. Left alone too long, it would weaken him. This had to be finished quickly.

He listened for sound from the corridor that he and his opponent had so recently quit, but the uproar had died down. There was no sound from his companions.

Had the Tawnians overcome them with another of their futuristic devices?

There was no time to turn, no time to think of anything but the battle at hand as the replica got his second wind and launched a new flurry of strikes. Now it was Clive who was put on the defensive, forced to retreat until his back was up against a wall. Their sabers met with a clang, the two blades locking, and suddenly the replica was pushing the false edge of Clive's own blade back against his face.

The replica had the superior strength—as Neville had always had.

"Weakening, little brother?" the replica asked.

"Damn you," Clive muttered as he strained to break the deadlock.

Through sheer force of will, he managed to put a halt to the replica's pressure. Sweat beaded both their brows. The replica's face was so close to Clive's that Clive could see every pore in replica's skin. The resemblance to Neville was frightening, it was that uncanny. It was as though he actually fought Neville—Neville, who invariably beat him, no matter what the game, except perhaps for chess.

But this wasn't chess now. No black and white pieces to

be moved on the board. It wasn't a game—it was life or death. Clive could see that plainly in . . . the replica's—his brother's?—eyes.

Suddenly, the replica brought up his knee toward Clive's groin. A true swordsman's sixth sense had warned Clive, however, and he turned just enough to catch the blow on his thigh. Clive's anger at the low blow was enough to fuel him with the strength to slip free of the deadlock. He faced the replica, features flushed.

"Always the gentleman, are you?" he said, forgetting in the heat of the moment that it wasn't his brother that he fought here.

He saw only Neville standing there.

"There are no gentlemen in this place," the replica replied. "There is only winning or losing—nothing else."

The tone of his voice, the spirit of his words, was so like Neville that it left Clive thoroughly confused. God help him, what if this truly was Neville? Neville, who could be so stubborn that all you wanted to do was throttle him, and still he wouldn't change his mind. Neville, who—

The replica grinned at Clive's momentary lapse. He renewed his attack with a bewildering flurry of strokes. It was all Clive could do to parry them. But then he had an opening and he thrust. The point of his saber entered the replica's chest, directly above his heart.

The replica's eyes widened and he faltered. As he stumbled back against a wall, his body pulled free of Clive's blade. Blood flecked his lips. It oozed from the wound to spread across his shirt. Slowly he lowered his own weapon and lifted his left hand to touch the wound. He stared at the blood, then his gaze lifted to meet Clive's shocked features.

"I . . . I never thought you had it in you. . . ." the replica managed.

His saber fell from his hand and clanged to the floor. His head slumped forward and he slid to the ground. And then he was dead.

"My God!" Clive cried, dropping his own weapon. "Neville!"

He no longer knew true from false, replica from original. Not anymore. All he could see was that his brother lay here—dead by Clive's own hand.

"Neville," he said, his voice breaking.

He reached to touch the dead man's cheek, but suddenly Smythe was there at his side.

"Sah!" he cried. "We've no time."

Clive turned slowly to look at Smythe. "I killed my brother. . . ."

Smythe shook his head. "You killed a replica of him. God knows, I'm hard put to tell the difference myself, but you saw the man, sah. He couldn't answer the simple question you put to him."

"Couldn't? Or wouldn't?"

For that would be very like Neville, Clive thought. Lord help him. How could he face their father now?

Smythe laid a hand on his shoulder. "We've no time for this, sah."

Clive gave him a blank look, the shock of his deed still just settling in.

Neville dead. By his hand.

"Some more of the buggers attacked us while you were fighting," Smythe went on. "Howlett took out one and Guafe used their own stasis ray back on them, but one of them had time to fire a projectile weapon and kill Howlett."

"There's no end to the killing," Clive said dully.

"Not if we stay, there isn't."

Smythe hoisted Clive to his feet. He bent and retrieved Clive's saber, cleaning it on the replica's shirt and replacing it in Clive's scabbard. Picking up the replica's blade as well, he steered Clive toward the vehicle they had commandeered.

"There are more of the buggers coming," Smythe said. "We have to go now."

"But, Neville. . . ."

Finnbogg helped Smythe tug Clive up onto the back of the cart. Guafe was behind the wheel. As soon as the cyborg saw that they were all aboard, he started up the cart and they shot down the corridor.

"That wasn't Neville," Smythe told Clive.

"But how can we *know* that?"

"We'll find the real Neville," Smythe told him. "He's here, somewhere in this Dungeon, and we won't rest until we find him."

But Clive only shook his head. Somehow, it didn't matter. Replica or not, it was still as though he'd killed his own brother. They had had their differences, God knew, but surely he never meant Neville that much ill?

It was true that Neville had led them a merry chase through the various levels of the Dungeon, but Clive had always expected that when they finally caught up with his twin, there would be a reasonable explanation for it all. He'd be angry—who wouldn't?—but it would blow over, because they were still brothers, in the end. Twins. Surely to God that still stood for something?

But he'd killed that man wearing Neville's face so easily. And what if it *had* been Neville . . . ?

Lord, but his head hurt to think of it all.

Smythe left him sitting beside Finnbogg, the dwarf seeing to Clive's hurt shoulder, while the sergeant climbed into the seat beside Guafe.

"Do we have a destination in mind?" he asked.

"I assumed we would continue to this Oracle Chamber, as we had initially planned," the cyborg replied.

Smythe nodded. "That's logical enough. What do you think of what just happened?"

Guafe shot him a sidelong glance, the look in his metallic eyes unreadable. "What is there to think?"

"*Was* that Sir Neville?"

"I really wouldn't know," Guafe replied.

"We turn here," Smythe said as they came upon a distinctive mural that Merdor had described to them back in his office.

"I know that," Guafe replied. "Here," he added, passing over the stasis ray control device.

"What is this for?"

But then there was no need for the cyborg to explain as they rounded the corner, the cart taking it on only two wheels, and they were aimed straight for another group of Tawnians. Smythe thumbed the device's control and the Tawnians froze in place. Guafe slowed the cart down so that Smythe could lean forward and push the rigid bodies out of the way without having to plow through them.

"Handy little toy," Smythe remarked as they entered the last corridor before they would reach the elevator taking them down to the Oracle's Chamber.

"It is more than a toy," Guafe said, "but not by a great deal. Judging by its size, it can't hold enough of a charge to immobilize a truly large creature."

"Like the brontosaurs?"

Guafe nodded. "They would be entirely out of the question. Even something twice the size of a man—it would slow down more than completely immobilize."

"Then, let's pray we meet nothing larger than men."

"Prayer is only superstition," Guafe said.

Smythe shrugged. They had reached the elevator now. He got down from the cart and pushed the control button beside its closed doors. As the doors slid open, he hopped back into the cart, looking back at Clive as Guafe drove the cart inside.

"Feeling any better?" Smythe asked.

Clive nodded, but the haunted look in his eyes belied his response.

As the elevator took them down, Clive sat up straighter, preparing himself for the next disaster that the Dungeon had to throw at them.

▪ Thirty-two ▪

There were twenty-two sarcophagi in the chamber. One belonged to the slain Oracle, and it remained shut. The one from which they'd rescued Neville was also empty. That left twenty stone lids grating open. Twenty Lords of Thunder stepping out from their coffins, like the walking dead in a Romero flick.

We really don't need this shit, Annabelle thought.

"BLASPHEMERS!" one of the Lords bellowed.

Ers, ers, ers. . . .

Other Lords took up the cry, until the chamber rang with the thunder of their furious voices.

"FOR THIS YOU WILL DIE!"

Die, die, die. . . .

Oh? Annabelle thought. Like you were gonna let us go before?

Shriek ran to the slain Lord and ripped free the bandoleers around its chest. She swung the leather bands experimentally, getting a feel for them. With the sharp blades that were stitched to the leather, they would make a better weapon than her hair spikes, which had already proved ineffective.

"That's not gonna be enough!" Annabelle cried, having to shout as loud as she could to be heard over the thundering voices of the Lords.

"What else can we do?" Sidi asked.

He started for the dais to rip the Oracle's bandoleers free as well, but he was too late. Two Lords had already blocked the route. Their movement made the curtain behind the dais flutter, and Annabelle caught a glimpse of what looked like wood, before the curtain fell back to cover it.

An exit, maybe? A way out? Unfortunately, they weren't going to be able to try it, as there were now five of the Lords between the dais and themselves.

The small party retreated, Sidi and Annabelle dragging Neville's limp form with them, until they had their backs almost up against the elevator doors. There was nowhere else to go.

Tomàs, as though atoning for his earlier cowardice, took up a stance a few yards in front of Annabelle, so that the Lords would have to attack him first. Shriek swung her bandoleers, waiting for the nearest of the monsters to come in range. Sidi stood at Annabelle's side, hands clenched into fists beside either thigh.

"Well, kids," Annabelle said, swallowing dryly. "It's been real nice knowing you."

"Perhaps we can make a break for the dais," Sidi said.

"You saw it, too?" she asked. "What looked like a door?"

Sidi nodded. "Some of us might make it."

Not bloody likely, Annabelle thought. But what did they have to lose?

"Okay," she said. "You and Shriek take the right—Tomàs and I'll go left."

But then she heard the elevator doors open behind her.

"Take 'em!" she cried.

She turned to meet the new threat, then darted aside as one of the Tawnian golf carts came whipping out of the elevator. It took her a long, shocked moment to recognize the cart's riders, then she gave a whoop of delight.

"Hoo-ha! The cavalry's here. Go get 'em, boys!"

Smythe leaned forward, holding out one of the Tawnians' stasis devices. He aimed it in an arc, sweeping the room. The Lords came to abrupt halts, then slowly began to lurch forward again, moving as though they were a film in slow motion.

"I told you," Chang Guafe said to Smythe.

Annabelle could have kissed the cyborg, never mind his know-it-all attitude.

"Where is the gateway?" Smythe asked her.

"There's one in here?" she replied. When he nodded, she pointed to the dais. "Then, it's gotta be behind that curtain."

She and Sidi began to hoist Neville's body onto the cart. A very pale Clive was there, with Finnbogg to help them.

"Hey, Clive-o—how's it going?"

"Who is this?" he said as he pulled the limp body on board.

"Your brother. Who did you think? Errol Flynn?"

"He's not a replica?"

Annabelle nodded. "I get the picture. Naw, the Oracle says he's the real thing."

Clive touched the pale cheek of his twin. "Thank Christ."

"Will the rest of you get on?" Smythe shouted.

Annabelle, Tomàs, and Sidi climbed into the back. Shriek stood on the front of the cart, whirling the bandoleers as the slow-motion giants approached. By weaving back and forth through them, and thanks to the Lords' now-slowed reflexes, they reached the foot of the steps leading up the dais without anyone being hurt.

"Take the wheel," Guafe told Smythe. "You help me," he added to Shriek.

The Lords were turning, slowly, slowly, but approaching them all the same. While Smythe got the cart moving, Shriek and Guafe helped it climb the steps by pushing it along, literally lifting the vehicle at times. Annabelle jumped off at the top and ran for the curtain, ripping it aside.

There was a door there, big enough to take the cart. But the door had a padlock on it. Shriek and Guafe each took a side of the large shackle and tore it apart. They pushed open the door to reveal another corridor, ceiling lit and running off into the distance.

"Okay, kids," Annabelle cried. "Let's go for it!"

Smythe drove the cart through. Shriek and Guafe

pulled the immense door closed behind them. A cross-beam lay to one side of the corridor, and they hoisted it up, fitting it into place to bar the door from their side. They heard the slow hammer of the Lords' fists on the wood, but the door held.

"I don't believe it," Annabelle said, leaning back against the side of the cart's bed. "It's like a miracle. Not only did we all survive, but we're back together again."

"This is really my brother?" Clive said.

Annabelle nodded. She gave Smythe a questioning look. Clive looked right out of it, as far as she was concerned.

"Major Clive fought an exact replica of Sir Neville," Smythe said. "Fought and killed him. It was an . . . unsettling experience."

"I guess," Annabelle said. "I'm not feeling so settled myself."

She turned to Sidi and put her arms around him, hugging him close.

"I can't believe we made it," she said.

Sidi stroked her hair. "Only this far, Annabelle."

"Sure. Rain on my parade."

She felt a weird tension in the air then, and looked over to find Clive watching her with a pained expression. Right, she thought. Fraternizing with the hired help, and a native, to boot.

"Don't you even thinking of saying anything," she told him, holding Sidi closer.

• Thirty-three •

With all that they had just gone through—their escape, killing Neville's replica, the monstrous Lords, finding Neville—Clive's mental state was in an uproar. Seeing Annabelle embracing the Indian was just too much.

"Annabelle—" he began, but Smythe gripped his shoulder, stopping him.

It was his hurt shoulder. The pain cut through him like a piercing fire. He turned, struck numb at this further betrayal, but Smythe was already letting go of his shoulder.

"Good Lord," Smythe said. "I forgot your wound, sah."

"Damn my wound. I—"

Smythe shook his head before Clive could continue. "Be happy they're safe," he said, "and that we're all together again. Companions in a bad situation, it's true, but together."

Finnbogg nodded. "We have found your brother, if not mine," he said. "Now we have a chance to escape. Together."

Clive frowned. "But. . . ."

"What they're saying, Clive-o," Annabelle told him, "is it's none of your business what I do or anybody else does, just so long as it doesn't screw up the party's chances as a whole."

"Fighting each other is *estúpido*," Tomàs agreed.

Slowly, the red flush left Clive's features. "You're correct," he said finally. "It's none of my business."

"Besides, it's not what you think," Annabelle said.

Clive touched his brother's brow and stroked the pale skin. For all his weakend state, Neville had never looked better, so far as Clive was concerned. He looked around at his companions, letting their presence sink like a balm through his troubled heart.

"I'm sorry," he said. "Truly I am."

Annabelle disengaged her arm from around Sidi's waist and leaned forward to give Clive a kiss. "Good seeing you again, ancestor."

"It's good to see you again as well . . . all of you."

Annabelle reached out and scratched Finnbogg's head. "Even you, Finn."

"Annie not mad at Finnbogg anymore?"

"Annie not mad," she said with a sigh. "I couldn't give up a friend like you. I'm too glad to see you again."

Annabelle settled back in her seat. "All right. So let's get this show on the road. We've got places to go, people to meet, stories to tell, like—" she drew Neville's journal from the inner pocket for her jacket and handed it to Clive "—what this was doing waiting for us in Tawn."

"How did you get this?"

"Better yet, how did *you* lose it?"

As Guafe got the cart moving once more, they began to exchange their tales. It was crowded on the back of the vehicle, but with Guafe, Smythe, and Tomàs squeezed into the front, there was room for everyone.

The corridor led them on. They left behind the thunder of the Lords, still hammering on the door, and all the dangers they'd survived so far. Ahead waited the next level of the Dungeon and, when Neville woke again, finally some answers. There would be more trials, of that they were all sure, but they would at least be together to face them.

For now, that was enough.

• Selections •
From the Sketchbook
of Major Clive Folliot

The following drawings are from Major Clive Folliot's private sketchbook, which was mysteriously left on the doorstep of *The London Illustrated Recorder and Dispatch*, the newspaper that provided financing for his expedition. There was no explanation accompanying the parcel, save for an enigmatic inscription in the hand of Major Folliot himself.

Our travels have led us through yet another level of the mysterious Dungeon. As our party temporarily split, I have recorded these images from memory and from Annabelle's recollections. How strange these images must appear to you, if you see them at all!

Now Annabelle's and my party have been reunited, and my brother has been found. May we escape this prison with godspeed and return to England alive!

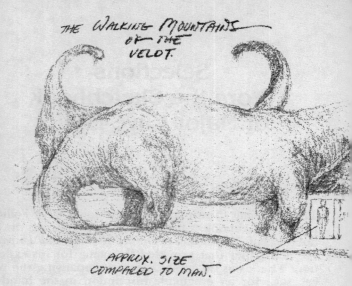

THE WALKING MOUNTAINS
OF THE
VELOT.

APPROX. SIZE
COMPARED TO MAN.

THE RUINED CITY of DRAMARAN.

WE WERE GREETED
BY THE DINOSAURS'
HERDSMEN, WHOSE
VEHICLES RODE
ON AIR.

KEOTI VECHLO -

FIRST SCOUT OF
THE DRAMARANIAN
DYNASTY AND OUR
WORTHY GUIDE.

FROM LIFE.

(FROM ANNABELLE'S DISCRIPTIONS)

A LANDSHARK PRIEST
BEARING THE SKULLS
OF THE ROGHA,
THE APE-PEOPLE.

LUKE DREW, THE NEWFOUNDLANDER, WHOM ANNABELLE'S PARTY ENCOUNTERED IN THE TREETOPS OF THE ROGHA.

BEENA - FETISH CHIEF - OF THE ROGHA WARNS ANNABELLE OF HER FATE IN THE DUNGEON.

CAVE CREATURES WE BATTLED AND
SLAUGHTERED BY THE THOUSANDS IN
THE MAZE BELOW DRAMARAN.

AS RECOUNTED BY ANNABELLE;
THE VILLAGE OF
DUAN AND THE GLOWING
STANDING
STONE.

THIS STONE
PROVED TO BE YET
ANOTHER
GATEWAY.

ONE OF THE HUGE WHITE WORMS OF THE CAVERNS. THE HYPNOTIC EFFECT OF THEIR EYES WAS EVEN MORE DANGEROUS THAN THEIR GREAT SIZE.

APPROX. SIZE COMPARED TO MAN.

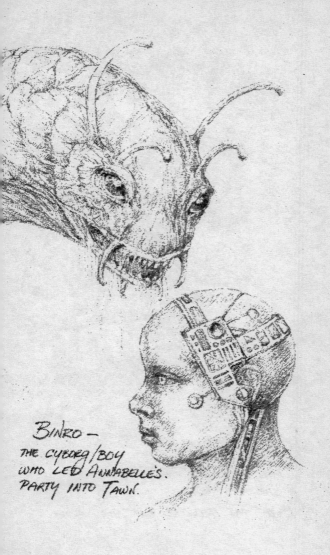

BINRO —
THE CYBORG/BOY
WHO LED ANNABELLE'S
PARTY INTO TOWN.

(FROM ANNABELLE)

THE ORACLE ON
A SARCOPHAGUS.
NOTE THE PIERCED FLESH!

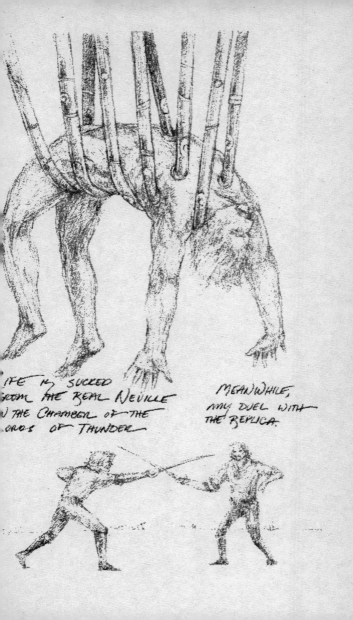

IFE IS SUCKED
FROM THE REAL NEVILLE
IN THE CHAMBER OF THE
LORDS OF THUNDER.

MEANWHILE,
MY DUEL WITH
THE REPLICA.

PHILIP JOSÉ FARMER'S
THE DUNGEON

BOOK FOUR
THE LAKE OF FIRE

ROBIN WAYNE BAILEY

T his book's dedicated with great affection to the incomparable Piranha Brothers: Bob Anesi, Vernon Nelson, Brad Strong, Brad Rainke, Rex Reeve, Steve Piland, Ellis Thigpen, David Stagg, Tom Ryan, Jonathan Nye, David Canaday, Mike Seimer, Mike Spenser, Forest Lewis, Rick Axsom, Tony Porter, David McGuire, Bryce Watterson, Pete Van Allen, Charlie Pierce, Jeff Diehl.

It's also for the incomparable spectators: Arthur Butler, Dennis Mitchell, Wayne Burge, Fred Pond, and Greg Hancks.

For Bob Johns, who provided technical assistance.

And always, for Diana.

Foreword

PHILIP JOSE FARMER

• Foreword •

First you go down. Then, you go up.

That is the opposite of what Heraclitus, the ancient Greek philosopher, said. He stated that it was a physical law that what went up had to come back down.

We know now that that is not entirely true. A rocket sent out of the solar system is not going to fall back.

Nor are the first two lines of this text entirely valid. But I am speaking of a general rule re the heroes of fiction. (By *heroes*, I also mean *heroines*.) They descend into a hell, and then, because they are fighters, they battle their way upward. This applies to both their psychic and physical struggles.

"Easy is the way down to Hell." But, oh, that way up!

So says Virgil, the ancient Roman writer (70–19 B.C.). *Facilis descensus Averni*. He was referring to the descent into the Roman underworld. Of course, he was not thinking about such an event over two thousand years later. That is, down into The Dungeonworld and the battling of a heroic band to climb out of it. At least, I do not think so. However, I would not be surprised if, in the course of the next two volumes of *The Dungeon*, our band ran into Virgil, snatched away from his sunny Mediterranean into the gloomy and peril-soaked Subterranean by its mysterious and malignant rulers. And then returned later to his own time and place. Perhaps Virgil, whose spirit was to guide Dante through Inferno, could aid our band in their search for the escape exit from the Dungeon. After all, the Dungeon, unlike Dante's underworld, does have hope for those who enter its ivory gates.

Upward go our heroes, though not only in a physical sense. In the sense of the light shed on the many enigmas and puzzles they encounter, they are also ascending. But this light brings with it more shadows. Every answer hurls more questions into their faces and strikes their hearts. Shriek, the female sentient spideroid, who is a walking pharmaceutical factory and missile launcher, is also telepathic. She detects two powerful telepathic observers of the band, though she knows neither where they are nor their identities.

I have no more idea than you or Shriek who these two are. But I suspect that one of the observers is evil; the other, good. Perhaps, they belong to two superraces not unlike the Boskonians and the Arisians. These were the supreme evil and supreme good powers, respectively, of the universe created by Doctor E. E. Smith in his Lensman series. They manipulated the lesser beings in their warfare against each other.

I could be wrong. Perhaps Richard Lupoff, who wrote the first book in *The Dungeon* series and will write the final (the sixth) will present another concept.

However it goes in succeeding books, we do know that when Clive Folliot, our main hero, enters this next level of The Dungeonworld, the diary of his twin, Neville, asks: "What will you do when you meet Hell's Sire?" Thus, Clive's destiny is to have a terrible confrontation with the prince of this underworld, in this volume or a later one. Whether or not this superformidable enemy, as powerful and malicious as Satan Himself, will be a clone of the Chief (W)retch or The Original, I do not know. At this point, what with all of the many surprises that have occurred, I'm not sure of anything. It's possible that Clive Folliot himself, User Annie, Sergeant Smythe, Sidi Bombay, and Shriek (and others) are clones. Anything can happen. Unlike the Hell of Dante, The Dungeonworld is open-ended, not a closed system. But it sure as hell has a lot of negative feedback—suffering and frustrating—for our heroes.

The parallel of this underworld to Dante's is obvious. And, as I have said in previous forewords, certain parallels—not strained—exist between The Dungeonworld and the worlds of Baum and Carroll. The main characters of *The Wonderful Wizard of Oz* are searching for something they lack or believe they lack. So are our heroes. All, like Dorothy, want to get back to their homeworlds. And the appearance and then fading away of some of the people and things our heroes encounter or their dissolving into other people and things reminds me of *Alice's Adventures in Wonderland* and *Through the Looking Glass*.

One of the major differences between our heroes and Baum's and Carroll's is that the latter do not bleed, sweat, fart, or suffer intensely. They also do not think about carnal lusts, sex, sexism, and racism. These elements are not necessary for their works and would ruin them if they were in them. But this is 1988, and *The Dungeon*, though fictional, is in "real" time.

"Real" time is a wearing down of things living and nonliving. An erosion, in short, like winds or waves grinding away rocks. This temporal erosion confuses and deceives us. If it were not for time, we would be fully aware of that unerodable part of us, that which exists after time has ceased to exist. We are incessantly bombarded by X rays and other radiation, pierced by neutrinos, and bent by gravitons. But the chronons, those wave-particles of time that surround and infiltrate us, most injure us. Chronons blanket with darkness that mental-spiritual light in us that does not know time.

The real essence of time is the never-ending smash of chronons. Helplessly, we are hurled along a path that would not exist if we could live within that glowing ball of timelessness that all of us have within us but of which we are either completely unaware or dimly aware.

Time was invented by The Devil, Some Thing, anyway, and this invention prevents us from knowing and using our timelessness. So, we erode—in this world.

Nevertheless, the timeless *Alice* books have enormously affected the fiction of our fake-real time world. This is not just because the more perceptive readers of them have a hemi-semi-demi-awareness of the timelessness embedded in the books. There is also the adventure, the like of which we did not have before Carroll wrote about it. There are his wild and distinctively individual characters. And there is the sense of Alice and all beings in the two books as pawns on a giant chessboard. That resonates with the feeling that I, and perhaps many of you, have of being pawns. (Though we are also pawns with, perhaps, free will.) Along with this goes the question of the identity and gamesmanship of the two Chess Players.

Aside from the Bible and Shakespeare's works, Carroll's *Alice* books and *The Hunting of the Snark* have inspired more references in literature and given rise to more plots and characters than any others you can name. Many mainstream, science-fiction, fantasy, and mystery books show evidence of this. There are Carrollian threads woven throughout the Dungeonworld books, some consciously put there. For instance, Clive and Neville Folliot, twins, are a sort of nonsilly Tweedledee and Tweedledum. Though, it can be said that their prejudices seem rather silly to us. Some of us. There are millions, perhaps billions, who in 1988 cherish the prudishness, racism, sexism, and superstitions of Clive and Neville. Neville may or may not be an evil twin, but Amos and Lorena Ransome, also twins, are undoubtedly evil. How could they not be, since they are so closely associated with the ironically named Philo B. Goode? Whom we may discover is the true Hell's Sire mentioned in Neville's pop-up diary. Or he may be a twin (or clone) of Hell's Sire.

Another Carrollian parallel, found in this very book, is the presence of the frogmen servants in Baron Tewkesbury's electronic gingerbread house. Remember the batrachoid

Footman who met Alice at the doorway of the Duchess's house? Bailey's Footmen, however, are tools of evil. So are the Wonderland robot characters misused by a murderess in the final book of my *Riverworld* series. Bailey must be aware of these and of the many other resonances à la Carroll in my works. Thus, writing this *Dungeon* novel in the spirit of my fiction, Bailey moves his frogmen along the chessboard derived both from Carroll and myself. But they are also moved by Bailey's own spirit and are far from being just derivative.

In the spirit of my writings, *The Dungeon* is a nexus where people and things from all times and places are collected by some unknown power for unknown reasons. But that nexus concept may have come to me (I really don't know) from the Sargasso Sea, which figured in so many pulp-magazine stories and hardcover adventure books in the late nineteenth and early twentieth century. (The last Sargasso Sea story I remember reading was a Doc Savage novel, *The Sargasso Ogre*, first printed in 1933.)

For those who have not heard of the Sargasso Sea, it does exist. It is an area of the Atlantic that encompasses the Bermuda Islands. Its surface is strewn with floating gulfweed, and it is a biological desert. The legends of early mariners related that this sea had trapped in its smooth and weed-filled waters many ships that had ventured into it. These ranged from fifteenth-century Spanish galleons to the ships then currently sailed by the storytellers. In the twentieth-century legend, the sea had also ensnared in its weeds abandoned steamers.

When I was young, the stories I read about the Sargasso Sea delighted me. I believed them. Then I found out that the stories were not true, in that this sea did not trap ships. However, this did not spoil the stories for me any more than knowing that Burroughs's Barsoom (Mars) did not exist. Not in this continuum, that is. Nor did that keep new writers from using some form of the sea in their plots. I used it myself, in *Venus on the Half-Shell*, though that sea was a nexus in outer space that attracted wrecked and abandoned spaceships.

The writers of *The Dungeon* series have been faithful to the spirit of my works in using both the pulp and classical themes used in my fiction. But I must stress that these writers have added a great deal of their own originality while paying homage to my spirit.

Our motto: Ever upward, onward, and outward!

—Philip José Farmer

• CHAPTER ONE •

Descent and Fall

Clive Folliot tried to stifle a yawn as the small horseless cart that bore his companions and him continued down the seemingly endless corridor between levels six and seven. The walls and floors were a sparkling, featureless white, as was most of the ceiling. He'd long ago given up trying to count the strange light-panels overhead, which provided an eye-aching illumination.

He longed to stretch his legs, but there was no room in the back of the tiny cart. Instead, he reached down with one hand and tried to massage away a cramp. How far to the end of this blasted passage, anyway? His stomach rumbled. *Not now,* he told it silently with no idea when he'd see his next meal.

He regarded his companions and let go a little sigh. They'd come through so much together as they'd descended the Dungeon's levels, faced one danger after another. It amazed him that they were all still alive.

He looked down at Annabelle. She slept with her head on his shoulder, her features peacefully composed. It pleased him to know that she was his great-great-granddaughter, a fact that filled him with pride. She had handled herself well through all their trials. It troubled him, though, that she reminded him so much of Miss Annabella Leighton, his mistress, whom he'd left behind in Plantagenet Court. In London. On Earth. Wherever that was.

He brushed a lock of short, dark hair from Annabelle's forehead and put on a weak smile.

Across from him, with his legs folded lotus-style, sat Sidi Bombay, the Indian guide who had been at his side even before they crossed the Shimmering Gate in Equatorial Africa. Well, his usefulness as a guide had been minimal in the Dungeon, but he had proved himself in other ways. Strange, to look now at the Indian. He had entered the Dungeon an old man, but an incident on the second level had aged him backward. Sidi was Clive's age, now, or even a little younger. And it bothered Clive that Annabelle and Sidi seemed to share a growing attraction.

Beside Sidi sat Tomàs, the Portuguese sailor from the fifteenth century. He'd drawn up his knees to make more room for the others, wrapping his arms around them. His head rested on his knees where it had been for some time, and Clive wondered if the man could possibly sleep in that position. Clive hadn't made up his mind about Tomàs, yet. He'd stuck with them and come in handy a time or two. Yet, Clive didn't particularly want the man at his back.

His former batman, Quartermaster Sergeant Horace Hamilton Smythe, sat behind the steering wheel, in one of the two front seats. The man was a rock. He'd been driving for what seemed like hours without one complaint or any indication of discomfort. Smythe had been with him through many a campaign in Her Majesty's service back on Earth, but only down here, in the terrors of the Dungeon, had Clive Folliot learned to call him friend.

He looked to the passenger beside Smythe, and his lips drew into a taut line. Chang Guafe was a cyborg, Annabelle had explained to him with her twenty-first-century knowledge. Yet, he didn't look to Clive like any of the other cyborgs he'd encountered on the Q'oonan level. Other than two arms and legs, a torso, and a head, there was nothing symmetrical about Chang's construction. He wasn't even human, but an alien from some distant planet.

Chang Guafe chose that moment to look over his shoulder, and their gazes met for just an instant. Clive found those ruby lenses that served for eyes completely unreadable, yet he waited until the cyborg looked away before giving in to a shiver.

Perched on the hood of the cart sat the strangest member of their company: Shriek, as everyone had come to call her, an evolved spider from another alien race. She had four arms and four legs and six eyes, and all the other attributes of a spider as far as anyone could tell. Oddly, Clive found that he'd developed a kind of fondness for the creature. They had touched minds in a weird sort of mental linkup and shared each other's histories and experiences, their very essences. Though undoubtedly, to his way of thinking, the most enigmatic of their company, she seemed also the most sublime, and he trusted her.

He yawned again and looked down at the bottom of the cart. Scrunched between them lay the unconscious form of his brother, Neville Folliot, whom he'd come so far and through so much to find. His twin, Clive reminded himself, though at the moment he felt nothing but a vast distance and detachment toward his brother. Oh, he'd felt bad enough, yes, when he killed a clone, thinking it was Neville. But that was then, and this was now. Neville had led them a not-so-merry chase, and when the blighter woke up, Clive intended to have some answers if it meant choking them out of his brother.

Something nudged his elbow where it rested on the side of the cart, and he heard a sniffing. Clive craned his neck around and raised an inquiring eyebrow. He'd almost forgotten Finnbogg.

"Not sleep?" Finnbogg asked softly in a gruff voice, his shaggy head bobbing up and down as he trotted alongside the cart.

"I'm okay," Clive assured him, reaching back to give Finnbogg a quick scratch between the ears.

That made Finnbogg smile. "Okay," he repeated, and then romped ahead of the cart to play scout. What there was to scout for in this featureless corridor, Clive couldn't imagine, but he watched over Smythe's shoulder as the creature ran ahead.

He smiled to himself despite his fatigue. If Shriek was an evolved spider, then Finnbogg was an evolved bulldog. Four feet of sheer canine muscle, the ferocious little being had pulled them out of more than one sticky situation. And if nothing else, he was the sense of humor the group so badly needed. Clive had long ago decided that an entire planet of Finnboggs was something he'd love the chance to see.

But he shared another bond with Finnbogg. As Clive had come to the Dungeon seeking his lost brother, so Finnbogg had come to find his missing littermate, his own brother. Clive realized with a start that he'd been fortunate in finding Neville. Finnbogg had been on the trail ten thousand years.

"Here's a piece of bad luck, Major," Quartermaster Horace Hamilton Smythe said suddenly without a trace of annoyance or panic in his voice.

"Another piece of bad luck is not what we need, Horace," Clive answered, rousing himself to see what the trouble was. As gently as he could, he eased Annabelle's head from his shoulder, inadvertently waking her in the process.

She batted her eyes, then rubbed them with one hand and tried to shield them from the overhead light. "What's wrong?" she asked, sitting straighter.

Sidi's eyes snapped opened and he regarded them placidly, not speaking, but waiting.

Clive leaned over the driver's seat and put his mouth close to Smythe's ear. He determined to remain calm whatever Smythe's news might be.

"Bad luck, he say? *Bad luck?*" That came from Tomàs in the back. So he hadn't been asleep after all, or not very deeply. "*Madre,* your man got some sense of humor."

Clive tuned out the Portuguese's grumbling.

"What is it, Horace?" Clive said quietly, peering ahead down the long corridor. He perceived no threat at all.

"Don't you feel it, sah?" Horace Hamilton Smythe said. "We're slowing down, and no matter how I step on that thing"—he pointed to a flat black pedal under his right foot—"we're not keeping speed."

Chang Guafe placed the palm of his left hand against the cart's dashboard. "Sensors reveal the power cell is depleted," the cyborg announced, his voice cold and mechanical, and to Clive's mind, chilling.

Clive pursed his lips, frowning. Damn all these mechanical contrivances. A good horse or even a mule wouldn't have let them down before the journey was over. And Annabelle had called this progress? Well, what about efficiency and reliability? He hoped they counted for something, too, in her world of the future. "Then I guess we walk," he said finally with some irritation. "And the next time we steal a cart, let's make sure we get something with four legs, too." Then he shot an embarrassed glance forward. "Oh, sorry, Shriek."

They clambered out of the cart amid a chorus of groans and joint creaks and bone pops. Clive was almost maliciously gladdened to discover he wasn't the only one who felt like a skin sock stuffed with gravel. He stretched with both arms over his head, and his vertebrae cracked into place one at a time. "A little trick I picked up while on duty in your country," he explained to Sidi Bombay when the Indian looked at him. Sidi put on a big smile and popped his back in the exact same manner.

"Enough of this exotic macho bullshit," Annabelle grumbled. "Somebody's got to carry this scrodhead, here." She pointed to the unconscious Neville Folliot.

As if his name had been spoken, Neville Folliot opened his eyes and sat up. He looked around, a big smile beaming on his face. "Are we there, yet?" he said cheerily. "I've had the nicest nap. Ready to face anything, I am!"

"Neville!" Clive shouted, turning to face his brother. A surge of relief and joy swept through him followed by a greater surge of annoyance.

"Bet this hacker's been awake the whole time," Annabelle accused, folding her arms across her chest, regarding Neville Folliot disdainfully. "Thought I felt him stir once or twice."

"*Seu irmão*—your brother—he is a big pretender," Tomàs mumbled, standing at the edge of the company apart from the rest. His dark eyes darted to each of them as if seeking approval for his contribution.

Neville Folliot nodded as he looked each of them over. "A very charming party, indeed, little brother," he said to Clive, grinning, "and very charming guests!" He brushed a finger along Annabelle's cheek, his smile widening as he looked into her eyes.

Suddenly, his hair crackled and stood straight on end, his eyes snapped wide with surprise and pain, and his entire body stiffened as he found himself flung three feet through the air. He crashed to the floor and lay there, stunned for a moment. Then, slowly he lifted his head and stared with puzzlement.

"You'll smoke a turd before you touch me again," Annabelle warned with a nasty little grin of her own as she fingered the array of small metal implants on her left forearm, the controls of her Baalbec A-9. Though the unit had numerous functions, its self-defense mode was formidable, as she had demonstrated time and again.

"You'll find your great-great-grandniece is not quite like the women you're used to," Clive Folliot told his brother with more than a fair share of smug satisfaction. In fact, Neville looked pretty good flat on his back like that, taken down a peg, as it were. And it delighted Clive that it had been Annabelle who'd done it.

Neville rose to his feet, rubbing his backside with one hand, watching Annabelle ruefully. "Grandniece, you say? From our future, then," he observed, proving he understood the nature of the Dungeon as well as any of them. "I'm not sure I like the change." Yet, he managed a wink in Annabelle's direction. "Then again, I might. Grandniece, you say? The devil take you, little brother! How about your hand, and it's good to see you, too!"

Finnbogg came bounding into their midst, alerted by the sound of the Baalbec A-9's zap. He looked at Neville and growled, rising on his hind legs. "Annie okay? Clive okay?" He growled again without taking his eyes from Neville. "Okay, okay?"

Annabelle put her hand on Finnbogg's head and scratched. "Okay, Finnbogg," she said, calming the creature. "Neville had a bug in his system, but he's user-friendly now." She gave Neville Folliot a piercing glare. "Aren't you, Uncle Neville?"

Neville made a sweeping bow. "As you say, dear lady." He turned to Clive. "Now, little brother, let's get this show back on the road, as they say, and you can make proper introductions as we go along. It'll help pass the time."

A deep crease formed between Clive's brows as he frowned. He knew that tone too well, and he didn't much like it. But Neville was right, they couldn't very well stay here. The others looked at him expectantly. At least he seemed to have their support. "Very well," he said, "let's go."

"*Ai!* Hope we find something to eat soon," Tomàs grumbled, following behind the rest. "And drink. I'm thirsty. Cart no fit place to sleep, either. Wish to get home. No place like home. . . ."

Clive tuned him out.

Clive filled in his brother, Neville, on all his adventures, beginning with the trip to Equatorial Africa, explaining how concerned their father, Baron Tewkesbury, had been for his missing son and how determined that Clive should find him. Father was fine, by the way, and codgerly as ever. He told of meeting his companions as he introduced them, and of the various races and peoples they'd encountered. The only thing he left out was his duel with Neville's clone on the level they'd just departed. He fully intended to forget that altogether.

He began to question his brother. "What is going on

here?" he said. "When Smythe and Sidi and I first got here, we found your body in a coffin. We also found a monster on a bridge with your face. We've found people impersonating you, and met a creature who—" He shut up suddenly, on the verge of mentioning the clone. "We've seen you half a dozen times around one corner or another."

"And how do you explain this?" Annabelle said suspiciously, taking Neville's diary from the inside of her jacket. "It turns up in the strangest places and says the strangest things."

"It has been a source of much trouble and misinformation," Chang Guafe agreed, his head rotating toward the book and away again.

Neville Folliot glanced back over his shoulder as he had done several times before. "I would love to answer all your questions and promise to do so at a convenient opportunity—"

"Neville!" Clive snapped, exasperated at being put off.

"Now look, scrodhead, we're tired—"

"Yes, I'm sure you are," Neville persisted as he turned to point the way they had come, "but doesn't it look to you as though the other end of this corridor is rushing at us awfully quickly?"

Annabelle gave a little scream.

"Good God!" Clive cried.

"Focusing sensors," Chang Guafe reported. "Confirming."

"*Christo!*" Tomàs turned on his heel and started to run without another word to the others.

Clive stood rooted to the spot, unable to believe what he saw even after all this time in the Dungeon. It couldn't be the same doorway they'd come through. Yet it was! The sound of huge hammering fists convinced him. It was the same door, and the Lords of Thunder battled to get through. The Lords of Thunder were still after them!

"Finnbogg, take Annabelle!" Clive shouted, taking Annabelle's hand as the beast came beside him.

"Hey, Clive-o, I can run as well as—"

"Just get on!" he snapped, practically lifting her onto

"Ooops" was the last thing Finnbogg said before he tumbled through the opening into the darkness beyond.

"Finnbogg!" Annabelle screamed, rushing to the edge. Then, she threw up her hands to protect her face, giving another cry of startlement, and nearly lost her balance.

Chang Guafe caught her around the waist and pulled her back from the brink.

Clive hurried to the doorway and stumbled back. "It's like a blast furnace!" he shouted in exasperation. He crept to the edge again, grimacing against the heat. "Finnbogg!" he called. "Finnbogg!"

Blackness and heat were all that filled the doorway, a vast yawning emptiness, frightening in its immensity.

"Sensor confusion," Chang Guafe stated.

"Great," Horace Hamilton Smythe snapped. "Finnbogg's gone, and now he's blind!"

"Not blind," Chang Guafe contradicted. "Unable to determine physical nature of environment which confronts us."

"Oh, pardon me," the quartermaster answered sarcastically.

Clive stared into level seven and beat his fist on the side of the door. "Can we survive in there?" he wondered aloud.

Something settled on his shoulder with feathery softness, and he felt Shriek's mind-touch. *Survival always possible is, Being Clive, especially with leader you.*

"I don't see that we have much choice, Englishman," Sidi Bombay said, coming to the edge.

Horace Hamilton Smythe joined them, shielding his eyes against the heat. "He's right, sah!" He jerked a thumb back over his shoulder. "It's either jump, it is, or get shot out like human cannonballs! The other end's coming fast on us!"

Clive looked back, and his eyes widened. There was no more time to hesitate. "Join hands!" he ordered. "We go, and we all go at once!"

"Well done, little brother!" Neville said, giving a small

round of applause before linking hands with Annabelle and Tomàs. Together, they crept to the brink and collectively drew a deep breath.

"Heigh-ho, Finnbogg!" Neville shouted cheerily, always trying to claim the last word. "Here we come!"

"What a jerk," Annabelle muttered.

Then, they jumped.

• CHAPTER TWO •

The Land of Darkness

How long or how far they tumbled Clive couldn't tell. He clung for dearest life to the two hands in his and hoped the others did the same. His eyes were open—at least he thought they were—but there was nothing to see, not even his companions. He listened, but there was nothing to hear. Except for the touch of the hands he held, all his senses failed him.

Suddenly there was solid ground under his feet. He couldn't say that he landed or that he hit bottom. It was just there under him. He didn't collapse from impact. There was no jolt, no shock to his knees or spine. It was as if the ground had been there all the time, and he had only just become aware of it, and considering the loss of his senses, he had to concede that, indeed, was possible.

But his eyes still refused to function. Was he blind? He squeezed the hands he held for reassurance. "Annabelle?" he called softly.

There was a pause before Annabelle returned his squeeze. "I can't see, Clive-o." She tried to sound hopeful, but a note of fear colored her voice.

"Nor I, little brother," Neville added, subdued.

Tomàs muttered under his breath, "*Ai, bento Maria!* Holy Mary!"

Clive tried to remember where the cyborg stood in their line and turned his head that way. Perhaps the cyborg's sensors would prove more reliable than human eyes. "Chang Guafe, can you see anything?"

"Negative, Clive Folliot. Visual-input systems remain inoperative. Running a complete light-spectrum scan."

Whatever that means, Clive thought to himself. Sweat began to trickle into his eyes. He tried to blink it back, then shook his head to hurl the droplets away. No use. The salt of his own perspiration stung like fire. He almost let go of Annabelle's hand, but he feared to do that. Until they knew what they were facing, he didn't want anybody to let go of anyone.

"Hold this a moment," he said to Annabelle, and he wrapped her fingers around a piece of his shirttail. Only then did he draw his sleeve across his eyes.

He took her hand again. "Now look, everybody keep hold of everybody," he said. "Don't let go, no matter what. There's got to be something down here, some clue as to which way we should go."

"But how are you going to find it in the dark, little brother?"

Clive almost snarled. He could just imagine the sneer on his twin's face. He could certainly hear it in that disparaging tone.

"I have a suggestion, sah," said Horace Hamilton Smythe, squeezing Clive's other hand.

"Yes, Smythe, speak up." Good old Smythe, he always had an idea.

"Let's lay your brother on his back, sah, give him a good spin, and go in the direction his head points when he stops."

Annabelle chuckled at that.

There was no amusement in Neville's voice, though. "I say, Smythe, you seem to have forgotten your manners, not to mention your proper station. Not good form for one of the queen's career men, I should think."

Annabelle chuckled again. "You've got a lot to learn, chipchewer. Attitudes like yours die hard, but don't make me sorry I hauled your butt out of that coffin thing back up there. Maybe I should have left you for the Lords."

Chang Guafe interrupted what Clive feared would turn into a serious argument. "Targeting," he announced suddenly. "Operational in the infrared spectrum." Twin beams of ruby light lanced outward from the cyborg's optic lenses, extending perhaps four or five feet before diffusing in the darkness. "Now indicating appropriate direction."

A chorus of grateful noises arose in response to Chang Guafe's beams. At least, that meant they weren't blind. One by one, Chang faced them, illuminating each face as he did so. Still, there was only darkness around them. They couldn't even be sure exactly what it was they stood on. The ground was just as black as everything else.

"*Obrigado, obrigado!*" Tomàs muttered, releasing his grip on Shriek long enough to cross himself. "Thank you!"

"Exactly what did you see, Chang?" Clive asked when everyone settled down again.

"A major heat source in the distance," he answered.

Annabelle interrupted. "The cause of all this heat, Tin Man? It's southern California in July down here. I'm melting!"

"Affirmative," he answered. "Also, a smaller heat source in proximity." He trained his eye beams in the proper direction. "Suggest we investigate."

"I agree," Clive said. "Let's not leave something at our backs without knowing what it is. Lead on, Chang Guafe."

"By all means, lead on," Neville chimed in.

They began to walk in a line, holding hands, stepping carefully. Their footsteps made no sound, yet the ground seemed completely solid. It was the eeriest thing Clive had yet encountered, he thought, resisting the desire to hold his hands out in front of him, fearing that any moment he might collide with something or trip on something or fall into something. Those two ruby lances of light were the only thing for the eyes to focus on, and just a bit of Chang's face where the light glinted briefly on the metal.

Clive heard a muttering. At first he thought it must be

Tomàs and more of his ever-running litany, but then he realized it was Annabelle right beside him.

"Lions, and tigers, and bears, oh, my!" she whispered. "Lions, and tigers, and bears . . ."

"What's that?" Clive said, wiggling his fingers among hers, leaning his head a bit closer to where he thought her mouth was.

"Oh, nothing," she said, sounding embarrassed, as if she hadn't realized she had been talking at all. "Just got the willies, that's all. Place gives me the creeps, Clive. It's like walking in space, only there aren't any stars."

He squeezed her hand again, then slid his palm up her arm without breaking contact between them and draped his arm around her shoulders.

"Clive?" she whispered again. "I think the Baalbec could give us a little more light."

"No," he told her firmly. "That's powered off your own body heat. It might drain you too much. We may have to risk it later, but for now we'll just follow Chang's light."

"Yes, Granddaddy," she answered meekly.

"Audio sensors receiving," Chang Guafe reported.

Clive gave a little start. The cyborg's voice just had that effect on him, especially in this infernal darkness. He drew a deep breath and determined to get his nerves under control. "What is it?" he asked. "What do you hear?"

Chang Guafe modulated his voice. "Camptown races five miles long, doodah, doodah!" he sang in a familiar manner.

"Finnbogg!" Smythe and Annabelle cried as one. "That's Finnbogg's voice!"

Indeed, moments later they all could hear the alien canine's crusty intonations roaring up from the gloom ahead, and they all joined in. "Goin' to run all night," they sang heartily with a little more bounce in their steps, "goin' to run all day!"

Only Shriek did not sing, because her vocal apparatus had such limited capability. But her thoughts brushed against Clive's mind. *What noise be this, Being Clive?* she asked curiously, amused. *Happiness, sense I do, and joy. Some ritual chant?*

Yes, Shriek, he answered gladly, *a ritual chant for the friend who was lost, then found.*

Friend? she inquired. *The Finnbogg being?*

He heard the echo of their song in Shriek's mind as she tried out the melody, struggled to make sense of it, and realized that, in her own way, she had joined in.

Finnbogg's voice stopped suddenly. "Annie!" His shout rose up out of the dark. "Smell Annie! Smell Clive! Smell Horace!" He pronounced it like "horse." He gave a long howl, then paused. "Ugh!" His voice rose again. "Smell Neville!"

"A fine thing," Neville said defensively. "After all, I taught him that song! Picked it up during a trip to America, I did."

For an instant two bright eyes gleamed at them as Chang Guafe's beams reflected on Finnbogg's face. Finnbogg threw up his hands and bounded at them. "Finnbogg friends!" he cried. "Happy reunion!" He rubbed up against Annie's leg and licked Clive's hand. Dropping the link, they clustered around the canine, everybody petting and scratching him at once, and Finnbogg preened in the sudden attention.

"Knew Finnbogg friends come!" Finnbogg said, grinning as he gratefully accepted a scratch on his left ear from Sidi Bombay. "So just sit down and sing Finnbogg! Friends hear and come. You hear Finnbogg sing? Sing good!"

"Sure, sure!" Annabelle assured him, rubbing his throat with long strokes. "Finnbogg hear Finnbogg friends sing back?"

"Ummm. Annie rub good. Annie smell good. Everybody smell good!" Finnbogg gave another long howl, and they all laughed, all but Neville and Tomàs, who stood a little apart.

"*Basta!*" Tomàs said abruptly. "Look there!"

Clive straightened. He could imagine the little Portuguese pointing, but he couldn't see the arm. He turned slowly, scanning the darkness. Far in the distance he spied an orange glow and the barest hint of what he thought were flames. The air, too, had gotten noticeably warmer.

"I've got a bad feeling about this," Annabelle said, coming to his side again.

"Chang Guafe?" Clive said over his shoulder.

"It is the major heat source I reported," the cyborg answered. "Indications are that it has just doubled in size and temperature output."

Clive turned to his brother. It galled him to have to ask Neville for advice. Neville had always lorded it over him, played the superior, and all because he'd been born a few minutes earlier, on one side of midnight, and Clive the other. But now his friends' lives might be at stake, and he swallowed his pride. "Do you know anything about this?" he asked as civilly as possible.

Chang Guafe's eyebeams happened to play over Neville's face. Of course, he wore that sarcastic smile. "No, nothing," he said. "You're now as deep into the Dungeon as I've been, so this is new for all of us, I'm afraid."

Sidi Bombay stepped between them and gave Neville a long, hard look. Then, he turned back to Clive. "Just an impulse, Englishman," he said calmly, "but check his diary. See if there's an entry."

"What diary?" Neville said with feigned exasperation. "All of you keep talking about my diary. I've never kept a diary in my life! And I've certainly been too busy down here just staying alive to start!"

Annabelle took the book from inside her jacket and passed it to Clive. "Sure, chipchewer," she said with a sneer. "Your program need another debugging?" She ran a finger over the Baalbec implants. "You know something about this place, you better upload."

Finnbogg gave a low snarl.

"Am I being threatened?" Neville said, laying a hand to his bosom in an exaggerated display of shock.

"Annabelle," Clive said. "You said the Baalbec could provide a little light. Chang's eyebeams are insufficient for reading."

Annabelle nodded. "Right up, Clive. Boy, I can't believe you came so far to find this piece of scrod!" She touched two of the implants on her forearm. An instant later she began to glow a with soft green light like a human firefly. "It's great for finding keyholes," she added with a grin. "Don't get too close, though, it still packs a zap."

Clive crept to the border of her light, opened the book, and thumbed the pages until he came to the last entry. He hesitated an instant, glanced up at his brother, then read aloud: " 'Out of the frying pan, into the fire; well done, little brother, well done. How will you feel when you meet Hell's Sire? Well done, little brother, well done.' "

" 'E's a bleedin' poet an' claims 'e don't know it!" Smythe said, putting on his best cockney.

"But I never wrote that!" Neville Folliot exclaimed in apparent indignation. "Here, let me see that bloody book!" He snatched it from Clive's hand and turned so Annabelle's light shone on the page. "Why, it's even in my hand! But I swear I never wrote this." He turned back to his brother. "Clive Folliot, you know I never. Why, I'm twice as good at poesy as the author of this bit of doggerel!"

Shriek quietly maneuvered behind the elder Folliot, and Chang Guafe moved to his right. Tomàs and Smythe stood shoulder to shoulder on Neville's left flank, looking like starved men regarding a good steak.

Sidi Bombay spoke up from the sidelines. "Actually, Major Folliot, I believe your brother, Neville."

All eyes turned toward the Indian.

"You do?" said Neville, as surprised as any of them.

Sidi Bombay folded his arms across his chest, closed his eyes, and bobbed his head up and down. He pursed his lips until they became a little brown pucker and touched them with a fingertip. "This book, which we are to assume is the diary of Neville Folliot's journeys, has turned up time and time again in places where your brother should never have been. And please to recall how every time you open it—or on some occasions, it opens itself—there is a new entry, whether or not it has left the possession of this party. Therefore, it is not reasonable to believe it is authentic."

"*Ora Bolas!*" Tomàs snapped.

"What's that?" Horace Hamilton Smythe said, raising an eyebrow.

Tomàs jerked a thumb toward Annabelle. "As she might say, 'shit of bulls'! Is his own writing, no?"

Sidi Bombay opened his eyes. "Handwriting can be duplicated. I believe this has happened. The question now becomes *who*? Who has done this, and to what purpose? Obviously, we are being led."

"Where led?" Finnbogg growled.

Neville pointed toward the fireglow in the distance. "Obviously, there. What else can it mean, 'when you meet Hell's Sire'? An invitation, if ever I heard one."

"And I know how you love parties," Clive responded caustically. "Do you think we should attend this one?"

Neville's saccharine smile returned. "Do we have any choice, little brother? That seems to be the only feature in this otherwise very dreary place. If there's a gate or doorway to the next level or to home, then it's got to be there."

Shriek's thoughts suddenly blossomed in Clive's head. *And if correct is the Bombay being, Being Clive? If led we are by secret Dungeonmasters, might they not also in strangeglowfireplace be?*

You are right, of course, Shriek, Clive conceded. Then, he said aloud, knowing Shriek would still understand, "I'm getting a little tired of being manipulated. Let's take it to them for a change."

"*Muito falar e pouca ação,*" Tomàs grumbled.

"Much talk and little action," Annabelle translated, much to the Portuguese's obvious surprise. She gave him a wink. "I'm beginning to crack your program, user."

Light from the Annabelle being dimming is, Shriek mind-whispered to Clive. The spider-alien was correct. The halo surrounding his great-great-granddaughter was only half as bright now.

"Annabelle, turn off the Baalbec," Clive instructed. "You're tiring."

"I'm all right, Clive-o," she told him, but she switched off anyway, plunging them into darkness again. "It works off my metabolic body heat, remember? The harder I work, the more heat the Baalbec has available to convert to power. Until I acclimate to this temperature, I can even use it as a siphon to delay the effects of heat stress."

Clive shook his head. "The harder you work, the harder the Baalbec works. It all adds up to a strain on your system, and that means exhaustion. We'll get by without it for now."

They had Chang Guafe's eyebeams to point the way, and the fireglow in the distance was now an easy mark to aim for. Still, Clive insisted they join hands again before they started off.

"You're turning into something of a worrier, Granddad," Annabelle said quietly, her hand in his.

"And you're using that 'granddad' business a bit liberally, aren't you?"

She nodded in Neville's direction. "A lot more aware of family relationships, lately," she confessed. "Before, we were just looking for your brother and a way out of this mess. Now, it seems there's more. Some—dare I say it?" She gave his hand a playful squeeze. "Plot?"

They continued walking. The orange glow slowly stretched out toward them across the vast dark expanse. Plainly now they could see the flames that leaped soaring and crackling into the air, searing white-hot tongues that might have licked the stars had there been any. A hot wind that stank of sulphur blew upon their faces and whipped their garments. It stung the eyes, and the humans in the company began to move in half-crouches, bent over against the scorching bluster. Even Finnbogg cowered down onto all fours. Only Shriek and Chang Guafe appeared unaffected.

Horace Hamilton Smythe stopped abruptly. "Do you hear that?" he asked.

At first, Clive thought it was singing.

"Begging the major's pardon, I don't think so, I don't," Smythe responded. They resumed their march.

It was Clive who stopped next. "What the hell is that?" he said suddenly with uncharacteristic crudeness.

"Just that, little brother," Neville answered quietly. "Hell, just as the book said."

They listened, rooted where they stood, to the terrible din that drifted to them. Lamentations and wails, cries and screams, moans and groans and shrieks: It chilled the blood in Clive's veins. Another groan sounded right beside him, and he nearly jumped out of his skin.

"You're crushing my hand!" Annabelle said, jerking free of his grip.

"Sorry," he apologized. "Guess it all got to me."

"I think it's supposed to get to you," Neville muttered. "Somebody's trying to soften us up."

"Friends of yours, maybe?" Annabelle said.

Neville didn't answer, and they started forward again.

The light from the fireglow was now bright enough for them to see easily. A huge black wall surrounded the fire, extending as far as even Chang Guafe could determine. Straight in their path lay an immense gate with double doors. The doors stood open invitingly, and through them Clive and his friends could see only fire.

As they drew closer, though, it became clearer that a path wound among the flames, a path of black-charred stone around which a pale smoke curled and eddied. Just outside the gate they stopped.

Annabelle looked up and groaned. "Oh, give me a break already!" She pointed overhead to the tall letters carved in the blocks that made the lintel. "Somebody's been working overtime at the scrodding funny farm! Is this supposed to be some kind of joke?" She whirled toward Clive, then

Neville. "I'm getting awfully goddamned tired of being fucked with, Folliot!"

Clive was unprepared for her angry explosion, but before he could say anything Tomàs fell to his knees in a heap. "*Ave Maria, cheia de graça!*" the Portuguese prayed at the top of his blubbering voice as tears streamed down his face. "*Ai, Christo, bendizo Christo!*"

Sidi Bombay ran to the little sailor's side and knelt beside him. Clive, too, went to his aid. "Get up, Tomàs, get up! It's all right. We're still all right!" He tugged on Tomàs's arm to no avail.

"*Analdiçoado!*" Tomàs screamed in terror. "Damned!"

"What a scrodhead!" Annabelle shouted, flinging up her arms. "You can't believe any of this is real. Come on!"

Clive snapped, "Annabelle, shut up!" He glanced at the Indian and whispered, "Sidi, take care of her. She's as hysterical as Tomàs."

Sidi Bombay went to Annabelle and slipped an arm around her shoulder. She shrugged him off angrily and paced off a bit, but at least she quieted.

"Tomàs," Clive continued, laying a hand atop Tomàs's head and gently rumpling his hair. "We must go on. Get hold of yourself!"

Tomàs caught Clive's hands and interlocked his fingers. "*Mi alma!*" he muttered. "My soul!" He let himself be lifted to his feet, but when he looked up, Clive thought he had never seen such pain and fear in a man's gaze before. "I'll stay beside you," Clive assured him, "right beside you."

Tomàs took a faltering step toward the gate, his entire body trembling like a leaf in the worst hurricane.

Suddenly Clive felt Shriek inside his mind. *Noting human reactions am I, Being Clive,* she said. *All right well are you?*

I'm a man of reason, Shriek, he answered with all the calm he could muster.

What, then, writing on gate that upset the Annabelle being is?

He looked up and translated for the spidery alien: "Abandon Hope All Ye Who Enter."

He glanced around for his brother. Neville stood in the gateway waiting for them, hands braced on his hips, the perfect image of the queen's military man. The fireglow even gleamed on his brass buttons. There was more than a hint of impatience in his stance as he regarded Clive's company.

"Smythe?" Clive called, looking around.

"Here, sah."

"Finnbogg?"

The alien canine turned toward him, tongue lolling. "Okay, Clive, okay, okay."

"Stay close to Annie, then," he instructed. "Keep an eye on her."

"Keep nose on her," Finnbogg assured. "Annie smell good."

He called to the last two, the strangest members of his strange troupe. Chang Guafe and Shriek both nodded and moved in closer on each of the company's flanks.

"Then let's go," Clive said, drawing a deep breath that threatened to sear his lungs. He wrapped an arm tighter about Tomàs, drawing the little man closer. "Let's go together."

• CHAPTER THREE •

Inferno

"Perhaps it's because I lost my turban." Sidi Bombay tried to inject a note of humor as they passed under the foreboding gateway. "God abhors a bare head."

The pathway was a craggy road of broken, blackened rock perhaps ten feet wide. Geysers of flames shot high on either side, spitting and leaping into the air like prominences shot from the sun. The ground itself seemed to burn with a low, blue fire that wavered hypnotically. Only the road offered safety.

Far in the distance Clive noted a feature that he quickly dubbed the Burning Mountains. Beautiful and terrible, they swelled on the far horizon, yellow and orange and red, with peaks so sharp they seemed to spear the darkness. They, too, wavered and danced with heat radiance so they were hard to look at for long.

Sweat ran down his face and neck, down his chest, making his garments sodden. He considered removing his shirt, but the skin of his face felt tight and tender already from the heat, and his hands felt as if they were slowly crisping.

"You don't seem to have much to say, Brother," he said to Neville Folliot, reflecting that his brother looked almost ridiculous in his crisp military uniform with its red coat and shoulder braids and brass buttons. He couldn't have entered the Dungeon in that outfit and must have had it made for him by the servants of the Lords of Thunder.

Neville stared straight ahead. "It is a sight that commands awe," he answered quietly. "If we get back home, little brother, I may amend my ways and return to the bosom of the church."

"Please!" Horace Hamilton Smythe interrupted. "We're going to get thirsty enough as it is. Don't make me waste what little spittle I've got left."

Neville shot the quartermaster a look of surprise, arching an eyebrow. "Smythe!" he said. "I really never knew you disliked me so!"

"Dislike you, sah?" Horace Hamilton Smythe responded with uncharacteristic bluntness. "I don't know you well enough to dislike you, having only met you a couple of times as your brother's batman. But that's enough to disapprove of you. I've been around in the queen's service, sah, and I know your reputation."

Neville Folliot looked at his brother with something of a frown, but he still addressed himself to Smythe. "Well, it's not your place, now is it, to approve or disapprove? After all, I am the Tewkesbury heir, and you? Well . . ." Neville turned up his nose and shrugged his shoulders.

"Let's move on," Clive suggested. "There's no point in lingering here." But Neville's words played over and over again in his mind. It was true, now that he'd found Neville alive, Clive had cut himself out of his inheritance. Neville had always been Father's favorite, while Father had always hated Clive, blaming him for their mother's death because he'd been the last from the womb.

Yet, even as he turned that over in his thoughts, it seemed like such a dreary old song. He just didn't care anymore. Right now he had good friends counting on him to lead them out of this mess, one of them his own great-great-granddaughter. Let Neville keep the money, and damn his father, and that was that.

Suddenly over the rush and crackle of the flames Clive heard another sound and called for a stop. He peered up, but it was hard to see. The brightness of the fires hurt his eyes, though he shielded them as best he could.

"Do you hear that, Chang Guafe?" he asked. The cyborg's sensors were far more acute than Clive's human senses.

"Affirmative," the machine man answered. "Unable to identify. Wait." He craned his neck and looked into the sky. "Something approaches from above."

They appeared right out of the flames, huge leathery batwings beating the heat currents as they soared downward toward the company and began to circle overhead. *Demons* was the only word Clive could find for the horrid monstrosities as he untangled himself from Tomàs and whipped his saber free from the scabbard.

"My God, sah!" Horace Hamilton Smythe exclaimed, taking his place at Clive's right side. His own sword was in his right hand, and in his left he carried the small stasis ray box he'd taken from the servants of the Lords of Thunder.

"Looks like we're in for a bit of a row," Neville said, stepping to Clive's left side. He brandished his own saber and gave Clive a wink.

Clive whispered to Smythe from the corner of his mouth, never taking his eyes off the winged threat above. "Give one of those to someone who doesn't have a weapon," he said. "Personally, I trust your sword arm."

"Sidi?" Smythe said without looking behind him, and he held out the stasis ray to the small Indian.

Above, one of the demons separated from the rest, folded its wings, and dropped feet first to the ground to stand before the company. Though otherwise gross in its monstrous nakedness, a hood covered its head and face.

"Welcome to Pandemonium, Clive Folliot," the creature said as it swept back the concealing garment.

"Philo B. Goode!" Clive stared at the familiar face. Despite the fangs that curled from the corners of its lips and the eyes that were slitted like a cat's, there was no mistaking the visage of the man who had tried to cheat him at cards aboard the *Empress Philippa* during the journey to Africa and whom he had seen on several occasions running loose throughout the Dungeon.

Philo B. Goode threw back his head and laughed a horrible laugh. "Ah, but down here, my good Folliot, I am known as Beelzebub!"

"The Lord of Lies!" Horace Hamilton Smythe interjected. "Hmmmph! It figures!"

Beelzebub looked down on the shorter quartermaster and smiled, showing the full razor-sharpness of his fangs. "Nice to see you, too, Sergeant Smythe. It's been a while since New Orleans, hasn't it?"

"I thought I killed you, then," Smythe said with some bitterness.

Beelzebub's smile widened until the flames reflected on the pearl whiteness of his teeth. "And so you did, and now I'm in hell. And you must join me, too, in spirit as well as in body!"

He threw back his head and gave a shrill scream as he leaped into the air, wings spreading, lifting high even as the other demons folded theirs and plummeted, screaming, down upon the company.

Clive steeled himself and thrust his sword through the chest of the nearest creature before its clawed feet ever touched the ground. Its scream took on a shriller note of terror all its own, and Clive ripped downward through its belly and jerked his blade free. Much to his relief, the creature crumpled at his feet and sprawled upon the road, bleeding a thick, black ichor.

"They can be hurt!" he shouted triumphantly. But Smythe and Neville had already learned that. The others, too, apparently. Behind him, he heard the hum of Sidi's stasis ray and saw one of the demons stop in midreach. To his surprise, it was Tomàs who gave a furious cry, leaped, and kicked the monster across the road and into one of the flaming geysers, where it sputtered and exploded. The little Portuguese stood there for a dangerous moment, shouting invectives in his native tongue.

It nearly cost him his life. A demon dropped out of the sky behind him and raised a clawed hand that might have severed Tomàs's head from his shoulders, but before the creature could strike, two of Shriek's envenomed hair-spikes suddenly sprouted from its back. It gave a hideous cry of pain and tried to reach back to pull the spikes free. It was too late. The venom did its work swiftly. The demon fell to the road, swelling and darkening as it twitched and kicked. Its flesh cracked open, and black blood oozed from its eyes and nostrils and mouth. It died horribly, but quickly.

Clive and Neville and Smythe worked as a front line, their sabers rising and falling, thrusting and cutting as the demons came at them. Overhead, the monster that called itself Beelzebub and looked like Philo B. Goode shouted curses at his minions and at Clive's company while his great beating wings kept him a safe distance away.

A loud zap behind Clive caused him to turn. *Annabelle!* he screamed inwardly, searching for her in the fray, fearing for his offspring. He should have kept a closer eye on her!

He needn't have worried. Many times she had proven herself on this journey. He watched as a demon lunged at her from the sky. She waited, waited, then at the last moment stabbed one of the implants on her forearm, and the Baalbec A-9 snapped on at full strength, stunning the monster. Finnbogg leaped on it, rending it with his own clawed hands and bared fangs. They made quite a team, Annabelle and Finnbogg. So did Tomàs and Sidi, he realized. So did Sergeant Smythe and Neville and himself.

That left Shriek, a deadly force all by herself. She didn't wait for the demons to land, but hurled her hair-spikes into the air by the handfuls, taking a devastating toll, and bodies rained about her.

And Chang Guafe. A mound of demon flesh piled at his feet. He had no weapons but his own armored strength. The creatures came at him, and their claws slid off his steel-sheathed body. He caught them in his hands and twisted their necks, stripped the wings from their backs, crushed their skulls. He moved like a juggernaut, unstoppable, like the golem of ancient Hebrew legend.

As Clive watched his friends, an angry passion surged through him. He felt stronger than he ever had, and more powerful. They had been through too much, suffered and experienced too much. And for this moment, at least, Philo B. Goode had picked the wrong time for a fight. As Annabelle had said, they were tired of being fucked with, whatever that meant.

He shook his saber at the sky. "Come on down here, Goode, or Beelzebub, or whatever you call yourself! Come down!"

The demon commander scowled and raked his claws through empty air. "You have this round, Major Folliot, you and your brother and your friends! But the minions of Hell are numberless, and the way is far to the Palace of the Morning Star! We will meet again!"

Shriek drew back to hurl a hair-spike, but before she could release it, a brown streak hurtled upward through the air, growling. Philo B. Goode gave a startled scream of his own as Finnbogg, at the apex of his leap, clamped powerful jaws shut on his ankle. The scream drew out into a long shrill note as he tried to shake the alien canine, flying high in a loop-the-loop, through a series of sharp twists and turns, and finally through the heart of a geyser of fire.

Finnbogg gave a yelp as they emerged and let go, falling ungracefully right at the edge of the road. Annabelle and Smythe ran to his side, Annabelle throwing her arms around him. "Good Finnbogg!" she cried, stroking him between the ears.

"Heh, heh, heh!" Finbogg answered with a gruff chortle. Then, "Phooey! Fly-thing not taste so good, but make a satisfactory snap, crackle, pop, in mouth!"

High in the air, Beelzebub/Goode glared down at them, cradling his broken foot. "Go, for now!" he raged. "But I have many surprises in store for you. Especially for you!"

He jabbed a long finger at Annabelle and then began to climb higher and higher into the sky until he disappeared from sight.

"And your little dog, too!" Annabelle mumbled as she scratched Finnbogg's right ear and watched Philo B. Goode depart.

"Hell hath no fury . . ." Neville started and left it there. He turned to Clive. "Well, little brother, I'm quite impressed. Quite impressed, indeed. These are some companions. I actually think we may stand a chance of finding our way home with friends such as these!"

"You handled yourself well, Neville," was all Clive said. He turned to see to his friends. All seemed well enough except, to his surprise and consternation, Chang Guafe. The cyborg was not entirely sheathed in metal, and the places where flesh was exposed were scored with seeping wounds.

"No cause for alarm," the cyborg told him as Clive examined his scratches and cuts. Some of them looked deep, and skin hung in ribbons. "Injuries well within design parameters. Damage-control systems functional and operating." Even as the others gathered around to watch, the bleeding stopped and clotted. "Antibiotics flooding system," Chang Guafe reported. "Healing in progress."

Well, that was that. "Let's get on the road, then," Clive said. "I believe I heard Goode say something about a Palace of the Morning Star and not letting us get there. That would seem to be our destination, then. Perhaps we'll find the next gate there."

"I believe you should check on Miss Annabelle, Englishman," Sidi Bombay whispered, leaning close. "She doesn't look well."

Clive felt a moment of terror grip his chest as he pushed through them. Had he missed something? Had Annabelle suffered some secret hurt and kept her mouth shut?

He found her sitting cross-legged on the side of the road with Finnbogg's head in her lap right where he had last seen her. She did look pale and as she would have said, "out of it." He touched her shoulder, then her cheek. Her skin was cool.

"Are you all right, Annabelle?" he asked.

Finnbogg rolled his huge brown eyes upward without lifting his head. "Okay, Annie?" he joined in. "Annie okay? Want Finnbogg to sing?"

Annabelle forced a smile. "That's okay, Finnbogg. I'm fine." She looked at Clive, and the smile faded. "The Baalbec," she said softly. "It took a bit out of me using it that much at that power level. I'll be fine, though. I'm just a little wobbly right now."

Clive helped her to her feet and supported her for a moment. "Finnbogg, will you carry Annie? I don't think it's wise to stop here."

Finnbogg sprang to his feet, then dropped to all fours again, and offered his back. "Happy to carry Annie. Finnbogg strong, and Annie smell nice, like littermates."

"There now, doesn't that make you feel better?" Clive said, helping Annabelle to straddle Finnbogg, making sure she could balance properly. "You smell just like his littermates."

"Want to know what you smell like, Clive-o?" she said with a gleam in her eye.

He turned back to the others and waved an arm. "Chang, can you monitor the sky with your sensors? They may try to attack us that way again."

"I am fully functional," the cyborg answered, "and monitoring."

Clive turned to Tomàs as they began to walk. "You did very well, my friend," he said. "Glad to have you back with us."

The expression the little Portuguese wore was one of near anger. "The *demonios* bled and died!" he answered through clenched teeth. "If this was truly *o inferno* that could not be. Before when I wandered through the Dungeon, I took things as they came to me. But now, I begin to think someone plays a deliberate game." He gave Clive a stare that was almost chilling. "I do not like games,

Englishman, especially when someone plays them with my faith." He looked down and made the sign of the cross, but as part of the last motion he drew a thumb across his throat and once more gave that cold, hard look ahead.

Clive only nodded.

For a while they walked with their weapons ready. Smythe was the first to sheathe his, noting that the grip was almost too hot to hold for long. Clive hadn't noticed during the battle, but Smythe was right. The metal was very warm to the touch. In fact, he was very warm, too. He ran his tongue over his lips. They were parched and dry. *Now, why did you do that?* he asked himself. *All you're going to do is think about how thirsty you are.*

Almost as if to tantalize him, the scenery changed. The huge roaring plumes of fire remained, but the burning ground came to an end, and they stood on the bank of an immense lake of brackish, black water. Its surface rippled and shimmered with firelight, and the water bubbled, frothed, and steamed. The air turned heavy and moist, in some ways a welcome relief from the searing, dry wind and heat they had encountered before.

But the sight of so much water made Clive thirstier. He could see the same thirst in the eyes of his human comrades.

"Will you take water from my mouth?" Chang Guafe asked, coming to his side.

"What?" Clive was uncertain of his meaning.

Chang Guafe said no more but knelt down by the roadside and plunged his head into the boiling lake. Horrified, Clive Folliot dropped down beside him, caught his shoulder, and tried desperately to pull him back up. The cyborg merely shrugged him off, and when he raised up again, his metal plating gleamed clean.

"Chang, are you all . . . !"

Before he could say more the cyborg caught his head in a viselike grip and pressed metal lips to Clive's. Clive resisted for an instant, uncomprehending, until he tasted the liquid that seeped between his lips. It was warm, but it was water!

Nevertheless, he pushed away, flustered, and shot a red-faced look around at the others. Neville's and Smythe's faces registered pure shock and bordered on outrage. Annabelle giggled, and because she did, Finnbogg did also. Only Sidi, Tomàs, and of course Shriek stood by quietly.

"The water can be consumed," Chang Guafe assured him. "I have analyzed its various compounds. The high sulphur content flavors it somewhat, but will not harm."

"That doesn't have anything to do with it!" Clive Folliot shouted. "A man doesn't do that to another man, even if he is some alien cyborg!"

Chang Guafe was unruffled. "Your life-form requires liquid sustenance. However, your flesh cannot tolerate this temperature extreme, and you have no container in which to collect and cool it." He continued with mechanized patience. "I can take and cool it in my mouth and pass it to you in the manner I have demonstrated. There is no other way."

"But, but . . . !" Clive looked to the others for help. He was thirsty as hell, appropriately. But this was an embarrassment, immoral! He wouldn't do it, he wouldn't!

Annabelle slipped off Finnbogg's back, came to Clive, and pushed him out of the way. "Oh, Clive, don't be a scrodhead! It looks kind of fun and kinky to me." She turned to Chang Guafe. "Down on your knees, cowboy. Fill 'er up, and give me everything you've got."

The cyborg's ruby eyes focused on her. "You will take liquid sustenance?"

Annabelle grinned. "I think that's what I said."

He bent down, plunged his head underwater, and surfaced again, then waited a moment while the water cooled in his mouth. He nodded when he was ready.

Annabelle's grin widened as she glanced at Clive. She locked her arms around the cyborg's neck, pulled him close, and set her lips right against his.

"No need to make a spectacle of it!" Clive snapped nervously. "It's broad daylight!" Well, it wasn't really daylight, but it was bright enough.

Annabelle backed away and licked her lips. She winked at Clive and said to Chang Guafe, "I think you enjoyed that, Tin Man!"

"I register alpha waves cerebrally when I serve good friends," the cyborg answered.

"I'll bet you do," Annabelle returned.

Sidi Bombay stepped up next. "I'm only a miserable savage," he said to Clive. "Completely uncivilized by the standards of your empire. What can you expect of me?"

Clive had to turn away from what followed.

Tomàs moved up next, and Clive groaned and closed his eyes. He, at least, had been a sailor. One might expect such behavior from a seaman.

"Begging the major's pardon," Smythe said apologetically, "but I'm just too thirsty to care how I wet my whistle, I am."

Clive grabbed his shoulder. "Not you, too, Horace!"

Horace Hamilton Smythe merely shrugged and stepped closer to Chang Guafe.

Neville Folliot came next. "You do think of me as a black sheep, after all, little brother."

Chang Guafe waited for Clive. "Will you not be reasonable?" the cyborg said. "There is no other way, and my sensors register a dangerous depletion in your bodily reserves."

Clive groaned again and looked at the others. As one, they folded their arms and grinned at him. It was a conspiracy! What was he to do? He bit his lip, trapped, and nodded. But he squeezed his eyes shut when Chang's lips met his, and he tried to think of his mistress, Annabella Leighton, in Plantagenet Court.

"That's it, little brother," Neville snickered. "Close your eyes and think of England."

"Don't worry," his granddaughter said laughingly over his shoulder. "It's just a phase."

A hearty round of laughter greeted him as he stepped away from Chang Guafe. Even Shriek chittered with the rest. Red-faced, he accepted their teasing. The water had refreshed him, he had to admit. When they stopped laughing, he turned back to Chang Guafe.

"We're just good friends," he said firmly. Then, he gave a laugh, too, and clapped the cyborg on the arm. "You must do something about your breath," he whispered just loud enough for the others to hear.

"It's the antibiotics," Chang Guafe told him, and even the cyborg laughed.

The road snaked across the lake, vanishing in the steam and mist that swirled over it. Clive insisted that Annabelle take her place again on Finnbogg's back, and she finally gave in. It wasn't as if Finnbogg minded. He lifted his head and began to sing.

"Oh, you take the high road, and I'll take the low road . . .!"

"Doesn't look much like Scotland to me, little brother," Neville confided.

"Oh, I don't know, guv," Horace Hamilton Smythe said, putting on his best cockney. "There's some good Englishmen what might think of it like that. Not a good pub in the whole bleedin' country, if you ask me, which you didn't."

The mist began to swirl up about their feet, hot and cloying, soaking through their trousers, seeping into their boots. Clive stamped on the ground to make sure it was still solid, that they weren't beginning to wade in muck or water. The road, though, was still the road, hard rock.

As they continued, the road took a sudden right turn, and they followed without a choice. Then, it turned left and doubled back on itself yet again. Suddenly, they came to a fork in the way and stopped.

"Finnbogg got a bad feeling about this!"

They all stared in surprise at the alien canine, and Annabelle gave a little whoop, then covered her mouth, though her eyes still twinkled. She scratched Finnbogg's ears. "I've got a bad feeling about this, too," she admitted.

"You don't think it could be another maze?" Horace

Hamilton Smythe asked, frowning, scratching the stubble on his chin. "Not another one, please."

"If it is," Clive said uncertainly, "at least we've got Neville. Mazes are a specialty of his."

"You've done well enough, yourself, sah, with the mazes we've encountered," Smythe commented.

Neville looked around kind of nervously and pursed his lips. "Are you referring to that hedge maze when we were kids? I've got a confession to make, little brother. I never solved its puzzle. I just crawled between the bushes in a straight line. Knew that would take me out eventually."

Clive's jaw dropped. "You cheated?"

Neville looked indignant. "Well, I wouldn't say it like that! I just played the game by my own rules!"

"We could apply the same rule if this is a maze," Annabelle reminded them. "The Baalbec took us all underwater once before and let us breathe."

"Negative," Chang Guafe said. "The Baalbec can electrolyze water into oxygen and hydrogen, yes, allowing you to walk underwater. It has demonstrated no capacity for ambient heat transference, however. In these waters you would be steamed to death within its field."

"Not a pleasant prospect," said Sidi Bombay.

"Then what?" Clive said in exasperation. "Which way to the Palace of the Morning Star?"

"This way, Clive Folliot."

They turned to stare in startlement down the left fork. A raspy-voiced figure sat cross-legged on the ground, shrouded in the swirling mist, at the center of what appeared to be a narrow crossroad. It was hard to see much about him until they drew closer. He wore an old suit that was mostly tatters and a high, black top hat. His skin was very pale, almost alabaster, and thin as tissue. His hands were mostly bone, the knuckles grossly swollen, and his feet were bare. The red-glowing tip of a stubby cigar flared briefly as he put it to his lips and inhaled. "Got to give these up," he muttered to himself as he stared at the butt with an expression of disgust. He flicked it away, raised his arm toward them, and beckoned with one crooked finger.

Clive stopped and laid one hand on the hilt of his saber as he peered at the figure. "Who are you?" he said in a barely audible whisper. Then he repeated the question.

The figure stared back, still beckoning with that thin, impossibly long finger. "I am called Baron Samedi."

· CHAPTER FOUR ·

A Guide by the Lake of Fire

"I say, chap," Neville spoke up sharply, "you're a bit out of place, aren't you?" He waved an arm around to indicate the landscape, if it could be called that. "I mean, a god of voudoun in a biblical hell?"

Samedi shrugged, a particularly gruesome gesture as Clive could almost hear the bones rattle inside that dry fleshly casing. "Hey, Jack, it's not my nightmare," came the raspy answer, and the thing smiled a smile that showed the roots of his teeth and colorless, receding gums. "Come." He turned and started along the mist-enshrouded pathway.

But Clive hesitated. "What did you mean, 'a god of voudoun'?" he asked his brother. "Who is he?"

"I spent some time in New Orleans," Neville answered, "and picked up something of the local voudoun practices while I was there. Voodoo, a lot of people call it. Just curiosity, really, and the fact that I met this really lovely girl who turned out to be something of a priestess, a mamaloi, she called herself. Anyway, this Baron Samedi fellow is sort of a spirit of the dead. You can find him at any crossroads, they say." He indicated the narrow paths that snaked off across the water and vanished in four different directions into the fog. "I guess this qualifies."

Sergeant Horace Hamilton Smythe stepped forward. "I spent time in New Orleans, too, sah, and I heard talk about this Baron Samedi, too, I did. Not a very pleasant fellow, the way I heard it. Turns men into zombies, he does."

"Whatever he is," Annabelle said, joining them, "he's a definite bug. He doesn't fit in this program. Somebody's made a mistake."

"But is it a mistake in our favor, beautiful lady?" said Sidi Bombay with a look of cautious doubt.

Ahead, Baron Samedi stopped, turned slowly, and beckoned to them again, crooking his finger and smiling. The tilt of that old black top hat gave him almost a comical look at a distance, when one couldn't quite see the pallor of his skin stretched taut over those cheekbones. "Come," he called.

Being Clive. Shriek's thoughts touched his with the gentleness of a single falling snowflake. *Choice is to wander maze pattern without Samedi being and perhaps lost be, or follow it, we. Destination it must have specific.*

Chang Guafe spoke up then. "I hear and agree with Shriek," he said. "If it will help you to decide, Clive Folliot, then my sensors reveal it is no spirit which confronts us. This ragged creature maintains a near-human heartbeat and radiates a body temperature of one hundred and five degrees. That is higher than human-normal, but no doubt allows it to function more comfortably in this heat extreme. I can probe deeper. . . ."

"No need," Clive said, holding up a hand. "I am convinced. As Shriek said, we really don't have much of a choice. But stay close together, and be ready for anything."

"Sound advice, little brother," Neville Folliot approved.

They followed the shambling figure of Baron Samedi through the thin mist. The path turned rockier. On either side now new pathways began to branch off, some wider, smoother, more inviting, but Samedi moved with surety, choosing the course without hesitation.

The path began to narrow and slope at odd angles. This mist made the black rock slick in places, and footing became uncertain. They were forced to walk single file.

On either side of the crazy, twisting road the bubbling black lake water lapped against the stone.

Clive's khakis clung to him, sodden with sweat and the dampness of the mist. At last, he cast propriety to the winds and dared to unbutton his shirt as low as his waistband. He might have removed it entirely, but that would have been stretching decency's boundaries too far with Annabelle and Shriek right behind him.

Out on the lake, a geyser of fire exploded upward from the surface. A blast of heat rolled across them, and the sudden flare of brightness caused Tomàs to cry out in astonishment and Neville to throw an arm across his eyes. The mist swirled in agitation, and the water lapped over their feet.

Barefooted, Sidi Bombay gave a shout of fear, but before the liquid could scald him Chang Guafe picked him up bodily under the arms and held him dangling in the air. The temperature of the water didn't seem to bother Shriek, whose four feet were also bare. Nor Finnbogg, who stood on somewhat higher ground.

"My thanks and gratitude, noble alien," said Sidi Bombay when the waves subsided and the geyser had disappeared. Chang Guafe merely nodded and set him down again.

"Come." Baron Samedi stood safely on a rock ahead of them, beckoning.

"Somewhat of a limited vocabulary, that chap," Neville muttered to his brother as they started up again. "Don't care much for his tailor, either."

The pathway took a sharp upward slant, and some of them had to help the others. For a change, it was particularly Chang Guafe who needed help. His metal-shod feet slipped and scraped on the damp stone, which had become obsidian-smooth, and more than once he fell to his knees. Clive discovered, to his surprise, what an expression of frustration looked like on a metal face. It might have been amusing had the situation not been so grim.

"Look here, isn't there an easier way?" Neville Folliot called ahead.

Samedi turned with a wide grin on his ashen face. "An easy road through hell? What a novel idea."

It was such a perfect imitation of his brother's voice and tone that Clive Folliot had to cover his mouth with a hand to keep from chortling.

"Well," said Annabelle with more than a trace of sarcasm, "his vocabulary is improving."

"If not his manner," Neville answered indignantly.

More geysers of flame erupted on their left and right, but now the path was too high above the lake to be flooded by the resulting waves. Hot winds whipped at them and tore at their clothes, and in the strange, wild flickerings they looked an odd company, indeed.

At the peak of their climb, Samedi stopped and reached into the pocket of his baggy old suit. His fingers unfolded to reveal a large lump of dirty wax. "Now, dudes, get this. You wear this stuff in your ears, see. We comin' up on the Lake of Lamentations, and you don't even want to hear that soulful sound, or the blues might hit you so bad you'd do somethin' real dumb, like throw yourselves into the water or somethin', dig it?"

Clive looked around, funny-faced. "What'd he say?"

"I say, that's very classical." Neville reached out to take his portion of the wax and began making small balls of it. "I guess that makes me Ulysses, braving dangers, trying to find the way home."

"So pass the wax, hero," Annabelle snapped. "You're not the only one on this ship, you know."

Clive ignored them both as he accepted his share. "The Lake of Lamentations?" he said to Samedi. He tried to remember his Bible verses, though he'd never paid much attention to that sort of thing. "You mean the Lake of Fire?"

Samedi made a sweeping gesture. "This all the Lake of Fire, brother!" He slapped his thigh. "But part is also the Lake of Lamentations. Don' pay no attention to what you see out there, either, and jus' tune your ears out completely. An' lemme tell you this, too, you step off that pathway an' you gonna be a sorry sucker! It ain't far where we're goin' when we get to the other side."

Clive immediately thought of Chang Guafe. "You don't have ears for the wax," he said.

"I will deactivate audio sensors," he answered. "I will not be in danger."

"Shriek, what about you?"

Hear, I do not as human beings think of it. Vibrations feel I on spike-hairs. Wax, nothing can help. Fine, will I be, though.

Baron Samedi beckoned and turned away to lead.

"Not yet!" Clive called. Samedi halted and regarded him patiently.

Clive turned back to Shriek. "Samedi says we mustn't step off the path, so I'd like us all responsible for each of us. The strong support the weak, and the entire group supports the strong, and all that. Can you web us together?"

Horace Hamilton Smythe clapped him on the shoulder. "Good idea, sah! A lifeline!"

Slender thread spin I, Shriek answered, *strong enough all to help.*

"Then do it now," Clive suggested.

But Neville protested. "Now wait a minute, I . . ."

Annabelle seemed to have appointed herself to keep Neville humble. "Oh, shut up, Neville," she said caustically. "Even Ulysses allowed himself to be bound."

Shriek moved carefully among them on the narrow path, circling each of them once, spinning a graceful strand around each waist. At first, the filament was sticky and wet, but in the hot wind it quickly dried, becoming a fine, strong line. Lastly, she approached Baron Samedi, who held up a hand and shook his head.

With deft agility and speed, she ensnared him before he could protest further. *Go down we, go down Samedi being,* she said.

"Looks like you done made Death your prisoner," Baron

Samedi rasped with some amusement, plucking the line with one finger as if it were a harp string.

"Turnabout's fair play, I say," Horace Hamilton Smythe muttered under his breath just behind Clive.

The road began to descend again, turning downward toward the lake's surface. The rock, so smooth on the way up, was cracked and battered now, providing surer footing.

Clive glanced at the small balls of wax on his palm and listened as the road descended almost to the level of the lake. If a geyser erupted, they would certainly all have scalded feet, he realized. He looked at the balls of wax again. The others had put theirs in their ears already.

A sound shivered on the misty air, a high plaintive cry, very distant. Still, it cut through him like a rusty sawblade. Another followed it. He remembered the screaming they had heard outside the Dantean Gate, as he had come to think of it, the shrill cries that had so terrified the company. They, at last, had faded, and he had almost forgotten them.

These were worse by far. They abraded the very edges of his soul! What creatures could know such torment? A sudden shriek tore at his nerves. He jumped, and before he could stop himself, he dropped one of the precious earplugs. It bounced on the rocky path and plopped into the water. He stared at the ripples, but the line compelled him onward.

"Horace!" he called over his shoulder. But there was no answer from Horace Hamilton Smythe, who had already stopped his ears.

Calm, Being Clive! Shriek's thoughts blossomed in his mind, soothing. *What remains, divide. Enough it may be.*

She was right, of course. There was nothing else he could do. Quickly, he tore the wax in half and made new balls. They looked so small, and his hands trembled as he rolled them. Another shriek sounded as if it came from right beside him, and he jumped again, but this time he closed his fist tight and the plugs did not get away. As fast as he could, he pushed them inside his ears.

He could still hear, he discovered, but at least the cries were muffled.

Something splashed out on the lake's surface. He caught the motion in the corner of his eye and stared. A hand! It was a hand that thrashed the water! And a head! A face broke the surface. A mouth opened in an almost soundless scream before the apparition went under again.

He knew that face!

"Du Maurier!" he shouted, terror roiling in his breast. "George, my God!"

But the line compelled him onward. He stared over his shoulder where his old friend thrashed and drowned without help or hope.

He didn't believe it, he told himself. He just bloody well didn't believe it! Somebody was playing tricks with them. George du Maurier was home in his London flat, sipping tea over his philosophy books and newspapers. That couldn't have been George!

Another motion caught his attention. A body bobbed up right beside the path at his feet. He glared at the bearded face as it opened its mouth and screamed. That terrible sound knifed even through the earwax. Weakly, as if the spirit were draining from him, Clive stumbled to one knee, and for an instant he came face-to-face with Maurice Carstairs, his former patron at *The London Illustrated Recorder and Dispatch*, the man who had funded the first leg of his journey to Africa.

But the line compelled him on.

He glanced over his shoulder, turning to his good friend Horace Hamilton Smythe for help, but Smythe only stared out over the water, tears streaming down his face as some great emotion wracked him. He wrung his hands around and around the line that bound him as if a part of him sought escape. Still, the sergeant walked on and left behind whatever part of his soul the lake called to.

Clive turned his gaze forward and tried to focus his attention on Samedi's top hat. *Don't look anywhere else,* he told himself. *It's all a trick, it's not real!*

There was a powerful tug on the line and a sudden splash. He felt himself pulled toward the lake and balanced precipitously on one leg until he braced himself. One toe slid into the water, and only his boot saved him from a burn as the water bubbled up. Still, the line shivered and vibrated and snapped taut around his waist.

"Finnbogg littermate!" The alien canine's roar cut plainly through the wax. "Stop! Finnbogg littermate! Need Finnbogg!"

His plaintive howl hurt Clive more than he knew he could be hurt, and the desperate sight of Chang Guafe and Shriek dragging Finnbogg back onto the rocky path moved him to pity and to anger. No one had the right to do this, no one!

He glanced at Annabelle before he turned around again. There was fear in her eyes, concern and puzzlement. He wondered what horrors she might be experiencing. But she was behind Horace and behind Neville, and he couldn't get to her, couldn't put a comforting arm around her.

On his right a geyser of fire shot into the sky, a tube of flame, carrying upward with it thousands of naked souls that writhed and squirmed over each other like snakes in a pit.

Dear God! He saw *her* there, screaming and crying, anguished tears streaming down her beautiful face as she clawed and scratched and dragged herself over and under the others, as they pressed and smothered and squirmed over her. As he watched, the fire caught in her lovely hair, setting her head ablaze. Her skin began to melt and burn, and her eyes exploded in their sockets. Flesh blackened, exposing bone, which blackened. Still, she churned and struggled with the rest, knowing no respite, no release.

"Annabella!" Clive choked. He had known she would come. The pattern of the lake was plain enough to see. It preyed upon the memories of their friends and loved ones. From the first instant he'd realized that, he'd prepared himself for this moment. Annabella Leighton was safe and sound back in Plantagenet Court, teaching literature to high-born young girls, eating crumpets, and waiting for his return. That thing in the flame, whatever it was, was not his sweet Annabella Leighton. Still, he choked again and muttered, "Annabella!"

Being Clive?" Shriek's mind-voice interrupted his grief. *Finnbogg being badly burned is. Jumped in hot lake did. Need treatment. Need help. Swiftly go must we to other side.*

Clive did his best to snap out of it. Finnbogg was hurt. He had to concentrate on that. All of his friends were in danger if they lingered out here. He tore his gaze away from the geyser and clenched his fists.

Tell everybody, Shriek, he said suddenly, *tell them to run. Tell them to hold on to the line and don't think of anything else except running.*

Slippery wet road is. Treacherous could be.

The greater danger is out here, he snapped. *Tell them!*

He stared at the back of the figure before him. Baron Samedi kept up his relentless shambling pace, eyeing the ground before him as he walked without looking back.

"Samedi, you old bag of bones!" he shouted as the others began to pile into him. "Get dragged or get carried if you can't make better time than that. We're coming through!"

Samedi cast a look of amusement over his thin, black-suited shoulder, then of utter surprise as Clive scooped him up. "You tell us the way, and it better be the right way, too, or I'll drop you in the lake and hold you under, myself," he muttered to the frail, nearly weightless creature.

"Mammy, how I love ya!" Samedi grinned, folding his arms as the tatters of his suit flapped around Clive. "Go right, young man! Does you like Cajun food?"

They wound their way through a series of narrow pathways, the water lapping at their heels, running as swiftly as they dared. Geysers erupted on every side, filled with images, and bodies bobbed and floated to the surface near their feet. Things thrashed and splashed and screamed and called to them, but the company ran on, each man pulled by the next, and Clive leading them all as fast as he dared.

Samedi kept up an endless stream of meaningless chatter, but the only words Clive listened for were *right* or *left*.

Sooner than he expected they reached the far shore. Clive set Samedi down and sank to his knees, breathless. Except for Chang Guafe and Shriek, the others did the same. The sounds of panting made Clive look up. Finnbogg sprawled with his head in Annabelle's lap, tongue lolling.

"I thought you said he was hurt?" Clive said to Shriek.

Clive being something needed did to focus energies. There was laughter in her thoughts, but also apology and desire for forgiveness. *Concern for friend beings stronger than griefselfpity.* She hesitated, and he felt her searching her mind for the right words. *Lied, I,* she added finally.

Clive flopped on his back and laughed, and the sound rapidly spread to the others, who did the same. Shriek, too, chittered, and Chang Guafe made that weird mechanical sound that passed for laughter. Finnbogg set up a howl.

Baron Samedi looked down at them. "Come," he said, crooking a bony finger.

They got to their feet and followed their strange guide, still chortling and snickering. It was relief, of course, from the terrors they'd just experienced, and welcome, good-sounding relief it was, too.

The screaming and wailing had stopped as soon as they reached the shore. At Samedi's instruction they removed the earplugs. Clive cast his into the lake with a lazy sidearm motion and listened for the slight *plop* that never came. He scratched his chin about that. One more small, inexplicable oddity, barely worth noting in this Dungeon.

They walked now mostly in silence. Only a thin mist lingered on the land, which took on a radical change as they journeyed. Gone were the flames and the hot winds and the bubbling waters. A featureless black landscape confronted them now, not unlike the land they had found surrounding Q'oorna on the first level when they first arrived in the Dungeon.

Gone, also, was the light provided by the flames. A gray, misty twilight hung over everything, bright enough to see by, but depressing to the spirit.

The road led now toward a range of low mountains. Clive looked over his shoulder, remembering the beautiful Burning Mountains he had named at the Dantean Gate. He couldn't see them now, though he didn't understand how that could be. He only shrugged. Things changed down here too quickly.

At the first of the foothills, Samedi led them to a huge cave just off the roadside. "Come," he said, beckoning. Clive was just too tired to be distrustful anymore. He went without questioning.

"Food!" Neville cried.

"Smell food!" shouted Finnbogg.

Deep in the cave, a fire burned in a hearthplace, flooding a large central gallery with warm light. Before it, a lavish spread had been prepared and placed on a long wooden table. Candles burned in brass sticks, and soft, comfortable chairs ringed the table.

"Get us out of this rope!" Tomàs shouted, tugging at the strand around his waist. "*Pressa*, I can't break it!"

Clive couldn't break it, either. "Shriek, can you help?"

The arachnoid plucked one of her hair-spikes and scuttled to each of them in turn. The spike gleamed wetly with an odorless chemical that swiftly dissolved the line, freeing them.

They swarmed around the table. In no time at all every last morsel was devoured, every crumb eaten.

Clive carried a glass of wine to Samedi where their host stood leaning by the fireplace watching the feast. He hadn't eaten a bite, himself, but he accepted the wine and tossed it back.

"Our thanks, Baron," Clive Folliot said gracefully.

"Lemme tell you somethin', Jack," Samedi said with a leer toward Clive. "I get tired of all this 'come' shit, you know? I mean, lookit these threads, man! How you like to have to go aroun' in public in somethin' like this? Shit! But like, it's my job, you know. It's why I was put here. Don' mean I'm not a nice guy inside!"

Clive shrugged, confused. He wasn't sure he'd understood half of what his host had just said. He thought for a moment and scratched the growing stubble on his chin. "I like you," he answered finally.

"That's very white of you, Jack." Samedi turned the wine glass upside down on the mantel. "Now you better get yourself some sleep, 'cause tomorrow we got to make the Palace of the Morning Star. Big Dude hisself's waitin' on you."

Clive almost hated to ask. "Are there beds?"

Baron Samedi rolled his huge eyes and crooked a finger. "Come," he said.

· CHAPTER FIVE ·

The Cave of Quiet Fears

Clive knew by now that Shriek didn't sleep; at least, not in any way that humans thought of it, and he felt perfectly safe knowing she stood guard while the rest of them caught a few winks. Nor had he missed the fact that she had set aside a few choice pieces of meat from the table to consume once she was alone, for she refused to eat in the presence of the others. All in all, she appeared as pleased to see them off to bed as they were to go.

Bearing a brand from the fireplace, Samedi led the way deeper into the cave. Numerous smaller galleries branched off from the main passage, and in each they found small pallets made from piles of thick, warm blankets. Beside each pallet stood a candlestick like the ones on the table. Samedi lit each candle with his brand as, one by one, the members of the company said good-night to each other.

Clive took the last gallery. So far into the cave, the air was still and close, but his belly was full and the pallet softer than he had imagined. He slipped off his boots and wiggled his toes, then wrinkled his nose at the smell. His feet had gotten wet inside the leather and needed a good airing.

He turned to say good-night to Samedi, but his host had already departed. Clive shrugged and stretched out for the night. He considered extinguishing his candle, then thought better of it. The tiny light it shed would hardly be enough to prevent his sleeping. He slipped off his khaki shirt and laid it aside. Then, folding one arm under his head, he closed his eyes.

Yet, as he lay there in the silence, it began to disconcert him how each of his friends had been separated from the others. Any of the galleries, though small, would have slept two or even three. He sat up suddenly, chewing his lip, his gaze searching the darkest corners of his chamber where the small flame did not penetrate.

At last, unable to stop himself, he slipped his shirt back on, picked up the candle, and padded barefoot back along the way they had come.

He found Finnbogg curled up around his lone candle, the blankets of his pallet rumpled and tossed into a designless mess that supported head and hips and little else. The canine creature yawned broadly and peeped out from under one droopy lid.

Clive shielded his flame and passed on.

Neville slept in the next gallery. His brother had peeled off his uniform and laid it in meticulous order on one of the blankets, which he apparently had spread upon the ground for the purpose. He lay naked with one blanket modestly across his middle, asleep as soundly as if it were his own bed in London he occupied. His thick blond hair made a mop around his face, and despite his size and musculature he looked ever so much the little boy.

Briefly, Clive felt a tinge of regret and frustration that he and Neville had never been close, never brothers in the fullest sense. But he still tasted the anger, too, and the bitterness. Neville had never made the least effort to close the gap between them, never done anything but ignore him while he lavished in the gifts and the favoritism their father showered on his so-called "firstborn."

A spot of hot wax dripped on Clive's hand, making him jump and curse silently. It was his own fault, he told himself, for letting his feelings run away with him and for clenching the candlestick too tightly in a fist that he'd much rather have used to give his brother the drubbing he so deserved. But that would have to wait until another time when they were all in much less of a fix. He gave Neville a last disapproving glance, then moved on.

One by one he checked his charges, for so he had come to think of them. Tomàs was curled fetally around his candle in much the same manner as Finnbogg. Sidi lay corpselike, stiff and straight with hands folded upon his chest, in what Clive guessed was one of the Indian's strange yoga trances. Annabelle tossed and turned restlessly on her pallet, but she didn't open her eyes when he lingered, so he passed on to the next gallery. Even his old friend Horace Hamilton Smythe, whom he might have expected to maintain an informal watch on his own, had surrendered to Morpheus' embrace.

Chang Guafe, though, was still awake.

"Can't sleep?" Clive asked from the gallery's narrow entrance. "Or don't you sleep, either?"

Chang Guafe stared at Clive for a moment, then turned his gaze on his own metal form. "My body does not require rest," he said with surprising softness in his mechanical voice. "However, my organic brain does. It eludes me, though, as you surmise."

Clive took that as an invitation to enter, reflecting on the incongruous sight that confronted him. The powerful cyborg had pulled his pallet next to the cave wall. He sat with his back against it, his legs sprawled open before him, arms at his side, looking much like a doll some child had placed there and abandoned.

"Ah, I know the feeling," Clive assured him. "Seems the more you need sleep sometimes, the harder it is to find. But can't you put yourself to sleep? With drugs, I mean?" Clive hesitated when Chang Guafe only stared back. "I mean, you had medicines inside yourself that healed your cuts and injuries. Is there nothing to help you sleep?"

It was Chang Guafe's turn to hesitate. He turned his head from side to side, and candlelight played eerily on his peculiar features. "I do not wish to," he answered finally. Then he reverted to his usual cold voice and added, "Alertness is a priority, observation an imperative."

But Clive wasn't fooled a bit. In fact, he was suddenly touched. Of all his strange new friends it was Chang Guafe who most unsettled him. Yet, now he found himself reaching out, laying a hand on the cyborg's shoulder. "Chang," he said, unable to keep the surprise from his tone, "are you afraid of the dark?"

"Negative!" the cyborg answered, then softening again, "And affirmative. Almost nothing can hurt this form," he said, rapping his metal knuckles on a metal thigh. "My sensors know this. The computer elements of my brain know this." He looked directly at Clive, his ruby eyes seeming somehow more human. "But there is still the organic brain, and deep inside it where the computer and the drugs do not reach, there lurk all the old archetypes and racial memories, the primitive fears and dreads that all beings know." He turned away and stared into the candlelight. The tiny flame reflected in his lenses. "Yes, Clive Folliot, in quiet moments such as this, even a Tin Man may know fear."

Clive thought for a long moment, silently recalling all the terrors he'd encountered in the Dungeon, able to face them with a sense of detachment because they were behind him. Then, he looked ahead and dared to wonder what still awaited them, and he bit his lip.

At last, he sighed and sat down beside Chang Guafe and leaned his back against the wall. "Well, I can't sleep, either," he said, setting his candle on the ground beside the cyborg's candle. "So we'll just bloody well look out for each other—how about that? Give me a blanket, will you?"

Two pairs of eyes met and looked away as the blanket changed hands, and two heads leaned back as one against the stone. Wordlessly, they waited for dawn, or whatever in hell passed for dawn.

*   *   *

Clive did sleep, however, and woke with a start, chiding himself for doing so. He glanced over at Chang Guafe. The cyborg, too, had fallen asleep, braced against the wall, his head lolled to the side. There was no gleam at all behind the ruby lenses.

Clive rose as quietly as he could and stretched. The sitting position in which he'd slept had left him stiff in the lower back. He rubbed his neck, picked up the stub that remained of his candle, and slipped into the cave passage.

Returning to his own gallery, he couldn't resist checking once more on his sleeping friends. When he reached Annabelle's gallery, however, his faint light shone on an empty pallet.

Clive chewed his lip thoughtfully, then returned to his own sleeping place to recover his boots. They had dried quickly in the warm air, and he pulled them on, buttoned his shirt, and tucked it into his trousers. Then, light in hand, he headed back to the cave's huge main chamber.

Up ahead, the remains of the hearthfire cast a soft red radiance. Hoping to find Annabelle there, he increased his pace. His candle flickered out suddenly as the wind slipped between his fingers, but he didn't need it now. He focused on the glow.

Something brushed his ankle, and a huge, dark shadow suddenly blocked his way. Clive's heart skipped a beat. His hand lunged for the hilt of his saber and tugged the blade half-free as he leaped back.

Being Clive.

Clive let go a sigh of relief and let the saber fall back into the scabbard. He should have recognized the silhouette before him. He squeezed his eyes shut for a moment and rubbed his temples.

"My apologies, Shriek," he said wearily. "Guess I'm a bit on edge."

Apologies mine for startlement, she offered. *Nervous, too, am I. See? Trigger-web everywhere. On watch, am I. Anyone moves, informed am I.*

Clive glanced down. Stretched across the passage between the galleries and the main chamber was a narrow, glistening strand. It was that his ankle had brushed. Similar strands, he noticed, were strung at various points, and all of them were ultimately attached to one of Shriek's legs. If anything touched the strands, the vibrations alerted her at once.

"Have you seen Annabelle?" he asked, concerned.

Shriek repaired the damage he had done to the trip-web and scuttled back to the hearthfire. In the light of the embers her six eyes glittered like strange jewels. *Annabelle being outside has gone,* she answered.

"What?" Clive's hands curled into fists, and he beat his thighs. "You didn't stop her?"

No words, but genuine surprise blossomed in his thoughts as Shriek considered the very novelty of the idea of one intelligent being attempting to regulate the nonviolent actions of another. *Egg-new is Annabelle being?* Shriek asked abruptly, grasping for understanding. *Youngling is?*

Clive growled in frustration and headed for the cave entrance. Despite his irritation, he stepped carefully, avoiding the trigger-webs. No reason to destroy Shriek's work, he told himself. It was his fault. Sometimes he forgot he was dealing with an alien.

He moved up the short passageway to the outside. Even there Shriek had placed a pair of webs, one at ankle and one at chest height. He couldn't fault her diligence.

A blast of warm air greeted him as he emerged. His sleeves made a crisp snapping sound, and his blond hair whipped back. In the stillness of Samedi's cave he'd forgotten the strength of the wind outside.

He looked up and down the path for Annabelle, but there was no sign of her. He braced his hands on his hips for an instant and cursed. What did she think she was doing, separating from the group like this? At last, reasoning that she wouldn't have gone back down the way they had come, he started up the path.

Higher and higher the road went, and steeper, too, as it wound among the mountain foothills.

He heard her before he saw her. Her voice rang down to him, clear and poignantly sweet, and he stopped.

> *Oh, Fortune's Child, where are you now?*
> *Oh, Fortune's Child, where are you now?*
> *I'd cry for you, but I don't know how,*
> *Oh, Fortune's Child.*
>
> *Unfortunate Child, I'm gone away,*
> *Gone to hell, like momma used to say,*
> *Gotta make it on your own, the price you pay,*
> *Child of an Unfortunate Child,*
> *But I think about you every day,*
> *And try to cry, Unfortunate Child.*

Clive found her sitting on a small black boulder, her knees drawn up to her chest with her arms locked around them. She rocked herself as she sang with her eyes closed, and the wind stirred her short dark hair. He knew in her own time in her own world she had been a musician, but he'd never heard her sing, never heard her talk about her music at all. He couldn't bring himself to interrupt her, and his chest tightened as he listened.

> *Oh, Fortune's Child, where are you now?*
> *I'd cry for you, but I don't know how,*
> *Oh, Fortune's Child . . .*

She opened her eyes suddenly as if she had somehow sensed him standing there. For an instant, fear reflected in her gaze, but as recognition came, that softened, and Clive saw such pain in those eyes as made him sit down beside her and gather her in his arms.

She didn't cry, just rested her head in the hollow of his shoulder and sighed, her arms hanging limply, her legs slowly straightening and sliding down the sides of the boulder, letting him take all her weight.

Clive held her and stroked her hair, and neither of

them spoke. Dimly, he recalled how she had stirred his senses before he realized their relationship. But she was his great-great-granddaughter, and suddenly that meant more to him than anything else in the world. He missed his own beloved Annabella Leighton painfully, and he might never make it back to her side again. But their love, at least, had produced this wonderful child in his arms, and he would protect her, protect her with all his being.

"Sorry," she said after a while, straightening. "Guess I was feeling sorry for myself."

Clive was reluctant to let her go. "You sing beautifully," he said with gentleness. "Was that about you?"

She shook her head, slid off the boulder, and leaned against it, instead, as she stared outward. "For Amanda," she answered. "I couldn't sleep for thinking of her." She hesitated and swallowed. "I miss my daughter."

And he missed Annabella. He hadn't really allowed himself to think about it, but he missed her terribly. What must she think of him? All this time gone, and no word from him. And why hadn't she told him about the pregnancy before he'd left for Africa?

He hung his head. If what his granddaughter told him was true, then he would never see his Annabella again. She would bear his child and raise it alone in poverty, never marrying, embittered and solitary, probably cursing his name.

How could he bear it? How could he ever respect himself again?

"There's almost a kind of beauty to it," Annabelle said suddenly, gesturing toward the vista that spread before them. "You have to open yourself to it, but it's there."

They were high on the side of a hill. A perpetual twilight hung over the land, but still they could see a vast panorama. A featureless, gray ashen plain lay below them, marked only by the occasional rock or boulder. Beyond that, the Lake of Fire glittered blackly, threads of mist drifting upon its surface like ghostly snakes. Flaming spumes shot up through the water here and there, casting red ripples that whipped and lashed the maze of narrow roadways, causeways really, that stretched from shore to shore.

Farther away, an orange glow lit the horizon, a dancing shimmer of heat and fire that marked the edge of the world on this seventh level. Like the sun at dawn, just as it peeked over the rim of the earth, it held the eye.

There *was* a kind of beauty to it, a terrible beauty that struck like an iron nail to his heart.

"Let's go back," he said, reaching for Annabelle's hand.

But she continued to stare outward. "That must be the Lake of Lamentations," she continued, pointing to a narrow inlet nearest them where the road met the shoreline. She glanced at him, then looked quickly away. "What did you see down there?"

He folded his arms as a lump formed in his throat and recalled that vision of Annabella lost in the fire with a squirming mass of souls, burning and rejuvenating, burning again as she screamed for him. It wasn't real, he reminded himself. Annabella Leighton was safe in London in her Plantagenet Court flat, probably reading to herself and worrying what had become of Clive Folliot. Or maybe by now she was cursing that name.

"Memories," he answered in a subdued voice. "Old friends."

"Old loves?" she prodded. "Did you love her, Clive? It's not my place to ask that, maybe, but it would matter to me to know."

"With all my heart," he admitted. "I wanted to marry her."

"Then why didn't you?"

Despite himself, he smiled at her directness. "Things must be so simple in nineteen ninety-nine," he said, laughing. "But in my time there is such a thing as propriety and responsibility. A man did not marry until he could afford to do so, and the salary for a major in the Fifth Imperial Horse Guards Regiment barely kept my horse fed and my brass buttons polished."

"But you did love her?" Annabelle Leigh persisted.

Clive looked her straight in the eye and answered with all seriousness. "I *do* love her. Present tense, for me, anyway."

She smiled and took his hand. "Let's go back, Clive Folliot." Then she added with a wink, "Granddaddy."

The smell of good English tea greeted them as they entered the cave again. Clive could hardly believe his nose. He forgot about Shriek's trip-webs as he rushed inside and nearly collided with the arachnoid as she jumped to investigate.

"Sorry, Shriek," he said, pushing past her, "but I thought I smelled . . ."

"Yes, it's tea, little brother!" Neville called, rising, cup in hand. "It seems even hell has a few amenities to offer."

The buttons of Neville's uniform gleamed in the light from the fire that their host had rebuilt in the hearth. For the first time Clive noticed it was all coal or some similar substance, not wood, that burned there. He usually prided himself on his observation of detail, and he took it as a sign of his fatigue that he had overlooked it. He should have slept longer.

But the tea refreshed him immensely, and Horace Hamilton Smythe poured a second measure of the precious beverage into the delicate china cups that looked so out of place on a rough wooden table in a deep dark cave in the depths of someplace someone wanted them to think of as hell.

"Almost like being home again, isn't it, sah?" Smythe said, setting the pot back on the table.

"I don't think I'd go quite that far, Horace," Clive said. "But it's certainly very welcome, isn't it, Annabelle?"

She looked into her cup and frowned. "Personally, Clive-o, I'd give anything for a Coke."

Granddaughter or not, Clive had long since given up trying to figure out everything Annabelle said. He shrugged and took another delicious sip and turned to Samedi, who stood by the hearth apart from the others.

"However did you manage to come by this here?" he

asked without setting his cup down. "Orange pekoe, I believe."

"Hey, Jack," Samedi answered with a snap of his sticklike fingers, "whatchoo need, baby, I got."

Clive took a second to figure that out. Samedi's speech was as odd to him as Annabelle's. Of course, why shouldn't it be? This was the Dungeon. "But *where* did you get it?" he persisted.

Samedi rolled his eyes and put on that big toothy grin that showed all his gums. "Friends in high places, baby, an' I done said too much. Ask me somethin' I can say straight."

But Clive wasn't ready to give up so easily. "What do you mean, 'friends in high places'? What friends? Did they provide the food last night, too?"

Samedi set his arms akimbo, leaned forward, and tapped his foot busily on the cave floor. "Look, man. What is it, rubber-hose time or somethin'? You itchin' or jus' bitchin'? Either scratch or get offn' my back, Jack, cause I ain't answerin' no more questions, dig it?"

Clive looked helplessly at Annabelle. "What did he say?"

Annabelle grinned as she swallowed the last of her tea. "He's running a limited function program," she said. "No queries."

Clive's brows knitted together in confusion. He turned to Horace Hamilton Smythe. "What did she say?"

Horace Hamilton Smythe leaned forward conspiratorially. "They said, 'Let's finish off the last of the excellent tea, sah, and get the hell back on the road.'" He picked up his cup and set it to his lips. "Wish I had a dollop of brandy, though—just for flavor, of course," he added over the china rim.

Clive drew a long breath and gazed at Shriek, Finnbogg, and Chang Guafe. He felt a lot closer to them, sometimes, he reflected, than to his own kind. Those three were aliens, after all. But sometimes he just wanted to set the others down and teach them the proper Queen's English!

"By the way," he said to Samedi, feeling a bit peevish about it all. "My name's Clive, not Jack."

Samedi strutted past, swinging his bony hips in a most foppish manner. "Clive," he responded, stretching the vowel to the point of breaking it, "no jive!" He sauntered on to the entrance, paused to adjust the top hat on his head, and turned back to face them.

Framed in the cave entrance, he crooked a finger. "Come," he intoned.

• CHAPTER SIX •

Deadly Echoes in the Hills of Hell

Higher and higher Samedi led them up the narrow mountain road. Jagged peaks rose like broken teeth on all sides. Sometimes, the road was little more than an uneven ledge that hugged the mountainside, and the tiny pebbles they kicked over the edge appeared to fall forever into a vast unending darkness. Other times, though, it was almost a lane, a broad ribbon of ebon stone, which took them through the highland-style valleys that nestled among those peaks.

> *What hills, what hills, so dark and low?*
> *Those are the hills of hell, my love,*
> *Where you and I must go.*

They were the words to an old British folk song, and they kept playing over in Clive's mind as he regarded their surroundings. He'd have to teach it to Annabelle someday. She'd sing it beautifully. Or—he grinned—perhaps he'd teach it to Finnbogg. Finnbogg would give it a distinctly different character.

He looked back at Annabelle, directly behind him in their single-file line, and two more lines came into his head.

> *And as they trod along the way*
> *She shimmered like glittering gold.*

Well, not gold, maybe, though she cut a nice figure in her red leather jeans and white camisole top with the black leather jacket tossed back over one shoulder. It occurred to him that she must be roasting in those clothes, yet she hadn't uttered one complaint. She was strong, his granddaughter, and she made him proud.

He reached inside his shirt and drew out Neville's diary from where it rested next to his skin. It was warm with his body heat, and the cover was damp with his sweat.

Neville claimed the book wasn't his, but could he believe his brother? He turned the diary over and over in his hands, rubbed off the moisture, rolled the balls of his thumbs along the binding as if he might discover some clue to the truth of the matter. The writing inside looked like Neville's, but Sidi's suspicions made sense. The thing had simply turned up in too many unlikely places.

So whose was it? Or rather, who was providing the messages and directions that kept turning up on the pages?

He stared directly ahead at the back of their guide. Samedi had mentioned "friends in high places." Clive tried to weigh the implications of that. What friends? Could he assume that someone somewhere was watching out for them? Were *they* the Dungeonmasters? Were these "friendlies" the ones providing the diary clues?

So many questions? He tried to turn his thoughts over, to look at the same questions from another view.

What if these "friendlies" Samedi had mentioned weren't the Dungeonmasters, at all? Did that indicate another faction in the Dungeon? Possible allies? Perhaps even something so unlikely as a brewing civil war? What if the diary entries were not the work of the "friendlies"? What if "unfriendly" forces sought to misguide and manipulate them? He fanned the pages with the edge of his thumb. Could he trust the entries at all or should he throw the damn thing away?

The Ren and the Chaffri: two names he'd heard on the second level, the names of two powerful alien races. He'd nearly forgotten them until now. The people on that level had suggested that one of them were the Dungeonmasters and spoke of both in fearful whisperings. But he'd learned nothing more of either race nor even heard the names again on any other level. Were they, then, just the products of local superstition, or were they, in truth, the architects of this fiendish place? He turned the names over and over in his head as he tried to make some sense of it all.

More than ever, he was convinced of this: He hadn't stumbled into the Dungeon by accident. He'd been brought here deliberately. So had Neville. So had all the others, probably. Annabelle, for instance. Could it be an accident that so soon after his arrival he'd found a granddaughter he hadn't even known about?

He put the book back inside his shirt. One question certainly remained hovering over all the others, and it made his head hurt.

What was going on?

He took a sip from the canteen he now carried. Samedi had provided several from his stores in the cave. Clive had one, and Smythe carried another. He mopped a hand across his brow and licked his lips. There would be no more drinking from the cyborg's mouth for him, or from anyone else's mouth. He took a second sip and put the canteen away. The heat and the searing winds had abated only slightly, and the exertion of the climb also exacted a toll. The muscles in his thighs ached, and he was glad for the sturdiness of his high-topped boots as he put one foot in front of the other.

> *What hills, what hills, so pale and high?*
> *Those are the hills of heaven, my love,*
> *But not for you and I.*

He tried to put the song out of his thoughts again. There were simply more important things to think about than folk songs.

There was Neville. What was he to make of Neville?

His brother seemed so quiet, almost cowed, not at all the Neville he thought he knew. Why, his Neville would be right up front with Baron Samedi trying to direct their course, himself, whether he knew the way or not, instead of following along docilely in line behind Annabelle. Why, from the first he'd expected Neville to wrest control of this little expedition away from him!

He glanced back over his shoulder. Filled with a sudden suspicion, he called back to his brother. "Say, Neville, remind me, will you? What was the name of Nanny's lapdog, anyway?"

Neville gave him a look of utter surprise. "Why, Tennyson, of course! Always thought the beast favored the old poet, she did. Strange notion, though, if you ask me. Whatever on earth made you think of that?"

Clive noted the expression of relief on Horace Hamilton Smythe's face. The quartermaster sergeant stood just behind his brother. Smythe knew the true intention behind his question. The Neville-clone they'd encountered on the sixth level had been unable to provide that simple answer, and so they'd discovered its pretense.

But this Neville had answered quickly and correctly. It was hard to doubt, then, that he was truly Neville Folliot, and Clive's brother. But he seemed so changed, subdued almost. Clive chewed his lip and thought and thought.

Gradually, the world became more muted. The gray near-light of perpetual evening segued down toward a more subtle and depressing shade that was not quite darkness. The mountains loomed all around them now like menacing giants unaware of the gnats that climbed their sides, and the sky closed in upon them like a hand ready to swat.

Still, Samedi led the way, unspeaking, never turning to look back, like Orpheus guiding nine Eurydices from the bowels of Hades.

"When will we get there?" Clive called suddenly. "How much farther?"

"Come," Samedi answered sullenly, stubbornly, lifting

one thin leg and setting it down, lifting the other, placing it carefully.

Clive wondered what time it was, day or night. It disconcerted him to look up and see nothing in the sky at all, just empty darkness, no sun, no moon, no stars, nothing by which to gauge the passage of the hours. He tried to count the seconds in his head and to order that count into minutes. It was a futile exercise, of course, one that left him frustrated and edgy.

For the first time he became aware of his shadow and of a gentle glow that cast it out like a thin line before him. He turned in wonderment and some relief, welcoming any source of light that might expel the cloying gloom.

Annie smiled wanly at him from within a pale green halo. She'd programmed the Baalbec A-9 for the effect despite the toll it would exact from her if she kept it on too long. But Clive could tell that the others welcomed the light, too, so he made no protest. Everyone knew enough to give her room while the Baalbec was operating, and the illumination, no matter how fragile, cheered them.

They reached the top of a narrow peak and rested for a while. The road wound down and down from that point into a mist-filled valley. Clive gazed that way, hands on his hips, his mouth in a pout. He wanted just to yell. They'd come so far, and there still seemed so far to go, and all around them nothing but this monotonous—nothingness!

Well, why not?

He set his hands to either side of his mouth, drew a deep breath, and yelled at the top of his lungs. It was great stress relief, he decided even before he'd gotten it all out.

"Goddamn you, out there, Ren, or Chaffri, or whoever you are!"

"You tell 'em, Clive-o!" Annabelle joined in.

"Good show, sah!" Smythe muttered approvingly. "Give the blighters what for!"

Finnbogg threw back his head and howled one long, loud note.

Samedi hurried to his side, his big eyes rolling. "Now you done it, boss. Done it good. Better get all your little asses movin' down this road fast now, cause the picnic is ovah!"

With that, Samedi gave a wave to the others, pushed his top hat down on his brow, and turned to run.

"Picnic!!!" Clive shouted, fury rising in him as he stared at the back of the so-called voodoo God. "What in God's name . . . !"

GODDAMN YOU

The volume nearly knocked Clive off his feet. He covered his ears against the pain in his skull and gazed upward, half-expecting to find the Deity, Himself, bending over them in all His glory.

OUT THERE

He staggered to one knee. Behind him, Tomàs lay rolling on the ground as he clutched his head. Sidi sat bent over, his head pressed between his knees. Annabelle sagged to the road, too, and Smythe bent over her, trying to shout over the thundrous assault, trying to convince her to turn off the Baalbec. Shriek had three of her arms around Chang Guafe, who looked awful even for a cyborg, causing Clive to wonder how high he'd tuned his audio receptors. Finnbogg, too, looked in terrible pain.

REN OR CHAFFRI

Neville looked white as a ghost, but he'd kept his feet under him. Clapping his hands to his ears, he sped past Clive in fast pursuit of the fleeing Samedi.

Now that was the Neville he knew, Clive thought bitterly, glaring at his brother's departing back.

OR WHOEVER YOU ARE

Those were his words, his own echo magnified tremendously and flung back at them. He felt his bones rattle as the force of it smashed at him.

YOU TELL 'EM

He struggled to get to his feet. He had to get up, had to get the others up and moving. But the pain! His head felt as if it were splitting!

CLIVE-O

He half-stumbled, half-crawled to Annabelle's side. She had managed to shut off the Baalbec, and Smythe had his arms around her. "Get her up!" he ordered his former batman. Smythe got his arms under her arms and pulled her to her feet. "Down the mountain!" Clive shouted. "Go!"

Sidi Bombay had heard the instructions and taken charge of Tomàs. He helped the little Portuguese up, and they followed the others.

"Não aguento mais!" Tomas cried, shaking his head in a useless effort to clear the ringing. "I can't stand this!"

"Shut up, shut up!" Sidi Bombay hissed. "Every sound you utter is a missile that comes back at us!" He gave Tomàs a kick in the pants and pulled him down the incline.

GOOD SHOW

"Oh, shut—!" Clive started to snap at the impossible echo. He caught himself. Sidi was right. Any sound was a deadly threat.

Shriek! he shouted in his thoughts, hoping she was there to hear. *Shriek! Can you handle Chang Guafe?*

In response, the arachnoid collected the cyborg in her four arms and scuttled downhill at astonishing speed.

That left only Finnbogg. The poor creature lay curled in a near-fetal position, its paws clasped tightly over its ears, emitting a low, pitiful howl of pain. Clive knelt down beside him and slipped an arm around his shoulder.

"Come on, Finnbogg, old boy!" he urged. "We've got to get out of here!" He kept his voice to a sharp whisper, his mouth close to Finnbogg's face. He forced the alien canine to look at him. "Let's go, Finnbogg!"

"Go! Leave Finnbogg!" Finnbogg cried, pushing him back with one powerful hand. "Owwww!" he howled, covering his ears again. "Clivefriend hurt Finnbogg!"

Rubbing a bruised backside, Clive crawled to Finnbogg's side again. "It's not me, Finnbogg!" he hissed, trying to keep his voice down. "I mean, it's me, but it's not really me. It's an echo." He tried to press a hand over Finnbogg's mouth. "Stop howling, Finnbogg!" he cried, forgetting himself. "It's all of us. Every sound we make comes right back at us. Now get up! Get up!"

But Finnbogg refused as thick tears ran down his cheeks. "Hurt too bad! Leave Finnbogg, Clivefriend!" He pressed harder still on his ears and squeezed his eyes shut.

Clive cursed and scrambled up angrily. "All right, pup!" he cursed, not bothering to keep his voice down. "I'm going, and you are, too! Cover your head if you must. This will do me just fine!" With that, he seized one of Finnbogg's legs and began to drag his whimpering comrade, bending all his strength to the task.

"Not leave Finnbogg, Clivefriend?" the canine moaned over one shoulder as he uncovered one ear.

"Not bloody likely!" Clive hissed between his teeth as he summoned his might and gave another massive heave. His heart hammered in his chest as he strained. *Good God*, Clive thought, *how much can the creature weigh?*

Finnbogg leaped up. "Then Finnbogg *must* go! Save Clivefriend!" He swept Clive up in huge arms before Clive could utter a protest and started down the road at a jostling run.

GODDAMN YOU! the echo started again.

"Put me down!" Clive demanded furiously. "I'm quite capable of running on my own two legs! I'm not a doll, you know!"

Finnbogg only squeezed him tighter and ran faster. "Save Clive Folliot!" Finnbogg repeated, panting. "Finnbogg's good friend! Yeah?"

"Yeah," Clive muttered helplessly under his breath, making up his mind to relax and enjoy the ride.

The road widened as they raced downhill. Their own voices rolled sonorously over their heads, shaking their senses and filling their eardrums with pins and needles. Finnbogg howled as he ran, no matter how Clive tried to convince him it only worsened the problem.

There was no sign of the others ahead, but Clive was sure he'd find them on the road somewhere. Down, down into the valley they descended, and the mist that Clive had seen rose up slowly around them.

It was a warm, damp mist that quickly permeated his clothing, a viscous fog that swirled in thick tendrils through the air and upon the road, obscuring it. At least, it muffled the voices that seemed to bounce unendingly among the peaks, muffled and diminished them so the pain left their ears. *How long can an echo last up there?* Clive wondered. He reminded himself this was the Dungeon, not his own native Earth. If the volume was so unnatural, how could he expect natural law to apply to duration?

Finnbogg slowed to a walk, but still he refused to set Clive down. *I am a doll to him,* Clive grumbled inwardly, *or a security blanket.*

The fog became a steam bath. The khakis were quickly soaked, and Clive's hair plastered to his forehead. Finnbogg's fur dampened, too, began to curl and hang in ropes. Clive almost barked a laugh when he looked up into his friend's face, but he held it back for politeness' sake.

They could see nothing ahead. Even the road beneath Finnbogg's feet had vanished. The air stirred like something alive when Clive blew a breath or passed his hand through it. "Nasty stuff," Finnbogg muttered. "Indeed," Clive agreed. He divided it with a sweep of his arm. It sealed itself again, leaving only a wispy vapor that clung to his sleeve momentarily before it diffused.

It was the fog of childhood ghost stories, exaggerated in the telling, surrealistically unreal. Impossible, like everything else in this Dungeon.

"Ooops," Finnbogg said.

Suddenly, Clive went flying through the air. He twisted and scrambled, uncertain exactly where the ground was. He hit it on his backside, on the same bruised spot he'd landed on earlier, and let out a yelp.

Unexpectedly, he began to slide. The road was steeper than he'd realized from above, and the mist had slickened the smooth black stone. *Where is the ledge?* a part of his mind screamed. *Was there a ledge?* He pressed his bootheels down to slow himself, with only marginal results until the left one caught briefly on some snag and he began to spin helplessly.

"Finnbooooogggg!" he cried, but the fog absorbed the sound with an impersonal efficiency. He reached out to both sides. There was nothing to grab hold of. How wide was the road here? Was he still on the road?

Abruptly, the slope flattened out and Clive lost momentum. He spun a few more times before coming to a stop, then lay still for a moment. His heart thundered in his ears as loud as anything at the top of the peak, and he waited for it to calm. Only then did he get to his feet.

The ground was still smooth and slick and he stood carefully, as if he were on ice, nearly slipping, and recovering only to slip again with the next step. He held his arms out for precarious balance.

"Finnbogg?" he called softly. Then, more boldly, "Neville? Annabelle? Smythe?" He waited, listening for an answer, and tried once more. "Anybody?" he said hopefully.

He considered what to do. Reason told him Finnbogg, at least, should be close. On the other hand, the creature's weight might have increased his momentum, carrying him along a lot farther. Clive scratched his head and wished he had paid closer attention to his physics studies during his years at Cambridge. But no sense regretting that now. He had to make a decision.

He decided to walk. Clearly, no one was within sound of his voice, though, he admitted, in this fog that needn't be far away. Nor could he see anyone. His own hand at arm's length was an uncertain proposition. The damn stuff made pea soup look like broth!

"Neville!" he called again, and waited for an answer. It was best to call out, he decided. Maybe someone would hear him if he passed close enough.

"Annabelle?" he tried hopefully.

"Shriek!" Then, he stopped himself. There was a better way to try that. Maybe he could touch the arachnoid's thoughts if he concentrated hard enough. He squeezed his eyes shut and called with all his mind, *Shriek!*

There was no answer from anyone. Still, he shouted the names of his friends, hoping they might hear and respond. He began to worry, though. Where could they have gone? Was it possible he was alone? Could he have fallen into yet another level of this Dungeon? He felt for the hilt of his saber. At least he still had a weapon.

After a while he tired of calling out names, so he began to sing. That old folk song crept back into his thoughts, and he found himself intoning self-consciously.

> *Well met, well met, my own true love,*
> *Well met, well met, cried he.*
> *I've just returned from the salty sea,*
> *All for the love of thee.*

When Annabelle tapped him on the shoulder, he nearly jumped out of his skin. He hadn't heard a footstep or a breath or anything to warn him of her approach. Of course not, over his singing.

"Guess I got my talent from Grandma," she said with a smile.

Clive threw his arms around her. "Annie!" he yelled. "Annabelle, thank God!" He hugged her close and breathed a sigh of relief, admitting to himself how much the thought of being alone down here had frightened him. It was easy to admit, now that it wasn't the case.

"That really gave a new meaning to the Miranda warning, didn't it?"

He looked into her eyes, reluctant to let her go. "What's that?"

"The Miranda warning," she repeated, thrusting a finger skyward. "Up there on the peak. You know, 'Anything you say may be used against you'?"

"Oh," he said without comprehension. He knew by her tone, though, it was some kind of joke. "Yes, that's funny. Wasn't Sergeant Smythe with you?"

She freed herself from the embrace. "Well, don't laugh yourself to death on my account," she chided. "We got separated. Slipped on the road or something. One hell of a ride, if you want to know, or did you come by the same route?"

"Yes, the same route," he assured her, rubbing his backside. It felt raw through the wet khaki. She giggled and rubbed hers, too, but the leather had offered more protection. Still, her laughter lifted his spirits. If they had found each other, then they could find the rest.

He took her hand and held it tightly. "Don't let go," he warned her. "We've got to find the others."

"Will you teach me that song?" she suggested. "You really didn't do it that badly."

He grinned and started from the beginning. It was better than shouting names, and more fun, and Annabelle was a fast learner. They sang together and pushed at the fog with the power of their voices.

• CHAPTER SEVEN •

The Goode Children
of the Mist

"Clive?"

"Neville?"

"Major Folliot, sah!"

The voices of their friends drifted to them as if from a great distance, mere whispers that flowed ghostlike through the fog. Clive and Annabelle shouted back hopefully, but the voices faded without response.

Clive imagined all his comrades wandering around, blindly groping for each other, unable to see through the dense mist that filled this mountain valley. He wondered how long they had been separated, how they would find each other, if the fog would ever lift. He felt like a shade in some Greek Tartarus.

Annabelle squeezed his hand. "Sing it again, Clive-o," she said.

But he didn't feel like singing anymore. They'd done the same folk song three times until she'd got it right, and it had buoyed their spirits for a while as they searched for their friends. But after a while the words began to sting a little, cut a little too deeply, and Clive stopped.

They had lost the road, of that he was sure. The surface under their feet felt soft and powdery like ash. The road had been hard stone, and smooth, like basalt. No doubt the others had lost the road as well. They could be anywhere in the valley by now.

Damn Samedi, anyway, why hadn't he warned them about echoes and the danger at the top of the peak? Why hadn't he warned them about this valley? Where was he?

"Annie," he said, using the familiar form of her name, probably because Finnbogg was on his mind, "how much light can you get from the Baalbec?"

She frowned. "I don't know, Clive-o, I've never turned it up all the way. The limit would depend on the body heat I'm producing. I'm game to try, though. Here, keep tight hold on my hand and don't break the coupling. That way you won't get zapped."

She grabbed his right hand in her left, then began fingering the implants on the inside of her left forearm. Slowly, they began to glow with a soft greenish radiance. Clive could feel the pulse under her skin as the glow began to brighten and build. Annabelle looked up at him, and their gazes met. His lips drew into a thin line as the light pushed at the fog.

But the fog only threw the light back at them. The brighter they glowed, the worse vision became. "Forget it," he told Annabelle disgustedly. She might have continued to glow and become a beacon for the others, but he had no guarantee they could see her light at all, and the toll on Annabelle would have been too great. "Turn it off," he said with firmness when he saw she was considering the same idea, and gradually the light diminished.

"Englishman!"

That was Sidi Bombay! Clive whirled in the direction of the voice and pulled Annabelle along. "Sidi!" he called. "Over here! Annabelle's with me!" He groped through the fog with his hands outstretched. But if Sidi heard him, he gave no sign of it. Again came the cry of "Englishman!"— but from farther away.

"I'm dying in these leathers," Annabelle complained melodramatically. "I swear these jeans could walk by themselves."

"Then don't take them off," Clive grumbled. "The last

thing we need is one more life-form stumbling around in this murk."

She nudged him gently in the ribs with an elbow. "Careful, Granddad. You're developing a sense of humor."

"I'd prefer a more useful sense right now," he answered irritably. "Speaking of senses, where is Chang Guafe? Shouldn't he be able to spot us by our body heat? What did you call that?"

"Infrared," she told him again. "And I don't know. Maybe this hot mist is scrambling his receptors. It's like a steam bath. Must be nearly a hundred."

He stopped, sighed, and bit his lip. "I don't know whether to keep going or just stand still. We could be wandering farther and farther from the road."

He waited, hoping she might say something useful, but Annabelle kept silent. Clive wanted to kick something. There hadn't been a situation in the Dungeon yet from which he hadn't been able to think or fight his way out, but this damnable fog had him stymied. He'd never seen anything like it! Now all his friends were separated, possibly in danger, and it was his fault. Because of his infantile display of frustration back on the peak, they were in this mess. It was almost enough to make him scream again.

Then, the mist unfolded to reveal a figure coming toward them. At first, it was a shadow, barely a dark outline in the fog. It approached them slowly, bearing something draped over one arm, reaching toward them with the other.

Clive thought he knew that silhouette. "Neville?" he called hesitantly. "Is that you?"

Annabelle's grip tightened on Clive's hand.

Neville Folliot stepped out of the fog. He wore the look of a dead man. His eyes focused on nothing, and his jaw hung slack. Deep creases furrowed his forehead where the brows pinched together. Rivulets of sweat and moisture streamed down his face. He had removed his uniform jacket and carried it over his left forearm. The cuffed sleeves of his white dress shirt he had pushed well above the elbow, and the front he had unbuttoned to the waist-band of his trousers.

Seeing them at last, his features recomposed themselves. His brow unfurrowed, and the gleam of life came into his eyes. He smiled suddenly and shook his brother's hand. "Clive!" he exclaimed. "Good God, I'm glad to see you. Glad to see anyone. And I see you found Annabelle!"

"She found me, actually," Clive admitted, withdrawing his hand coolly, frowning at his brother's appearance. His own khakis were soaked with sweat, and his shirt clung uncomfortably to his chest and back, but he had not exposed himself in such a flagrant manner. He was embarrassed for Annabelle's sake, even though she obviously was not. "Have you encountered anyone else?" he continued. "What happened to the others?"

Neville wiped a sleeve across his eyes and stared at each of them in turn. "I haven't the foggiest notion—you'll pardon the expression, I'm sure. I think I've been wandering for hours down here. Called out until I was hoarse, I did." He rubbed a hand under his chin. "Still a bit of a sore throat. Worse than the bloody wharf district, if you ask me."

"Watch your vulgar language!" Clive snapped. But he agreed London had nothing to match this. "Take hold of Annabelle's hand," he said to his brother. "Let's not get separated again."

"My most charming relative," Neville said, lifting Annabelle's fingers to his lips. He planted a delicate kiss on her knuckles, winked, and smiled.

"You're slime, but you're my slime," Annabelle answered, putting on her best, most formally exaggerated British accent. Then, with a brother on either side she let go their hands and linked her arms through theirs, instead. "Now," she proclaimed, "let's go see the wizard."

Clive and Neville looked at each other over her head. They both shrugged at the same time. "Who knows?" Neville said. "Down here there may actually be one."

Well, Clive thought, *we are three now.* Three down and

six more to go. Seven if he counted Samedi. They moved slowly, peering into the mist seeking shadows and outlines, listening for voices. Every so often they called out a name and waited for an answer. The only sounds they heard were the soft scrapings of their own steps on the ground.

Clive began to feel lightheaded. He wiped the sweat from his eyes, from his face. He knew he was losing moisture too fast, dehydrating in the constant, relentless heat. He took out his canteen again, sipped, and offered it to his companions, who also drank. While Annabelle tipped her head back, he glanced at his brother. Their gazes met, and the message passed between them. Neville knew they were in trouble, too.

"Did you hear that?" Annabelle asked suddenly, passing the canteen back to Clive.

"Hear what?" he answered. "I heard nothing."

"Wait," Neville said, holding up a hand. "I thought I . . ."

They froze, straining to listen, and it came again like a plaintive cry. Out from the fog that single small sound issued, sending a shiver up their spines. There was no mistaking it, a tiny child's voice, weak and uncertain, fearful. And the single word it spoke was:

"Mommy?"

Annabelle slipped her arm from Clive's and covered her mouth. She stared into the fog, her eyes wide and bright with doubt and horror. She shriveled, drawing into herself. Her elbows pressed into her ribs, her shoulders slumped forward and down. Even her knees pressed together. She chewed a fingertip, then stopped. "Amanda?" It was a soft whisper and quickly swallowed by the fog.

"Don't be silly, Annabelle," Clive started. "It can't . . ."

Annabelle leaned forward as if in a desperate effort to see through the curtain of mist. "Amanda?" she said again, louder, more certain.

"Mommy?"

Perhaps it came from straight ahead, Clive couldn't be sure, but before he could do anything, Annabelle tore her other arm free from Neville and ran toward the sound, crying, "Amanda, baby! I'm here, Amanda!"

"Don't lose her!" Clive shouted at his brother, trying his best to keep his great-great-granddaughter in sight. A vague outline, a racing shadow, was all he had to follow, and the mist seemed determined to obscure even that.

Neville passed him. Neville always had been a better runner, winning at footraces and steeplechases and those sorts of things. He caught up to Annabelle easily and tackled her in a most ungentlemanly fashion. For an instant, they both disappeared as the fog rolled over them, and Clive's heart stopped. But then, they were on their feet, scuffling and struggling. One shadow kicked at the other and shouted angrily in Annabelle's voice. The low-throated curses were definitely Neville's.

"Amanda! Amanda!" Annabelle screamed hysterically as she kicked and kicked Neville's shins. He held both her wrists in unyielding fists, determined not to let her trigger the Baalbec A-9. He'd already had a taste of that.

"Pardon me, lady," he said suddenly just as Clive caught up. He let go of Annabelle's left arm just long enough to draw one hand up and slap her to the ground.

"Neville!" Clive cried in outrage. "Damn you, Neville!"

Both men knelt down beside her as she sat slowly up. Neville, Clive noted, was careful to keep a grip on the hand that would activate her self-defense unit, intent on stopping her if she tried to use it. "They weren't your shins she was beating on, little brother," Neville said unapologetically. "And she's a strong one, besides. The way she was twisting, she was bound to get loose long enough to turn that thing on. Where would either of us be then? I'll tell you where she'd be, all right. Running free and crazy in this pea soup, that's where."

He hated to admit it, but Neville was right. If Annabelle had used the Baalbec they wouldn't have been able to touch her, and it would have been only a matter of instants before they'd have lost her. He slipped one arm around her shoulders and bent close to examine her.

There was a darkening place on her left cheek where Neville's blow had landed.

Tears trickled from Annabelle's eyes as she looked into Clive's. "I was sure it was Amanda," she said weakly. "I heard her, I know her voice!"

Clive wrapped her in his arms. She trembled against him, even as her gaze darted frantically around. One hand clutched his shoulder, then she pressed her face against his and wept. Neville let go of her arm and sat back with a sigh, folding his legs under him. Clive looked at his brother as he rocked Annabelle and held her close and waited for her grief to pass. He wanted to tell her that they'd get out of here, find the way home, and that Amanda would be waiting for her. But he was no longer sure of that, himself, and he wouldn't lie to her. So instead, he held her and pretended to be strong and kept quiet. If he said nothing, there would be no quaver of doubt to hear.

"Mommy?"

He felt Annabelle lurch as he jerked his head around. Neville sprang to his feet, poised, ready, the saber already half out of its scabbard as he stared at the shadow emerging from the mist.

The child might have been four years old, not more. Dark, shiny hair hung down over her shoulders and into the glittery moist eyes that stared back so widely. Her naked little body shone palely in the shifting vapor as she reached out with one plump, stubby-fingered hand for Annabelle.

Annabelle screamed with delight. "It was Amanda!" she shouted at Clive as she pushed him away and reached for her child. "I told you I knew her voice!"

"Mommy!" the child said again. Then, as Annabelle's arms went around her, Amanda made a noise like an angry cat. The pudgy little hand she had carried behind her back in what had seemed a posture of childish shyness slashed out at her mother's throat.

Annabelle screamed and fell back, blood spurting dark between her fingers as she clutched the wound. Amanda leaped on top of her mother, spitting and hissing like a small, furious beast. Again and again those tiny clawed hands struck, and Annabelle rolled and screamed and tried to cover her face.

Then Neville grabbed the child from behind. It spat at him, making that terrible feline sound, and clawed at his bare arms as it also tried to kick him. He shook it angrily in an effort to make it stop, but it continued to spit and scratch, and blood ran thick into Neville's sleeves and soaked his shirt. At last, he gave a furious roar and heaved the creature away from himself.

"I'm sorry!" Clive shouted, his heart pounding in his chest as he came to Neville's side. "I was just too stunned to move. I couldn't move. It was a child!" He gripped his sword's hilt and shot a glance into the fog. There was no sign of the child, if it was a child at all.

Neville gave a moan and sagged to his knees, holding his arms limply out before him as he uttered a string of curses and oaths. Clive tried to examine the wounds, afraid some artery had been breached. But Neville growled and pushed him away.

"See to Annabelle!" he ordered. "That damn thing got her throat!"

Annabelle lay sobbing on the ground, curled into a fetal ball that Clive had a hard time prying her out of. Her arms and shoulders were a bloody mass of scratches. Clive felt a tightening in his gut as he bent over her, and tears filled his eyes. He wiped them away, though, as he ripped a piece of his khaki shirt and folded it into a useful square. Four jagged cuts pumped blood on the right side of her neck. Clive poured water from his canteen onto the square and daubed at them as he wept. Annabelle moaned and jerked at the touch of the cloth, but Clive kept up a pressure.

Neville crawled to his side. "Let me see," he said, and Clive lifted a corner of the wet square. "Good." Clive shot him a look that said how could anything be good about this, and Neville explained. "The carotid artery is here."

He drew a finger gingerly down the side of his own neck. Clive looked under the square again and realized the cuts stopped just short, but by only a hair's breadth. "She'll have a lovely set of scars, though, little brother, if you don't strangle her."

Clive frowned and eased off the pressure. The bleeding had slowed. He poured more water from the canteen onto the strip of shirt cloth and tried to wash her other cuts. Mercifully, Annabelle seemed to have passed out. She resisted and helped no more than if she were a doll as he worked. When he could do no more for her, he turned to Neville with the water and the cloth.

It was then they heard another, more familiar sound, the beating of great leathery wings. Side by side, the brothers looked up as Philo B. Goode, who now called himself Beelzebub, descended before them. His ankle seemed completely healed, nor was there any evidence of Finnbogg's teeth or jaws on his unblemished flesh.

In his arms, he cradled the child-monster who had attacked them.

Annabelle sat up. "He's got Amanda," she said painfully.

"That's not Amanda," Neville told her firmly, still on his knees as he regarded Goode.

Clive licked his lips as he noted how Neville and Goode stared at each other. "I never thought to ask after our last encounter," he ventured, "but have you two also met?"

"He did me a disservice back in Africa," Neville explained, never taking his gaze from their winged foe. "Passed me a note from one Lady Baker, wife of one Lord Samuel Baker, of whom you might have heard. They're on the social register. A charming couple, really. They were enjoying a safari in the Bukoba country, and I chanced to meet them. Anyway, the note suggested a, well, an amorous liaison to which I responded in person. Lord Baker found us and took great affront, though I assure you nothing untoward transpired. Not that it mightn't have," he added with a wink at Clive, "had we more time and a good bottle of brandy. The note, needless to say, was a practical joke, one of this chap's forgeries. He's quite good at them."

Clive glared at his brother. "You've done business with him?"

Neville shrugged. "I met him in a wharfside tavern after leaving the ship in Zanzibar, and we played a few hands of cards. Some blokes robbed us both in an alley after it was over. Took all my money, they did." Neville Folliot nodded toward Goode, who listened patiently with a big grin. "Goode, here, helped me obtain supplies anyway by, uh, charging them to certain other wealthy individuals."

"Such as the Sultan Seyyid Majid ben Said?" Clive suggested, recalling an unpleasant episode of his own stay in Zanzibar.

Neville shrugged again. "And a few of his relatives. You met the chap?"

Clive rolled his eyes and turned to Philo B. Goode. "You look better in this incarnation, Goode," he said. "It suits you."

Before Goode could answer, Annabelle slapped her head. "System malf! I've been on downtime! I know him, too!" She shot an accusing look at the archdemon. "Weren't you a roadie on my band's tour? Sure, I remember, chipchewer! You set up the equipment for the Piccadilly show!"

Philo B. Goode fluttered his wings, causing the mist to churn and swirl while he flung back his head and laughed. "Ah, my darling Ms. Leigh," Goode acknowledged. He licked his lips and ran his tongue over the tips of his fangs as he leered at her. "I'm a man of many places and many times. But come now, tell me how you like my little pet." He flipped the child over in his arms. The Amanda-thing arched its back and uttered a low growl as Goode ran a palm along its spine. "Mommy," it said, but there was nothing human in the sound.

"Bastard!" Annabelle muttered, her temper barely under control.

Philo B. Goode clucked, "My, my, Ms. Leigh, such

language. What must your grandfather and your uncle think?"

"Well, I, for one, think she's quite right," Neville volunteered offhandedly.

"Leave her alone, Goode," Clive threatened, low-voiced, rising slowly to his feet, laying a hand to the hilt of his saber.

"Leave her alone?" Again, Goode laughed, flexing his wings as he did so, stirring the fog and causing waves of damp heat to wash over them. He continued to stroke and pet the Amanda creature on his arm in an almost obscene manner. "My dear Major Clive Folliot, you fail to understand! It was a miscalculation that brought you here, an error which I plan now to correct." His catlike gaze shifted from Clive to Neville as, again, he licked the points of his fangs. "And you, Major Neville Folliot, you have been such a disappointment. Barely an entertainment. Your poor little brother, whom you referred to on the occasion of our acquaintance as 'inept and unprepossessing' has proved much more of a challenge."

Clive looked at Neville and raised an eyebrow. " 'Inept and unprepossessing'?"

Neville shrugged and tilted his head sheepishly. "I misspoke myself." It was the closest he'd ever come to apologizing to Clive.

Philo B. Goode sprang into the air. His pinions beat a powerful rhythm as he hovered just above their heads, still clutching his precious pet. "It's checkmate, Clive Folliot. Even with your friends you never really had enough pieces to play out the game."

"Whatever you think, Goode," Clive said, easing his saber from the sheath, "this is no game."

"Oh, but it is, Major!" Goode roared, laughing. "And I've an inexhaustible supply of pawns."

Without further warning, Philo B. Goode tossed the Amanda-thing at Clive's face. It came to him, screeching and hissing, claws reaching for his eyes.

Clive saw in plenty of time and drew back his sword.

Still, though, it was a child's face that he saw, and he couldn't quite bring himself to strike. At the last possible instant, he dodged it altogether. It gave an angry shriek, twisted, and landed on its feet. Hardly a heartbeat passed before it leaped at him again. He threw up his left arm to intercept it. Claws dug into his flesh; teeth tore his khaki sleeve. With a cry of pain, Clive flung the creature away.

Overhead, Philo B. Goode roared with mirth as from deep in the mists more shadows emerged, spitting and hissing, all Amanda-things, all identical, all reaching with razor claws. Clive stared in horror as dozens of little girls, all resembling Annabelle, rushed at them out of the fog.

Annabelle gave a scream of anger and dismay.

The children swept upon them like a wave, scratching and tearing, biting like little animals. Clive found his own moral code playing him false. He pushed and kicked at his small attackers, but halfheartedly. He couldn't bring himself to use the saber.

"Don't be soft, little brother!" Neville called, but before he could bring his own blade to bear one of the little beasts jumped up and sank its teeth into his wrist. Neville screamed and dropped his sword before he could shake free.

He heard Annabelle's cries, saw her rolling on the ground under the weight of half a dozen tiny Amandas. She didn't lash out at all, didn't even push them away. She tried only to protect her face and head as tiny fists pummeled her and tiny claws raked her skin.

Suddenly, Clive pitched backward under the onslaught. They pulled his hair, clawed at his eyes. Tiny teeth closed on his throat. Somehow, he lost his sword. With a furious roar, he swung out with his arms and sent his foes sprawling, but others took their places before he could catch his breath. Despite himself, he screamed in pain and threw up an arm to protect his eyes.

Then, for the first time, he heard the Baalbec. It sounded a second time and a third. Annabelle was fighting back! He knew what it must have cost her to make that decision, remembered how badly he'd felt about facing and slaying the Neville-clone on level six. But these were her daughters—that is, creatures made to resemble her daughter. Still, the emotional price . . .

With a wrench he freed one arm, caught the hair of the Amanda-thing nearest his face, and snapped its head back. It gave a screech of agony as he hurled it away and reached for the one that took its place. He punched and slapped and struck with his fists, elbows, any part of his body he could free, and managed to sit up.

A pile of stunned little bodies grew around Annabelle. All she'd had to do was activate the Baalbec. The children did the rest. They threw themselves mindlessly at her in wave after wave, touching her field. The sound of its energy whip-crack filled his ears.

Neville stood just beyond her, flinging the creatures right and left, a complete madman. He growled like an animal, himself, and his face wore a bestial expression. The shirt had been ripped from his body, and his trousers hung in tatters. As Clive watched, he lifted a child, broke it over his knee, and flung it away with all his might.

Philo B. Goode broke into enthusiastic applause. "Oh, this is delicious! Is it not special, Annabelle Leigh, as I promised you it would be?"

"You monster!" Annabelle raged, shaking her fist. The Baalbec A-9 implants gleamed with mingled blood and sweat on her bare upraised arm. "You think this is a game? That you can just play with us?" Hysteria burned in her eyes. Five more Amandas leaped at her, screeching, and hurtled unexpectedly backward to twitch and writhe before collapsing unconscious.

Goode clutched his belly with laughter as more and more of his pets swarmed out of the fog and flung themselves at Annabelle. The Baalbec's zap made a constant staccato as they reached out for her.

But Annabelle ignored them. Her gaze focused angrily on Philo B. Goode as she waded through the children to stand before him. "You fucking scrodhead!" she stormed. "I'm gonna crash your whole fucking program!"

Her right hand slapped against the implants.

Clive's horrified exclamation died before he could utter it as every inch of his skin crawled with sudden electricity and every muscle in his body convulsed. He hit the ground, his fall softened only by the bodies of several of the Amanda-things as they succumbed to the same force.

His chest burned, but he didn't lose consciousness. He saw the look on Goode's face as the force hit him as well. The huge leathery wings snapped out straight and locked, and Philo B. Goode fell like a very surprised stone.

Annabelle picked up Neville's saber and walked with hysterical calm to her tormentor's stunned form. Clive gained enough control over his muscles to ease up onto one elbow, but not enough to do much else. There was no way he could stop Annabelle from what she obviously intended.

She set the point of the blade to Goode's heart as a groan issued from his lips. "Shove this up your disc drive, you bastard!" she hissed as she leaned her weight on the saber.

Goode let go a sharp sigh of pain. His head lifted from the ground, then sank back. "Fool!" he whispered through clenched teeth. "The game goes on. I am but the servant who goeth before the master!" Another long sigh fled his lips, and with it his life.

Annabelle looked down at Goode. Slowly, she let go of the saber and stared, instead, at her hand. Then, she turned and stared in horror at all the tiny bodies that so resembled her daughter. She bit her lip, let go the meekest of whimpers, and slipped to the ground in a faint.

▪ CHAPTER EIGHT ▪

The Unexpected Ferryman

"I didn't realize she could push the field that far from her body," Neville said worriedly.

"Neither did I," Clive answered, grim-voiced, as he bent over her. "Her skin's cold as ice."

Every muscle in his body burned and ached, but he began to rub her as briskly as he could. Neville joined in. The hot mist should help to bring her body temperature back up, too, if it wasn't already too late. But such a tremendous power surge must have been a strain on her system.

"Thank God the thing shut itself off," Neville muttered as he worked. "There must be some kind of safety feature, an automatic shutdown point."

Clive massaged her left hand, then recoiled, appalled, as he noticed the smear of blood spreading on her pale flesh, his own blood that ran down the underside of his arm and into his palm. Well, he couldn't think of his own wounds now. He and Neville both were scored and lacerated with scratches and cuts. So was Annabelle. There simply was nothing he could do about them now.

He bent over Annabelle and listened for her heartbeat. "It's there, but faint."

"Take off your shirt, Clive, or what's left of it. We've got to get her warm."

Clive removed the tattered garment and spread it over

Annabelle's chest and shoulders as best he could, then settled back on his haunches and looked at his brother. Neville was nearly naked. Only his boots and strategic remnants of his trousers remained. His flesh was a bloody lacework, and blood matted his blond hair into ropes and knots. He appeared altogether a wild man. Nor was that an inappropriate description, perhaps. He remembered the vision of his brother hurling their attackers right and left, growling like a beast. It was not a pleasant vision.

Neville, too, settled back. "It's up to her now," he announced. "The air's hot enough to warm her fast." He picked up the arm with the implanted controls for the Baalbec A-9 and cradled it gently. "Unless this damn thing did damage that we don't know about."

The twins regarded each other then, their gazes locking, lingering upon one another. There was nothing of a challenge in those gazes. It was a mutual exploration on a very subtle level. Clive had thought he knew Neville. But he wasn't sure he knew this man across from him. Clive had thought that he hated Neville. But he didn't know if he hated this man at all. Clive had thought that he envied Neville. He wasn't sure if he envied this man.

All the childhood wrongs that Neville had done him, all the insults and injuries came rushing back into Clive's mind, and he tried desperately to fit them to the face of the man he saw now. Yet, he failed. The memories broke and blew away like a fine powder, like dust that he could see and smell and taste, but that eluded his grasp.

He looked away, confused.

Neville spoke first. "Hello, little brother."

Clive looked up. "I am not your *little brother*," he said stiffly.

Neville's lips parted in a slight smile as he nodded his head. "But you are my brother," he affirmed, "my twin."

Around them, the Amanda creatures began to awake. The brothers started and reached for their swords. Neville came up empty-handed, and he shot a look toward the corpse of Philo B. Goode. His blade stood at attention in the dead man's chest.

Slowly, the little girl-things sat up. They snarled and hissed as they shrugged off the effects of the Baalbec. "Mommy," they uttered in low, unnatural voices, "mommy, mommy." There was no love in the sound. It was a hunting cry, a lure, no more. They seemed uninterested in Clive and Neville and Annabelle as they stirred. They arched their backs and stretched, catlike, rose to tiny feet, and tottered toward the still form of their master. "Mommy," they whispered, the sound an eerie susurrus in the mist. One by one they moved toward Philo B. Goode, touched him, explored with their fingers, licked his face and hands, his chest and wings. They crawled over him in slow motion like maggots, and when he didn't respond, they eventually drifted off into the fog.

"What is that weird sound?" Neville snapped with some irritation as he rubbed the back of his neck.

Clive had been too awed watching the children to note the distant shrill ululation that barely penetrated the fog. "That's Shriek!" he exclaimed, leaping to his feet only to fall sideways. He looked at his right leg in surprise. A long rip in his trousers allowed the material to flop open, exposing a deep gash in his thigh that pumped a steady crimson stream.

He pressed his hand over the wound and squeezed his eyes shut in an attempt to ignore the sudden pain. He had to concentrate. Maybe Shriek had been too far away to hear him earlier, but she was closer now. He crossed his fingers.

Shriek! he called, firing his thoughts in all directions like warning shots. That was how he tried to imagine it, like a hunter alerting his comrades by shooting into the air. *Shriek!* he shouted silently over and over. *Shriek!*

"What are you doing?" Neville entreated as he stepped around Annabelle and knelt by Clive. He pushed his twin's hand away and looked at the gash. He made a face. "Nasty, that," he said. He tore away Clive's trouser leg and began stripping the fabric into bandages. Before he could bind the injury, though, a white silky spray snagged his arm. Neville gave a startled cry and sprang up, trying to rip free.

Before he could do so, Shriek appeared. Her eyes were unreadable as she glanced at the twins and hurried to Annabelle's side. The arachnoid kneeled on her front legs as she bent over the unconscious human female, chittering and clacking her mandibles.

It was then Clive saw the strands of webbing attached to her left rearmost foot. They trailed behind her and disappeared into the fog.

An instant later, Tomàs joined them. The strand encircled his waist and continued to snake back into the fog. He stared at them for an instant with horror on his face. "*Senhor* Clive! *Senhor* Neville! *Ai, Christo!* What has happened?" He glanced in all directions as if searching for danger as he knelt down between them. He spied the body of Philo B. Goode partially obscured now by the drifting mists. "Who is that?"

"The good Mr. Goode," Neville explained through clenched teeth. One hand rested now along his ribs. His expression betrayed the pain he had denied too long.

Clive tried to sit up. "How did you find us?"

Tomàs saw the gash on Clive's leg and gasped. Seeing the small pile of strips that Neville had started to make from the khaki material and discerning their intended purpose, the little Portuguese got to work. He washed the wound by pouring water from his own canteen over it, folded one strip, pressed it over the cut, and tied another around it.

"I found Shriek wandering in this cursed fog," he explained while he worked. "We wandered long time, very far from road, sometimes hearing voices, but finding no one."

Clive thanked the little sailor for the bandage, but he suspected it was Shriek who probably found Tomàs.

"*Ai*, you are a mess, so much blood!" Tomàs exclaimed,

dampening a strip and wiping at the scratches around the gash as he continued his story. "Suddenly, Shriek she go *demente!* Crazy!" He threw his hands up and made a face. "She catch me in her web and run into fog. I follow fast as I can, and she shoot her web everywhere blindly, just shoot it into fog!" He gestured again and rolled his eyes. "Once, she pause long enough I catch up and jump on her back. She not care. She stop again as if to look around. I relax one minute to catch my breath, and *ai de mim!* she start running, and I fall off." He smacked his palm against his forehead and smiled broadly. "But here I am!"

A shadow took form at the edge of the fog and merged into the familiar shape of Chang Guafe. The ruby lenses of his eyes burned at full intensity, causing a red glow that diffused spectrally in the mist that surrounded him. Shriek's webbing made a thick coil over one of his arms. "No apparent hostilities," he observed. "All sensors nominal."

Clive grinned, recalling the previous evening and his conversation with the cyborg. "Hello to you, too, Chang. Good to see you again."

Chang Guafe moved closer to the center of the growing gathering. "Monitoring accelerated blood pressure rhythms in both Majors Folliot," he reported, "accompanied by inefficient respiratory rates."

"We've had a little excitement," Neville explained with droll amusement as he winked at Clive. "But you'd better take a look at Miss Leigh."

Shriek's thoughts brushed into Clive's mind. *Problem her body is not, despite lacerations,* the arachnoid told him. There was a knife edge of fear in her thoughts that spread to Clive across their neural linkage. *Reach, though, her mind I cannot! Closed, she is!*

Clive pushed Tomàs back and crawled on his knees to Annabelle's side. He looked up at Shriek. "What's wrong with her, Shriek? Was it the Baalbec?"

Shriek clicked her mandibles and trained three of her eyes on him. The other three remained on Annabelle. *Shock, it is, Being Clive, deep shock. Even over great distance her mindcry heard I. Egglings, saw I. Her egglings. Then, madness, madness! Fear of Annabelle being*—she put two of her hands to her head as she shook it from side to side—*very powerful.*

Clive laid a hand tenderly on Shriek's shoulder. "Are you all right?"

Shriek swallowed as she nodded. *Frightened. Mindfear of Annabelle being lingers, but fades. Well, am I.*

He pointed to the webbing attached to her foot. "Do you have all our friends?"

The question seemed to trouble her. *Many beings in the web,* she answered. *Luck my spinning guided. Blindly worked I, casting my web. Much struggling, many vibrations. Too many beings, friends just to be.*

Clive rubbed his chin and winced, finding new cuts even on his face. "You've probably snared some of her egglings," Clive explained. "Shriek, we'll care for Annabelle. Can you backtrack and find the others? Samedi, too? Cut the rest loose. They seem to be harmless without Philo B. Goode to lead them."

Can find all I, Shriek answered, rising. *Vibrations lead I very fast.* She somehow slipped the strands of webbing from her rear foot, pressed them to the ground, and rubbed her spinnerets against them, making a firm anchor. Then she disappeared into the fog.

In no time at all the entire company was reunited. Finnbogg set up a grievous howl when he saw Annabelle. The others crowded around them. Cuts and scrapes were washed and bandaged with scraps of cloth. When the strips of khaki were exhausted, Smythe donated his shirt. Neville had a deep and very painful rake along his ribs and a serious trio of wounds down his back. There was no way they could bandage Annabelle's throat, but her arms and back were also severely clawed. Clive surveyed his own injuries and declared them minor, but the others pushed him back down when he tried to get up.

Baron Samedi hung sheepishly back at the edge of the fog, top hat in hand.

"Why didn't you warn us about this place, Samedi?" Clive demanded.

Samedi looked at his hat and shrugged. "Hey, Jack, everybody slips up now an' then, ya know? I panicked, okay, when you started flappin' your tiny Caucasian lips up high, right? So sue. If we'd taken it all slow an' kept together, things'd gone slick as satin, no problem."

Sidi frowned. "Tiny Caucasian lips?" he said pointedly. "Though you have been my gracious host and guide, I must insist that you, noble sir, are as white as my friends. Indeed, as white as any man I have ever seen."

Samedi looked at him as he tilted his head and cocked an eyebrow. "Well, *pahdon me!*" It was a perfect imitation of Smythe's voice and accent. Samedi donned his hat and patted it down over his brow.

Clive frowned at their guide. The creature still confused him with his funny speech, and more, with his elusive background. He claimed he'd been sent to show them the way. But who'd sent him? Could Clive trust him? Could he trust Samedi's employers?

Clive knew he'd have to answer those questions soon, but now it was best they get out of this fog. He had no more fear of the Amanda-things, but there might be other dangers lurking beyond the range of vision. "Let's get out of here," he said suddenly.

He started to rise, but Horace Hamilton Smythe pushed him back down. "No, sah," Smythe insisted. "You can't walk, yet. That leg wound is too deep and needs time to close."

Clive tried to push him back. "Don't be silly, Sergeant," he responded. "We can't stay here in this muck. The bandage will have to do. Now help me up."

But Smythe was adamant. "Shriek or Chang Guafe will carry you, sah, and Major Neville, too. Finnbogg will take Miss Annabelle."

Finnbogg looked enthusiastic. "Okay, okay!" he agreed. "Finnbogg carry Annie gentle as litterpup!"

"Don't be absurd, Horace!" Clive snapped, appalled at

the idea of being carried like a doll. After all, he was a grown man and an officer of Her Majesty's army. A certain decorum must be maintained. "I'm perfectly capable of walking on my own." Again, he pushed Smythe back and sat up, intent on rising to his feet.

"Better listen, little brother." Neville grinned weakly at him. "I don't think they're going to give you a choice."

Too late, Clive noted his brother's eyes, the way his gaze flickered to something behind Clive. He jerked around just in time to feel a new scratch on his right shoulder, followed almost immediately by a rapidly spreading sensation of numbness. He folded helplessly sideways into Smythe's arms. A moment of terror seized him as he resisted the chemical's effect, uncertain of exactly what had been done to him.

Shriek moved into his field of vision, a hair-spike still grasped in one hand. She'd drugged him again as she'd done twice before. Was that a smile on her alien face? It was so hard to tell.

"Shriek . . ." His mouth refused to obey, to form the words he wanted, and he tried to focus his thoughts enough for her to hear: . . . *you traitor.*

Something tickled his brain that must have been Shriek's laughter. *Fear you must not, Being Clive,* she said to him. *Powerful anesthetic have I made. But more subtle than last time, more human-suitable. No bad effects. Human blood from the Annabelle being have I tasted. On my hands it was when examine her I did. Blood having tasted, analysis my body does, new chemicals to know and produce.*

Clive forced himself to concentrate. His thoughts seemed to spin and tumble. It took an effort to think coherently. *What have you done to me?* He realized distantly just how much fear tinged his response. He had seen the effects of Shriek's hair-spikes before.

Sedate, have I, she answered, *and medicated, healing to speed. Same will I do to the Neville being and the Annabelle being. Care for you will all friend beings.*

He gazed upward at all those clustered around him:

Shriek and Sidi, Tomàs and Smythe. Samedi, too, with that funny, crooked grin. Beyond and above them, the fog swirled almost milk-white. For the first time, Clive thought, he knew real fear. Always before, whenever danger had threatened, he'd had his sword or his fists or his feet to run if necessary. But now he was helpless, completely helpless, and he didn't like it one bit.

Dimly, he heard a commotion and an outraged squawk that must have been his brother. That, at least, made him feel a little better. If he had to be carried like a sack of vegetables, it heartened him to know that Neville would share the same embarrassment.

Shriek's face appeared again above his, and he felt himself lifted with her lower set of arms. With her upper right hand she brushed a lock of hair back from his face. The gesture struck him as strangely, tenderly human, but he still didn't forgive her.

Untrue forethought, she said with a chiding, almost motherly tone. *Deepthought of Clive being forgives*.

From far away Clive heard a familiar word, but it oozed into his head with liquid slowness. "Cooommmmee." That had to be Samedi.

Horace Hamilton Smythe came to his side and squeezed his hand. "Don't you worry none, sah," he reassured confidently. "We're all going to be just fine, we are. You just rest."

Tomàs also moved close. *"Não se afliga,"* he said conspiratorially as one confidant to another. "Don't worry. I have your sword." He held the blade for Clive to see. "I give back soon when you are well. Now, though, Tomàs keep it and protect companions."

Clive could see Neville in the arms of the cyborg Chang Guafe. His brother wore a thoroughly idiotic expression as his head lolled over his bearer's huge arm. Likewise, Finnbogg carried Annabelle, but it was Finnbogg who wore the idiotic expression as he gazed with worshipful concern at his burden.

"Best be about it, lads."

That was Smythe's voice. Apparently, the sergeant had assumed the leadership role with Clive incapacitated.

They began to move. Shriek carried him with great care, and yet he chafed at his powerlessness and vulnerability. With a great effort of will he turned his head forward and tried to focus his vision. Samedi and Smythe led the way just as he'd figured. No one else walked in front of him. At least, he could see something of what lay ahead. At the moment, that was nothing but the mist.

Shriek had provided the way back to the road. They had indeed wandered far from it, but she had left a strand of webbing, which they now followed like Theseus from the labyrinth. In little time they were back on the smooth surface.

After a while, Clive thought he detected the smell of water in the air, and his ears began to pick up a dull rushing roar. *A river?* He sent the thought to Shriek.

River, there must be, she agreed, and indeed they shortly reached its bank.

From the sound of it he had expected a swiftly flowing body with a treacherous current, perhaps rapids. But the "rush" was not the rush of motion, of water between two banks. It was the bubbling and furious churning, rather, that he'd heard so far away, for this river boiled!

How would they ever get across?

The others gathered around in a tight group and stared with trepidation at this newest obstacle. It was then that Samedi reached inside the pocket of his jacket and extracted a small whistle, which he set to his lips. He walked as close to the water's edge as he safely dared and blew. A long, high-pitched note sailed evenly over the river's surface and faded into the misty distance. He returned to the group, then, and folded his arms expectantly.

Moments later, a similar note only slightly lower in pitch drifted back in answer. They stared toward the sound. A small ship crawled slowly out of the milky curtain of steam that hung over the river, powered by a pair of slender oars that rose and dipped with metronomic regularity. Long minutes passed before it finally touched the shore.

The oarsman sat with his back to them as the bow bumped the stony bank. Only when the oars were carefully shipped did he rise and turn to face them.

Gasps sounded from Tomàs and Smythe. Even through the sedative Clive managed to blink.

"Hey, Jack!" the oarsman said, grinning as he doffed his top hat. "High five!"

The oarsman and Samedi slapped palms with a loud smack.

They looked exactly alike.

• CHAPTER NINE •

Under the Shadows of Death

The journey across the river was steamy and miserable. Clive, Annabelle, and Neville were placed as comfortably as possible in the bottom of the vessel while the others seated themselves on small benches. The two Samedis took positions in the fore and aft.

The ship resembled a Viking Oseburg craft. Its prow swept upward in a high graceful curve, and a single sailless mast stabbed the heavy mist. Small enough to be rowed by one man, it nevertheless contained oars for three. Each of the Samedis worked a pair. Tomàs manned the third set.

The vessel's construction material fascinated Clive. It was not wood, not even metal. Completely smooth, it glistened blackly, and though the hull seemed quite thin, it conducted none of the water's terrible heat. There were no visible joints or seams. The entire ship, even the benches, the mast, the prow, all appeared molded from a single piece.

Shriek's potent anesthetic had begun to wear off. Clive could move again, but weakly, and that required concentration. Still, he wiggled his fingers on the bottom of the boat—he couldn't call it a proper deck—and marveled.

It was then he noticed the others. Food! They were eating! The sight instantly made him hungry, too. He tried to sit up, but he only made a thumping with his elbows and shoulders. It was enough to attract attention, though, and Horace Hamilton Smythe quickly bent above him.

"Sorry, sah!" Smythe apologized. "Assumed you were asleep like your brother, sah." Smythe slipped an arm under his shoulders and helped him to sit against the side of the boat as the others leaned closer. "Are you hungry, sah? Can you eat?"

Clive gave his sergeant what he hoped was a withering look. What kind of idiotic question was that? He forced himself to nod and stared pointedly at the strange concoction in Sidi Bombay's hand, something that looked like beef chunks between thick slices of bread. "Eat," he said, forcing movement into lips that felt like mushrooms.

Sidi Bombay twisted on his bench and reached into a box apparently made of the same material as the ship and withdrew some kind of packet. He unwrapped it carefully, and amazingly a tiny cloud of steam rose, bearing a potent savory odor.

Clive's hand came up shakily to accept it.

"That's what Samedi calls a sandwich," Smythe told him. He pointed toward the prow. "That Samedi there, that one," he added. "He's the one that brought the boat and the box of food. At least, I think he is." He turned back to Clive. "Don't look like any sandwich I ever saw in England, though, sah. Whatever that bit of meat is, it isn't ham, it isn't. And see, there's two pieces of bread, and not a spot of butter on either of them. It's hot, too. Tasty, though, I'll say that."

Clive Folliot didn't care what it was called or by whom. He brought the sandwich to his mouth, took a cautious bite, and chewed slowly. It tasted wonderful, and his brain seemed to clear with every passing moment. All he cared about right now was his stomach.

When he finished his meal, he licked his fingers. Then, he held out his hand again, this time toward Tomàs. "I'll have my saber back, if you don't mind," he said.

The little Portuguese continued at his oars, but the

blade lay ignominiously at his feet between his bench and the bulkhead. He pushed it with his toe toward Clive. "Thank you," Clive said. He looked back to Smythe. "How wide is this river? Is it the drug, or haven't we been crossing for some time now?"

"Some time, sah, yes," Smythe agreed. "It seems impossibly wide for these mountains, doesn't it? The bubbling and churning, combined with the effect of the river current, make for tough going. But Tomàs and our twin guides are doing their best."

"Annabelle and Neville?" he asked, gazing down on his relatives.

Smythe shook his head. "No change for Miss Annabelle. Neville finally went to sleep. The drug and the rocking of the boat, no doubt. We thought you had, too. Truth to tell, I was a bit envious."

Clive smiled. "Tired, Horace?"

Horace hesitated, then grinned. "Tired of the Dungeon, sah, that's for sure. What I wouldn't give to curl up by a fire in a London pub with a pint of stout."

A curtain of warm mist rolled over them. For a few moments it was impossible to see either end of the boat. Horace Hamilton Smythe drew nose to nose with Clive, and the two men stared at each other for an uncomfortable space, then glanced from side to side, anywhere but at each other.

Clive felt jittery, and the sudden thickening of the fog had actually made him jump inside. He knew that his sergeant had seen the brief flicker of fear in his eyes before he'd been able to suppress it. To his surprise, though, Smythe's eyes had betrayed the same momentary fear. It was an embarrassing revelation for them both.

A muttered curse in Portuguese caused Clive to look toward Tomàs. Except for Smythe, the little sailor was the closest person to him, yet a vague form in the mist was all he could see. It bent forward over the oars and pulled with a sure, easy stroke, but it could have been any spirit that rowed.

"When we get out of here, Horace," Clive said at last, wiping a hand over his damp face, "I'll join you at your pub. Damn it, man, I'll even buy. But I warn you, I'm going to have more than just a pint. A lot more."

"Be careful, little brother. You'll spoil your image."

It was a bare whisper, but Clive heard it plainly. A muffled scuffling accompanied the speech, the sound of uncooperative elbows and bootheels scraping on the hull.

"Lie still, Neville," Clive instructed. "It wears off slowly at first, then more quickly. "When the fog parts again, we'll sit you up and give you a bite, but right now let's not have anyone moving around and falling overboard."

"Thank you, brother," Neville answered stiffly, "but I am sitting up."

Clive peered hard through the mist and saw the dim form of his twin resting against the other side of the ship. He couldn't resist a frown. Neville would shrug off the effects of Shriek's drug just fine on his own without any help from anybody. Neville never needed any help. Neville always did everything just right.

Clive tried to straighten his injured leg, and a sharp twinge of pain shot up his thigh. A sudden intake of breath alerted Smythe, but Clive gently pushed him back when the sergeant leaned to see what was the matter.

Shriek's thoughts brushed against his. *Your painsong heard I, Being Clive. More healing venom need?*

"No, Shriek," he snapped aloud. "What I need is a clear head and a good leg!"

Healing venom good make leg in time. Transparency of bone brain casement effect I cannot.

Several snickers followed that, and Clive realized with some irritation that Shriek had generally broadcast her answer. Everyone had heard. Well, everyone had heard him snap at her. He sighed and laid his head back against the hull.

They emerged from the heaviest fog, and moments later the prow thumped solidly against the bank. They had reached the far shore. The Samedi at the front of the boat leaped over the side onto firm land and held the boat as steady as possible. Sidi and Tomàs followed.

Clive started to rise on his own despite the pain that screamed through his leg. Then, Shriek lifted him and carried him ashore. Chang brought Neville, and Finnbogg gently bore Annabelle. The thick mush of puppy-dog tears had matted the corners of his eyes.

The other Baron Samedi came last, bearing what remained of the box of food. He set it down on the ground and beckoned to his look-alike, and together they dragged the boat out of the water. Clive dismissed his pain long enough to marvel at how light the ship must be and wondered again at the material of its construction.

"Not wanting to be a bother, old boy," Neville said with polite patience, "but I could use some of whatever smells so good in that container."

Clive nodded and waved a hand at the box. Sidi Bombay dragged it closer, and they all made a circle around it. Only Shriek hung back as the Indian passed out the contents. Finnbogg accepted a bit of meat and munched it disconsolately as he cradled Annabelle's head on his lap and stroked her hair idly with the fingers of one hand. Tomàs devoured his portion wordlessly, licked his fingers, smacked his lips, and reached for more.

Neville Folliot ate with a pristine elegance that irritated Clive. As he swallowed his last bite and brushed crumbs from his mouth and mustache, he said, "Might I suggest we save just a little something for later?"

Neville looked at them all with that expression of utter reasonableness, and Clive mentally kicked himself for not thinking of it first. He stared at the untouched sandwich in his hand and frowned as he started to return it to the box.

"You my kinda man," said one of the Samedis, slapping the side of his leg. "Hey bro'! Ain't he my kinda man?" The other Samedi nodded and smiled. "Always thinkin'!" the first one continued, addressing Neville with a keen stare. "But you got to trust, man! Now, the palace ain't far away, an' the Big Dude hisself is waitin'. All you wanna eat, there, man. Pig heaven!"

The second Samedi bent down close and patted Clive's shoulder sympathetically. "So you jus' eat that, now, an' don' worry none 'bout savin' it. Get yo' strength back, Jack."

Horace Hamilton Smythe scooted next to Clive. "Shall I tuck some away, sah, just in case?" He nodded subtly toward Neville. "The major brother does have a bit of a point."

Clive thought about it, then shook his head. It wasn't just to spite Neville, he told himself, not just another instance of taking the opposite side. "No, Sergeant. Samedi has done well by us so far, and I think we should trust him as he says." He lifted his sandwich to his mouth and took a big bite.

Neville's gaze met his for just a moment. Then, his twin shrugged and helped himself to a second sandwich, too.

While they ate, Shriek filled all the canteens from the river and set them aside until the water cooled enough to drink. When everyone was refreshed and full, the company prepared to get underway again.

Shriek bent over Clive, but he thrust up a hand. "Wait," he said. "If you insist on carrying me, there must be another way. I am not a sack of potatoes, ma'am."

The arachnoid's brief chitter sounded embarrassingly like a snigger as she grabbed Clive with her top two hands and swung him high onto her shoulders. Two hands clapped over his thighs, carefully avoiding his worst wound, and the other two locked on his ankles. He caught his breath, then let it out. It was better than being carried like a baby.

Chang Guafe lifted Neville and placed him similarly on his shoulders. Clive didn't miss the way his brother flinched and caught his ribs, and he felt a twinge of guilt about some of the thoughts he had toward Neville.

"Where to, Samedi?" Clive asked.

Both creatures turned and smiled. "Movin' on up," one

of them said. "Outta this valley o' the shadow of death, man," said the other. They both raised an arm, looked at each other for a moment, and grinned. "Come," they said in unison, beckoning.

Clive rolled his eyes as Shriek lurched under him, and their two guides turned to lead. He stared at their backs, at their tattered black suits and worn old top hats. There had to be some way to tell them apart, but it eluded him. They were the same height, looked and talked alike, even walked alike. Their garments, too, were studiously identical.

Clones. He didn't understand how such a thing could be. Two living things grown from the same tissue. He and Neville were born from one womb, but that wasn't the same, Annabelle had told him. But what if they'd been identical twins instead of fraternal ones? Would the same egg, divided by whatever mysterious process at fertilization, have made them clones? Annabelle said no. He still didn't understand it, he admitted, and determined to quiz his great-great-granddaughter about it again later.

He twisted around so he could see Annabelle in Finnbogg's arms. She hadn't so much as stirred since her killing of Philo B. Goode. Finnbogg had wet her lips to keep them moist and continued to coo and whisper to her as if she could hear, but so far, nothing had reached her.

Shriek, Clive mind-whispered, *would you try again?*

Touch her mind have I tried, the arachnoid responded, her thoughts tinged with sorrow and concern. *The Annabelle being deep within herself retreated has. Find, I cannot, Being Clive.*

He looked at Annabelle and bit his lip. There had to be a way to help her, and he'd find it. "Take care of her, Finnbogg," he said worriedly.

The alien canine glanced up with sad eyes. "Okay, okay," he answered. "Finnbogg here, have no fear. Want to sing?"

Clive shook his head. "Not now, Finnbogg. No telling if there's anything else lurking in this damn fog. Let's not draw any more attention than we have to."

"Okay, okay," Finnbogg agreed. He looked at the woman in his arms and rocked her as if she were a child. "Let Annie sleep quiet, then."

They trudged onward, and the ground began to gradually slope upward again. Soon, the mist began to thin, and the path steepened. Clive locked his fingers under Shriek's chin to keep his balance. When at last they achieved a point above the mist, they stopped and looked back. A thick white sea stretched below, obscuring the valley and the river, swirling and eddying with a sensuous slow movement.

Samedi called them to look as he pointed to the highest peak that rose in the distance. "There rests the Palace of the Morning Star," he said with unusual formality.

They resumed the climb, picking their way carefully, for the path was still slick with moisture. Clive had hoped that once the fog was behind them he'd be able to look up and see blue sky again, or at least a normal sky full of normal stars. But there was only a flat black expanse. *Like the sky of Q'oorna on the first level,* he remembered, *but without even the spiral cluster to break the monotony.*

It grew darker as they climbed, too. The ridge of mountains behind them now obscured the fireglow from the east that had lit the earlier part of their journey. Perhaps they would rise above it in time, but there was no indication of that, yet. The two Samedis seemed unconcerned, as if they could see in the darkness, and perhaps they could.

But Clive was concerned. He didn't want anyone to get separated from the group in the dark. With Annabelle unconscious there could be no illumination from the Baalbec A-9. Maybe he should ask Shriek to web them all together again? He didn't care much for that idea, either. Even though Philo B. Goode was dead, the threat of attack still niggled in the back of his mind. He didn't want to be bound to someone if he had to fight.

"Chang?" he said over his shoulder, breaking the silence that had fallen over the company. The cyborg quickened his pace and came up beside him, bearing Neville. He glanced briefly at his twin before continuing. "We could use a little light."

The cyborg's eyes began to glow with a familiar red light. It wasn't much radiance, but at least the others could see it and follow it and know they were still all together.

"Perhaps we should stop for a while," Neville suggested. "Maybe this is night and it will get a bit lighter when morning comes."

It was Sidi Bombay who spoke up. "We've seen nothing to indicate there are such things as night and day on this level, Englishman. Only a perpetual darkness from which the flames provided a little relief."

Clive concurred. "Remember what it was like on the other side of Dante's Gate? It may come to that again."

"*Não agüento mais!*" Tomàs muttered. "No more of that!"

Horace Hamilton Smythe smirked. "Oh? You preferred the fire, then? Or the Lake of Lamentations?"

Tomàs grumbled something incoherent but undoubtedly rude.

"Come!" the Samedis insisted as one. "Not much further to the promised place," they chanted, slapping palms, "where milk an' honey gonna stuff yo' face!"

Clive used his vantage high upon Shriek's shoulders to keep a continual lookout. There was little to see, though. The mountain peaks were deep shadows against the general blackness, featureless and indistinguishable except for the tallest one, their destination. To fight the monotony he tried counting paces, but that, too, became boring.

At last, he sought out conversation. *Shriek?* She didn't answer at once, and he called again with his mind.

What?

The word cracked like a pistol shot inside his skull. Clive clutched his temple and waited for the shock to pass.

Sorry, am I, Being Clive, Shriek said apologetically. *Distracted, was I.*

But Clive sensed something behind the words, some puzzlement or concern that colored her thoughts. *Is something wrong, Shriek?*

The arachnoid shook her head. *Know I do not. Tense am I.* She chuckled, but Clive could tell she felt no true mirth. *Deep in your mind a phrase there is that fits, Being Clive.* She hesitated before continuing. *Itch have I, but scratch I cannot.*

She made a mental frown, and Clive withdrew. Whatever was bothering her, he sensed her desire for solitude.

The ground leveled out suddenly, and they found themselves atop a high plateau. The warm wind gusted over them as it had not done for some time. It blew Clive's hair straight back, and he dared to hope it might dry his tattered garments, which were saturated from sweat and from the steam bath they had left behind.

The Samedis led them to the far edge. A vast, black abyss yawned at the plateau's rim, and Clive felt a moment of vertigo as he peered down into it from Shriek's shoulders.

Smythe leaned outward precariously and stared, rubbing his chin. "Wonder how deep it is?" he said.

Neville was droll. "Personally, I'm not going to go crawling around for a pebble."

"Why bother with a pebble, sah?" Smythe retaliated. "We could drop you over."

Chang Guafe moved to the edge.

Neville gave an unexpected yelp. "Wait. I'm sure he didn't mean it!"

Even Clive gave a shout. "Chang!"

The cyborg stood with his toes right at the rim and extended a hand into space. A dull green light winked briefly on his palm, and a tiny, high-pitched *beep* sounded once. He balanced there a moment more before moving away from the edge. He looked at Horace Hamilton Smythe.

"In answer to your query, my sensors receive no sonar response at all from the signal tone."

Smythe looked around for help from the others. The confused look on his face was almost comical. "Do you mean to say there's no bloody bottom?"

"Affirmative," answered Chang Guafe, "or if there is a bottom, it is too far away for sensor detection."

"That means it's deep," Neville volunteered caustically.

"Do not sneer at my friend, *senhor*," Tomàs spoke suddenly. "But a moment ago you thought Chang Guafe meant to drop you. Your little yelp betrayed your fear. You are smug, but you are no better than the rest of us."

Clive grinned inwardly. Point to the little Portuguese! Neville didn't even have a good comeback. He looked away from his brother and stared across the chasm.

A tall shadow loomed above them, the peak toward which they had been journeying. At its summit they would find the Palace of the Morning Star and meet whoever had sent Samedi—the Samedis, he corrected—to guide them. Again, he considered the idea of warring factions in the Dungeon, one of which might at least be friendly. But which one? The Ren? Or the Chaffri? Or some other group, altogether?

Perhaps he'd find new clues at this palace. He considered its name again, turning it over and over in his mind. Clive knew mythology well, and he knew the only possible significance of that name in this starless place. He wondered if he should tell the others.

Finnbogg gave a low growl that made Clive twist around. "Finnbogg?"

The others noted it, too.

Finnbogg stared up into the empty sky and gave another throaty growl. Then, slowly, without taking his eyes from the air above them, he stooped and placed Annabelle on the ground.

Clive drew his sword. "Put me down," he told Shriek. "Put me down."

Too late, he heard the rush of air. Clive threw himself

backward to avoid the down-sweeping leathery wings and unbalanced both himself and Shriek. They tumbled over in a tangle. Clive managed to keep his grip on the sword, but the wind was knocked from his lungs. Still, he tried to scramble to his feet.

A pair of shrill screams ripped from the Samedis as they cowered at the plateau's rim. But two hideous creatures sank clawed talons into the clones' shoulders, and their folded pinions opened suddenly to beat the air. The clones fought and struggled as the monsters swept them up into the sky. They hammered with their fists as they kicked and flailed above the chasm, screaming and begging for help.

Clive stood helplessly at the edge, cursing, tears burning on his cheeks as he watched. The fight was far beyond him now. There was nothing he could do but clench his fists in bitter frustration and stare horrified.

Shriek drew back with an envenomed spike-hair, but he stopped her. "What good would it do?" he said despairingly. "If you kill the creatures, they will drop our friends."

A quick death could I give, Shriek insisted, drawing back again, taking aim. *Better than to fall endlessly*.

Clive caught her arm again as he reached out for the smallest hope. "Maybe they only mean to capture them!"

Shriek hesitated, her body trembling with indecision. In that instant came two long despondent cries that faded quickly into the depths.

Clive's own scream followed, long and anguished and full of rage as the winged demons turned their backs and flew away. He took a step as he shook an empty fist, calling curses, and his leg gave way and he fell toward the yawning blackness.

Smythe saved him from tumbling off the edge and pulled him safely back. The others quickly gathered around. Only Tomàs stayed where he was.

Something in the way the little sailor stood alerted Clive. "What is it, Tomàs? What's wrong, man?" He pushed at all the hands that tried to restrain him and sat up. "Tomàs?"

"Their faces!" the Portuguese said, unable to hide the trembling in his voice. "I got a look at them! *Impossivel*, but I know those faces! A man and a woman, they were standing on the dock in Spain when the *Pinta* set sail. Only then, they looked normal. I remember! They stared right at me!"

Clive clutched his leg and winced and he leaned forward. "Tomàs, are you sure . . . !"

Neville Folliot interrupted as he looked down from his perch on Chang Guafe's shoulders. The cyborg hadn't even had time to set him down. "I saw their faces, too, little brother, and I knew them. They traveled with the good Mr. Goode for a while when I first met him. A brother and sister, I believe. Twins, just like you and me. Ransome, the name was, Amos and Lorena." Neville scratched his chin and frowned. "I must say, her looks have certainly taken a turn for the worse."

CHAPTER TEN

Across the Black Abyss

The loss of the two Samedis cast a pall over the company. The black landscape seemed twice as black, and the mountain peak that was their destination seemed twice as far away.

Chang Guafe stood at the edge of the chasm and watched for the pair of demons with all his sensors at maximum. He blamed himself for the deaths of their guides. Had he attuned his audio sensors, he claimed, he would have heard their swooping attack in time to warn everyone, but he had foolishly given his attention to the argument between Horace Hamilton Smythe and Neville Folliot.

Clive alternately cursed himself, the Ransome twins, the soul of Philo B. Goode, and the unknown Dungeonmasters. The screams of the Samedi clones still echoed in his ears, and the vision of them tumbling into the depths burned inside his head. Maybe he didn't understand exactly what a clone was, but those final cries had been human.

And what did that mean, anyway? Would he feel any better if Shriek had been killed? Or Finnbogg? Or Chang Guafe? Though they were aliens, they were no less his friends. Their souls were as noble, their spirits just as fierce, their loyalties just as strong as any man's.

He looked at Sidi Bombay in that instant, as if for the first time seeing the black man from India, and he understood at last the depth of his own English-bred prejudice.

Dark skin or white skin, four arms or metal arms—what did any of it matter?

And why had it taken the deaths of two beings—he understood now the honorific and the honor inherent in Shriek's form of address—to teach such an obvious lesson?

Slowly, painfully, he pulled one foot under himself. With a rocking motion he rose and straightened, putting just enough weight on his injured leg to balance himself. The thigh muscle screamed, and he clapped a hand over the bandage, but instead of easing off he put more weight upon it and limped in a small circle. He squeezed his eyes shut for a moment to hold back the tears that threatened. Then he opened them again and began to force the pain to a dim back corner of his mind.

He glanced around at the others, unsurprised that Neville, too, had mastered his discomfort. His twin clutched his side as he moved, but he limped purposefully around the lip of the chasm as if searching for something.

"Being Shriek," he called aloud, and the arachnoid scuttled swiftly to his side. "Our guides are gone. We've got to find our own way to the mountain peak."

Before Shriek could respond, Neville sang out. He had wandered far from the group and stood barely visible in the darkness on the plateau's far side. "Over here, little brother. I believe I've found it for you."

Clive frowned, then chided himself for the misplaced sense of competition he felt toward his twin. This was no time for childhood rivalries between grown men. The lives of his friends were in danger every moment they remained in this open space. He unfastened the belt that held his saber and scabbard, wrapped the leather strap around his hand once or twice, and leaned on it. A bit of folded ornamental steel tipped the scabbard, which protected it from wear and scuffing, but that would make it somewhat unstable on hard stone if he used it as a cane. Still, if he was careful, it would do, and it was all he had. He hobbled toward his brother to see what he had found.

"Oh, not goody," Finnbogg said, creeping up beside

them with Annabelle cradled in his arms. "Not my idea of funtime, no."

Horace Hamilton Smythe came up on Clive's other side, stared, and made a face. "Good lord, sah! I'm really beginning to hate this place!" the sergeant muttered in disgust.

The others quickly gathered around.

"Do you think if we waited five or ten minutes you could find another route?" Clive said to Neville with some sarcasm.

Despite his injuries, Neville put on his usual grin and pulled himself erect. "Come now, chap, where's the spirit? It would be ungentlemanly of us not to take advantage of what our hosts have provided."

"I don't know about that, Englishman," Sidi Bombay said unhappily, "but this must be why Baron Samedi brought us here. It must be the way to the Palace of the Morning Star, if that is still to be our destination."

"Don't see that we have a choice, really," Neville said, heading off any argument. "The Ransome twins or demons or whatever they were deprived us specifically of our guides, so they must not want us to reach this palace. That's one reason I say we should continue. The most important reason, however, is that if there is a gate around here to the next level and hopefully, home, we stand the best chance of learning about it there. It may even be there."

Clive stared over the edge of the plateau and squirmed. He didn't like it, but Neville was right. Besides, he was too angry and too curious now about the architects of this Dungeon. He and his friends had wandered blindly through the upper levels, guided or manipulated by the authors of the so-called diary, escaping from one threat after another without ever really learning much about this strange place in which they found themselves.

Here, though, on this seventh level, there seemed to be a chance to change that, to gain some understanding of what was going on. Clive was quickly beginning to realize that such understanding would be crucial if they were ever to get home.

"I hadn't realized the Ransomes were twins," he whispered to his brother. "That's interesting, a new piece of the puzzle."

Neville nodded and answered quietly, "Actually, they made quite a point of it when I met them. Now here they are, twins, and here we are, twins again. I'd really like a bit of a chat with them about that."

Clive let go a sigh as he turned to the rest of his party. "I think Neville's right," he said finally. "We really have no choice but to go on."

Tomàs rolled his eyes. "¿Por quê, Christo, por quê?"

Clive stared once more over the edge. A narrow stairway of carved black stone descended into the abyss. Each step appeared barely as wide as a man's foot, and no end to the treacherous incline could be seen. The chasm wall flanked the left-hand side, but a careless misstep to the right spelled doom. A small doubt plagued him. What if they were wrong? What if this wasn't the way the Samedis had intended to bring them? What if the stairway went nowhere but ended in midair? For that matter, what if it wouldn't support their weight?

"Let's go!" Neville said, descending the first step.

"Not yet!" Clive caught his brother's arm and pulled him back, ignoring the wince of pain on his twin's face. He turned worriedly to Shriek. The narrow stairs might prove a problem for her four feet and greater size. "Being Shriek," he said formally, "can you navigate these safely?"

Much care shall I take, Being Clive. For your concern, much thanks.

Clive resolved to worry anyway and to keep an eye on her. He turned back to his brother. "Just get back, Neville. You're not going first. Chang Guafe's sensors will see where you cannot. If the stair just ends, I want to know before anyone drops off. And if the stone won't take all our weight, again his sensors stand the best chance of detecting the stress."

Chang Guafe stepped forward. "You choose logically, human, I will test the way."

"Everyone go slowly, and keep close to the wall," Clive ordered quietly as the cyborg took the first step. They watched as Chang descended, his ruby lenses burning into the dark. "Stay away from the edge and watch out for the updrafts," Clive reminded.

"For a brother," Neville interrupted lightly, "you make quite a mother."

"And you make quite . . ." Clive stopped himself and looked away. Childhood rivalries, he remembered, were things best left to children. "Quite a good second choice. Down you go." He tapped his twin on the shoulder and pointed to the stair.

Next went Sidi Bombay, followed by Finnbogg with Annabelle in his arms. Tomàs waited, swallowed hard, and crossed himself, then descended behind them.

"After you, sah," Horace Hamilton Smythe bade with a short bow. "And mind your leg. I'll be watching you, I will."

Clive had a different idea. He planned to stay next to Shriek so *he* could keep an eye on *her*. Despite her reassurances, such narrow stairs weren't made for four arachnoid feet.

"No, old friend," he said to his sergeant, "you go first, and if I stumble, I'll have you to support me, just as you've always done."

Smythe stiffened as if he'd been insulted. "If it please you, sah, with these steep steps the last thing we need around here is that kind of grease." He gave a stern glare that quickly turned into a grin to let Clive know he was kidding. "Besides, Major, you've never stumbled, yet, but what you didn't pick yourself up smartly."

"Now who's spreading grease?" Clive answered, returning his sergeant's grin. "Get going."

After you will come I. Shriek's thoughts brushed against Clive's, but with a strange saw-edge that he had never felt before. She tried unsuccessfully to mask some irritation by ignoring it. *The Smythe being watch you from the fore he will, from behind watch will I*.

Clive raised an eyebrow, leaned on his sheathed sword to ease the ache in his thigh, and wondered what could be bothering Shriek. "Now, wait," he said with a cautious grin. "Who's watching whom?"

He sensed the tickle of her laughter as she forced herself to relax. *Watch all, all watch*, she responded, *so live all safe*.

Clive regarded her for a moment and scratched his head. That sounded to him suspiciously familiar. Did her planet have its arachnoid equivalent of Alexandre Dumas? "Say it this way," he told her. "All for one, and one for all."

All one, one all, came her response.

No, no, he thought. Too existential that way. Voltaire, not Dumas. But he'd have to teach her later. The others were getting too far ahead. He limped to the first stair and began a cautious descent.

If only there'd been something to make into torches. As they dropped beneath the plateau's rim, the darkness began to approach that on the other side of the Dantean Gate. Clive pressed his left shoulder to the wall and took the steps one at a time, stepping with his right and bringing the left foot down to meet it and stepping right again. It eased some of the stress on his injury.

A few steps ahead he could see Horace. Tomàs before him, though, was a dim shadow easily identified by the string of foreign epithets proceeding from it. Beyond Tomàs he could see nobody, though he knew by the shuffling of their footsteps they were there.

He glanced back at Shriek. She leaned with three of her hands against the wall, using it for balance as she negotiated the narrow stairs. Her front two feet moved in unison, descending three stairs while her back two supported her weight. Then, she shifted her weight forward and brought her back legs down. The stairs were clearly not made for her kind. They were too narrow for her feet, putting her in constant danger of slipping, and Clive considered that perhaps he'd made a mistake in positioning her last, for if she fell forward, she'd sweep them all over the edge. The steps were also too narrow for her girth. Though she hugged the wall, her right arm and shoulder dangled in space.

She stopped suddenly and gazed upward.

Clive stopped, too. *Being Shriek?* he called silently.

She didn't respond, though she started once more down the stairs. Only two of her six eyes, however, appeared focused on her passage. The others darted upward, around, as if she searched for something in the darkness. Though it was hard to tell for sure, her mandibled mouth seemed fixed in a frown.

Are you unwell? Clive inquired, concerned, as he resumed his descent.

She hesitated before sending a response, and when she did, it came tinged with confusion. *Understand I do not, Being Clive,* she said at last. *Something . . .* She waved her free hand in a sweeping gesture toward the sky, then frowned again, and touched her temple.

Oh, great, thought Clive, *an arachnoid with a headache.* He clapped a hand to his mouth as if he'd spoken out loud and wanted to catch the words before they escaped. But Shriek read minds. She didn't react, though. Either she hadn't heard or didn't understand the reference or chose simply to ignore him.

Should we go back up? he asked, pushing his thoughts at her. *We can search for another way across.*

No, she answered firmly. *Only way this is. Certain am I, or the Samedi beings . . .* She stopped again, shook her head and rubbed her temple, then resumed. *A scratch I have, itch I cannot,* she said as if that explained everything.

An itch you can't scratch, he corrected, remembering she'd said something about that earlier. *Are you sick? Can you tell me anything more about this itch?*

She shrugged all four of her shoulders, a rippling effect that traveled up and down her torso, and again shook her head. Her frustration shivered the neural web that linked them.

He bit his lip, then gave his concentration back to the stairs. Again, he'd fallen behind the rest of the group. Smythe's back was barely visible. Clive quickened his pace, though it cost him in pain. He leaned heavily on the sheathed sword and against the wall.

After a while, he could no longer see the top of the plateau. Memories of the dreadful darkness they had first encountered on this level began to nag at him again. He hadn't realized or even admitted before now how the time they had spent wandering on the other side of the Dantean Gate had unsettled him. It had happened, and he'd survived it, and that was that. But now that he recognized the possibility of finding himself in the same situation again, it discomforted him all the more. It was shameful for a grown man to fear the dark, and he wasn't *afraid*, really. It just made him nervous. Not because he feared any fairy-tale bogeyman, either, but because he'd seen the very real things that crawled around in this Dungeon.

He snapped out of his reverie at the sound of voices. Horace Hamilton Smythe called his name, and the others ahead muttered and whispered in excited tones.

"Watch your step, sah," Smythe whispered. "It levels off quite suddenly, it does!"

The sergeant was right. Clive nearly stumbled when he tried to descend one more step and there wasn't one. The staircase had become a narrow ledge that continued on around the chasm wall. At least, he hoped it continued on and didn't just end somewhere. He pressed his back firmly against the wall and felt for the edge with the tip of his sword. Then he felt for it with his toe and caught his breath.

The ledge was maybe two feet wide.

"Shriek!" he called back. The arachnoid had stopped just above him before the bottom step. "For God's sake, be careful!"

The arachnoid nodded as she stepped cautiously onto the precipice.

Clive thought suddenly of Finnbogg, too. Finnbogg couldn't have much more room to maneuver, either, and he was further burdened with Annabelle. Well, at least, he only had two legs to worry about, and if he stayed flattened against the wall, he'd be all right.

They began to move again. This time, though, they stayed within reach of each other, sliding their feet sideways in a slow shuffle that took them around the rock facing at a snail's pace. A metallic scraping accompanied them for part of the way until Sidi Bombay paused long enough to shift the canteen he carried. Neville and Smythe took the opportunity to unfasten their sword belts, deeming it safer to bear the weapons in their hands than to risk tangling their legs, however remote that possibility.

Neville was first to break a long silence. "Any of you chaps read any good books?"

Clive recognized a gallant try at breaking the gloom that seemed to have settled upon them, but no one responded.

"Ummm," Neville continued. "An illiterate bunch, eh? Well, perhaps we can find more common ground for communication, anything to pass the time, eh?" He snapped his fingers. "I know." He paused, cleared his throat theatrically, then began, "There was a young lady from France . . ."

Clive felt his cheeks go crimson. If he could catch his brother's eye he might silence him with a look of disapproval. Of course, he couldn't see his twin in the dark, and he had no intention of trying to lean out to do so. "Neville!" he hissed.

". . . and if you should meet her, by chance, she might give you a wink, and for the cost of a drink . . ."

Clive's face burned. "Neville," he tried once more, outraged, extremely grateful that Annabelle, at least, could not hear.

". . . you could spend the whole night in romance!"

"You what?" Clive sputtered, surprised. "Why, that's not the way I heard that last line!"

Horace Hamilton Smythe chuckled. "Something about spending an hour in her pants, sah? Wasn't that the way you told it?"

"Sergeant!" Clive snapped.

Neville clucked his tongue. "I'm shocked, little brother, and I'm sure Father would be, too. You simply hold out with too rough a crowd."

"There was a young girl from New Delhi," Sidi Bombay started, "who sported a jewel in her belly. Some called it a sin how she danced for her men, as slowly she turned them to jelly." The Indian gave a little chuckle and called back to Clive. "It is a universal verse form, Englishman."

Clive gave a low groan, frowned, and shook his head. Then, Chang Guafe began, much to Clive's surprise. *Oh, no! Not the aliens, too?*

"There once was a cyborg named Sue," he recited in his coldest mechanical voice, "who wound up on the scrap-heap, it's true. What a vicious caprice—she was missing a piece, and perished for want of a screw."

Chang's laughter sounded much like a sudden crackle of static, but the others joined in heartily. Even Clive had to admit he liked that one.

"You see, Englishman?" Sidi Bombay said when the laughter died a bit. "It *truly* is a universal form."

They continued along the precipice, trading old limericks and composing new ones, and gradually Clive forgot his fear and surrendered to the mirth of the game. It felt good to hear his friends laugh again. It cheered him, and the pain in his leg seemed to lessen. The medicine of the gods, some poet had called laughter, and perhaps it was so.

The ledge began to slope gently downward, and they moved with great caution until it leveled again. Sergeant Smythe had just begun a new limerick when Chang Guafe's single word silenced them all.

"Alert," the cyborg said.

They stopped absolutely still. Clive listened for the dreadful sound of leathery wings in the darkness above, suddenly aware of their vulnerable position as his hand closed around the hilt of his sword. He didn't draw, though. There wasn't even room for a good fighting stance. He stared ahead, straining for a glimpse of Chang Guafe, and barely made out the cyborg standing at the very edge and looking downward.

"Visual receptors scanning at infrared," Chang Guafe reported when Clive called his name. The cyborg hesitated as he continued to peer into the abyss, then he spoke again. "Heat patterns of unknown origin or purpose appear along the lower wall opposite." He paused again. "Computing probabilities." Another pause. "At this distance, analysis must combine with logical supposition. They are vents."

"I say, vents?" Neville interrupted. "Whatever would anyone be venting down here?"

"Heat," Chang Guafe repeated, looking at Neville as if he were an inattentive schoolboy. "My readings, though subject to error at this range, suggest the probability of some underground industry."

Clive pursed his lips and peered over the precipice. The hot updraft blew his hair and stung his eyes, but he saw nothing in the yawning blackness. Yet, he had no doubts that the cyborg spoke truly. "How far below us are these vents?"

"As I understand your units of measurement," Chang Guafe answered patiently, "approximately seven hundred meters."

Clive chewed his lip. This new discovery intrigued him immensely. Yet, there was no way they could reach the vents from the ledge, and there was every possibility that all they would find there would be danger. It might even be home for the demons they had encountered.

"It's too far below us to bother with for now," Clive said unenthusiastically. "Let's move on."

"¡Sim, adiante!" Tomás agreed. "But quietly, amigos, so we don't disturb our neighbors."

"He has a point," Neville concurred.

There were no more limericks, no more jokes. They proceeded around the ledge with their backs pressed to the wall as if to hide from unseen eyes that might be watching from below. They inched their way slowly, and the scuffle of their boots on stone made the only sound. Clive watched the sky and half-expected the wingbeats of their enemies.

Then, they stopped again. "Oh, you're going to love this, Clive, old boy," Neville said distastefully.

"Perhaps it's a good thing that Miss Annabelle is not awake for this part of the journey," Sidi Bombay added.

"What is it?" Clive whispered with some irritation, unable to see what they were talking about. "Can we go forward or not?"

"Affirmative," Chang Guafe responded. "We could go forward. The ledge continues as far as my receptors can detect. However, this span offers a route to the other side."

"Span?" Clive said, leaning forward. "You mean there's a bridge?"

Neville sniffed. "If you care to dignify it with that word. It looks like four ropes and a lot of old boards to me. Why the hell do you suppose they put it down here?"

"I've stopped asking 'why' about a lot of things in this Dungeon," Clive answered smartly. "But if it goes to the other side, then we've got to take it."

"Would you care to go first, little brother?"

Chang Guafe interrupted as his metal heel scraped on wood amid the creaking and straining of old ropes. "I am chosen to test the way," Chang told Neville firmly. More steps sounded along the boards. The ropes creaked horribly, then stopped. "Are you not chosen to come second?"

There was an unspoken care in the cyborg's voice that almost made Clive grin. Chang's ruby lenses and the twin beams of light he radiated illuminated a small portion of the bridge, though, and he understood his brother's hesitation. Clive had seen such bridges only in picture books, and a part of his heart quailed at the idea of crossing this one. The ropes sounded ancient, and the boards looked rotten and riddled with wormholes. And yet, another part of his heart lifted with a kind of boyish excitement. He kept that part in check. This was the Dungeon, after all, and on that bridge they would be even more vulnerable than they were now.

Still, it was the way across.

"Either go, or get out of the way," Clive told his twin firmly.

"I'm going, I'm going," Neville snapped. "You're getting to be a bit of a pushy twit, Clive."

Clive ignored that. It was only Neville's way of summoning courage, and the sound of his boots on the boards was all that Clive listened for. Chang Guafe turned and moved farther along the span. His eyes burned like two glowing coals that seemed to float in the dark emptiness above the chasm. The line moved forward as Sidi, then Finnbogg, bearing Annabelle, and Tomàs and Smythe stepped onto the bridge.

The ropes creaked in his ears like a discordant music. Clive took the time to strap on his sword again, then gripped one rope in each hand and stepped onto the boards. There was a disconcerting moment as it sank under him, and the updraft swirled suddenly about him. He gripped the ropes tighter and gritted his teeth and took another step and slowly another. His heart raced around in his chest as it seemed to him the bridge took a strange pitch and righted itself. The boards bounced under him, vibrated with the tread of those before him, and the whole structure swayed frighteningly in the hot, rising winds.

Then his foot touched solid ground again, and Horace Hamilton Smythe reached out to steady him. "It's another narrow ledge, sah," his sergeant told him, but Clive was grateful for it, anyway. Narrow it might be, but it didn't shift or buck, and it didn't creak.

They crept along the edge, and the way at last began to rise at a gentle slope toward the chasm rim. The wind blew stronger on this side, though, and they hugged the rock face. Again, Clive unfastened his sword, preferring to carry it rather than have it slap his leg. But this time, as he undid the buckle, he felt something slip against his skin and catch in a rip in the side of his shirt.

Neville's diary! He made a grab for it, but the scabbard began to slide off its belt, and he made a grab for that. He didn't dare lose his sword. That motion, however, dislodged the diary from the rip, and the book tumbled out. "Grab it!" he shouted.

Shriek made a lunge for it. It bounced off her top right hand and went spinning, pages fluttering, its leaves opening like the wings of a precious bird as her lower right hand stretched out for the capture.

Then, the arachnoid gave a cry and teetered over the abyss. She fanned the air with all four arms, struggling for balance on a ledge barely big enough for her. Clive let go of his sword belt and tried to snatch her back. The scabbard clattered against stone, directly in the path of his foot as he moved, and went tumbling end over end into the darkness.

His fingertips brushed Shriek's, but it was too late. She screamed and pitched backward, following book and blade into the black emptiness as Clive and company stared in numbed horror.

· CHAPTER ELEVEN ·

Shriek's Flight

A billowy white substance blossomed far down in the chasm depths. Moments later, Shriek floated upward, borne aloft by the hot updrafts that filled the rippling, diaphanous strands of an immense sail-web. She hung limply, though, and the frivolous winds shifted and stirred and blew her away from the rock face where no one could reach her.

Clive screamed her name as she drifted higher above them.

Well, I am, Being Clive, the arachnoid answered without moving a muscle, *though fall I may yet. Violent, these winds. Tear my sail they may.*

"Throw out a line!" Clive called. "We'll haul you in!"

Another web I cannot spin, she replied, and a note of worry played among her thoughts. *Maintain this sail I must or fall.*

Horace Hamilton Smythe touched his arm. "But where will she go, sah? How high?"

So Shriek had sent her thoughts to all of them. Clive opened himself slightly and felt a jangling on the neural web that Shriek had spun about them at their first meeting. It was not a pleasant thing to him, nor to many of the others. It allowed far more than just silent speech if one didn't guard oneself carefully. But he reached out now and felt his friends, all but Annabelle, whose mind was closed, and all but Neville and Sidi Bombay, who had not been party to the arachnoid's mind-gift.

Go I where the winds blow, Shriek answered Smythe as she rose higher and higher on her strange delicate parachute. *Fly I where the hot breezes flow. Pass under me the land and sea. Freedom will I know.*

A poem? Surprise filled Clive's thoughts as Shriek ascended beyond sight.

Translation, came the arachnoid's answer. The worry seemed to have faded from her thoughts. A sublime joy filled her mind. *A song of my people at flight time, a special time for us. Not completely accurate, but close it is.* She paused, and everyone sensed the awe that consumed her as the winds bore her farther and farther away. *Drifting toward the mountain I am, Being Clive. Meet again we will. Meet again we will, friend beings.*

Clive didn't know if she simply stopped answering or if she had floated too far away to hear him. He called and called, but Shriek didn't respond. He watched helplessly as she floated away into the darkness and disappeared.

Horace Hamilton Smythe put an arm around his shoulders. "It's all right, sah, it is. She'll meet us at the top, you'll see, just like she said."

Clive Folliot looked his sergeant straight in the eye, then blinked and looked away. He let go a sigh. "I thought I'd lost her, Horace, just as I lost the Samedis, as I may have lost Annabelle." He drew a deep breath, held it, then sighed again. "I shouldn't be leading this outing. Let Neville do it. He's a natural leader."

"He's a horse's arse, if you'll pardon my saying so, sah!" Smythe whispered tersely. "Now you didn't *lose* nobody. The Ransome twins, or some mockery of the Ransome twins, killed the Samedis. As for Annabelle, she's right here, and we'll find a way to make her well if she doesn't snap out of it herself, as I expect she might when she's ready. And Shriek's not dead, either. She's alive because she's got the skills to keep herself that way, she has. It's all any of us have got, our wits and our skills. Well, it's your wits and skills that's going to get us out of this mess. Not Neville's. He may be your brother and all, but don't forget, he got himself caught by the Lords of Thunder, and he'd be last week's news, if you'll pardon the expression, but for you and Miss Annabelle thinking and acting so quick to save his hide."

Clive still wasn't convinced, but he put on a weak smile. "Good old Horace," he said, "always there to kick my backside."

"Only when it needs kicking," Smythe answered sternly.

Clive cast another glance upward, hoping for a glimpse of Shriek, but the darkness was unblemished. Well, there was no point in standing on this ledge debating the finer points of leadership with Horace Hamilton Smythe. "Let's go," he said at last. "We've got a friend waiting for us at the top."

They resumed their cautious trek and came to another set of steps just as steep and just as treacherous as the set that had carried them down to the ledge. After a long and arduous climb, they found themselves on the other side of the chasm, in the shadow of the mountain that was their destination.

"Okay, okay!" Finnbogg said with faint enthusiasm. "Not so dark as big pit. Easier to see." He shifted Annabelle's weight as he stared toward the mountain.

It was a subtle difference in the darkness, and the reason seemed to be the mountain itself. A nebulous halo radiated from it, as if the mountain obscured some greater light that burned palely behind it. The gloom was still pervasive, but they could at least see each other, and they could at least see their way. Yet, why had they not noticed it before from the other side of the chasm? The view of the mountain had been just as clear.

At Clive's suggestion, Chang Guafe searched with his electronic senses for some sign of Shriek. The cyborg found no trace of her, though. Who knew where the winds would carry her, or where she would touch down, or if in her strangely ecstatic state she even wanted to? He reached out with his thoughts and called her name, but only silence echoed back, bringing with it an odd loneliness.

The canteens were passed around and everyone drank. Clive's leg felt stiff and sore, and yet it bore his weight better than earlier. He limped ahead of the others and paused, the mountain filling his vision. At its summit rested the Palace of the Morning Star. That meant food, he hoped, and perhaps sleep as well. Maybe they would find the gate to the next level, too. He would welcome the chance to leave this one behind.

But would there be friends there? Maybe allies? Samedi had claimed he'd been sent to guide them to the palace. Philo B. Goode and the Ransome twins had seemed bent on preventing that. Why? One side for them, and one side against them. What did it mean?

Clive Folliot was beginning to feel more and more like a pawn in some kind of chess match, and he didn't care much for the feeling.

He turned and beckoned to the others to follow. "Come," he said automatically.

A short march across a relatively flat stretch of terrain brought them to the foot of the mountain. While the others rested briefly, Clive wandered a bit, searching unsuccessfully for Shriek. Returning, he knelt down beside Annabelle and took her hand in his. She still showed no sign of stirring. He lifted one of her eyelids. Her iris had drifted far up, and her dilated pupil was an empty well of blackness. He kissed her lightly on the forehead, then patted Finnbogg's arm. "Take care of her," he whispered.

"Annie okay, will be okay," Finnbogg answered with assurance.

Sergeant Smythe rose and came to his side. "You should let me check that bandage, Major, sah," he said.

Clive waved him off. "It's okay, Sergeant." But when his batman looked away, he pressed his hand over the wound and winced. The soreness was still there, and the stiffness. He'd succeeded in pushing the pain to the back of his mind for a little while, and he'd just have to do so awhile longer. If he sat down and rested like the others, he had a feeling he wouldn't get back up.

At first, it was an easy climb. The gentle slope took a minimum of effort and the footing was sure. They maintained less of a line now as each found his own path up the hillside. Horace Hamilton Smythe, though, stayed close by Clive's side, and Clive noticed with some reluctant gratitude how Chang Guafe watched over Neville.

The delicate light surrounding the mountain grew subtly stronger and illuminated the cracks and crevices that might have tripped them up, the rocks that might have turned underfoot. Clive began to reflect that he had seen no blade of grass, nor any living creature on this level except the demon-things that had attacked them. The other levels had been peopled with beings of all different kinds from all different times and planets. But apparently not this one. Why was that?

The climb became steeper. Now Clive felt the strain on his wounded thigh. He touched the bandage with his fingertips and found a warm wetness. Blood. The wound was seeping. He covered it with his hand to hide the fact from Smythe and kept climbing. Some of the inclines, though, were so sharp they had to lean forward and scramble up on all fours. He always tried to position himself so that the sergeant couldn't see his leg.

Halfway up they rested again. Chang Guafe and Finnbogg showed little evidence of fatigue, though the alien canine's tongue lolled a bit as he cradled Annabelle in his lap. Sidi Bombay also appeared fit and ready to continue, and Clive wondered if perhaps he'd spent some time in the mountains of northern India or some of the more rugged regions of Africa during his career as a guide and gunbearer.

On the other hand, Tomàs looked ready to drop, which was just what he did as soon as they stopped, just collapsing onto his back and throwing an arm across his eyes. He let go one long, miserable moan and fell silent.

Neville was the one he worried about most. His brother

refused to be carried anymore, but he looked pale, and his mouth had drawn into a taut lipless line. His right hand never left his ribs, and he was having some trouble breathing. Sergeant Smythe and Sidi Bombay both had examined him, though, and assured him that none of the ribs were broken.

Chang Guafe extended a slender tentacle from a small panel in his chest and passed it near Neville's ribs. Though he possessed numerous such appendages, the cyborg seemed to use them less and less, and Clive paused long enough to wonder if it was some latent aspect of Chang's lost mimicking power that he unconsciously relied more and more on his humanoid form as he spent more time with humans.

A tiny red light on the very end of the tentacle winked on and began to blink rapidly as it moved back and forth over Neville's ribs. "Difficult to be accurate," the cyborg reported, retracting the tentacle into his body again. "This sensor is calibrated for the study of alien flora. However, allowing for that, analysis indicates a higher-than-mean probability that Neville Folliot has torn cartilage between the ribs, which will cause pain, but will easily heal with rest and time."

Clive scratched his chin and wondered how much he should trust an alien's diagnosis of a human's injury. On the other hand, there was nothing else he could do, at least about Neville's ribs. Many of the cuts and scratches on his twin's shoulders and back, though, looked almost as nasty as the cut on his thigh. Clive thought they both probably needed stitches, but that, of course, was out of the question.

They sipped from the water canteens again, then after threatening and prodding Tomàs to his feet, they resumed the climb.

They ascended to another flat plateau and looked back the way they had come. It wasn't much of a view. The mountains they had already crossed looked like jagged shadows against a backdrop of night, starker and more ominous than when they had stood upon them. There was no sight of the mist-filled valley or of the river that had carved it.

Nor was there any sight of Shriek. Everywhere, Clive watched for the arachnoid. He missed her calming presence in his mind, and he missed the security of her fierce fighting skills. He scanned the plateau, thinking she might have been able to land safely there, but there was no trace.

Horace Hamilton Smythe stepped up to his side. "You're bleeding, sah," he said. "You should have said something."

"Get away from me, Horace," Clive whispered. "You're like a mother sometimes. And keep your voice down. We're high up now, and I don't know if there's an echo or not up here, but let's not find out, huh?"

"But your leg, sah . . ."

"It's all right!" Clive insisted quietly. "I'm keeping an eye on it, and it's all right, I tell you."

They crossed the plateau and began to climb again. The mountain turned more rugged. Sections of black rock shot up like splinters. Stone piled upward like stalagmites in a cavern for no apparent reason. Some toppled at a touch; others proved strong enough to lean against. Sheer rock faces loomed. Yet every time the trail looked too rough to follow someone found another trail conveniently close.

Tomàs complained of blisters, stopped, and massaged his feet. Smythe rubbed his palms together, wincing. Everyone's hands were raw from scrambling. Clive, too, felt the beginnings of a blister inside his boots. He wiggled his toes and let go a long, silent curse using words no true English gentleman should even know.

A rude awakening, Being Clive.

For an instant, Clive Folliot thought he had imagined it. Then, he snapped to alertness. He almost shouted but thought better of it. "Shriek!" he hissed, staring wildly about. "You're alive! Where the hell are you?"

The others heard him and regarded him with something

approaching the suspicion one harbored toward an idiot on the street.

Up here, Being Clive, she answered with a hint of sleepy amusement. *Above you, am I.*

Clive looked up sharply and caught his breath. Suspended between a tall, needlelike pinnacle and a cliff face hung the hugest web he had ever seen, and Shriek bobbed and bounced in the center in the gentle wind that rocked it. He pointed, and the others looked, too, with similar amazement.

"The barest hint of light on the strands," said Sidi Bombay in awe. "This is a work of art, my friends, a work of woven art."

Shriek stirred and stretched in her web. *The Sidi being kind is. Primitive, barbarous, disgusting this would be on home world of Shriek. Fly we do not on home world. Fly only ill-mannered or poorly raised egglings.* She paused, reached out with two arms, and plucked strands of the web, making it vibrate and to Clive's surprise, making it sing. Two musical notes shivered in the air. She plucked two shorter filaments and two higher-pitched quavers were the result. Then, her thoughts brushed against them all. *Yet, learning am I how much of our past, our evolution renounced have we. Sacrificed for affectations of civilization have we. Perhaps, basic nature of self rejected have we.*

Clive sensed something deeper under her thoughts, though. Suddenly, the back-and-forth motion the web made as the wind blew through it reminded him of a mother consolingly rocking her child. He reached out with his thoughts instead of his voice, offering the greater intimacy. *What is it, Being Shriek? What's wrong?*

After a hesitation, she answered. *Fear I do, Being Clive, and wonder. Home can I go? Fit there, will I? Learned much have I in this Dungeon. Changed much.*

A chill rippled down Clive's spine, and he looked at the others. They had all heard their arachnoid friend, and he knew by their faces they all felt the same chill.

Only Chang Guafe reacted differently. "Change is the nature of all things," he said coolly. "On my planet each new thing we touch we absorb into our beings. It becomes a physical part of us. Each new thing we learn causes us to change. We do not even look alike, but wear our changes and our learning as our skin." The others turned slowly to look at him, remembering no doubt his own story of his planet's evolution, of how life there had been just a primordial muck until the first spaceship landed there and both ship and crew were absorbed, giving intelligence and form that was both mechanical and organic. "I travel with you, fight with you," he continued, "because the Dungeonmasters have taken away my power to change, my power to grow and evolve. I want it back."

"Perhaps it is not the change we fear." Sidi Bombay spoke with a quiet wisdom. The little Indian turned his thin, dark face to each of them, and his eyes glittered with a sad compassion. "But the isolation. The veneer of custom, of civilization, locks us into certain patterns of accepted behavior. Shriek fears she has seen through that veneer, that the pattern is no longer acceptable to her." He looked at each of them again. "And so, I think, do many of us. And yet, if we do not conform to those patterns, whether they be English manners or Hindu beliefs, we face rejection and ostracism, perhaps even imprisonment, by our people."

"Or they lock us up in a bloody loony bin," Horace Hamilton Smythe added gloomily.

"How illogical and confining," Chang Guafe responded. "You are truly alien creatures."

Clive listened to the argument with one ear, but it was still Shriek's simple statement that struck him most deeply, maybe because with the mind-touch he caught something of the complexity of her fear, while Chang Guafe and Sidi attempted to simplify it with mere words. That was an important thing to understand, he realized suddenly, that language could only encapsulate. It could never express fully.

He wondered how he would ever fit back into Victorian society knowing that other planets harbored life in such an infinite combination of forms. What did that say about man's place in the universe and his relationship to God? Which of them, Clive, Shriek, Chang Guafe, or Finnbogg, was truly made in the image of the Lord? That was not the only question, though it alone was enough to rock the foundation of his culture, should anyone ever believe him and care to seriously debate the issue.

How would he fit knowing—*knowing*, not just speculating as did his friend George du Maurier—that one being might speak to another being with the power of thought alone?

How would he fit knowing the shape of the future to come, knowing of a nightmare world ruled by things called computers and populated by people who had harnessed themselves to strange machines in an obscene symbiosis, machines such as the Baalbec A-9. Chang Guafe was not the only cyborg he had met in the Dungeon. Chang, at least, came from another world, where other mores and customs were prevalent. It was not for Clive to judge Chang's world. But he'd met human cyborgs, too. Annabelle's Baalbec was an almost inoffensive example.

For that matter, how would he fit in having realized that women were not the fragile creatures he'd been taught they were, that they could plan and scheme and fight right beside any man if they chose to do so, that they didn't require a man's protection, let alone his supervision? Annabelle had taught him that much, his own great-great-granddaughter.

Yet, as he looked at his granddaughter, he saw suddenly the sad face of not Annabelle Leigh, but Annabella Leighton, the woman he loved and had unknowingly left in unfortunate circumstances alone in a flat in London.

He drew a deep breath and hardened his resolve. This time he spoke so the others would hear. "It's a fear we all have to face, Being Shriek, each in our own way and as best we can. But we have to go home."

Why, Being Clive? Shriek responded, the doubt in her thoughts easy to taste. *Perhaps here now belong we.*

"Then let me amend that," Clive answered stubbornly, moving to Annabelle's side and touching Finnbogg between the ears. Finnbogg growled appreciatively. "I have to go home. Matters compel me."

"Father?" Neville asked dubiously.

"Father be damned," Clive responded forthrightly. "I must get back for my own reasons, not for his. I've played his puppet for the last time."

"Puppet?" Neville said. "That's a bit disrespectful, isn't it? He sent you to find me."

"And I've found you," Clive snapped. "Now it's time to get home." He turned to the others. "For all of us."

"*Bom idéia,*" Tomàs muttered, "if we can."

· CHAPTER TWELVE ·

Annabelle in Wonderland

The source of the faint light was no longer a mystery. The mountain itself had obscured a familiar spiral of stars that floated up from some invisible horizon higher and higher into the sky. It was not the same spiral as the one that shone over Q'oorna, however. That one hung in the night, cool and picturesque and indifferent, like a faraway galaxy of icy diamonds. This one burned with the same cool light, but the stars swirled and danced in a cloud of churning gases. The entire mass seethed against the darkness with an unnerving and soundless fury.

Its light fell upon an equally unnatural structure that stood at the top of the mountain. The pinnacle, itself, had been sheared away by some great and inconceivable machine, leaving a surface like polished onyx that gleamed smoothly in the spiral's radiance. In the center of that surface loomed the strangest of houses, an immense dwelling whose lines and angles all seemed subtly wrong. It seemed to *lean* in three or four different directions all at once, and the roof sagged in some places, bulged oddly in others. The several chimneys tilted left and right, refusing to stand straight. None of the windows made a square or a neat rectangle either, but pinched in at one corner or the other.

"I say, the architect must have drawn his blueprint on a

napkin over drinks," Neville Folliot whispered to his brother.

"You mean *after* a couple of drinks," Clive suggested.

They crouched at the edge of the mountaintop, feeling nakedly exposed, almost afraid to stand. The hot winds blew in sudden gusts strong enough to sweep them from the edge if someone got careless. The final part of the climb had taken a lot out of them, for it had been the steepest and most difficult part, and the path had zig-zagged back and forth along a towering rock face.

Clive's thigh throbbed painfully, and the muscle trembled and quivered whenever he rested it. A thin trail of blood had trickled down into his boot, then clotted mercifully. The bandage that bound his wound, though, was saturated. All his lesser cuts and scratches ached and stung, too, from the strain and from the sweat that continually irritated them.

Neville didn't look any better. Neither twin said anything, though, or gave any complaint. They glanced at each other from time to time out of the corners of their eyes as if checking on the other. It was almost as if they were in a competition to see who would hold out longest, who would be the strong man and who would break. Annabelle had had some word for it, something shocking, but Clive couldn't recall what it had been.

Macho bullshit, Shriek thoughtfully provided.

Clive jerked around, appalled. "Thank you," he said dubiously.

"Who do you think lives there, sah?" said Horace Hamilton Smythe in a whisper as he crouched next to Clive.

"Oh, I think that's pretty obvious, Sergeant," Neville Folliot interrupted.

But Clive interrupted his twin. He'd solved that puzzle some time ago, and he was darned if he'd let Neville have the satisfaction of taking the credit. "We've had two very good clues, Horace. First, the diary entry when we first came here. "How will you feel when you meet Hell's Sire?"

it said. Then, there's the name of this place, the Palace of the Morning Star.

Neville broke in. "Obviously, it's—"

"Lucifer," Clive snapped before his brother could finish. "At least, that's obviously who we're supposed to think it is."

Tomàs folded his knees under himself and made the sign of the cross. "*Ave Maria, cheia de graça. . . .*"

Clive just frowned and tuned him out.

"Hell's Sire is an obvious reference," Chang Guafe agreed, "but my memory index provides no data on the second."

Clive explained. "Both my brother and I were provided with a solid education in the classics. Among the ancient Romans, a culture that once thrived in our world's past, the morning star bore the name Lucifer, or Light-bringer. Later, that name was attributed to the angel who led the revolt against God and fell from heaven. He became the ruler of hell, a place made specifically for his punishment."

"Your God punished him by giving him a place of his own to rule?" Chang Guafe looked from Clive to Neville and back. "He was victorious in his revolt, then?"

Clive and Neville looked at each other. Neville couldn't hold back a crooked grin. "You must introduce him to Milton sometime if we get out of this."

Chang Guafe looked at each of them again. "I register confusion," he said.

Sidi Bombay tapped him consolingly on the shoulder. "Their beliefs have always confused me, too, my friend." He tilted his head and made a face of mock-sympathy. "But they are English."

Chang Guafe turned his ruby eyes toward Sidi. "Are you not one of them?" he said evenly.

Sidi clutched his heart and put on a look of shock and offense so extreme they could not but know he was teasing. "I am Hindu!" he answered with exaggerated dignity. Then he waved a hand of dismissal and wrinkled his nose. "They are Christian."

Chang Guafe eyed them all one at a time as his eyes

brightened and dimmed, brightened and dimmed. "I register confusion," he repeated.

"It would take too long to explain," Clive responded, grinning at Sidi's antics. "Suffice it to say that although humans may all look alike to you, we have as many differences among us as your people. But none of this matters now." He rose slowly, cautiously with the aid of his sheathed sword to a half-crouch. The winds pushed against his chest, and he took a half-step back to catch his balance. "This is the place where Baron Samedi intended to bring us. I say we go knock on the door and see who answers."

"And if it's Old Nick, himself?" Neville said, also rising.

Clive cast a glance at their Portuguese companion, who still knelt muttering into folded hands. "Then we'll get Tomàs to scare him off with prayers."

The company clustered around Clive and began to walk toward the house. "Food, okay?" Finnbogg inquired. "Food for Annie, food for Finnbogg, food for everybody?"

"We'll hope so," Clive assured him.

"Probably devil's cake," Horace Hamilton Smythe grumbled.

"Or a fallen angel cake," Neville suggested.

Sidi joined in. "Or hot cross buns."

"Something from the oven, no doubt," Clive agreed. He looked up at the lighted windows that shone from the house and felt his gut tighten. He watched for shadows moving within, for a face appearing from behind a curtain. Wasn't anyone aware of them? He simple didn't believe they weren't observed. He was beginning to think every move they had made since entering the Dungeon had been observed by someone. He felt like a bug under a microscope. Or a student taking a test.

The house seemed even larger as they approached. An ornate trim of swirls and spirals bordered the windows and the eaves. Leering gargoyles jutted from the guttering. A kind of petrified hedge sprouted up on either side of the path to the main door, with ebony leaves and branches that sparkled in the light and shattered at a touch.

A huge knocker made of iron or some black metal hung upon the door. Clive reached out for it, then hesitated. He looked back at the faces of his friends and saw the same mixture of hope and anxiety in each of them. Only Chang Guafe's face remained impassive, yet in one night in Samedi's cave Clive had learned how to read his cyborg friend.

He grabbed the knocker and slammed it down twice.

The door swung back. A small, frog-faced creature perhaps four feet tall peered suspiciously out from a brightly lit entrance. Opaque membranes nictated over a pair of large round eyes that settled first on Clive's face, then on Neville's. An immense, toothless smile split the curious little face nearly in half and he flung the door open wide.

"You've arrived, arrived!" The creature began to spring up and down on powerful legs, and it clapped webbed hands gleefully. "We didn't know when to expect you, expect you! Come in, Clive Folliot! Come in, Neville Folliot! Welcome all! Welcome, welcome, welcome!"

The twins exchanged glances.

"Hardly my idea of Lucifer, little brother," Neville commented dryly.

"The Frog-prince of darkness, maybe?" Clive shook his head.

They followed the creature down the hallway. Their guide moved in tiny lurching hops, twisting its neckless head around to smile at them, maintaining a constant stream of chatter. Gold bracelets jingled on its wrists as it moved, and a robe of purple silk fluttered about its legs.

Horace Hamilton Smythe watched those legs with a gleam in his eye and licked his lips until Clive Folliot gave him a stern look. "It's devil's cake for you, remember?" he reminded his former batman.

"I don't suppose you have a name or anything?" Neville asked, interrupting their guide.

"Herkimer," came the rapid-fire answer. "I'm Herkimer, Herkimer. Now come this way, please. We have rooms for all of you, and hot baths and fresh clothes and everything to make you comfortable, comfortable! And later, when you're rested, there will be dinner. The master will be awake, awake by then. He's so looking forward to seeing you at last. You're all he's talked about lately, you know, all he's talked about. Oh, and your injuries, injuries! We'll send fresh bandages and medicine right along, along, along. Then, you must tell us all about your adventures. The master will know, of course. He knows everything. But he'll want to hear your stories in your own words, your own words. It'll be such fun!"

Clive followed but tuned out much of Herkimer's chatter. It surprised him as they passed from one hallway into another how the furnishings were from his own period. Here and there were paired overstuffed chairs, sometimes a delicate table or a framed mirror. Gaslight even provided the illumination. The walls were covered with a flocked, floral-patterned paper not unlike that in his very own home.

How strange, he thought, to find such Victorian tastes in such a faraway place. In many ways it reminded him of his own home, with many of the same finishing touches, and a moment of homesickness stole unexpectedly upon him.

They climbed a flight of steps to a corridor that was lined with doors. Herkimer pointed to the first with a mottled-green-and-brown hand. "Here's your room, your room, Mr. Chang Guafe, and there is yours, Miss Shriek." He indicated the door opposite from the first. Surprisingly, he knew all their names as he led them each to his room and opened the doors for them.

"Please," Clive said suddenly when Herkimer made Annabelle's assignment. "I'd like Annabelle to have either the room next to mine or directly across from it."

"Of course," Herkimer said with a smile. "That's easily arranged, easily. We'll just change her room, her room, for Mr. Smythe's." He turned his smile on the sergeant. "Since you're both of the same species there should be no problems, no problems at all."

Sergeant Smythe moved into the doorway but stood on

the threshold watching as did Shriek and Chang Guafe, Sidi Bombay, and Tomàs from their doorways. Finnbogg noted his room assignment but followed along after Clive and Neville with Annabelle in his arms.

There were exactly enough rooms to guest them. Clive and Neville took the last two at the farthest end of the corridor. Their rooms faced each other, and Herkimer flung back the doors, revealing a glimpse of lavishly furnished bedchambers.

Herkimer made a curt bow, his frog-smile never fading. "You'll find hot baths drawn and waiting, waiting for you," he said, "and fresh clothes in all the closets, closets. Never fear, the sizes are each yours. My master has seen to it, seen to it."

"I thought you didn't know when to expect us," Clive said suspiciously.

"Oh, we didn't!" Herkimer insisted. "But never fear, the water *will* be hot, hot. Trust my master. And when you are washed, dressed, and rested, then supper will be ready, will be ready."

"Will we meet your master then?" Neville asked casually, peeking around his door, surveying his room as he spoke over his shoulder.

"Most assuredly," Herkimer answered as he hopped back toward the stairway. "Most assuredly."

Clive watched him go and watched his friends as they glanced his way, then slipped into their rooms. He listened to the quiet closing of the doors until he found himself alone in the hall. He went to Annabelle's door, then opened it and passed inside.

The room was done in a rather Spartan military style reminiscent of an officers' quarters, and he remembered it was originally intended for Horace Hamilton Smythe. There was a bare desk and a chair with a small pile of stationery and an inkwell in one corner of the desk. A wardrobe stood in a corner of the room, and a wooden footlocker sat at one end of the bed. The odor of warm, herb-scented water emanated from a tiny side room.

Annabelle lay composed on the bed where Finnbogg had placed her. Clive sat down on the edge of the mattress, looked at her for a long moment, then drew one finger along her soft cheek. Wherever her mind had retreated to she looked so utterly at peace. He turned her head a little to the side. The wounds on her throat had scabbed over, but he feared they would scar and leave three fine, delicate lines. Her other scratches were relatively minor.

Clive felt a sudden fatigue wash over him, bringing with it a familiar guilt. Though part of him had learned better, another part chided him for failure. He should have taken better care of her, looked after her more closely, protected her. It should have been his hand on the sword that killed Philo B. Goode. He should have spared her that shock.

He drew a deep breath and cradled his head in one hand as he closed his eyes. No, even by then it was too late. He remembered the look in her eyes, the expression of terror as Annabelle waded through the creatures that wore her daughter's face, as she flung them right and left and drove them back with the machine that was part of her body. Even before she killed Philo, her mind had begun its retreat.

Well, if he had been unable to help her then, perhaps he could do something now. He had to, she was his own granddaughter, and his only link to another woman he loved in a world to which he might never return.

Shriek had provided him with a way. At their first meeting the arachnoid had drawn each of them into her psychic web so that they might all communicate on a speechless level with her, or by touching, with each other if they wished. It was not something they did often. Shriek, to whom such telepathy was entirely natural, was able to shield the passageways that led to her deeper thoughts and emotions, and her skill or courtesy was great enough that she didn't intrude too deeply into another mind when she initiated such communication.

But everyone else shied away from using the power without her guidance. It was too easy to tumble into the personality and secret intimacies of someone when you'd only wanted to say hello. In that first encounter before the shock made them all recoil, Clive had glimpsed not only the memories and personal experiences of all his comrades, but their biases and desires, even the bits and pieces of their own cultures as seen through their eyes.

It was all a bit too personal, and by unspoken agreement they had refrained from doing it again except in direst circumstances.

He touched Annabelle's cheek again, feeling the warmth and flush of his own blood under her pale skin. This was such a circumstance, he told himself. Maybe Annabelle would disagree, maybe she'd consider it the cruelest of all possible invasions. But he wasn't just going to let her lie there like that the rest of her life.

He was going to go find her.

He took her hand and pressed it firmly between his, then closed his eyes again. *Annabelle,* he called softly, *Annabelle.* But no answering thought stirred against him, no voice echoed gently up out of the black empty well that was all he perceived.

Clive opened his eyes and looked at her stubbornly. He wasn't at all ready to give up. He rose, moved around to the other side of the bed, and stretched out beside her, adjusting his body on the mattress so that their shoulders touched. He squeezed her hand again and pressed it down between their bodies. Again he closed his eyes.

Annabelle, he called, moving to the edge of the well, bending over it, shouting quietly down into it. *Annabelle, it's Clive.* He waited, staring down into the emptiness. Still, no reply. *All right, granddaughter, I'll come to you.*

He hesitated for the briefest of instants and stepped over the edge. An impossible wind rushed past his face as he fell straight down into the well, deeper and deeper, faster and faster. He began to tumble end over end. All Annabelle's memories, all her desires flashed by too swiftly to taste, all blurred, all tiny little images that cowered and trembled in cells and shallow tunnels that lined the sides of the well.

Either he fell for a very long time, or despite the evidence of his senses, he fell very slowly. Down, down, down—would the fall never come to an end? Down, down, down. *Annabelle*, he called, looking down past his toes into the darkness, though actually he might have been looking up into the darkness, he couldn't tell anymore. *Annabelle, if you're down there, look out below!*

Then, suddenly, *thump, thump!* He landed on something soft and firm. Unhurt, he got to his feet.

Annabelle stood with her back to him, crouched, and fingers extended clawlike. Her clothes hung in tatters, and her hair stood in a wild tangle.

After this I shall think nothing of falling down a stair, Clive said to her, trying to sound light and cheerful. She didn't even turn around to greet him. An animal sound escaped her lips. *Annabelle,* Clive called. *It's all right. Everything's all right. I've come to get you. You can wake up now.*

She whirled then, and a catlike scream issued from her mouth. Startled, Clive jumped back, stumbled, and fell on his backside. Only then did he see what he had landed upon. It was a pair of bodies—bodies of two of the Amanda creatures.

Annabelle gave another cat scream, and he looked up again. Suddenly, emerging from the darkness came scores of the furious little creatures, all looking sweetly childlike, all hissing and spitting, scratching and biting. Annabelle flung them away as they charged at her. She used the energy of her Baalbec and burned them to crisps. She sliced them in halves with a saber that seemed to appear and disappear in her hand.

Then the creatures simply vanished. Annabelle waited in exactly the same crouched pose as Clive had found her. He didn't even call out her name this time. She turned and screamed exactly as she had.

It all began again.

Annabelle, don't! he shouted. *This isn't real, it's a dream! It's all over! Wake up!*

But she didn't hear or didn't respond. Again and again she fought the same battle, slaughtered creatures who looked exactly like her little daughter, sometimes with her sword, sometimes with her machine, sometimes with her own bloody bare hands.

Clive couldn't reach her, couldn't touch her or run to her side. No matter how he ran or walked or jumped, he seemed to stay on the same spot. He could move, he just didn't seem to get anywhere!

But he had to do something. He thought of going back for help. Maybe Shriek would know what to do. Yet, when he looked up, he suddenly realized he had no idea how to get back. He tried to imagine himself back in his body, but that didn't work. He tried to imagine a well or a tunnel that would lead him back to reality, sort of a reverse route to take him out of Annabelle's nightmare, but that didn't work, either.

He was trapped!

With a sudden chill of fear he saw that for the first time the Amanda creatures were noticing him. They didn't attack him, yet, just watched. But he realized intuitively that the longer he stayed the stronger his fear would become, and the stronger his fear became the more Annabelle's nightmare would become real to him, too. Then the creatures would turn on him.

No, Being Clive, not to be that is.

The thought brushed against him with gentle reassurance, and immediately his heart lightened as he felt Shriek's presence nearby. Suddenly she stood beside him.

Negative, came another thought simultaneously with Shriek's, and Chang Guafe was also there.

Finnbogg bite nasty-things. Save Annie, okay?

Clive found himself surrounded by his comrades. Sidi and Tomàs and Horace Hamilton Smythe with saber drawn were there, too. They ringed him closely, and at once the Amanda creatures lost interest in him.

Where's Neville? he asked abruptly, spinning around.

Yer bleedin' brother's not yet part o' the mind-web, Smythe answered in his best cockney. It seemed to Clive an inappropriate time for such foolery, however.

It's Shriek's idea, Englishman, Sidi Bombay said, reminding Clive that every thought was open now. *We must maintain a good humor and allow no fear whatsoever. Then we must surround Miss Annabelle.*

Clive stared at the Indian. *But you're not part of the mind-web, either,* he said in confusion. *You were trapped in that damned egg-thing when we met Shriek. How can you be here?*

Shriek brought him in just now for this, sah, Smythe hurriedly explained. *Can't say the same for Neville, but we all trust Sidi Bombay. More importantly, Annabelle trusts him and cares about him. Shriek says that Annabelle needs us all right now.*

The arachnoid interrupted. *Caught in a memory loop the Annabelle being is. Find her I could not. Only to you a path did she open. Trust you most of all she does.*

Then how did you find us? Clive asked, his spirits buoyed by the presence of his friends.

Trapped here you almost became, Being Clive. Called out to me you did. Closed your mind is not, so follow I did, bringing all friend beings. Friend beings it is can save the Annabelle being now.

How?

We must surround the senhorita, Tomàs jumped in eagerly. *Shriek has explained it to us. The monstros would not attack you, and they will not attack us. When they cannot reach her the . . .* The little Portuguese hesitated and looked to Shriek.

Memory loop, she supplied.

Si, the memory loop, the pattern, will be broken. Then, she may awaken.

Clive turned back to Shriek. *May?*

She shrugged her four shoulders helplessly. *Try and hope. No more can we do.*

Clive nodded his head and put his arms around as many of them as he could and drew them close. *Well, let's do that much.*

With Shriek beside him, guiding his steps and all their steps, Clive found he could move toward Annabelle. He linked his right arm through one of hers and his left arm through Smythe's. Each of them linked with someone else, and they marched toward Annabelle, surrounded her, and closed a tight circle about her.

The Amanda creatures jumped about, making their obscene animal noises, slicing the air with their claws. They ran around the circle in agitation, long black hair flying, ragged blue pinafores fluttering about their legs. But they could not reach Annabelle. One by one they began to fade. Just an arm or leg at first, followed by another, then an eye or a nose. Always, the last thing remaining was a mouth. Then that, too, faded.

I think she's read Mr. Carroll's new book, sah, Horace Hamilton Smythe said with a grin.

Clive Folliot nodded to his old friend. Horace Hamilton Smythe never ceased to surprise him. *I didn't know you'd read it, sergeant,* he said. *It's rather recent.*

Smythe's grin widened, and he gave a wink. *A man's got to stay abreast of things, sah.*

Clive returned the wink, recalling Smythe's skill at disguise and his activities on the queen's behalf as an agent provocateur. *Especially a man like you, eh, Sergeant? I guess there's a little bit of Alice in us all.* He turned to see about Annabelle, but before he finished the movement his legs disappeared, leaving him hanging in midair. He looked at Horace in astonishment.

Be seeing you topside, sah. There was nothing left of Horace but his head, and that began to ghost away feature by feature. *Always wondered what a Cheshire puss was, anyway.* The sergeant put on his biggest smile. The corners of his mouth strained upward toward the tips of his ears, and he held it frozen playfully that way. It was the last part of him to go.

Clive looked over his shoulder at Annabelle. She stood with her eyes closed, but the terror was gone from her face. In its place he saw the same peaceful expression that her real body wore in the real world. He had a feeling she would be all right now. He'd come through for her after all. They all had.

Me, too, Horace, Clive admitted, putting on his biggest grin as he watched his right arm fade away. The others stared at him, uncomprehending. How peculiar they all looked half there, half gone. Chang Guafe had no torso at all, just two legs, two arms, and a head with lots of space between. Clive laughed. *The most curious thing I ever saw in all my life!*

¡Ai de mim! Tomàs exclaimed, making the sign of the cross with only three fingers and his smile showing. It looked like three little sausages teasing a hungry mouth.

Indeed, Clive laughed again. *Curiouser and curiouser.* Then he, too, was gone.

CHAPTER THIRTEEN

At the Palace of the Morning Star

Clive opened his eyes, immediately aware of the warmth of Annabelle's hand in his and of the softness of the bed upon which he lay. He rolled his head to the side to look at his granddaughter. She had a nice profile, such a lovely face.

With a start he sprang up. Whatever was he thinking of? It was a bed they were on, after all, and she was a lady, and he was a gentleman. It was no proper place to conduct business, or at least, to linger after business had been conducted.

"It's a nice blush yer wearin', guv, but don't be embarrassed." Horace Hamilton Smythe looked up at him from the floor and grinned as he still played the cockney. Clive had nearly stepped on him. "You did the right thing by her, sure."

All the company minus Neville sat on the floor around the bed, hands still enjoined.

"Is the *senhorita* all right?" Tomàs asked as he released the hands of Sidi Bombay and Finnbogg. He stood up slowly. It was plain he'd cramped his leg.

"I hope so," Clive answered, turning his attention back to Annabelle. Her eyes were still closed, though, and she hadn't stirred.

Awaken soon she will, friend beings, Shriek said to all of them as awareness returned to her six eyes. She released the hands of Chang Guafe and Smythe, and she, too, stood, rising to her full seven feet of height. She laid a hand gently on Clive's shoulder. *Find her I could not when before tried I. But a secret path unconsciously left she for you alone, Being Clive. This brave attempt had not you made, lost she would be still, perhaps forever.*

"Observation," Chang Guafe said in a cool metallic voice. "You are a hero."

"*Allons enfants de la patrie . . . !*" Finnbogg began to sing at the top of his lungs the French national anthem, and Clive decided at once he was going to have to chide Neville for the choice of songs he'd taught the alien canine at their first meeting. Before he could say anything directly to Finnbogg, however, Tomàs leaned over and clapped a hand around Finnbogg's mouth. Finnbogg's eyes rolled toward the Portuguese and they regarded each other for an instant. Then both smiled, and Finnbogg shut up.

"Oh, I've had such a curious dream!"

Everyone looked toward the bed at the sound of Annabelle's voice as she rose up on her elbows and looked at them all with an expression that beamed with joy. Sidi and Finnbogg and Chang Guafe scrambled to their feet and bent near the bed. Annabelle blinked at them for a moment, then her eyes twinkled.

"Why, it's the scarecrow, the lion, and the tin man!" she exclaimed, sitting up quickly and crossing her legs in the bed. "But that's another story." She reached out and patted Finnbogg on the head, and his ears pricked up. "Besides, you might be Toto," she said to him alone.

"I don't know about the other story," Horace Hamilton Smythe said, moving closer to the bed. "But Mr. Carroll seems to have made quite an impression on you. The major and I have both read his newest book, and I'm pleased to see it must still be popular in your time."

"It's one of my two favorites," Annabelle admitted. "But you wouldn't know Mr. Baum. I used to read both stories over and over when I was a kid, and later I read them over and over for Amanda." She looked down suddenly, and her face clouded over.

Decorum be damned, Clive thought, and he sat down on the bed beside her, put an arm around her shoulder, and drew her close.

"Guess I fell down a hole of my own this time," she said, looking up at them all again and forcing a little smile. "Thanks, everybody." She squeezed Clive's hand and gave him a kiss on the cheek. "Thanks, Grandpa."

Clive blushed again and stood up. Inside, though, he felt better and bigger than he ever had in his life, as if in some way he had just kept some unspoken promise to a lonely woman in a flat back in London. Emotions rushed powerfully upon him, and he knew he had to get away from everyone.

"If you can manage," he said quickly to Annabelle, "we're invited to dinner. There's a hot bath through there"—he pointed to the small side room—"and clothes in the wardrobe." With that, he stepped around the others and headed for the door.

"By the way, just where are we?" she said, but Clive didn't turn around.

Chang Guafe answered for him. "The Palace of the Morning Star."

As he stepped through the doorway, Clive heard her sigh and her comment, "I didn't think it was Kansas."

He closed the door and hurried to his own room. There, he sat down heavily on his own bed and held his head in his hands. Slowly, he mastered the emotions that had nearly caused an unseemly display.

Someone knocked on his door.

He hesitated but a moment, stood, and turned. "Come in," he called, expecting Horace Hamilton Smythe. His sergeant had a habit of looking after him, "mothering," he sometimes accused his friend.

It was Shriek who opened the door and stepped inside. She closed it quietly behind her. *Another problem there is*, she informed him.

"Of course there is," he answered, using speech. A smirk flickered across his face. "This is the Dungeon."

Her mandibles opened wide in what might have been her imitation of a human smile, and she shrugged her four shoulders. Clive started to wave her toward one of two overstuffed chairs that furnished the room, then realized wearily they wouldn't accommodate her four-legged form. For that matter, he had never seen her sit at all.

"Well . . ." He looked around helplessly, then gave it up. So much for Victorian hospitality. "What is it this time?"

Shriek paced to the far side of his room, looked around, then paced back. *No windows, Being Clive,* she pointed out. *None in my room. None in room of Annabelle being.*

She was right. Clive hadn't noticed, but she was right. His brow furrowed, and he ran his tongue along the back of his teeth. No windows, and only one door in or out of the rooms. The hackles on the back of his neck rose slowly. *Perhaps we've been careless, Being Shriek.* He sent the thought to her. No one could overhear their private thoughts.

More there is, she continued. *Irritated have I been. Distracted.*

The itch you couldn't scratch?

Identify it could I not until linked in the psionic web were all friend beings. Not in myself could I see it. Too well it disguised itself. But in all of you burned it, glaring to my senses.

Clive unconsciously ran a hand over his chest. *In all of us? What?*

Scanned we are being, very subtly, by powerful telepath beings.

"Well, who the hell are they?" Clive shouted and clenched his fists. So offended and angered was he by her revelation that he forgot himself and slipped into speech. Not that it mattered any goddamned way if someone could hear his thoughts as well as his words! A man didn't have any privacy at all!

Know them I do not, Shriek answered, projecting calm. *Find them I cannot. Far away they are and well-shielded. But no secrets can we be sure to keep. This I thought you should know.*

Clive thought. "Are they scanning us now?"

Shriek shook her head.

"Then it's not a constant scan," he said. He moved about the room uneasily. Even if Shriek said they weren't being monitored, he still felt like a bug under observation or under the shadow of someone's heel. "Is there any pattern? Anything in particular that they seem interested in?" He scratched his stubbled chin as he paced. "Could they be the Dungeonmasters—the Ren or the Chaffri—that run this place?"

No time have I had to learn these things, the arachnoid apologized. *Beyond my meager power are these telepath beings, but try will I.*

He stepped up to her and patted her left upper shoulder affectionately. Odd, how once he had considered her so ugly and strange. He saw none of that now. She had taken on a unique kind of beauty to him, an alien beauty to be sure, but something even his human senses could appreciate and trust.

And there was also about her a tranquility, a serenity that he tried to emulate. "There is no more we can do then, but bathe and dress and go down to dinner. You're sure our telepath isn't here?"

She clasped one of his hands and then released it. *Far away,* she assured him. *But more there is to do.* She pointed a finger at the wound on his leg. The blood had clotted, but traces of fresh red seeped around the edges of the clots. *Help I can, better than before.* She plucked one hair-spike from her body and held it up. On the tip a bead of clear fluid gleamed in the gaslight that illuminated the room. *Medicine for blood of human beings. More time have I had to assimilate blood-taste from the Annabelle being. Infection could I prevent and pain relieve the first time—*

"And Mickey could you slip," he interrupted, remembering a phrase he'd learned from Annabelle. He folded his arms and raised one eyebrow.

Pain will this relieve again, she continued. *And pain you have though deny it you do. Behind your every thought sense it I can. But heal this droplet will, also, and swiftly. Stop your bleeding, seal your wound, heal the scratches.*

"Can you do the same for Annabelle and Neville?" he asked, hesitating, then extending his arm.

Accepted medicine the Annabelle being has already, she told him. *The Neville being, too, if allow it he will.* She jabbed him quickly with the hair-spike. A drop of blood welled up around the puncture in his forearm and mingled with the clear droplet.

"I don't recall that you asked him the first time," Clive said with a teasing grin. He flicked the drop of blood away. A tiny hole marked the skin underneath, but no more blood appeared.

Urgent it was that we move swiftly then, she said, looking askance and shrugging. *Argument there was no time for.*

Clive barely heard her. The pain flowed out of his body as if he were a glass vessel with a crack in his foot. With it went all his fatigue. The tension in his neck and shoulders vanished. The sting of his scratches faded away. He flexed his thigh. There was some stiffness there and the mildest twinge, but even that lessened as he tested the muscle.

He beamed at Shriek. "Well, you ask him politely then and with all courtesy, but if he says no"—he winked at her—"jab him anyway."

His door opened and Annabelle entered wearing a disgusted look and a large damp towel. Actually, the towel wasn't *that* large. Clive let go a moan and squeezed his eyes shut.

"Oh, grow up, Clive-o!" she snapped. "And help me!"

With a patient sigh he opened his eyes again and looked. Over one arm she carried a man's khaki outfit. Over the other she bore a full dress uniform for a regimental quartermaster sergeant in Her Majesty's Fifth Imperial Horse

Guards. Her short black hair clung wetly close around her face, and her legs seemed to go on forever, and the towel just seemed to float there.

"My entire wardrobe is full of garbage like this!" she complained.

"Perhaps this would be more to your liking, miss."

Horace Hamilton Smythe appeared just behind her. He held up a white cotton dress in one hand and a pair of leather trousers in the other.

Clive rubbed his eyes and the bridge of his nose and sat down weakly on the foot of his bed. His own Annabella Leighton had never dared to appear before him in so little or in so much light! Well, that wasn't strictly true, he admitted wryly. There had been a very memorable night in her boudoir just before he left London. But there had been just a single candle, and she certainly hadn't been so brazen about it. His granddaughter, though, had made it plain that things were different in her century, but how different he hadn't guessed. Still, it was her life; she'd made that plain, too. Slowly, he let go the breath he'd been holding.

"Take your pick," Smythe told her, "or there's a lot more to choose from. We switched rooms while you were"—he paused, searching for a suitable word—"asleep. We can trade back if you like."

Annabelle dumped the two men's outfits in Horace's arms and turned up her nose at the dress and pants. "Just let me grab something else to wear—"

Please! Clive thought to himself.

"—and we'll switch after dinner. I've already used the bath, and I can tell you haven't, Sergeant." She patted him with mock condescension on the crown of his head and marched out of the room. Smythe followed.

"Well, she's back to normal," Clive said to Shriek. He rose to his feet. "I guess we'd better prepare for dinner. I'm suddenly eager to meet the lord of this manor." He frowned. "On second thought, 'lord' might not quite be the appropriate word. Well, no matter. I just hope his food is good."

Shriek moved toward the door and regarded him from the threshold. *That he knows the way to the eighth level hope I*, she said.

"You have a positive talent for the practical, my dear," he answered, making a short bow. Then, he turned serious again. "Let me know if you learn anything more about our mysterious monitors. If they're as powerful as you say, they may hold the key to this whole Dungeon." Then, he grinned again. "Now go give Neville hell." He made a jabbing motion with his hand.

Shriek made the soft chittering sound that passed for laughter and closed the door on her way out.

Alone, Clive turned and surveyed his room again. If it was a cell, it was a velvet-lined cell, and for now, at least, he intended to take advantage of it. He stripped off the rags that were once his clothes and kicked them into a corner near the wardrobe.

He stepped up to a full-length mirror that had been framed in an exquisitely carved antique wood and tilted it to an angle that best reflected his body. He had lost weight since coming to the Dungeon. Not that he had ever been fat, but the slight padding around his waist had disappeared. He'd grown thin and rangy in his time here, and his stringy muscles had strengthened.

He examined some of his scratches. They were no longer tender to the touch, and when he brushed a couple with a fingertip, the scabs fell off easily to expose patches of fresh pink skin. All the stiffness had left his thigh now, and a hard scab had formed over the wound. *Thank you, Shriek*, he thought silently.

Welcome you are, Being Clive.

He jerked around, covering his groin with both hands and blushing hotly, but there was no one else in the room. He relaxed, but kept his hands low.

That's not fair! he protested.

But she was gone already, in and out of his head almost

before he'd been aware of her. *Come on, old boy, you weren't aware of her at all*, he admitted. And if anybody else was prying around in his head, he wasn't aware of that, either, but just in case, he offered them a very rude thought having to do with the conduct of their mothers and strode into the bathroom.

The bath was still hot. He lowered himself cautiously into the tub, expecting to feel some stinging in the scratches despite Shriek's medicine, but he experienced only the delicious sensation of the warm water. Drawing his knees up, he sank to his neck. Undoubtedly, it was the closest thing to heaven he expected to find in this hell.

He found a bar of perfumed soap, along with some scented oils, on a small table at the foot of the tub. He disdained the oils, but the sandalwood odor of the bar he deemed not too unmasculine, and he scrubbed himself gently. Also on the table he found a small razor and hand-mirror. In fact, his host had provided for all his needs.

When at last he stood, he discovered more patches of exposed new skin. Toweling dislodged even more of his scabs. It amazed him how fast his body seemed to be healing!

He didn't stop too long to marvel, though. His stomach grumbled threateningly. He'd felt hungry before the bath, but now he was starving! A side effect of the arachnoid's medicine? he wondered. No matter. He hurried to the wardrobe, chose a pair of sturdy khaki jungle slacks and a loose shirt of white cotton. Everything fit him perfectly, even the boots he found at the bottom of the wardrobe.

He checked his appearance in the mirror. He barely recognized the man who looked back at him. He'd almost forgotten how blond his hair was, so long had it been since he'd last washed it. It shone now, as did his thin golden mustache, all the facial growth he'd ever allowed himself. He ran a finger over it, considering how it would look if he let it grow a little thicker. No, he decided. Then he'd be chewing on the ends, and a gentleman did no such thing. Better to keep it neatly trimmed.

He stretched one final time in front of the mirror, feeling better than he had in ages, then started to leave his room and join the others. He stopped, though, suddenly noticing a new sword, which lay upon the bed.

He picked it up and examined it carefully. It was an extraordinarily generous gift, a finely crafted blade. Yet a gentleman would not insult his host by wearing a weapon to dinner. It just wasn't done, not even if that host was Lucifer, himself. If anything went wrong he'd just have to rely on his wits and on his companions. He placed the sword back on the bed, then stepped through the door, and closed it quickly before he changed his mind.

Sergeant Smythe paced the hallway, obviously waiting for him. He cut quite a figure in his regimental uniform.

"I'd hoped to see you in the white, Horace!" Clive joked, clapping his batman on the shoulder.

"Hadn't the knees for it, sah," Smythe answered glibly, "and it pinched a bit in the middle, it did. So this will just have to do."

Sidi Bombay came out of his room. The Indian looked almost regal in white slacks and a white embroidered shirt. A sash of soft blue silk encircled his waist, and a turban of the same fabric perched upon his head. A small silver brooch sparkled in the center of it. "Ah, Englishmen!" he said by way of greeting. "My head is covered again. Perhaps God will favor me once more."

"In this place, old friend?" Smythe scoffed. "You're an optimist."

"Am I wrong," asked Clive abruptly, "or isn't this the first time the three of us have been alone together since we crossed the shimmering mist and found ourselves in Q'oorna?"

The three men looked at each other curiously. "I think you may be right, Englishman," Sidi agreed.

There was an awkward moment of silence. Then Clive spoke. "I'd like to thank you both. You've been good friends and stalwart companions. I consider it the highest honor to know you." There was another awkward moment before he asked to shake their hands.

"I also consider it an honor to know you, Clive Folliot," Sidi Bombay said. "You are, indeed, a credit to your race." He grinned broadly, showing lots of teeth.

Horace threw an arm around Sidi, clapped his back, and hugged him playfully, reminding Clive that the two had been friends for longer than he knew.

"Forgive him, sah," Horace begged, showing the same grin. "He's not a bad fellow, as dirty little fakirs go."

"I am quite clean after my bath," Sidi assured him defensively.

Smythe sniffed and wrinkled his nose. "You should have skipped the perfumes."

Sidi sniffed. "We Indians are unburdened by your English concepts of manliness. I find the floral oils quite pleasant." He sniffed again. "You certainly might have benefited from them."

"Enough!" Clive suggested, chuckling. He enjoyed their banter, though, and it felt good to laugh again. Still, it was time for dinner, and he was famished. "Where are the others?"

"Already gone down, sah," Horace informed him.

"Then what are we waiting for?" Clive made a bow and gestured toward the stairway. "Gentlemen?"

They descended together. At the bottom they looked up and down the long corridor. Not far away, Herkimer stood near a set of oaken double doors. Clive blinked and considered just how peculiar a four-foot frog looked in formal wear.

"This way, this way, sirs!" Herkimer said. The frog made a deep bow as they approached, and with one hand he pushed wide both doors. A red carpet led the way to an elaborate dining table. In the center of the carpet stood another frog who bowed, then smiled at them. "This way, please!" it said, and gestured toward the table where the rest of the company was already seated.

"Who are you?" Clive asked the second frog.

"Herkimer, sir," the frog answered politely. "You may choose your own seats, your own seats. Will you take wine with your meal, sirs?"

Clive grinned at Horace and Sidi. "That would be delightful, Herkimer, Herkimer," he answered for them all.

"We have a considerable cellar, sir," Herkimer continued. "May I suggest a claret, a claret?"

Clive deferred. "I trust your judgment, Herkimer."

The frog moved aside and made another bow as Clive, Horace, and Sidi took seats at the table. There were just enough chairs for them all, he noted, plus one at the head of the table for their host, who had not yet made his appearance. Then, he recounted.

"Where is Shriek?" he asked with sudden concern.

Annabelle waved him to a seat she had saved at her left hand. "She wishes to be excused," his granddaughter told him. "You know she doesn't like to eat in front of people."

Clive took the chair and sat down. The table settings were elegant by any standards. The silver had been polished to a high gleam. He could see his reflection in the china settings. The candelabra appeared to be gold, as did the butter dishes, the creamers, and the sugar bowls.

He turned to Annabelle. She had chosen the white cotton dress, after all, and she looked radiant.

"You look nice, too, Grandpa," she whispered.

Two more frogs appeared from a side entrance. One pushed a small metal cart with various covered dishes. The other bore a tray with three glasses of deep-red wine. Clive quickly noticed the others already had glasses.

"Herkimer, I assume?" he asked as the frog placed his glass on the table.

"Of course, sir, sir, sir," came the throaty answer, and the frog returned to other duties.

Neville sat directly across from Clive. He leaned forward now, placing his elbows on the table in unseemly fashion. "And where," he muttered conspiratorially, "do you suppose, is our host? I always expected to meet the devil someday, you know."

"And I expected the same for you," Clive admitted wryly.

As if on cue the double doors swung open again. Clive pushed back his chair and rose to his feet. Everyone except Annabelle followed suit and looked toward the entrance as their host appeared at the threshold, hesitated, and came toward them.

Clive's jaw dropped, and Neville, for once, was speechless.

Herkimer stepped to the edge of the red carpet. "My master, master," the little creature called in his best frog's voice, "and the lord of this manor. Also, your host, your host!" Then, he paused with needless drama before announcing the name.

After all, Clive knew his own father!

· CHAPTER FOURTEEN ·

Hell's Sire

"That don't look like *el diablo* to me," Tomàs muttered.

"Look again, sailor," Neville whispered. "It's the devil, himself."

Clive shot a look at his twin, surprised by the anger in Neville's voice and the poorly concealed contempt on his face. He'd never seen such a look before! Neville was Father's favorite, the chosen heir to the family estate and rightful heir to the Tewkesbury title as well. He didn't understand his brother's reaction at all.

Neville, though, noticed Clive's reaction, and his face went stony, then completely passive again as if nothing had passed between them.

Baron Tewkesbury walked forward, picking up speed with every step, beaming with paternal pride and joy as he approached the table. He cut quite an imposing figure in his brown velvet jacket and silk ruffled shirt. He was taller than either of his sons, and the years had not yet stolen all of the blond from his thick mass of curls or from his carefully trimmed beard. He still carried his broad-shouldered bulk with power and grace.

Clive stepped away from the table. "Father, what are you doing here?"

It shouldn't have surprised him at all when Baron Tewkesbury ignored his question and walked to Neville's side of the table. He'd had a lifetime of that kind of treatment.

Still, it smarted when, holding out his arms, the old man embraced his favorite son and clapped him on the back with enthusiasm. Clive's hand closed on the back of his chair and gripped it until his knuckles turned white. He was barely aware of it when Annabelle's hand covered his.

"My son!" the baron cried. "My prodigal son is found!" He embraced Neville again, wrapping him in great bearish arms. "Dear Neville, I thought I'd never see you again! But here you are!"

"So, kill the fatted calf," Neville muttered halfheartedly over his father's shoulder. He stared at Clive. Nothing but coldness filled his gaze.

"Sit down, sit down!" Baron Tewkesbury held Neville's chair for him and slid it under his son when Neville returned to the table. The old man patted him on both shoulders and planted a kiss on the top of his head, which brought a frown of annoyance to Neville's face. Though his father didn't see, it didn't escape Clive's notice.

He could wait no longer, though. "Father, how did you get here?" he blurted. "I don't understand. . . ."

"Of course you don't, Clive." At last his father acknowledged his presence. The old man looked at him strangely as he gripped the back of Neville's chair, and Clive trembled inwardly under that scrutiny, an old feeling that he remembered all too well. Automatically, Clive straightened his shoulders and drew in his stomach.

"Clive, Clive!" the baron said suddenly. He strode decorously around the table and opened his arms again to gather Clive in. Clive felt himself nearly crushed against his father's chest. He sputtered. In all his memory his father had never hugged him, never shown him any affection at all!

"Clive, can you ever forgive me?" His father pushed him back at arm's length and looked at him. "I've been an old fool. I've blamed you all these years for your mother's death, but I was wrong, Son." Tears barely held in check sparkled in the corners of his father's eyes.

Clive didn't know what to say. What was he to make of

such behavior? He'd wanted his father's love for so long, worked so hard for it until he'd finally given up. Now, at last, it was being offered unconditionally. His father had even asked his forgiveness. But could he forget so many years and so much indifference so easily?

Baron Tewkesbury kept one arm draped around Clive's shoulder as he turned to face Neville and the others. He made a sweeping gesture with his free arm. "My sons are home! I never thought to see this day! Welcome, welcome to all of you!"

He embraced Clive again, then moved to his seat at the head of the table between his sons. He sat down with great dignity, composing himself once more. "Herkimer," he called to the frog who had announced him. "You may serve now."

Herkimer bowed and clapped his webbed hands together. At once three more frogs, all exactly alike, came through the side door. Two pushed small carts, which they parked beside the first one. The other one carried trays of small steaming bowls, which turned out to contain rice. A dollop of green sauce rested atop each dish, along with several small shrimp.

The delicious smell crept up Clive's nostrils, reminding him how hungry he felt. Still, he couldn't believe his father was actually here in the Dungeon. He leaned forward on his elbows. "Father, how in hell—"

His father clucked his tongue and gave him a stern look. "Where are your manners, Son?"

Clive looked sheepish and took his elbows from the table at once.

"That's better," his father said, smiling again. "Now introduce me to your friends. By the way, isn't someone missing?"

"Our friend Shriek," Annabelle spoke up. "She preferred to stay in her room."

The baron frowned, then shrugged. "Ah, well. I'll see that a meal is sent up to her."

Horace Hamilton Smythe cleared his throat and glanced

at Clive. "Uh, she has rather peculiar needs, milord, she does."

"Nothing we can't meet," the baron assured. He picked up a spoon and tasted the rice dish. One of the frogs stood close by awaiting his approval. The old man chewed delicately, then smiled. "Please, everyone, we may converse as we dine."

Clive quickly made introductions, then took several bites from his own bowl. He had never tasted anything quite like it, but it was superb.

Abruptly, Tewkesbury put down his spoon. "Is the rice not to your liking, Mr. Guafe? You're not eating."

The cyborg had not touched the dish or the wine. He looked coolly at his host, and his ruby lenses glowed. "I do not need to ingest organic matter," he stated. "This body extracts single atoms from the air and converts them to the energy I require."

Clive looked at Chang over the rim of his glass. He knew, in fact, that his cyborg friend could eat and drink if he chose. He'd seen him do so, sometimes just to experience the pleasure of taste, sometimes as a means of analysis. But he said nothing now to contradict Guafe, though he watched him carefully.

The cyborg placed his hands in his lap and spoke to the baron with even more flatness of tone than usual. "You have repeatedly ignored the inquiries of your son, Clive Folliot. Respond to my inquiry, please."

The baron's eyes narrowed, and Clive saw the father he remembered sitting next to him. Tewkesbury's stare rivaled the cyborg's for coldness as he sat back and folded his hands across his stomach. He said nothing but waited for Chang Guafe to continue.

"Why do you attempt duplicity?" Chang said. "This dwelling structure conforms outwardly to the conventions of the period your son has described as Victorian." He touched a finger to the edge of his rice bowl. "Yet this food bears faint traces of microwave radiation." He touched the wineglass. "This vessel contains few of the minerals from which glass is usually made." He waved his hand in a casual gesture. "This structure, itself, the walls and floors, the ceiling—all seamless in construction, impossible for the level of technology Clive Folliot has described. Nothing here is exactly as it seems."

The baron relaxed somewhat. "And how do you know these things, sir?" he asked.

"His sensors are quite remarkable, Father," Clive interjected, "far keener than eyes and ears." He looked down the table at his friends. Everyone stopped eating, and all spoons were quietly set aside as they waited for their host to provide an explanation.

Tewkesbury picked up his glass and sipped the red liquid slowly. With great deliberation he set the glass back down. "You are quite right, Chang Guafe," he said. "And if we can allow the dinner to continue, I will explain how it is that I am here. We really have an excellent roast beef, and my servants get quite upset if they are not allowed to carry out their duties. Nervous creatures, really they are."

At his word, the frog-creatures rolled up the carts and uncovered plates containing steaming slices of rare and medium roast beef. Clive felt his senses reel at the fantastic odor, and despite himself, he picked up his fork and knife as soon as his plate was set before him. Alongside the beef were buttered small potatoes still in their skins and served with parsley.

From another cart came bowls of stewed tomatoes, corn, and peas. Another bowl of apples and oranges joined those. On yet another cart parked at the far end of the table sat three kinds of pie.

Two other servants, Herkimer and Herkimer no doubt, waited close at hand with wine and iced water.

Iced water in hell, Clive thought with an incongruous grin as he chewed and swallowed.

Then, he stiffened a bit as Annabelle's hand settled on his thigh under the tablecloth. "You were about to tell us how you came here, Mr. Folliot," she said, using a very improper form of address.

The baron pretended not to notice. "Thank you, my dear." He smiled at her, then reached out and caught the hands of each of his sons and smiled warmly at them, too. "I don't understand it all, myself, but I'll tell you what I can."

Tewkesbury sat back and twirled his wineglass between his palms. He seemed to gather his thoughts before speaking. Then, he looked up at Neville. "When you didn't return from Africa, I sent your brother, Clive, to find you and bring you home. You'd been missing for a year, and no one knew if you were alive or dead." He turned to his other son. "To my great shame, Clive, I waited two years after we lost track of you. Then, word came that someone had found some of your belongings in a shipwreck off the coast of Zanzibar, a suitcase or something with some of the articles you'd been writing for that unsavory scandal rag that your friend—Carstairs—edited."

His father paused and took a sip of wine to wet his throat. Clive didn't bother to explain that Carstairs was no friend of his, that the man had paid him for those articles, only enough to supplement the inadequate sum the baron, himself, had provided to outfit his expedition.

After a brief while, his father continued. "I don't mind telling you that, faced with the loss of both my sons, I set about to examine my entire life. Shortly after that, I set sail, myself, for Africa, determined to do whatever I could to find you both."

Clive felt Annabelle's hand tighten on his leg, and he caught it in his own hand. Anyone else might have misinterpreted her action, but he knew she only meant to reassure him. Still, he could hardly believe what he was hearing! His father, an esteemed noble of the realm, stealing through the fetid jungle like a common adventurer? Surely other lords and ladies had done as much. But his father?

He glanced across the table to see how his brother was receiving this, but Neville was uncharacteristically quiet. He listened politely, but his face remained unreadable, and he went through the motions of eating without consuming much.

"With some difficulty I traced your steps, until in Bagamoyo I encountered a Father Timothy O'Hara who remembered you both." He turned his gaze on Neville and shook a finger. "You with some consternation, I must tell you," he said to his son. "He charged nothing specific, mind you, but hinted at some highly improper behavior on your part." He sipped his wine again and beckoned to the frog-servant with the wine. "Thank you, Herkimer," he said.

"Father O'Hara," Neville said with a bemused smirk as he leaned back in his chair. "Now there's a man who knows more about this place than he pretends."

Clive agreed with a barely perceptible nod. "I suspect the same," he said. Then, with another nod and a wry tilt of his head toward his father, he added, "Though I charge nothing specific."

But the baron seemed to ignore them, lost, as he was, in his own tale. "Strange thing about Bagamoyo," he continued. "Never saw such lights in the sky in all my life." He thought for a moment, remembering, then shrugged. "Anyway, it was this Father O'Hara who told me about the Sudd. He said it was the last place anyone had seen either of you."

"You encountered the sparkling mists," Clive interrupted excitedly.

The baron nodded. "But not the first time. After I made it across the swamp—nasty place, that—I asked about you in a village on the far side and determined that neither of you had made it that far. I don't mind telling you I feared the worst then. If the Sudd had claimed you both, there'd never be a trace. I started back, intending to question the priest again or anyone else in Bagamoyo who might have seen you." Again, he took a drink of wine and dabbed at the corner of his mouth with his napkin. "I never made it back across."

"You didn't see the mists the first time?" Clive asked.

He'd forgotten his own meal as he listened to his father's tale. The idea that his parent had, indeed, come looking for him filled him with a rare and pleasing warmth.

"Not the first time, but there it was the second. I and two bearers were poling a small boat through the muck when the stuff suddenly closed about us. I tell you it came up faster than a London fog!"

"What became of the bearers, Lord Folliot?" Sidi Bombay inquired, speaking for the first time.

"They panicked and jumped overboard, I'm afraid. Whether they got away or died in the swamp I don't know. Perhaps the mist got them anyway and carried them to another part of the Dungeon. I wound up here alone. When the mist cleared, I found myself on the shore of the Lake of Lamentations."

Clive had met only a few people in the Dungeon who had not entered at Q'oorna, the first level, and worked their way to the other levels. None ever seemed to have any idea why they landed where they did, though.

Sergeant Smythe clinked his glass on the edge of his plate as he set it down. He glanced at Clive, then at the Baron Tewkesbury. "Pardon me, your lordship, but you said you waited two years after Clive disappeared before coming to look for him? But we can't possibly have been here that long!"

"I'm afraid it's true," the baron answered. "Certainly you realize by now that time in the Dungeon has a nature all its own. It's certainly different from time on Earth. It may even be different from one level to the other. I, myself, have been here for quite a while, I don't mind telling you." He waved a hand toward the other end of the table. "How about some pie, everyone? Herkimer is really a very good cook."

"Herkimer? Really?" Neville said with sarcastic liveliness. "Which Herkimer?"

The baron looked at his son with something of a frown. No one at the table had missed the note of unpleasantness or failed to notice how little Neville had spoken during the meal.

"All of them or any of them," his father answered quietly. "They are very talented creatures and learn quickly."

"They all look alike to me," Neville said curtly. He pushed back his chair suddenly and rose. "I hope you'll excuse me, but I'm quite tired. The dinner was excellent."

Clive watched his brother march stiffly away. Herkimer reached to open the door, but Neville beat the little frog to it, planting his hand against the smooth wood and giving a shove. Clive glanced at Annabelle, then, and she returned his gaze. There was a troubled look in her eyes that he'd learned to recognize. Under the table she squeezed his thigh again.

Finnbogg pushed back his chair and rose, also: "Finnbogg go make sure Neville okay. Maybe learn new songs." He followed the way Neville had gone.

The baron stared toward the door as Finnbogg departed. Then he rubbed his eyes and stood up. "I think I, too, shall retire," he said. A heavy weariness showed in his features as he pushed back his chair. "It has been quite a day seeing both my sons again, and an old man grows tired easily. But please, continue without me." He gestured toward the dessert cart and forced a smile. "There is still the pie. Herkimer will be disappointed if no one partakes."

None of the company spoke until Clive's father was gone. Then, one by one, they each pushed back their chairs and rose. Only Tomàs kept his seat. The little Portuguese sailor forked the remaining roast from Neville's plate and proceeded to devour it and anything else that was within his reach.

"Observation," Chang Guafe said, turning to Clive. "He did not respond to my inquiry. This technology remains unexplained."

"It may be worth noting, Englishman," said Sidi Bombay calmly, "that, as we have proceeded to the deeper levels of the Dungeon, the technology evidenced has become increasingly complex."

Horace Hamilton Smythe harrumphed. "You sound like our cyborg friend."

"But he's right, hacker," Annabelle agreed. "We should have noticed it before. Chang, what else have you observed?"

The cyborg answered without hesitation. "The gaslight is not gaslight at all. The food was molecularly reconstituted from other organic material—"

"You mean it wasn't real?" Horace blurted, passing a hand over his stomach.

"Real?" The cyborg shrugged. "The nutrients are perfectly balanced and without traces of preservative or pesticide or any foreign chemical contaminant. It is real, Horace Hamilton Smythe. It is wholesome. It is perfect. This can only be achieved through highly advanced nutriment design."

"Fake food!" Annabelle exclaimed. "No wonder the meat tasted a little bland. The vegetables were great, though. You know, they've just begun to dabble with this stuff in my time."

"What else?" Clive asked Chang Guafe.

"There are many energy patterns," he answered. He turned, and the candlelight from the table lent his armored body a burnished luster. "The walls are full of circuitry, some of it beyond my analytical capacities."

"I think we should be on our guard, sah," Smythe said quietly.

"But this is my father!" Clive protested. "Sure, he has to explain some things, but you all look ready to go to war again. I say let's grab some sleep and see what we can learn tomorrow when we're all fresh and rested. Coming, Tomàs?"

The little Portuguese looked at Clive as he chewed, then looked around the table with a frown. At last, he stood up, grabbed one whole pie off the dessert cart, and smiled. "*Sim*, coming, yes," he answered.

They filed out of the dining hall, leaving the cleanup for the frog-servants. There was no doubt they had just been served one of the finest meals set before them since coming to the Dungeon, and yet there was a strange air of quiet over everyone as they headed up to their rooms.

Herkimer, or at least one Herkimer, stood waiting for them at the foot of the staircase. From the smart dinner jacket he wore, Clive assumed it was the same one who had served as doorman to the dining room and who had announced his father. He looked down at the short little creature. Nothing but their clothes differentiated one from another. They were identical. *Clones*, he realized.

"Excuse me," Annabelle said to the patient-faced servant. "But I was wondering if there might be a program or something I could scan before powering down. There's really plenty of room left on my disk yet."

The frog put on a big smile that faded quickly. "Program? Scan? Disk, disk, disk?" He hopped up and down and a troubled expression settled across his features. "My master orders me to please, to please, but I don't know these things, don't know these things."

Clive was both touched and amused by the cute creature's near panic. He could almost hear the little being's heart hammering. "Calm down, Herkimer!" he said, setting his hand on its head so it couldn't bounce up again. "She means she's not sleepy, yet, and is there, perhaps, a book she could read?"

"Book?" Annabelle made a face. "Well, yeah, that'd do, too."

"Book, book!" Herkimer repeated excitedly. "Plenty of books. The master has a library. Want to see?"

The others had already gone up the stairs, so Clive decided to accompany Annabelle and Herkimer. The frog led them down the hallway and back past the dining room. They turned a corner and passed down yet another hall. Halfway, Herkimer stopped and pushed open another set of oaken double doors. He bounced twice and bowed with a sweeping gesture. "The master's library, the library," he announced grandiosely, and one webbed hand fluttered, inviting them inside.

It was a huge room, and a fire crackled needlessly in a great stone fireplace opposite the door. The house was too warm, already. The flames made the room a small inferno. Nevertheless, they went in.

The walls were lined floor to ceiling with books. The bindings looked old and worn, and a faint dust lingered in the air. An old wooden ladder hung suspended on hooks from an iron bar that circled the bookshelves, giving access to the higher volumes. In the center of the room sat two stuffed leather chairs on either side of a low wooden table.

"Shall I bring brandy, some brandy?" Herkimer asked. "Or a pot, a pot, of coffee?"

Annabelle and Clive moved to different sides of the room as they eyed the titles. Both muttered "no thank you" to the drinks, and Herkimer excused himself, leaving the doors open. The happy sound of his flat feet could be heard as he retreated down the hallway.

"He reminds me of a dashboard toy," Annabelle chuckled from across the room.

Clive turned around with a book in his hands. He glanced at the title on the spine, then at her. "A what?"

"A dashboard toy," she repeated. "In my time it's a little figure mounted on a spring. People stick them in the windshields of their vehicles, and they bounce around a lot."

Clive set the volume back in its place on the shelf. "To what purpose?" he called over his shoulder, choosing another book and opening it carefully. There was an audible crack as the dry pages separated. He shot a look guiltily over both shoulders and toward the open door, then shut the book, put it back on the shelf, and moved away from it.

"I saw that," Annabelle said accusingly. Then, "To no purpose, really. A lot of people in my time are pretty simpleminded. You know, easily amused."

"You mean their programs were buggy," Clive offered, moving the ladder out of his way. It scraped along the rail as if rust had formed where it couldn't be seen and it needed a good oiling.

"Hey, you're really hacking now, Clive-o, getting down to BASIC!"

She craned her neck sideways to read the spines as she moved around the room. "This is wonderful stuff," she muttered as she examined titles. "Just like home when I was a little user. Mother kept stacks of books in every corner of the house, and made sure I read them, too. Not diskettes, but real books. And old videos. She loved old classic videos." Suddenly, she stopped and pulled a book off the shelf. Lovingly, she ran a hand over the front cover, then looked at her palm and made a face. "Yucko," she muttered as she wiped her hand on her dress, leaving a smear of thick dust on the bodice.

"You've ruined a lovely dress," Clive chastised, selecting yet another book and placing it back.

"So, who cares?" she answered, moving toward one of the leather chairs with her volume. "There's like a whole wardrobe full of 'em. Your dear old dad really has a thing for virgin white, you know? And not much fashion sense."

She sat back and propped her feet up on the low table while Clive continued to peruse the titles. There were books on world history, English history, military history, ancient history. All the classics were there, and works on Plato, Aristotle, and Thucidides' *The Peloponnesian War*—another history. He found the plays of Shakespeare and Marlowe, and collections of poems by all Romantics. There was a book of colored plates by William Blake and next to it a volume of his poems. In another section he found Homer and Virgil and Ovid, the Norse sagas and the Pearl Poet, Chaucer and Bunyan and Jean de Meun.

He stepped back in awe and put a finger to his lips. He had not gone even a fourth of the way around the room. With a sigh, he turned back to Annabelle. She didn't notice, so deeply involved was she in the open book on her lap. He didn't get the chance to ask her what it was.

" 'It was many and many a year ago,' " said his father's voice from the doorway,

> " 'In a kingdom by the sea
> That a maiden there lived whom you may know
>   By the name of Annabel Lee;
> And this maiden she lived with no other thought
>   Than to live and be loved by me.' "

The baron walked into the library, a faint smile flickering across his face. He'd changed out of the brown velvet jacket and into a smoking gown of softly radiant blue silk. In one hand he carried an unlit pipe, in the other a small pouch of tobacco.

Annabelle closed the book she held, marking her place with her index finger, and turned a cool face toward her host. She didn't bother removing her feet, however, from his table.

" 'For the moon never beams, without bringing me dreams . . .' "

She spoke evenly, meeting the baron's direct gaze without flinching.

> " 'Of the beautiful Annabel Lee;
> And the stars never rise, but I feel the bright eyes
>   Of the beautiful Annabel Lee:
> And so, all the night-tide, I lie down by the side
> Of my darling—my darling—my life and my bride,
>   In the sepulchre there by the sea—
>   In her tomb by the sounding sea.' "

She took her feet from the table, then, and stood. "I never cared for Poe," she informed him, "and I particularly never cared for that poem."

Baron Tewkesbury settled heavily into the other leather chair and set the tobacco pouch on the table. He leaned forward, tapped the bowl of his pipe against the palm of his hand, and reached for the pouch. "But it's a beautiful poem, my dear, full of romance and mystery!"

"That Annabel dies," Annabelle pointed out, glancing at Clive as he came to stand opposite her by his father's side. "And her boyfriend is a sicko. Lie down by her dead body in its grave? Give me a break. Anyway, we spell our names differently." She backed toward the door, clutching her book to her chest with both arms. "Now, if you'll excuse me, I'm sure the two of you have all sorts of father-son shit to talk about, so I'll get out of your way."

She pulled the doors closed on her way out.

Clive took her empty chair. His father's jaw still hung open, and he still stared at the space Annabelle had just vacated. His hand had paused in midair, the reach for the tobacco pouch not quite completed. Slowly, he turned his gaze toward Clive, who forced a big smile.

"Quite a girl, isn't she?" Clive said innocently.

His father swallowed. "Uh, quite," he agreed. "Very colorful language. Very . . ." He swallowed again. Then he tilted his head quizzically and tapped his pipe.

"She'll grow on you," Clive assured him. "She's your granddaughter, several 'great's' removed."

His father looked at him. Again the jaw dropped, and again the hand hesitated as it reached for the tobacco. "You don't say," the baron finally managed. "The result of one of Neville's peccadilloes?"

• CHAPTER FIFTEEN •

Home

Clive had never spent such a night with his father in his life.

Herkimer brought a bottle of brandy and two glasses with fine gold rims and left them alone while they sat facing each other over the library table, sipping the liquor, and talking as they had never done. The baron had never talked about Clive's mother. Now, he told his son everything he wanted to know: the color of her hair, her favorite flower, how his parents met, what they had hoped for out of life together. Lord Folliot described their wedding. They had married on the lawn of the Tewkesbury estate before hundreds of guests with not one but five wedding cakes, and all the notables of the realm had attended, including even the Prince of Wales, who bore a short congratulatory note from the Queen, herself. They had honeymooned in Lausserk, Switzerland, and spent an entire month in the sleepy little town nestled gently among the snowcapped mountains. They had followed that with a whirlwind tour of the capitals of Europe before returning exhausted to England and beginning the business of establishing their household.

It was upon their return to London that his bride had made her happy announcement. They could not have been more joyful over the news and set about preparing for a long and contented family life, as had always been the Folliot way.

By that point, the brandy was half-consumed. Clive stared into his glass, mesmerized by the rich amber contents as he swirled his drink round and round the crystal snifter and mesmerized by the soft sound of his father's voice. He felt incredibly warm and maudlin. For half of his life he'd wondered what it might be like to actually be close to his father, to feel that his father cared for him and about him as much as he did his other son. Clive could recall not one single time when his father had spent more than ten minutes alone in conversation with him unless it was to scold him for a bad grade or castigate him for some other real or imagined shortcoming. But now, all the barriers between them seemed suddenly to have collapsed, and they were talking for the first time man to man, father to son, and his heart felt simply too big inside his chest. He wanted to push away the table so not even that stood between them. He restrained himself, however. There was, after all, a certain amount of decorum they must maintain.

His father leaned forward and refilled both their glasses, then sat back and stared at his son for a long quiet moment. The baron took a swallow, then began again.

Clive knew instinctively that not even Neville had been privileged to hear what passed between them now. It could only have been the brandy that loosened his father's tongue. He spoke in a low whisper of the pain of losing his young bride in the first year of their life together, of how even now after so many years he dreamed of her and longed for her in the nights. He had never touched another woman, not even for a single night of pleasure, but kept himself for her, alone, when they met again in heaven. His hands reached out as he talked. One held his glass, but the other moved gently in the air as if he were caressing the face of a ghost that Clive couldn't see. It was a strange pantomime that made Clive lean forward, one elbow on his knee, and it was then he saw the tear that trickled down the old man's cheek.

Clive's breath caught in his throat, and the snifter nearly

fell from his numb fingers. He had never ever seen his father cry, and the sight sobered him for all of five or six heartbeats. Then he tumbled over that fine drunken line of self-control, set his glass down clumsily, and came around the table to embrace his father even as the elder Folliot rose to do the same. They clung to each other weeping before the fireplace.

"I've been such an old fool!" the baron cried. "Forgive me, son, say you forgive me!"

"I do!" Clive cried into his father's shoulder. "I forgive you! I forgive you for getting me so embarrassingly inebriated!"

The baron clapped his son on the back, still hugging him close, refusing to let him go yet. "Yes, we Folliots always had a taste for the grape, I'm afraid." He sniffed and ran a hand through Clive's hair. "To think it took a bottle to bring us to this. I never held you when you were little. You always wanted me to hold you. I saw it in your eyes. But I never did!" He put his face down beside his son's so their damp cheeks touched.

"It's all right," Clive whispered, when he could finally shape words through a throat too swollen with emotion. How odd it felt that he should have to console his father after so many years. "It's all right," he repeated again. "We don't have to speak of the past anymore. We can start again right here, Father!"

The baron lifted his head, sniffed again, and looked into the fire. "Yes, we can start again," he agreed, "right here." He backed away a bit, pulled an embroidered handkerchief from his jacket pocket, and wiped at his eyes and nose. "I'd like that, Son."

"I'd like it, too," Clive said, withdrawing a bit.

"It must be very late," the old man reasoned. "I think I'd better get Herkimer to see me to bed."

He didn't look at Clive again but stumbled to the library door. Herkimer was there without needing to be called. The little frog-servant took the baron's arm and helped him down the hall.

Clive stood by the fireplace for a long time and tried to sort out the jumble of emotions that whirled inside his head. He felt like a little boy who had just won his father's approval, and he felt like an old man who had needlessly embarrassed himself. All his life he had competed with his brother, Neville, for the old man's attention and always lost. But that was over, past, and all the old anger drained out of him as he picked up his glass and drained the last of the brandy.

His father's glass sat, empty, on the edge of the table beside the empty bottle. On an impulse he would never be able to explain, he leaned over and clinked the rim of his own glass to it. A pleasant ring floated upward at the contact, a sweet crystalline note that penetrated and stuck in his thickened senses.

He smiled, and the room spun a little, and he knew he had imbibed too much. He really had to get to bed before the others saw him. But first he would sit down just for a moment.

When he woke, a dull throbbing beat behind his temples. He peeled his eyes open slowly and recognized the room as his own. Who had put him to bed? Vague memories of a patient Smythe came to him. His former batman had carried him upstairs, then, if he remembered correctly. He touched his head and winced.

He practically oozed out of bed and into the bathroom. To his surprise, the tub was full again and hot. He eased into it and kneeled and filled his lungs with a deep breath. Then, he plunged his head under the water.

Fifteen minutes of soaking and scrubbing made him feel almost human again. A soft toweling and a fresh shave helped, too. He checked his appearance in the small hand-mirror by the tub and smoothed down the hairs of his thickening mustache.

Almost as an afterthought he checked the wound on his thigh and received his second surprise of the morning. There was nothing but a pink scar along the muscle, and no pain at all. In fact, he recalled now how Annabelle had squeezed his leg under the table at dinner, and there had been no pain. He hurried into the main room and to the full-length mirror. Most of his scratches were entirely gone, without trace.

He took clean clothes from the wardrobe and dressed and went downstairs. He found Herkimer in the hallway. The little frog wore an apron and brandished a feather duster. "You must be hungry, be hungry, Clive Folliot," the creature said. "I'll bring some breakfast to the dining room, dining room." With that, Herkimer hopped away.

Clive found the dining room easily enough and sat down alone. Herkimer came through the side door with a tray of hot rolls and butter and marmalade, a selection of cheeses, and a pot of hot tea. It was a different Herkimer who served him, though, at least to judge by the baker's whites and the chef's cap the small frog wore. He watched the awkward little servant depart and buttered his first roll.

"So you're awake at last, you are, sah." Horace Hamilton Smythe peered at him from the open doorway and ventured in.

Clive waved to him with the butter knife. "I vaguely recall your carrying me to bed, Horace," he said sheepishly. "Hope I wasn't too heavy."

"A gallon or so more than usual, sah," Smythe answered blithely. "But nothing to speak of."

"You're a paragon, Horace," Clive responded. He gestured toward the rolls. "Help yourself."

Horace explained that everyone had eaten breakfast early, a much larger meal than the one before Clive now. He launched into a description of the succulent piles of bacon and sausage, the eggs, the biscuits and gravy. Clive stopped him. Even the sound of such heavy fare made him feel queasy.

"Where is everyone?" he asked suddenly. Herkimer and Horace were the only ones he'd seen this morning.

"Well, sah, now 'morning' is a relative term, it is." He rose and moved to a huge curtained window at one end of the dining room and drew back the curtain. It was black as ever outside. "As for the others," Smythe continued, "they're all about different things, occupying time. Sidi and Tomàs are wandering around outside. Finnbogg's with them. Chang Guafe said something about running a systems check on his sensor circuits, whatever that means, and he's in his room. That's where Shriek and Neville are, too. Neville's been real quiet, he has, and Shriek hasn't come out since dinner last night."

"Leave her alone," Clive said quietly. "She's doing something for me." He'd already decided it wouldn't do any good to tell the others about the mind scans Shriek had detected. They couldn't do anything against an enemy they couldn't see, and it would just put everyone on edge. Right now was a time to relax, the first chance they'd had for some time. Soon he'd tell them, but not now. "What about Annabelle?" he asked.

Horace dipped one finger in the marmalade and put it in his mouth. He made a smacking sound with his lips. "Good as anything in London," he remarked. "Can't figure how he gets it here." He tasted another fingerful, looked around hastily, and wiped his hand on the border of the tablecloth. "Annabelle, now, she's been in the library ever since she woke up, sah. In fact, she took her breakfast in there. Still there as far as I know. In love with all those books, she is."

Clive buttered another roll and took a drink of his tea. "Have you seen my father?" he asked.

"No, sah, but then I suppose he had his own share of that brandy, and he's not as young as you, though he wouldn't like to hear me say it." Smythe hesitated, put his elbows on the table, folded his hands, and leaned his chin on them. "Did you ask him about the gate, sah? You know, to the next level?"

"No," Clive answered slowly. "Not yet. But there's time. I think we're going to stay here for a while, Horace. Not long, but long enough to rest a bit. We're all tired, and so far it's been one fight after another. We could use an interlude. I'll ask him tonight, though." They separated shortly after that. Since rest was the plan, Horace intended to get some, and he left Clive at the foot of the stairs.

Clive, for his part, took the opportunity to explore the rest of the house. He found a large sitting room filled with beautiful Queen Anne furniture. A heavy, brocaded paper of peach swirls covered the walls. A large window caught his attention, and he pulled back the drapes. Outside, the softly glowing spiral floated across the sky. He lowered the curtain and turned away. The smell of a clove-and-cinnamon potpourri wafted through the room, and he inhaled the rich fragrance.

Next to the sitting room he found a conservatory. Four concert harps occupied the center of the room. In one corner stood a piano. He shuffled idly through the sheets of music that lay open on the bench. Chopin, Brahms, Beethoven. He brushed his fingers over the keys. It had been so long since he'd played. He knew he wouldn't be very good. Nevertheless, he sat down and made a few runs at Beethoven's Piano Concerto Number Three in C Minor before giving it up in disgust. He looked around self-consciously to make sure no one had heard, then closed the lid quietly over the keys and left the room.

He returned to his room after that. The throbbing in his head had become a mild but persistent pressure. A nap, he figured, would relieve it.

Herkimer woke him with a knock on his door. His nap had lasted until dinnertime. He went down, eager to see his father once more.

The meal passed in quiet conversation. Almost everyone seemed occupied with their own thoughts as they ate. Annabelle had a book on her lap all the while she ate and answered questions only in grunts and monosyllables. Neville looked sullen and said next to nothing. Tomàs and Sidi and Finnbogg conversed among themselves, as did Clive and Baron Tewkesbury, while Chang Guafe hung on every word the old man said. Shriek again ate in her room.

"We have some small entertainment tonight," the baron announced when the last morsel was finished. At his direction they carried their teacups or wine glasses into the conservatory and took the seats that had recently been placed there.

When they were all comfortable, the four look-alike Herkimers filed in. They wore identical dinner jackets and sat down at the four harps. The instruments looked huge before them, but they touched the strings in unison, and the sweet strains of Beethoven's Sonata Number Fourteen in C Sharp Minor filled the room.

The music entranced Clive, who had long counted the *Moonlight Sonata* among his favorite pieces of music, but next to him Annabelle put down her book and hid the lower half of her face behind her cupped hands. She struggled not to laugh, but she convulsed with a fit of barely contained giggles.

"Don't you like Beethoven?" Clive inquired in a whisper, leaning close to his granddaughter. "I've never heard him on harps before. It's enchanting!"

Another fit seized Annabelle as she looked at him wide-eyed over hands clapped tightly to her mouth. Merriment twinkled in her dark eyes. "Enchanting?" she dared to murmur. "That's the word, Clive-o!" She looked toward the four performers and uncupped her fingers long enough for him to overhear. "Pluck your magic twangers, froggies!" she whispered. Quickly, she picked up the book from her lap and hid her entire face behind its covers while she rocked with silent mirth.

On Clive's right side, the baron tapped the back of his hand with one fingertip and gave him a stern look. After that, Clive ignored Annabelle and settled back to enjoy the concert.

Midway through, Neville stood suddenly and left the room. Clive bit his lip as he watched his brother depart, but the first notes of Bach's *Arioso* made him forget about his twin.

When the music ended, everyone returned to the dining room for dessert and more conversation. When that was finished, the baron took them all on a tour of his home, apologizing for not doing so earlier. A mild headache, he explained. Smythe coughed and grinned at Clive, and Tomàs openly snickered.

After the tour Clive and his father drifted away from the others. Again, they began to talk as they aimlessly wandered the halls and rooms of the estate, cautiously at first, gradually letting down the barriers, this time without the benefit of alcohol. Clive told him about his years at Sandhurst, the friends he'd made there, and about his course of study, which had been literature and the classics. Then, he talked about his military life, his career in the army, the time he'd spent in Madagascar, and his promotion to the rank of major.

The baron listened attentively like a kindly father, shaking his head frequently, and chiding himself for ignoring his son for so long.

After a while, they wandered outside into the darkness. The spiral overhead lit the way as they drifted toward the very edge of the mountaintop. The wind blew against their faces as if to push them back, but they held their ground and stared outward. In the far, far distance, Clive thought he could just make out the hazy orange glow of the fiery land they had crossed. A vast sea of blackness spread between it and the mountaintop.

At last, Clive told his father about Miss Annabella Leighton and how he knew he'd found the love of his life in her. She was of a good family, he explained, but not of noble stock. He didn't care. She supported herself by teaching literature at a school for wealthy, aristocratic young girls and kept a small flat in Plantagenet Court, and Clive had wanted to marry her for a long time. Only his poverty had prevented it, for he felt life on a major's small salary too much of a sacrifice to ask such a lady to make.

"And yet you carried on a dalliance with this woman?" his father asked, brows furrowing.

Clive knew what he was hinting at, and he raised his

head proudly, if a little defiantly. "We were in love," he said defensively. "There was no sin in what we did, and certainly no shame." Then, he lowered his head. "The shame lies in my leaving her to find Neville. I didn't know she was carrying our child, I swear I didn't, and I admit that I was even eager to make the journey, for a chance to get away from England for a while. I thought I might be able to find my fortune and go back with money enough to wed her then." He looked away and shook his head sadly. "It just didn't work out that way. At least, as Annabelle tells the story."

"Your great-great-granddaughter?" his father said.

"Your great-great-great-granddaughter," Clive responded. He stared upward at the spiral, daring its swirling gases and dizzying stars to steal his senses, almost hoping they would succeed and leave him numb to the ache that suddenly filled him. "She says I never made it back to London, that I disappeared in Africa just like Neville. Neither of us made it back."

The baron reached out and laid a hand gently on Clive's shoulder. Then, he drew his son close and embraced him. "Because you found your home here," he said in Clive's ear. "We're together again, Neville and you and me. That's all that matters. There's no way out of the Dungeon. I know. I've tried to find it. This is our home now, Clive, right here, and we must make the best of it." He held Clive out at arm's length and peered intently at his son. "This is our home," he insisted.

Clive hugged his father with a trembling intensity. "Home," he uttered, half-believing it, wishing to believe it.

• CHAPTER SIXTEEN •

Blood Relatives

Outside, the sky and the land remained black and foreboding. Only the pale spiral provided any light at all as it moved slowly, slowly across the sky. Clive learned to count the days by the cycles of dinners and sleeping periods.

He spent more and more time with his father. They talked and played chess in the sitting room, or he played the piano while his father listened, pleased at how quickly he improved on the keys. Sometimes, they shared wine in the library by the fireplace, or tea and crumpets in the dining room. Sometimes, they walked side by side along the rim of the mountaintop or along some of the easier trails that led down the far side.

"I can see so much farther now," his father confided. "To the edge of the world if I concentrate. So I saw you when you approached the Dantean Gate. I erected that myself, you know. A sort of jest to ease the loneliness I felt when first I came here." He touched his son's arm. "Now I will never be lonely again."

Clive saw less and less of his friends. Neville kept mostly to his room, coming out only to eat or to chat with Annabelle in the library or to wander solitary outside the house. When he spoke at all to his father, it was with brusque indifference or barely concealed anger.

Annabelle buried herself in some research. She showed

up for meals, usually with a book in hand. Otherwise, she could be found in the library or in her room reading.

Shriek did not show herself at all. The arachnid ceased even to eat the meals that Herkimer carried to her room. Clive dared to look in on her once and found her deep in a trance. She roused herself long enough to assure him she was well and to ask him to leave. He bothered her no more.

As for the others, he couldn't really say how they occupied their time. They milled about listlessly, and Clive began to sense a general restlessness in his friends. Still, he gave the matter little thought, and when Horace Hamilton Smythe came to his room after dinner one evening and said he might be gone for a while and not to worry, Clive merely shrugged. If his sergeant wanted to explore some of the other mountain trails, he saw no reason why he shouldn't. Smythe was a competent man.

At dinner the next evening Chang Guafe expressed his quiet dissatisfaction with the decision to let Smythe go. "There is still the matter of the implants in Sergeant Smythe's head," he reminded them. "We have not fully dealt with that. Instead, we have assumed, without evidence, that merely knowing about the implants would enable him to resist outside influence. But how can we be sure that leaving us was his own idea? We do not know who put them in his head, or why."

When Clive waved aside the objection, the cyborg raised a new, more sensitive, issue, openly questioning the clarity of Clive's judgment. "Perhaps, Clive Folliot," he challenged, "you are becoming too comfortable here."

The baron intervened to prevent an argument, though, and ordered Herkimer to serve the special surprise he had prepared—hot chocolate with marshmallow. No matter that the temperature of the air remained uncomfortably warm. It was a delicious treat.

The following morning Clive and his father passed Neville near the library. Neville closed the book he held in one hand and glanced curiously at the baron. "Tell me,

Father," he said with a lightness that made Clive hope his twin's mood had improved and the three of them might spend some time together. "I've been trying to remember the name of Nanny's dog."

Clive felt the heat rise in his cheeks, appalled at his brother's insinuation, but the baron answered nonchalantly. "Why, I'm surprised at you, Neville. How could you forget a thing like that? The poor woman fastened your first nappy! It was Tennyson, of course."

Their eyes locked for the briefest instant. "Oh, yes, that was it," Neville said, touching one finger to his chin and feigning a thoughtful look as he tucked his book under his arm. "How silly of me." His gaze flickered over Clive, full of something his brother didn't understand, before he turned away and went upstairs.

Later, Clive walked with his father along the petrified hedge. "I sent Samedi to guide you through the dangers to my side," the baron said. "I shall miss the little man. Because I was a baron, he decided to be one, too. Baron Samedi, he called himself, but I suppose you know that. And what did I care? What do such things mean in the Dungeon?" He looked sad as he remembered.

"Where did he come from?" Clive asked idly.

The baron shrugged. "We're not alone here, Clive. There are other creatures."

"The demons?"

Tewkesbury nodded as he whispered. "And more. But they stay away. They leave me alone."

What was it about darkness, Clive wondered as he hugged himself, that made men whisper? He took a step back and looked at his father, measured his huge silhouette against the shadows of the looming mountain peaks. When the old man turned toward him, the light from the spiral caught his eyes just so, giving them a weird catlike glow that made Clive shiver unexpectedly.

His father must have seen his reaction. "I am part of this world now, Son. I don't even want to go back to London. I'm changed, and there is no place for me there."

They stood again on the rim of the baron's high mountaintop, and the hot wind blew against their faces as he spread out his hand. "Your poor eyes cannot see," he said, "but there are lands beyond us. You've seen the Hell That Is Fire and the Misty Limbo, and you've crossed the boiling Phlegathon River to come to me. But below us there is the Kingdom of Ice, the Marsh Hell, and the Mud Hell, and more hells than Dante ever dreamed or imagined."

He took his son's hand and drew him closer to the brink. The darkness whirled about them as if it were alive, and the wind rushed in Clive's ears. "It is mine, my son. Ours, for whomsoever I will, I will give it."

Clive stepped back trembling, uncertain of the words that burned in his ears. Was it his father's voice, or was it the wind? Why couldn't he think? He had to think!

He untangled his fingers from his father's grip. "Let's go back inside," he said.

"Of course," his father answered. "I'm sure there's even a little chocolate left."

Clive felt strangely tired after their chocolate, however. He returned to his room without a word to anyone else and slept until dinnertime. Only once did he awaken. His sheets were drenched with sweat, and his head throbbed with a dream he couldn't remember.

A knock at his door awakened him for good. He called out, and Finnbogg peeked around the door. "Clivefriend awake?" he asked needlessly. Clive propped his back against the headboard and waved his friend inside.

Finnbogg wore a strange expression as he seated himself in one of the chairs. He glanced from side to side as if to avoid Clive's gaze. He tapped his foot and dragged the point of one claw nervously over the padding of the chair's arm.

"What is it, old friend?" Clive asked, for plainly Finnbogg wanted to talk.

The alien canine rubbed his nose with the back of one paw and cleared his throat with a deep *harummmp*. "Okay," he said at last. "Finnbogg promised Clivefriend to help find Clivefriend's littermate, Neville Folliot. Neville Folliot found now, okay?" He paused and cleared his throat again. "But we find not just Clivefriend's littermate, but Clivefriend's littersire. Happy for Clivefriend is Finnbogg at this joyous reunion!" He rose from his chair and began to pace at the foot of the bed. "But now Finnbogg thinks of Finnbogg's littermate. Finnbogg is lonely, too! Where is Finnbogg's littermate?" He stopped pacing directly in front of Clive. The look on his face was so sad and touching that Clive finally looked away.

"When do we go, Clivefriend?" Finnbogg pleaded. "When do we go?"

Clive got out of bed and went to his friend, placing both hands on Finnbogg's brawny shoulders. "Soon, Finnbogg, soon," he answered, feeling a band tighten around his chest as he spoke. "But not yet," he added. "A little more time. Just a little more time."

Finnbogg accepted that and left. Clive went into the bathroom and washed his face. Then, he picked up the hand-mirror and looked at his reflection for a long time. The mustache had grown out nice and full. Yet the face displeased him. On impulse, he reached for the razor and prepared to shave his upper lip bare. He looked at his reflection again, studying what he saw. It felt wrong. Everything felt wrong! He slammed the unused razor down, and the mirror, cracking it.

He changed into a pair of soft khaki pants and a white shirt and pulled on boots. Without meaning to, he slammed his door on the way out.

Annabelle was halfway down the hall coming toward him with a stack of books. "Clive," she called in a low voice. "We've got to talk now. I've overloaded my disk on this thing, and you'd better hear the voice-out!"

"Not now," he muttered, crossing to his brother's door.

"Clive!" she insisted.

He whirled on her. "I said, 'Not now,' goddamn it!"

With that, he pushed open Neville's door without bothering to knock and slammed it shut again.

Neville sat on his bed with his back to his headboard, much as Clive had sat earlier. But his hands were folded behind his head as he stared off into space, and a book of poems lay open on his lap. With an irritating self-assurance and calm, he rolled his head to the side and looked at his twin.

"Well, little brother—"

Clive didn't give him a chance to speak. "What in God's name is wrong with you?" he raged. "What have you got against Father, anyway? You haven't had a kind word for him, not one! You insult him at his table, and you're rude to him everywhere! And I want to know why."

Patiently, Neville closed the book and set it aside. He swung his legs over the side of the bed and rose.

"I just don't understand you, Neville!" Clive continued in a fury. "He gave you everything, and you treat him like this? You were always his favorite. He gave you everything you ever—"

"Stop it, Clive. You don't know what you're talking about."

But Clive wouldn't stop. His head felt as if it were about to explode, and his face burned as he shook his fist under his brother's nose. "He gave you every goddamned thing!" he continued. "And I got nothing! I didn't have a father, and I didn't have a brother, either! The two of you were too bloody busy having a good time to remember I was around! Now, we find him here. He came looking for us, for God's sake! And finally, for the first time in my life, he acknowledges that I'm alive, and you act like a silly prig about the whole thing!"

Neville's calm exterior began to melt. He clenched his fists at his sides, and his face colored. "You want him so bloody bad?" he said, trying to keep the anger from his voice. "Then take him. Keep him. It's time I was leaving, anyway. But I'll tell you this, little brother. You were better off when he ignored you. You didn't have his arm locked tight about your bloody throat!"

"And I didn't have my hand locked tight on his bloody pocketbook, either!" Clive shot back.

"He's a bastard, Clive, but you're too stupid to know it! You're getting your ears scratched a little now, and you think it feels pretty good, and maybe it does to a dog that's been starved for affection. But you damn well better learn to fetch his stick when he tells you to, and you damn well better bring his slippers."

Neville paced to the far side of the room, putting distance between them. "You don't know what he's like, little brother!" Neville shouted. "All you saw were the favors you think he did me. You don't know how he can push and drive and suffocate a man! Sure, he sent you to Sandhurst and me to Oxford. I got the better school, and that sticks in your craw, no doubt. But he picked the goddamned school for me without ever asking my opinion! He chose my course program, and my tutors. I studied what he wanted me to study! And when school was done, he pushed me into army service. He even picked my regiment and pulled the strings to see I wound up there. It didn't matter what I wanted! You think you know me? You think you know him? You don't know what my life was like. You don't know anything! You're just a stupid little sod who thinks he's been cheated out of something."

Clive trembled with rage as he faced his brother. He knew one thing, all right. He knew this had been coming a long time, and he didn't intend to back down now.

"I was cheated!" he shouted back, the words ripping out of him like sharp knives. "You might have turned around at any time and said, 'Father, let's take Clive fishing, too.' But you never did. You loved having him to yourself!"

Neville jabbed a finger at him. "You were lucky he ignored you, Brother! He left you alone. Yes, I probably flaunted the relationship a bit, I don't deny it. But it was because I envied you your *freedom*! You could do practically whatever you wanted. It didn't matter to him. But he was always breathing down my neck. Why do you think I started traveling so much? Even in the army I couldn't get free of him. Not until I volunteered for India. Not until I went to America. The world was the only thing I could find to put between us! Why do you think I went to Africa, you bloody fool?"

"Don't call me a fool!" Before Clive even knew what he was doing, he struck his brother. The impact tingled through his fist and up his arm, as Neville crashed backward over a desk, spewing blood from his lip.

Then, Neville came at him. His brother's momentum carried them into a wall, which shook beneath their weight. They fell over a stuffed chair and rolled on the floor. Bright stars flashed in Clive's temple, and he knew the taste of his own blood in the corner of his mouth. He lashed out wildly with both fists, pummeling his brother's face as he fought to push Neville off him.

Somehow, they both got to their feet. Clive's heart hammered furiously in his chest, and a red haze clouded his vision, but he saw well enough. As Neville straightened, Clive punched him again, sending him to his knees. But when he closed in, Neville struck. An incredible pain exploded between Clive's legs, and he sagged to the floor.

"This isn't the Marquis of Queensberry, little brother!" Neville hissed, spraying blood from his lip. "Get up! Let's see what they teach at Sandhurst these days!"

Clive's hand brushed against something, and he grabbed it and flung it. The pages of the poetry book fluttered like the wings of a terrified bird as it flew through the air and caught his brother in the face. It gave Clive time to get up. Neville, unhurt by the book, launched himself again, his arms reaching.

Clive grabbed the nearest thing at hand, a pillow from the bed at his back, and swung it with all his might. Neville crashed sideways into his wardrobe, bounced off it, and collapsed on the floor again in a shower of down feathers that swirled in the air. Clive looked stupidly at the ruined pillow and sputtered.

Neville rolled over just as the framed full-length mirror

teetered on its stand and fell on him. He swept it aside with his arm, and silver glass scattered everywhere.

The shattering crash was enough to make them stop. The anger drained from Neville's face. He raised up on one elbow and looked at the mess. "Well, that's seven years of bad luck," he said, and a grin spread weakly over his bloodied lips.

Clive felt out of breath and suddenly sheepish as he waved a hand through the feathers that swam around him. Then, he grinned, too. "As funny as time seems to be in the Dungeon, that should pass soon enough. And it's appropriate. It's been seven levels of bad luck, so far."

Their gazes met. They looked away, then looked at each other again, grinning.

"It was kind of fun, wasn't it?" Neville said. He picked up a piece of mirror, checked his reflection, smoothed his hair back, and tossed the piece over his shoulder. It shattered with a tinkling sound.

"Kind of fun," Clive agreed. He bent and recovered the book he'd thrown at his twin. He thumbed through the pages, then glanced at the title on the spine. "Didn't think you were the poetry type, big brother." He sagged down onto the bed as his breathing returned gradually to normal. *I'm going to need more of Shriek's medicine,* he thought to himself. *I hurt in a hundred places.*

"A small weakness in my otherwise completely manly self," Neville quipped with an exaggerated wave of his hand. He stood slowly and uttered a low groan. Then, he dabbed at his lip with the back of his hand. "I wonder if Shriek is in a charitable mood? I hurt all over. Not bad, for Sandhurst."

Clive nodded, acknowledging the compliment. "Not bad, for an Oxford softie," he returned.

"Shall we go down to dinner?"

"Let's."

"You know you look like hell?"

Clive looked at the rip in the front of his shirt and the sleeve that hung by a thread. All the buttons on Neville's shirt had flown off, and there was a tear in the knee of his trousers. As for their faces, Neville's lip was taking on a thick purple, but—Clive suspected—so was his left eye. "I look just like you," Clive countered with a wink. "And I'm starving."

They got up and went to the door, wearing their rips and bruises like badges of honor. They found their comrades waiting for them in the hallway. Even Shriek had roused herself from her trance. They all wore such anxious expressions. Annabelle was the only exception. She stood right in the doorway, her arms folded across her chest as she regarded them.

"Well, you're both still on your feet," she said with amused disgust. "You've got this macho bullshit out of the way?"

Clive looked at Neville. Neville looked at Clive.

"How she talks!" Neville said, clucking his tongue. "You really should have reared her better."

"It's her mother's fault," Clive answered disdainfully. "I could never do anything with her."

Annabelle half-turned and said over her shoulder to Shriek, "Isn't it cute? They're in the full ruddy glow of masculinity."

Embarrassment, I thought it was. Shriek's answer brushed them all.

Annabelle folded her arms again and tapped her foot. "If you two are finished playing in the sandbox, I've got an interesting pieces of news." She looked at them expectantly and impatiently.

Clive realized it was the first time in days he'd seen her without a book in her hand. She looked almost unnatural without one. "Something you found in the library?" he asked, suddenly serious. He knew that look in Annie's eye.

"I've been researching my ass off," she responded, turning eager again. "There's a lot of stuff down there about the Folliot family: histories, genealogies, biographies, that kind of stuff. Well, I've read it all now, and I've made a lot of notes and double-checked everything. I could have done it faster on a computer, but I'm finally sure I'm right."

Neville leaned on the doorjamb and folded his arms in imitation of her. "Well, what?" he asked.

Herkimer appeared at the top of the stairs, immaculate in a fresh tuxedo. He hopped up and down impatiently and called to them. "Dinner! It's time for dinner! My master waits, he waits!"

"Can it, froggie!" Annabelle snapped.

Herkimer looked stricken. His wide jaw dropped open, and his tongue lolled slackly while his eyes grew rounder and rounder and his shoulders slumped. He tilted his head quizzically, then turned and hopped back down the stairs.

Annabelle watched him go, then turned back to the others. "I didn't want the little critter to overhear," she whispered. "The two of you can decide whether or not to tell your father."

"Tell him what?" Clive said with some exasperation. He rather liked Herkimer, and Annabelle had plainly hurt the little creature's feelings.

She grabbed Tomàs by the arm and dragged him forward. By the look on his face he didn't know what was going on, either. The others gathered closer as Annabelle prepared to reveal her new-found secret.

"*Senhor e Senhor,*" she addressed Clive and Neville as she placed one hand over her heart. "*Eu apresento . . .*" Then a look of intense frustration crossed her face and she slapped her thigh. "Oh, damn!" she muttered to Tomàs and threw her hands up helplessly. "I still can't break down your verb forms! Well, never mind." She turned back to Clive and Neville and let go a sigh. "Oh, say hello to your long-lost cousin."

Clive looked at Neville. Neville looked at Tomàs. Tomàs looked at Clive. Then, they all looked at Annabelle.

"What?"

"What?"

"¿Qûe?"

Annabelle grinned. "Yep, it's true. The little scrodhead's a relative. I'll show you the research after dinner." Her grin faded and she turned serious. "Kind of brings us back to an old question, doesn't it? Who, exactly, is so interested in the Folliots?"

Clive looked Tomàs up and down and nodded gravely as he added, "And why?"

· CHAPTER SEVENTEEN ·

The Council of War

"I'll show you the details later, if you like," Annabelle said. "But one of your ancestors married a young woman of a poor Spanish commoner family in 1463 and took her to England. She apparently didn't fit in very well, though. Before a year was up she ran home to mom and dad with a small baby boy. Of course, since she'd shamed the family by marrying one of the hated English, they would have nothing to do with her or the child, whom they couldn't really afford to feed, anyway. She finally wound up living with some lowly relatives on the Portuguese side of the border."

Tomàs looked dazed as he stared over Annabelle's shoulder at the writing on the page. "*¡Pobre mãe!*" he muttered. "My poor mother! She never told me any of this!"

Neville pointed a finger at Clive. "Must have been your side of the family," he accused wryly.

Clive was silent for a long moment as he and Tomàs regarded each other. He couldn't quite read the expression on the little Portuguese's face, but there was no doubting his own confusion. He needed time to think, time to understand. "Let's go down to dinner," he announced quietly. "We'll talk more about this later, but for now let's keep it to ourselves."

Also must talk we, Being Clive, Shriek said to him privately. *Information have I to share.*

After dinner, please, Being Shriek, he answered. *We'll talk then. Will you join us now?*

No, Being Clive, she responded. *Repulsive you find my feeding habits. But grateful am I.*

Shriek went back to her room, and the rest went down to dinner. The Herkimers served yet another sumptuous feast, but the meal passed quietly. Clive and Neville studiously avoided their father's gaze while glancing surreptitiously at each other across the table.

"You seem to have a rip in your sleeve, Clive, my boy," the baron finally said between bites.

Clive swallowed a sip of the wine. "Um, I fell down the stairs, I'm afraid," he lied. To avoid his father's gaze he glanced at Annabelle. The scars on her throat, he noticed, were almost completely gone.

The baron rubbed his chin and glanced at both his sons. "I see. You also have ruined your shirt, Neville. Did you also fall down the stairs?"

Neville set down his knife and fork and smiled sweetly as he looked his father straight in the eye. "Why, yes, I did. Damn near landed on Clive, I did."

The baron crimsoned at Neville's epithet and leaned forward to chastise him, but at the last instant he appeared to think better of it and settled back in his chair with a glower. For the rest of the evening he watched them over the rim of his glass.

Again, Tomàs was the last to finish. The news about his family ties certainly hadn't harmed his appetite. Clive could only watch in amused appreciation as his Portuguese cousin wolfed half of an apple pie and washed it down with water. Fortunately, no one else had wanted dessert.

"Tomàsfriend eat like Finnbogg's littermates!" Finnbogg remarked at Tomàs's elbow. "Why doesn't Tomàs grow?"

"He's big where it counts," Annabelle answered from across the table.

Clive, in the process of taking a drink, started to cough, then sealed his lips tight to avoid spewing wine. Unexpectedly, though, it surged up his nose and down his throat, choking him. He spilled the glass's contents as he tried to set it down and get his napkin up in time, but some dribbled into his mustache before he could catch it. He coughed, trying to get air, and coughed again.

Annabelle watched him, grinning, and she tapped a finger over her chest. "His heart," she assured him ruefully. "He has a big heart."

Dinner ended quickly after that. The others retired to their rooms while Clive walked outside with his father. The spiral was low in the direction of the Dantean Gate now. Clive avoided looking at it, fearing its hypnotic effect.

He felt strangely uncomfortable in his father's presence as they walked between the pertrified hedges. They made the same idle small talk as they always did before turning to more personal matters. But this time Clive felt the old barriers erecting themselves once more. He looked sidewise at the figure of his father as they walked along the edge of the mountaintop where the winds blew on their faces.

When his father spoke, Clive barely heard. "Clive?" the baron repeated, touching his son's arm.

"Father," Clive said, turning away from his sire to look out into the vast darkness that enshrouded this world. Darkness, darkness everywhere. *I am half sick of shadows,* he thought, recalling a favorite line of poetry. It was one of the few things, the love of that poem, that his father had ever given him. "Father," he started again, "when I was a child you used to recite 'The Lady of Shalott' to Neville and me, and you'd get this faraway look in your eye." Clive hesitated, filled with a sudden realization. "It was Mother you were thinking of, wasn't it? She was your Lady of Shalott."

Baron Tewkesbury moved to the very edge. A sudden wind might have cast him to his death, yet he balanced there as if daring such a fate, and the only things the wind blew were his hair and the ends of his jacket. He didn't say anything, just stood there, lord of all he surveyed, or so he claimed.

"Recite it for me now, Father," Clive begged. He wanted suddenly to reach out and pull the old man back from the brink, to wrap his arms about him as he heard that deep voice and those lines he had loved so well when he was little, that he still loved. "Please?" he urged, taking a step closer to his father, his hands trembling to reach out and grab a jacket sleeve, but his hands remained strangely at his sides. "What was the first line? How did it go?"

The baron didn't move, didn't turn to look at Clive, didn't shrug even his shoulders. He might have been another distant shadowed mountain, a splintered fragment of the darkness itself, for all the indication he gave that he had heard his son.

Then, the Baron Tewkesbury raised a hand and extended it into the infinite, and his voice rumbled deep and rich as thunder though he spoke in only a whisper. "Whomsoever I will, I will give it. Stay with me, Son. Stay here with me."

Clive stared at the back of the towering figure. He trembled all over now, and his eyes stung as he blinked furiously. "How did it go, Father?" His voice was strained and fearful, and he thought of Neville and home and Nanny and her dog, Tennyson, and their mother he had never known. "How did it go, damn you?" His voice went up a note and quivered with emotion. "Don't you remember? Don't you know? 'On either side the river lie long fields of barley and of rye that clothe the world and meet the sky.' You remember, don't you? It was your favorite poem. You taught it to me. You couldn't have forgotten!"

Slowly, the mountain moved and turned and extended a hand toward him. "Stay with me, Clive," it said. "We don't need Neville. We don't need the others. Let them go. It will be just you and me, the way you've always wanted it. Stay with me."

" 'And through the field the road runs by to many-towered Camelot'!" Clive shouted, clenching his fists at his sides. "You know it! Why won't you say it? Why?" Even as he pleaded with his father he began to back away.

"I love you, Son."

The words struck Clive like painful blows and sent him reeling backward.

"I need you. Stay with me. Stay here."

Clive no longer felt fear or anger or desperation. He felt only empty and a little bit dirty. There was nothing more to say, for he knew the truth now. Neville had guessed it before him. He turned his back on the baron and walked sadly toward the house. When he reached the petrified hedge, he paused long enough to look up at the odd structure. *Four gray walls and four gray towers,* he thought wearily, recalling more of the poem his father had taught him. Then, he sighed as he started up the long walk to the door. "I am half sick of shadows," he muttered softly to himself and went inside.

He crept softly up the stairs and to his room. There he stripped off all his clothes and climbed into the bath. The water was cold now, but he didn't care. He wasn't even sure if it had been changed or if it was the same bath he'd soaked in earlier. He laved the water over his body, trying hard not to think of anything, seeking just a few moments of precious numbness before he had to start making decisions.

When he was ready, he rose, toweled himself, and dressed in fresh khakis from the wardrobe. He disdained the new boots he'd worn the past few days and reached for his old ones. They were scuffed and battered, but they were broken in well and would serve him better on the rugged trails.

Dressed, he stole from his room, crossed the hall, and rapped lightly on Neville's door. When Neville failed to answer, he twisted the knob and cracked it gently. A beam of light lanced across the gloom of the unlit room and touched Neville's empty bed. Clive closed the door quietly and wondered where his brother had gone.

He turned then to Annabelle's door. This time when he knocked, the door opened. Annabelle pulled him quickly inside and closed it again. All the others were there, too. "What's all this?" he said.

Annabelle shushed him, a finger at her lips. "Keep it down, hacker," she warned him. "It's a war council. We've been comparing notes, and none of us seem to care much for what we've learned."

Finnbogg got up from where he'd been sitting by the foot of the bed. He wore a child's troubled expression, which Clive found touching. "Smythefriend is missing," the canine said.

"I know that," Clive answered, moving into their midst. There were no more seats so he stood and leaned against the wall. "He said he was going exploring. The mountain trails, I think."

"Three days have elapsed since then," Chang Guafe said emotionlessly, "as you insist on measuring time by periods of ingestion and somnolence. We must consider that the implants in his head may have yielded him to someone else's control."

"Something has happened to Smythefriend!" Finnbogg insisted. "Finnbogg says we go look for Smythefriend, okay?"

Annabelle resumed her seat on the edge of the bed near Finnbogg. She reached up to scratch his back. That always seemed to quiet the excitable creature. "It's more than just Smythe," she reported in a low voice. She seemed to be in charge of this meeting, and Clive guessed it was she who had called it without bothering to wait for him. "Chang?" she said, turning toward the cyborg.

"Primary Anomalies, Report One," he responded, directing his ruby lenses toward Clive. "I have been in continual scan and analysis modes since we entered this structure. Though the artifacts of the interior appear familiar to your eyes in shape and form, they are each completely alien in molecular construction. They defy analysis of material and composition. All artifacts," he insisted. "Bed or bedsheets, clothes, chairs, books, walls. All are of unknown composite materials.

"Primary Anomalies, Report Two," he continued. "The interior of this structure gives the appearance of what has been referred to as 'the Victorian period.' Yet, I detect radiations and power fluctuations that are incongruent with such appearance. The walls, ceilings, and floors are interlaced with electronic circuitry of uncertain purpose. It is possible this structure is some kind of energy-receiving grid-station. But that is only speculation." He paused and ran the fingertips of one hand along the wall at his back. Clive knew the cyborg could sense the pulse of whatever circuitry lay behind the plaster.

"Report conclusion," Chang Guafe said formally. "On each level we have encountered increasingly advanced technology and increasingly sophisticated culture groups. Much of the technology on this seventh level reaches beyond even my knowledge, yet someone has attempted clumsily to disguise it behind familiar facades or in familiar forms. Of culture groups, we have observed few. Perhaps this is because so few of the Dungeon's captives ever survive to reach this level, whereas the gateways between the other levels were comparatively easy to breach." The glow of his lenses dimmed somewhat. "This is the general summary of Primary Anomaly Report. Details may be provided for specified areas of inquiry."

"That'll do for right now, Chang," Annabelle said. She twisted so she could see the other side of the room. "Shriek?"

The arachnoid had crouched down into a corner. All six of her eyes seemed to focus on Clive, but he knew that she directed her thoughts to all of them. *Under constant telepathic scan we are. Not word-thoughts, but images do they lift from our minds.* She turned three of her eyes toward Chang Guafe. *Believe do I in the Chang being's power grid. Believe do I that, at least in part, it boosts the telepathic powers of they who scan us.*

She hesitated then, but Clive knew her well by now, and he sensed before she could hide it that there was more. "Give it all," he said aloud for the benefit of the others. "Hold nothing back."

Very hard it was for me, she continued at last, *but this much more know I. They are two, our observers.* She hesitated again, then shrugged reluctantly. *And most interested are they in the beings Clive, Neville, Annabelle, and Tomàs.*

Neville sat at the top of the bed with his back against the headboard, but now he sat up. "In the four of us, you say?" He tapped Annabelle on the shoulder, and she twisted around. "I've been meaning to ask, but since everything in the bloody place seems to be fake, how can you trust what you read in those books? How can we know if the little sailor is really related to us? What if someone just wants us to think he is?"

Annabelle shrugged. "We can't know for sure, hacker. But whoever's got a modem hookup in our heads seems to be as interested in him as in us, so that lends some credence."

Sidi Bombay spoke up for the first time, rising carefully from his seated lotus position on the floor until he stood. "It is believed by some people in my land that God chooses special men for special testing."

Neville held up a hand and rolled his eyes. "Please, I think we've had enough religious nonsense. . . ."

But Sidi was firm. "If *you* please, Englishman. I brought it up only by way of example. I have meditated on this. I think the time has come to consider that this adventure— perhaps the entire Dungeon, itself—has been constructed as a test for the Folliot family."

"A test?" remarked Tomàs. He sat on the side of the bed between Chang Guafe and Annabelle. "*De qûe, amigo.*"

Sidi Bombay shrugged. "Of your character, perhaps. Of your courage, or your intelligence. Or perhaps through you, all of humanity."

"That's an awfully big burden for four pairs of shoulders," Annabelle said doubtfully. "Besides, where would that leave Shriek and Chang and Finnbogg, not to mention you, Sidi? Along for the ride?"

Sidi shrugged again. "Who am I to understand the ways of gods?"

"Whoever these Dungeonmasters are, they're not gods!" Neville muttered. "They're aliens! Maybe Ren, maybe Chaffri, or maybe somebody else. But they're not gods. Just damned inscrutable aliens!"

Annabelle got to her feet and began pacing back and forth at the foot of the bed. She held up the fingers of one hand and began to tick them off as she spoke. "Okay, here's the menu as I read it. First, Sergeant Smythe is overdue. Second, this whole place is a lot more than it seems. Third, someone besides Shriek is able to see into our minds." She stopped in the middle of the room, folded her arms across her chest, and looked at each of them in turn. "I think we've been sitting on our backsides long enough. Let's get some straight answers from Granddaddy Folliot, then go look for the sergeant. How about it?"

Clive shifted uneasily as he leaned against the wall. "I'm afraid you won't get many answers from him," he said quietly. "Granddaddy is a clone."

Neville sat up and slapped his thigh. "I knew it, old boy. I just had a feeling. But he threw me when he knew about Nanny's lapdog. How ever did he work that, do you suppose?"

"If our minds are being read," Clive suggested, "then maybe our observers heard you give the answer when I asked you the same question. Maybe they fed it back to their clone."

"How'd you trip him up, then, little brother?"

Clive's lips drew into a tight line as he remembered the scene on the mountain edge. "A different question," he answered curtly. He didn't feel the need to explain any more. The emotions were still too raw to probe now even with his friends.

Finnbogg sprang to his feet. "Okay, we go then. No safe place here. Go find Smythefriend."

"I guess that's one vote," said Annabelle, "and I'll add mine to it."

They all agreed.

"Then, everybody make a light pack of the things you'll need," Clive said, resuming his role as leader. "Neville, you and Finnbogg sneak downstairs and see if you can pilfer a little food to take along. We'll meet in the hallway. Let's go."

A few minutes later, Annabelle slipped into Clive's room. She'd changed into a pair of black denim jeans with a metal-studded belt and a white cotton sleeveless shirt. She carried her familiar leather jacket over one shoulder. "No matter how many times I open that wardrobe," she commented, "it has something new and exactly to my taste. I wish I could take it with me."

"Let's join the others downstairs," Clive said. He really had nothing to pack. He'd only come back to his room to retrieve his sword. He fastened the belt around his waist and adjusted the sheathed blade.

But Annabelle put a hand against the door. "Wait," she said gently. "Clive-o, I know you think you're hiding it, but the hurt on your face is as plain as a wart between the eyes." She caught one of his hands in hers and interlocked fingers. Her eyes were a misty blue as she forced him to look at her. "I don't know what went on between you and your . . ." She stopped herself before she said *father*. "I mean, I don't know what happened to you after dinner." She hesitated and bit her lip as she regarded him, and he felt her fingers tighten around his. Finally, though, she pressed on. "But Clive, how could they make a clone of your father? I mean, how would they get the tissue samples or the cell cultures to do it? I mean, he's back safe and sound in England, isn't he?"

He had already turned the question over and over in his mind, and he still only had one answer. "I don't know," he told her. "I don't know."

CHAPTER EIGHTEEN

A Walk on the Deadly Desert

The Baron Tewkesbury met them at the bottom of the stairs. He blocked the door, flanked on either side by the four Herkimers. In his hand he held a weird kind of gun whose barrel appeared plugged with a small emerald jewel. It was leveled on Neville and Finnbogg.

Clive went cold with anger and hesitated halfway down the stairway. Right behind him, Annabelle stopped, too.

"Please, Son," the baron said evenly, "just turn around and return to your rooms. They should hold you quite securely. I had hoped to convince you to stay of your own will. But you will stay."

"You did a good job, whatever you are," Clive answered acidly. "You told me everything I wanted to hear, played your part just right. You bastard."

The baron looked pained as he waved the gun. "No, I'm not your father. But I could have been. Perhaps you'll understand in time, but now, please, return to your rooms."

Finnbogg gave a low growl and dropped his bundle, a stolen tablecloth apparently full of the supplies Clive had asked him to gather. But before Finnbogg could move, the gun shifted. A blinding green beam lanced forth lasting but a fraction of a second, leaving a smoking black scorch mark on the floor near Finnbogg's feet.

"Oops," said Finnbogg, touching the mark with the tip

of one toe and snatching it back. He forced a big smile that showed plenty of canine teeth.

"The beam is quite lethal, I assure you," the baron warned. "Now let's have no more unpleasantness."

The stern expression on the baron's face only made Clive angrier in its perfect resemblance to his father. The same expression and the same ruthlessness were in the voice that Clive remembered so well. He had no doubt that this imitation was capable of using the gun.

"Please, tell your arachnoid friend not to reach for a hair-spike." The baron raised the barrel of the weapon ever so slightly.

Clive ground his teeth. There was nothing he could safely do. Trapped on the stairway they made easy targets for the strange burning beam. One sweep of his arm and the baron could kill them all. They wouldn't be able to retreat quickly enough to get away, nor could they descend except straight into the beam. Someone would get burned even if the rest of them managed to overpower their host. He wasn't prepared to take that chance.

"Back up," he told the others over his shoulder, but his gaze didn't waver from the baron. Slowly, as the others gave way, he crept up the steps.

The baron motioned with the gun barrel for Neville and Finnbogg to follow. Neville placed a hand on the banister and took the lowest stair. "Now this is the father I remember, old chap," he said with a wink to his twin. "But instead of a gun to the head, it was a purse string around the throat."

Finnbogg gave another dumb look at the scorch mark on the floor, then stepped daintily over it. The smile faded from his face as he moved toward the stair.

The baron moved up behind him.

With speed that belied his squat bulk Finnbogg whirled. His hand closed swiftly on the baron's wrist, and the snapping of bone made a loud crack that was audible over the sizzle of the beam as it burned a scar in the ceiling.

The baron gave a sharp cry of pain and stared wide-eyed with surprise.

"Oops, your ass!" Finnbogg growled as he seized the gun from the baron's numbed grip. He passed it back to Neville behind him. He pulled the baron's face close to his and showed his teeth again. "Okay?" he asked.

"Okay by me," Neville answered lightly.

Finnbogg drew back a fist and sent the baron crashing backward into the Herkimers, who scattered like formal-dress tenpins. Amid much slapping and flapping of webbed appendages the frog creatures regrouped, and the baron rose painfully and leaned against the door that was their way out.

"Daddy dearest," Neville said nonchalantly, gesturing with the gun as he moved by Finnbogg. "I'm so glad we had this time together—"

"Just get him the fuck out of the way, hacker!" Annabelle interrupted, pushing past Clive to get downstairs. "And let's get out of here!"

The baron looked pleadingly up at Clive. "Son," he begged, giving another tug on Clive's heartstrings, "don't let him kill me."

Neville looked back over his shoulder and started to say something. As he did, the nearest Herkimer opened its mouth. A long, slick tongue shot out and snaked around Neville's hand. The frog jerked its head, and the gun went flying down the hallway. Neville leaped on top of the creature as it released his wrist and darted for the weapon.

The baron, spying the gun, dashed around the scuffling tangle of arms and legs that belonged to Neville and the frog. From halfway up the stairs Clive launched himself over the banister and landed in a crouch. Before he could chase after his father, though, something pink and slimy zipped around his ankle and pulled him off balance. He hit the floor with a crash that ignited stars in his head.

At the same time he heard another crash, a curse, and a growl. From the blurry corner of one eye he saw Finnbogg sitting astride the baron while the baron scratched and clawed after the gun, which was just beyond his reach. Finnbogg sniggered and smacked his captive playfully aside the head.

Clive started to rise to his hands and knees, and something leaped up on top of his back. He looked cautiously over his shoulder into the eyes of one of the Herkimers. Its tongue lashed out whiplike at his eyes. Reflexively, he threw one hand up to protect his face and caught the icky little organ in a tight grip. The frog looked at him in wide-eyed panic and grew quite still. "Oon'n oort ee!" it begged incoherently. Carefully, it slid off Clive's back and stood beside him. Clive held on to the tongue as if it were a leash.

He looked around as the others came down the stairs. In the corner by the door the two remaining Herkimers crouched side by side clutching their mouths behind folded hands and looking as if they'd swallowed something terrible. "What happened to them?" Clive asked as Annabelle came to his side.

She chuckled and fingered the controls of the Baalbec A-9. "They tried to trip me the same way they tripped you," she said, "but I had a low-power field on."

"Ouch," Clive muttered.

"Quite a pet you've got there," she said, laying a hand on the head of the Herkimer at Clive's side. The creature stood absolutely docile as she kneeled down and stroked it sympathetically. "They're so cute in their little tuxedoes. What do we do with them?"

"I saw a key in the library," Neville called from the hallway. He straddled the chest of his Herkimer and pinned both its hands in one of his. His other hand held its mouth pinched shut. A pair of little feet flap-flapped on the floor as the creature struggled helplessly. "We could lock them in there."

"¡Ora bolas!" Tomàs sneered. He had one hand on the doorknob ready to go. "Cut their throats and let's go, *amigos*."

Clive glanced at Annabelle. "¿*Ora bolas?*" he said. "Is that an insult?"

She frowned impatiently. "It translates roughly as 'baloney,' " she lied with a grin. "You know him by now. He only thinks in terms of food."

Clive thought for a moment. He didn't want to kill anyone, especially the baron. It still troubled him how easily he'd been able to kill another clone that resembled his brother. There was still a strange, lingering guilt about that. He wasn't at all prepared to deal with the idea it might be as easy to kill his father's look-alike.

"Get him on his feet, Finnbogg," Clive ordered. "We'll lock them up as Neville suggested."

He led the way to the library with his Herkimer in tow. Finnbogg followed with the baron, whose arms the alien canine held twisted up between his shoulder blades. Next came Neville, Chang Guafe, and Shriek, each carrying one of the Herkimers, all of whom were quite passive now.

When the baron and his frog-servants were safely within, Clive took the key from the inside lock and prepared to close the door. His father made one last appeal. "Stay with me, Son," he said quietly in a voice full of regret and despair.

Clive hesitated as conflicting emotions raged within him. "I wish you had been my father," he answered softly. "Maybe I would have stayed. Or maybe I would have come back." He shut the door before any more could be said, slid the key into the hole, and turned it. The lock made a solid click as the bolt slid home. Clive tossed the key on his palm for a moment, considering, then made a fist around it.

Finnbogg had gathered up his bundle again, and Annabelle had retrieved the baron's weapon. She offered it to Clive, but he shook his head and told her to keep it for now. When they were all outside, he drew back and hurled the key as far away as he could. In the darkness he had no idea how far that was.

Clive wiped his hand on his pants. His palm was sticky as the devil from the Herkimer's slimy tongue.

He gave a final look at the strange old house where for a short time he had realized a dream of getting to know his father as he never had. Only it hadn't been his father at all, and the dream had become another Dungeon nightmare. Someone had dug inside his head and found his heart's desire and turned it against him.

For that, he owed someone, and he intended to pay in full.

He called to Finnbogg. "Can you pick up Sergeant Smythe's scent?" he asked.

Finnbogg's face brightened. "Look for Smythefriend? Smythescent Finnbogg knows!" The canine set aside the bundle of supplies, dropped to all fours, and began to sniff the ground. For several minutes he ran back and forth before the door and along the petrified hedge, his nose twitching and sniffing.

Clive bent and retrieved the bundle and slung it over his shoulder.

"I will take it, Clive Folliot," Chang Guafe said, and he took the bundle before Clive could protest. "I do not tire as you humans do."

"Smythescent!" Finnbogg announced suddenly, standing erect again and waving his arms to attract the others. He had worked his way to the far side of the mountaintop rim to a trail Clive knew from his walks with his father.

Not my father, he reminded himself bitterly. *With the clone.*

Clive had absolutely no sense of direction on this level. But he knew that the Dantean Gate was behind him, so he thought of that as gateward. Whatever lay before them was unknown, and he thought of that as darkward. Everything else was left or right of the spiral, which seemed to cut a straight swath as it rose out of the darkness and descended toward the gate.

The downward trail on this side was not so steep as it zigzagged its way from the summit. Still, as they dropped beneath the rim, they lost the little light provided by the setting spiral at their back, so Annabelle took the lead and used the Baalbec to provide a faint illumination. Since the trail, itself, dictated the way Smythe must have traveled Finnbogg only made spot-sniffs and nodded his assurances.

At least they had had a chance to rest, Clive reflected as they climbed lower and lower. He felt fresher, stronger, almost glad to be on the move again. Everyone had recovered from their wounds and injuries. They'd had time to bathe and relax. They'd eaten well for a change. And it was nice to be wearing something besides rags. Maybe, all in all, they hadn't come away from the Palace of the Morning Star too badly.

Maybe.

At the bottom of the mountain they paused and shared sips of water from the canteens Neville had filled. Annie switched off the Baalbec at Clive's suggestion. It wouldn't do to tire her too quickly.

The hills and mountains loomed ominously in the darkness. The higher peaks still sparkled in the light of the spiral, but Clive and his company were deep in the shadows where no light ventured. The wind whispered through the valley in which they found themselves, a soft rustling susurrus that reminded Clive of dry leaves in autumn. But there were no leaves here and no seasons, only the darkness and the wind scraping against the stone.

"Smythescent!" Finnbogg announced. He had been sniffing about while the others rested. "We go, okay?"

Annie reached for the Baalbec controls on her left forearm, but Clive stopped her. The trail was smoother here and less dangerous than the mountain descent. There was less need for her energy-draining light.

He turned, instead, to the cyborg. "Chang, can you . . . ?"

"Affirmative," Chang Guafe answered. Instantly, his ruby lenses began to glow brighter, and the metal of his face and chest gleamed redly as it reflected the new light. Wherever he turned his gaze the black ground bled under his stare. It was a poor substitute for Annabelle's purer light, but it served, and it wouldn't tax the tireless cyborg to maintain it.

They resumed their march with Finnbogg leading the way. A narrow natural path wound among the hills, and they followed it, just as Smythe had done before them. In some places the ground turned softer, almost ashen, and Clive remembered the shores of the river they had crossed. It, too, had been ashen. Perhaps, then, these were antique stream beds, all that remained of the waters that had carved these mountains.

"Why ever do you suppose your man came this far?" Neville asked once when they achieved the summit of a rather tiring slope.

"He's not 'my man,' " Clive answered patiently. Neville's patrician attitudes could still be so annoying. "As for why?" Clive shrugged. "You had your poetry to occupy your time. Annabelle had her research. Sidi had his meditations, and Tomàs was busy stuffing himself. Shriek and Chang Guafe, too, found mysteries to keep them busy. But Horace is a soldier. He probably found himself with too much time on his hands, so like any good soldier he decided to scout the terrain."

Annabelle moved closer and took Clive's hand. "Do you think something's happened to him?"

"He's overdue," Clive answered tersely. "Good soldiers are never overdue without reason. If I hadn't been busy making a fool of myself, I'd have noticed sooner."

She looked at him sympathetically. "Hey, hacker, you weren't making a fool of yourself. There's never been a human born that didn't wish for the chance to sit down with his parents and really download, you know?"

He smiled secretly at her language but kept any further comments to himself. The episode was past. It was better if he put the whole thing behind him.

"Oops, bad news!" Finnbogg suddenly stood erect and sniffed. He looked around sharply in all directions, then bent down to the ground and sniffed again. "More scents, many scents, okay. All mingling with the Smythescent."

The glow from Chang Guafe's ruby lenses focused on Finnbogg, lending a weird spectral appearance to the bulldog features. "He encountered other sentients?" the cyborg inquired.

"Many scents, yes!" Finnbogg repeated in agitation. "They go this way together, all scents. We follow, okay?"

They continued darkward and sooner than anyone expected found themselves out of the foothills and on the edge of a vast plain. At least, they thought it was a plain. In the velvet gloom it was impossible to guess just how far it actually extended.

"The Deadly Desert," Annabelle whispered to herself. Her voice held a mixture of awe and dread.

After a brief discussion they decided to eat something from the bundle and rest at the edge of the plain, then resume the search for Smythe after a bit of sleep. It had been quite a trek from the mountains, and they'd made it in good time, but Clive didn't want to exhaust the company. They nibbled on celery, apples, and cheeses, a bit of bread, and washed it all down with a bottle of claret that Finnbogg had also appropriated.

Sleep all, Shriek said when the meal was finished. *Stand watch will I.*

They huddled close together on the hard stone. After the soft beds they had slept in at the Palace of the Morning Star, no one expected a comfortable sleep.

"*¡Ai de mim!*" Tomàs grumbled. He reached into his waistband and extracted a small wooden box. "Why did I steal these matches? There is nothing to build even a small fire."

"*¿Pequeno incêndio?*" Annabelle grinned, hugging her knees to her chest and rocking back and forth. "A small fire?"

Tomàs returned her grin and tucked the matches back into his trousers. "*Incêndio pequeno,*" he corrected. "You learn fast, *senhorita,*" he said with appreciation, and he clapped his hands in soft glee. "*¡Muito rapidamente!*"

Annabelle gave a lighthearted laugh. "Very fast," she

translated as she inclined her head. "¡Obrigado, senhor! Thank you!"

The little Portuguese smiled a crooked-toothed grin, and a twinkle came into his eyes as he answered shyly in his peculiar accent, "You have much high-speed ram in your hard-drive, hacker." He curled up, then, and lay back on the hard ground to sleep.

Annabelle stared at him for a moment, then hid her mouth behind her hands and gave a muffled chuckle. "He's so cute for such a little slime!" she whispered to Clive when she recovered herself. "You think he can really be a relative?"

Clive shrugged. "Since I never expected to inherit, I never bothered much with the family history. Beyond my grandfather I know very little about who did what with whom or when, if you get my meaning."

She lay back and folded her hands under her head while Clive sat beside her. Then, she rolled on her side and curled up into a fetal position. Then, she returned to her back. At last, she sat up again and glanced at the others.

Only she, Clive, and Shriek remained awake.

"I keep thinking about Sidi's idea," she said quietly, "that all this is some kind of testing ground. Why? Why would a race of creatures powerful enough to build all this be even remotely interested in us?"

Clive only shrugged. Tomàs, though, was right. He wished there was a campfire, not for warmth, but for the soothing comfort of its flickering light.

"And if they are interested in us," Annabelle continued in a low voice, "in the Folliots and their descendants and offspring, then what does that make everyone else, pawns?"

Clive drew a deep breath and let it out slowly. "Maybe it's Shriek, or Chang Guafe, or Finnbogg they're interested in," he suggested as he put an arm around her shoulder. There was a certain comfort and reassurance in the touch of another person that he had never appreciated before, and he pulled her close. Maybe it was even better than a fire. It didn't keep away the cloying dark, but he didn't face it alone. "Maybe we're the pawns."

She didn't say any more, but he felt a slight tremor run through her body. After a while, they both lay down. She put her head on his shoulder, and he folded one hand under his head for a pillow and they both stared open-eyed at the featureless sky. There was no other sound in the world but the ghostly stirring of the wind, which finally lulled them both to sleep.

• CHAPTER NINETEEN •

Down to the Underworld

"Are you sure Smythe came this far?" Neville complained. Sleeping on hard stone without blanket or pillow had left him stiff and grumpy. He walked along in a black mood, sullen and petulant.

Finnbogg lifted his nose from the ground long enough to answer. "Aye," he said. "The nose have it. Smythefriend have distinct odor."

"He'll be happy to know that," Annabelle quipped. She gave a toss of her head and a light laugh as she patted Sidi Bombay on the shoulder. "He's your friend," she said to Sidi. "You be sure to tell him."

"This is hardly a joking matter," Neville snapped. "We could be very lost."

Annabelle caught Tomàs's hand and pulled him up beside her so that she, Sidi, and Tomàs walked arm in arm. "Well, you've certainly lost it, hacker," she responded. "You need to reboot your system."

Tomàs muttered under his breath, "*Sim,* I've got a boot for him."

"I don't mean to interrupt," Clive said patiently, "but has anyone else noticed those flashes to our right? You have to watch carefully. They're not very regular."

They stopped and looked where Clive pointed. After a few moments a short flicker of dim blue light colored the darkness. They waited as it repeated, one flash, two, a sporadic burst, then nothing, and Clive signaled they should move on, but they kept their gazes trained toward the phenomenon.

"What do you make of it, Tin Man?" Annabelle asked offhandedly. She had relinquished her grip on Tomàs and Sidi as her interest in the flickering grew.

Chang Guafe kept his gaze straight ahead as he walked beside Clive. The light from his lenses illuminated the ground at their feet and spilled around Finnbogg as the canine sniffed out the way. "All sensors scanning," he reported without turning to look either at Annabelle or the phenomenon. He hesitated, then added, "Monitoring a marginal increase in the number of negatively charged ions present in the air."

"Thank you," she said impatiently. "What's that mean?"

"Sudden violent electrical field fluctuations," Chang Guafe continued. An array of tentacles emerged from small panels on his face, chest, and left shoulder. Tiny lights at each of their tips activated and turned in the direction of the phenomenon. "Brilliant surges of luminosity," he reported. "Current discharges in excess of twenty kiloamperes. Specific flash temperatures vary from two times ten to the fourth power to three times ten to the fourth power in your Kelvin degrees."

"Never mind!" Annabelle muttered, cutting him off with a sigh. "Whatever it is, it's beautiful!"

"It looks like lightning to me," Neville said.

Chang Guafe's gaze left the ground for an instant and focused on Neville. "I believe that is what I indicated." The sensor-tentacles recoiled into his body, and the panel doors behind which they hid popped seamlessly shut.

"Is it coming this way?" Clive asked, suddenly concerned.

"Affirmative."

Clive exhaled slowly. "And me without an umbrella. Can we make better time, Finnbogg?"

Finnbogg stopped, drew himself up to his full four-foot height, and puffed out his considerable chest. "Very strong wind makes tricky task, okay?" he grumbled. "Must keep nose very close to ground to sort many scents. Not easy. Not human work. Let Finnbogg do it, okay?"

"Testy little beast," Neville mumbled in a low voice.

Annabelle glared at him. "I'm looking at the only beast around here, hacker."

"I apologize, Finnbogg," Clive said politely. "I know you're doing your best. Why don't we take a break and everyone have a drink of water."

"If that is lightning," said Sidi Bombay, "we may soon have more water than we want."

The flickering in the distance intensified. There was no longer a question that it was lightning, or that it was moving in their direction. The wind blustered about them and pelted them with airborne particles of ash and dust. A low thunder rolled ominously through the sky.

Finnbogg led them in a straight line across the plain. They moved at a brisk pace, fighting the wind. More than once, Clive nearly lost his balance as an unexpected blast caught him in midstride. Once, Annabelle gave a yelp and stopped suddenly to pick something from her eye. After that, she walked with one hand shielding her face.

The lightning drew closer. No longer was it a sheeting flash on the horizon. Blue-white snakes slithered with electric grace through the darkness. Tiny darting tongues licked groundward as Clive watched with growing concern. Every deadly bolt seemed to have a pair of eyes that stared in his direction.

Chang Guafe stopped so abruptly that Tomàs and Sidi Bombay collided against him from behind. "Scanning a heat pattern directly ahead," the cyborg announced, ignoring Tomàs's muttered cursings.

"What is it?" Clive said curtly, anxious to keep everyone moving. "How far ahead?"

"Unknown, but the pattern is similar to those I recorded in the chasm," Chang Guafe answered. "Distance approximately one thousand Earth meters."

"The vent shafts?"

Change Guafe shrugged. "Uncertain. But the pattern is similar."

Clive glanced again toward the storm. The cyan lacework reflected eerily in the smoother gleaming patches of stone that dotted this world's surface, making ephemeral pools of blue fire that burst into existence and died in the space of a human heartbeat. He smelled no rain in the air, no moisture. Pure electrical fury bore down upon them, and it would catch them in the open without a hope of shelter long before they crossed a thousand meters.

Clive chewed his lip worriedly, and every hair on his neck stood on end. He knew better than to trust anything in the Dungeon, even the weather. "Finnbogg," he shouted over the rising wind. "Is there a chance Smythe headed for that heat source?"

Finnbogg didn't stop, keeping his nose close to the ground as he answered. "Smythefriend and many scents moving easy path straight for long time. Nose says still straight okay."

Clive called back to Chang Guafe. "Your heat source," he shouted, "it's also straight ahead?"

"Affirmative," the cyborg assured him.

The air sizzled suddenly, and the world rocked under them and turned stark white. Thunder exploded with deafening force, and the ground shivered as a crackling cobalt sledge smashed against the stone, sending fragments and splinters flying.

Clive clutched his face with both hands. The burning behind his eyes was an exquisite pain, and when he peeked out between his fingers, the world danced with shimmering afterimages.

"I don't come with a surge-protector, goddamn it!" Annabelle shrieked. "That was too scrodding close!"

The world screamed with whiteness, harsh and terrifying. Clive flung up his hands to protect his vision and felt the flesh on his arms crawl with galvanic sensation. All the world turned to thunder, and the thunder turned to a wave that lifted him up and dropped him on his back.

"Run!" Clive shouted, picking himself up and snatching for Annabelle's hand. "Chang, take the lead. Head for the heat source!" He waved to the others. "Follow Chang!"

Finnbogg straightened, looking sad. "Oops, Finnbogg fired!"

"¡Ai, Christo!" Tomàs muttered, crossing himself and looking to the cyborg. "¡Adiante! Go on!"

The next blast of thunder was as good as a pistol shot. With Chang Guafe in the lead, they raced across the plain. The sky hurled white knives that scarred and burned the black stone, that stabbed their vision and gouged the darkness from the world. They ran half blind, barely able to keep their eyes on the cyborg's back, which rippled blue and white and red as his metal body shimmered with the reflection of the storm.

A sudden bolt hammered the ground off to the right. Tomàs gave a scream and stumbled. Before Clive and Annabelle could reach his side, Shriek sped past them and swept the little Portuguese up in her arms.

Go! came the arachnoid's insistent thought. *Carry him will I!* Then she fell back again to bring up the rear while Tomàs cursed and clutched a bleeding cheek.

Since Clive couldn't see where they were running, it was impossible for him to judge how far they had to go. His heart pounded in his chest, and his breaths came in short gasps. His legs felt like lead, and too quickly he felt himself giving out. Still, he pushed himself, urging his limbs to greater effort as he fought to keep up with Annabelle, who ran tirelessly.

Then Neville stumbled. Without thinking, Clive caught his brother's arm and pulled him to his feet again. "We're almost there!" he lied encouragingly. He had no idea whether they were or not.

The lightning strobed with increasing fury. The world roared with thunder and wind.

Ahead, Chang Guafe and Finnbogg stopped. Sidi caught up to them an instant later and sagged breathlessly to his knees. Clive and Annabelle arrived next with Neville and Shriek and Tomàs close after.

Clive gripped the cyborg's arm and leaned on him for a brief moment. "What is it?" he asked between gasps. "Why are we stopping? Are we there?"

Chang Guafe pointed. In the lightning flash Clive spied a patch of blackness that remained black even under the brightest coruscation. They stood ten meters from its edge.

Cautiously, he crept toward it. It appeared to be a hole in the surface, perhaps five meters wide and perfectly round, and as he peered over the edge a rapid series of bolts illuminated the narrow metal ladder that descended into its depths.

Finnbogg sniffed around the rim. "Smythefriend and many scents go down!" he shouted enthusiastically from the top of the ladder. "Finnbogg not fail! Smythefriend come this way!"

Clive drew a deep breath and let it out. "Then we go, too," he said, stepping delicately over the side and setting foot on the first rung of the ladder. "Ditch that bag, Finnbogg. You can't negotiate this with your hands full."

"Wait just a bloody minute!" Neville objected. "Don't you think we should discuss it? I mean, we've got no bloody idea where this goes, or if it goes anywhere!"

Annabelle shouldered Neville aside and moved to follow Clive down the shaft. "You want to stand out here and get a galvanic haircut, scrodhead, that's your business. You and the barber can discuss anything you want. But get out of my way!" She dropped to her hands and knees and carefully explored with her toe for the first rung.

"Remember, Nevillefriend, what you teach Finnbogg!" Finnbogg slapped Neville on the back, practically knocking the poor man over the side. "Heigh-ho, and God save the Queen, and stiff upper lip! Let's go! Finnbogg after Annie!"

Down into the darkness they climbed with no bottom in sight until the lightning storm became no more than a round flickering moon above them, a silver-blue disk that grew even smaller as they descended. No wind blew in the shaft to menace them, though the air was as warm and close as ever.

"Never have I seen such a storm," Sidi Bombay said somewhere above Clive. "No clouds, no rain. It was as if the hand of Shiva had reached out for us."

A quietness settled upon them, and they concentrated on climbing. Clive felt gingerly for the next rung, always trusting it would be there.

Sometime later, Neville broke the silence. "Do you think this is the way to the next level?"

No one answered. There was no way of knowing for sure, though Clive doubted it. The deeper they descended through the Dungeon's levels, the more disorienting the transitions had become. A simple ladder from one level to the next seemed just too easy.

"I think I see a light," he said at last, keeping his voice low and calm and hoping the others would take the hint. If there was light at the end of the tunnel, there might also be someone waiting for them. Chang had mentioned back at the chasm the possibility of underground industry. He listened for the sounds of pumps, of engines, of any kind of machinery, and heard nothing. As he climbed lower, the silence made him edgy. He felt too much like prey. He could almost feel the gunsights on his neck.

It was definitely light—artificial light, in fact. The shaft in which they found themselves broke through the roof of yet another tunnel. "Stay here," Clive ordered the others when he estimated no more than twenty steps remained before they emerged. As quietly as he could, he moved toward the opening.

The ladder ended at the lip of the air shaft. Clive paused again and listened. Then, gripping his sheathed blade, he dropped lithely down to the floor. He blinked and shielded his eyes from the painfully bright light and waited for his vision to adjust.

It was not a tunnel at all, but a huge corridor. Glowing light panels placed at regular intervals in the ceiling provided an illumination that, after a few moments, proved soft and comfortable. The walls were perfectly smooth, and the floor tiled with great polished stone squares. To his right the corridor proceeded a short distance and turned a blind corner. To his left was some kind of crossroads.

Still, he moved quietly, nervously, with one hand at the hilt of his saber as he stole toward the crossroads and peered in all directions. Both ends of the new corridor curved out of sight. *Great,* he thought to himself. *Another bloody maze.*

He tiptoed back to the air shaft and whispered up to the others that it was safe to descend. Once down, Annabelle stayed close by his side, and Finnbogg began to sniff around. "Oops," he said apologetically, "no scent on this funnystuff stone."

Shriek emerged last from the air shaft, for everyone realized now that was clearly what it was. She looked both ways and chittered softly in appreciation.

"Hey, it's cooler down here," Annabelle noted, rubbing her arms briskly. "That's a welcome relief."

"Mechanically conditioned," Chang Guafe reported. "Olfactory sensors detect very faint traces of chemical coolant."

"Well, well!" Annabelle responded, brightening. "Civilization."

Clive looked around uncomfortably. "That's a word with a lot of different meanings," he warned. "Let's reserve judgment."

Suddenly, a soft purring noise vibrated in the air. As one the company turned toward it and saw a section of the wall rotate outward. Clive and Neville reacted as one, drawing their swords. Annabelle dropped into a crouch and brought up the business end of Baron Tewkesbury's strange lightbeam weapon. Shriek plucked a hair-spike and prepared to throw.

Someone moved behind the panel. "Hey, Jack! I know that voice! No-jive Clive, as I do live and breathe! Lay some skin, man!"

Baron Samedi pushed his top hat to a jaunty angle as he stepped into the corridor light and grinned his big infectious grin.

· CHAPTER TWENTY ·

Twisted Selves

"Forgive me for seeming ungracious, Samedi," Clive said, keeping the point of his saber level and steady, "but please stay where you are until you explain how you got here. We saw you die."

Neville also kept his blade high. "We saw two of you die."

"But don't you see?" Annabelle said, lowering her gun and relaxing. "That's the answer. This must be another clone."

Samedi let go a melodramatic sigh. "The last o' the line, I'm 'fraid, Jack."

Clive lowered his blade cautiously. "What do you mean?"

Samedi sighed again. "I mean, somebody's wiped the data bank containin' my genetic code and personality programmin'. There can't be no more Samedis. And there's a whole lot more you should know, but not here. Ain't safe."

But Clive was not yet quite ready to trust. "How'd you know we'd show up at this particular point? There are other shafts into this place, so why decide to wait at this one?"

Samedi put on a pout and braced his hands on his bony hips. "Hey, like I been hidin' out down here a long time, passin' as one o' the defectives an dodgin' the rat-catchers an' all, an' keepin' my eyes open. I seen 'em when they brought in your friend. They wander around on the surface sometimes, but they always come back, cause ain't no food up there. I figured odds were good you'd come runnin' along pretty soon to save him. Took your sweet time, though, you did. Thought I'd suffocate in that storage closet."

At mention of his sergeant Clive's brows knitted together. He lowered his weapon. "Save Smythe? From what? Who's got him?"

"A bunch o' defectives," Samedi answered disdainfully, "an' you better save his ass quick. Ain't pleasant what they're gonna do." He glanced back down the corridor suddenly. "Ain't pleasant what's gonna happen to us, neither, if we keep standin' here."

Clive sheathed his sword and gestured for Neville to do the same. Annabelle hid the gun again inside the waistband of her jeans and tucked her shirt over it so it couldn't be seen. "Can you lead us to Smythe?" Clive asked.

"Depends," Samedi answered, staring wide-eyed past the group.

"On what?" Clive snapped.

Samedi pointed. "On whether you can ditch the rat-catcher, Jack. Bye!" With that, he turned and ran.

Clive whirled in time to see a bright flash. At the same time, Chang Guafe spread his arms and swept them all to the floor as a searing beam scorched the air, barely missing them. Clive pulled himself from the tangle of bodies, ignoring the pain in his side where someone's elbow had smashed his ribs, and rose into a crouch to get a look at their attacker.

The rat-catcher was a robot, a legless metal monster that moved on nearly silent treads like a small tank. Its arms ended not in fingers but in yellow glowing lenses from which it had fired the beams that had so nearly claimed their lives. As he watched, those lenses began to glow again, and the creature's huge single eye focused directly upon them.

"Look out!" Annabelle cried, pushing Tomàs out of the

way with her foot as she tugged the gun from her waist-band. "Get out of the way!" She pushed Finnbogg out of her line of sight and brought the gun up to bear on the robot.

The emerald beam lanced outward, shattering the robot's eye-lens. Again Annabelle fired, desperately swinging the beam in a wide arc. Metal squealed and sizzled as coherent energy raked across the monster's throat. The head tottered for an instant, then fell forward and dangled from an array of colored wires and cables.

The rat-catcher went crazy, spinning on its tread, waving its arms and spraying the corridor with deadly force rays. The company scrambled for their lives, twisting, dodging, and rolling to avoid death.

Then, Shriek voiced her horrible battle cry and launched herself at the rat-catcher. Her seven-foot bulk struck the machine from the side and knocked it over. Its treads whirred uselessly as she stood on one arm with two of her four feet and ripped the other arm from its socket. In a fury she beat and tore at the machine until it crumpled under her fists like an empty can. Wires and circuits popped and shorted and sparked, and smoke exuded from joints and splits in the armor. Still, the treads continued defiantly to operate. Shriek gave another frustrated scream, lifted the broken robot in her four powerful arms, and heaved it against the wall. The crash made a terrible noise, but all that remained of the rat-catcher was a pile of junk.

Shriek stood victoriously over the rubble, breathing hard. Slowly, she looked at them and parted her mandibles in what served her for a grin, and Clive felt her in his mind. *Good that felt.*

"Hey, baby, I am *sooo* impressed!" Samedi peeked at them from around the corner far down the corridor. "I never seen nobody do that to a catcher before. But you all better haul ass now. Sound's what attracts 'em. That's how they locate the defectives, an' it's probably how they found us here."

"Then take us to Smythe!" Clive ordered, containing the urge to shout angrily as the others gathered around him.

Samedi grinned and beckoned. "Come," he said.

They moved quickly, but quietly, through one corridor after another, through closet-sized rooms and chambers as large as warehouses. The deeper into the complex they journeyed the more mysterious the place became. Crystalline tubes of various dimensions hung suspended from the ceilings. Within them coursed strange chemicals and viscous fluids. Some traveled in steady, streaming flows while others pulsed as if driven by an immense hidden heart. Some radiated with soft shades of golden color.

Another chamber contained vast numbers of square plastic boxes piled in orderly fashion from the floor to the ceiling. Each bore a series of unreadable symbols that Clive assumed were lot numbers. The seamless boxes defied all attempts to open them until Samedi showed them how. He approached the nearest container and touched the first two symbols simultaneously, and the top opened in a slow, controlled manner.

"What is it?" Clive asked, looking inside at a colorless mass.

Chang Guafe leaned forward and placed his hand on the substance. "In simplest description," he answered after a moment's pause, "raw organic compound. Do you wish a detailed analysis?"

Clive declined, and they continued on.

A short distance away they found another chamber full of the same cartons, but some of these had been opened. Empty containers lay scattered about randomly, and greasy smears stained the floor and walls as high as Clive could reach. A mildly unpleasant odor hung in the air.

An old shirt lay crumpled in a corner. A rusted set of keys lay discarded nearby. Neville found an old shoe. Annabelle slipped on a broken pencil. Sidi Bombay slipped in something else.

"Yuck," Finnbogg remarked, wrinkling his nose.

"Better watch your back, Jack," Samedi whispered in a low voice.

"The defectives you mentioned?" Clive inquired, and Samedi nodded. "What are they?"

"Defectives," Samedi repeated, straightening his raggedy suit jacket self-consciously. "Clones who couldn't cut it in the real world, you know? Clones who didn't grow right or whose programin' didn't take right." He shrugged and nudged one of the empty cartons with a toe. "Just meat, that's what they are, sometimes overcooked an' sometimes undercooked, but not fit for servin' up."

"You mean the Dungeonmasters make mistakes, hacker?" Annabelle said. She still carried her gun in her hand, and her eyes flitted now and then toward the shadows.

Samedi shrugged again as he looked at her. "Any assembly line has its share o' bad parts," he told her as he led them out of the chamber. "But some o' these parts can still think, an' they manage to avoid the regular disposal. Course, there's nothin' for 'em to do but hide out here. There's nothin' to eat on the surface, an' they can't get near the Gateway."

"The Gateway?" Clive said, catching Samedi's arm and jerking him around. "You mean the gate to the next level? Level eight? It's here?"

"That's right, boss. You'd o' found that out at the Palace o' the Mornin' Star, but I bet that turned into a bad scene, huh?"

Clive snatched Samedi's top hat and rubbed his sleeve against a spot on the brim. He hesitated, then passed it back. "You put it so politely," he said to the clone. "I suppose you didn't know it was my father, or rather his doppelganger, that we found waiting there."

"Didn't know what you'd find after I died," Samedi answered with a straight face. "Oh, yeah, you should o' found another me, but better dressed, like someone who lives in a palace an' talks better. But somebody killed him just like they dropped the other two Samedis into the chasm, the same people who wiped my gene bank. I felt it, you know."

"You felt it?" Sidi Bombay asked.

"Course, man!" Samedi answered. "How can you not feel it when your entire program an' all your copies get wiped? I mean, you can hear the scream down here!" He tapped his temple.

"Interesting," Sidi said quietly. "As if you were in touch with all your lives, past, present, and future. My faith speaks of something similar."

Finnbogg crept forward a bit and broke into the conversation. "Okay, how come Samedifriend still lives when littermates all die?"

" 'Cause I hid my ass in a closet, Jack," Samedi answered honestly. "I was supposed to guide you from the palace to the gate in the central chamber an' send you on your way to the next level, but I'm jus' a walkin' dead man, now, a zombie, like what my original patternin' was taken from. But zombie or not, I didn't much feel like jus' walkin' into whatever trap was waitin' at the palace. I saved my skin, instead."

Clive stared into the creature's hollow eyes, then backed up a pace.

"That's right, Clive Folliot," Samedi said, meeting his gaze evenly, unapologetically, and dropping the inconsistent accent. "I resisted my programed task. I'm a defective, too."

"I don't give a bloody damn if you're Queen Victoria in drag, old chap," Neville said impatiently. "Just get us to Smythe and to the gate so we can get out of here."

"Wait," Clive insisted, cutting his twin off with a wave. He turned back to Samedi again. Everything the clone had said only convinced him that he was right about different factions operating in the Dungeon, perhaps warring with each other. "Who dumped your gene bank? Do you know who?"

Samedi shook his head, and a look of frustration flickered upon his pale face. "First, they grow us real quicklike," he answered, slipping back into his accent, "then they fill our heads with a preprogramed wet-ware personality and whatever knowledge they want us to have. But the more I resist that programin'—the more I insist on thinkin' my own thoughts an' doin' things my way—the faster their stuff fades. Course, the answer you want might never have been in my program anyway."

"Let's ditch this scrodding place," Annabelle suggested.

They started across the chamber toward the open door on the far side. Abruptly, the chamber lights went out, and they stopped in midstride. It was not completely dark. Light spilled in from the doorways before and behind them, enough to see their way. Cautiously, they moved forward.

A huge, hulking figure suddenly blocked the door, and a grotesque shadow stretched toward them. Two red eyes blazed, and the corridor light gleamed on powerful metallic shoulders.

"Back out the way we came," Clive said slowly without taking his eyes from the figure before them. There was something darkly familiar about it.

" 'Fraid not, hackers," Annabelle answered. "It's blocked, too."

Clive drew his saber and risked a hasty glance over his shoulder. Four figures shambled through the rear doorway. Two stood as tall as Shriek. One appeared much shorter, perhaps Finnbogg's height. The last seemed more reasonably proportioned.

"Forward, then," he decided. "There's only one."

He spoke too soon. Two more creatures joined the tall silhouette. Worse, Clive detected motion in the corridor beyond, and since none of the three turned to look, it had to be more of their friends.

"Looks like feeding time," Neville said, coming to Clive's side. He drew his saber as well.

"I don't mean to be depressing," Annabelle muttered, "but have you ever thought of yourselves as raw organic compound?"

"They won't eat you," Samedi said with assurance.

"That's a relief, *amigo*," Tomàs grumbled.

"They will strip you for genetic material and feed your pieces to the machines," the clone continued unpleasantly, losing his accent once again, "after they have drained your psyches and recorded your every memory and entered those in the master data banks."

"Why would they do that," Sidi Bombay inquired, "if their creators are trying to destroy them?"

"Not kill 'em all, Jack," Samedi answered quickly. "Just keep the numbers low. Some o' the defectives do menial service work, though most o' the clone bank is automated. But to drag you to the analyzers, the machines have to also give 'em access to central processin' where, if they move quick an' know what to do, they can punch up another copy o' themselves. Most o' the time the machines recognize the false command an' dump it, but not always."

"Reproduction with a cookie cutter," Annabelle commented dryly. "I don't mean to be pushy, hackers, but I think it's time to party. I've got the Baalbec, so Tomàs, you'd better take this." She passed him the beamer weapon.

Tomàs cradled it in his palm and looked up coldly. "*Obrigado.* I take out the big monster first, then." He brought the weapon up and pointed at the huge silhouette in the doorway.

"No." Change Guafe's hand closed firmly on Tomàs's forearm, and he pushed the gun barrel down. "He must be mine."

Of course, thought Clive. No wonder the shape seemed so familiar. Chang Guafe's visual sensors must have confirmed it immediately. "It's you, isn't it?" Clive said worriedly. "They've made a clone of you."

"Oh, the Dungeonmasters probably have genetic samples from all o' you by now. Drops o' blood, small skin samples. Easy enough to get, you know, especially what with all the scrapes you been in. It's your memories an' personalities they probably want most."

Being Clive, Shriek said quietly. She'd been silent for quite a while, but there was a sense of urgency in her thoughts. *More beings behind us there are. Numbers growing are.*

"All right, let's get out of here," Clive answered grimly.

Clive, Neville, and Chang Guafe advanced in a line. But as soon as they made a move, the defectives charged from both directions. Shriek made the horrible sound after which they'd named her as she hurled a handful of hair-spikes at the rear attackers. Five bodies gave equally horrid cries of pain and fell as their flesh swelled frighteningly, purpled, and split open, and pouring blood onto the floor. At the same time Tomàs muttered a hasty curse, leaped to the side, and pointed the gun. The emerald beam flared, but his aim was off. The deadly light missed the Chang clone but severed an arm from the creature right behind him. Its scream echoed in the vast chamber.

Chang Guafe and the Chang clone met with a crash. They struck the floor in a tangle of arms and legs and thrashed about until suddenly one of them obtained an advantage in leverage, planting armored feet in the chest of the other and shoving with mechanically enhanced power. A heavy form smashed backward into one of the neat stacks of plastic cartons and was quickly buried in the collapse. Almost instantly, though, containers flew everywhere as the cyborg fought free and attacked again.

Chang Guafe and the Chang clone looked identical to Clive, and he had no time to sort one from the other. He brought an arm up to sweep aside an empty carton that waffled through the air toward his head. Too late he saw the defective that followed it. Outstretched arms locked around his waist, pinning his arms and lifting him off his feet. He looked into a face that was almost human except that one eye was a good inch lower than the other, as if the flesh on one side had slightly melted.

Its strength, though, was superhuman. Clive felt the breath rush from his lungs as the creature squeezed, and his ribs started to give. Desperately and with all his force, he butted his head against the offered nose and heard it crack. Blood spurted, and his foe loosened its grip as it flung back its head in a gurgling outcry. Clive repeated the trick, smashing the tortured nose a second time, drawing another wail. The creature released him and clutched its face. Clive drew back with his saber and prepared to dispatch it, but at the last instant he uttered a low curse and slammed his fist into its exposed jaw, driving it to the floor, where it lay unconscious. Quickly, he looked around to see who needed help.

Four creatures cornered Neville against a pile of cartons. Unburdened by Clive's respect for Queensberry rules, his twin slashed two of them across the gut with smooth rapid strokes and kicked a third between the legs, which gave him time to thrust through the chest of the fourth. Barely breathing hard, he finished off the third as it sagged to the floor clutching its groin.

Tomàs's green beam blazed everywhere through the darkness as yet more defectives poured through the doorways. The little Portuguese had found himself a perch atop a stack of containers, and screaming strings of Portuguese epithets and curses, he raked the lethal ray back and forth across the entrances. Many made it safely inside, dodging his beam, but the bodies swiftly piled, and still he fired and fired.

Then, the two Chang Guafes, locked in each other's arms, encoiled in tangles of snapping tentacles that emerged from every part of their bodies, pitched backward like enraged juggernauts, and stumbled against Tomàs's perch. Cartons and Tomàs went tumbling.

Clive had no chance to help as a true monstrosity launched itself at him. It resembled a jellyfish on legs, and barbed tentacles snapped whiplike toward his face. He brought the saber up in a rapid arc, intersecting the deadly limbs, severing a few, which writhed and squirmed at his feet. But still the beast came on, forcing him to retreat even as he struck and struck again. Cold, malignant eyes regarded him from the mass as the thing advanced.

Suddenly, Clive dropped low, one knee actually brushing the floor, and swung his blade with all his might. The razor edge drew a deep ichorous line across the creature's knee. It gave an inhuman cry of pain and hesitated. For an instant, it stared uncertainly at Clive, then it came on again. But it moved more slowly now, more cautiously. Clive's foot nudged a carton as he backed. As he moved around it, he caught the open lid with his booted toe and flipped it upward at his unnatural attacker. He blessed his stars when the tentacle shot up to intercept the flying carton. He stepped in close, drove his blade deep into the central mass, and jerked it downward in a savage slicing motion as he withdrew. A pale vitreous humor rushed out through the rent in the skin-sac, and the thing deflated like a ruptured bladder and flopped hideously in its death throes.

Another carton hurtled toward him. In annoyance he reached up to bat it aside. Unexpectedly the full weight of its unbreached contents caught him in the face. Bright stars exploded in his skull as he crashed to the deck. The sword went skittering from his grip. Dazed, he struggled to reach it, but a booted foot pushed it farther away. He looked up into the eyes of Baron Tewkesbury.

"Father!" Clive cried in dismay.

The clone sneered as it reached a huge hand toward Clive's throat. "Forget it, human," it said in a horrible, rasping voice that in no way resembled his father's. "The programing didn't take! You're nothing to me but meat for the grinder!"

Clive crawled back a pace, seeking escape from that grasping hand and those almost mesmerizing eyes.

Then, Annabelle stepped between them and brushed her fingertips along the top of that hand. The baron gave a short, choked cry as the jolt from the Baalbec A-9 flung him backward off his feet. Immediately, Finnbogg pounced upon him and with a horrible growl, locked his jaws on the old man's throat.

A spurt of crimson shot across the floor, and Clive squeezed his eyes shut with a groan.

"Are you okay, Clive-o?" Annabelle said, turning. "I can shut off the field if you need help."

"You keep that thing on!" Clive shouted, recovering himself and scrambling to his feet. He looked around for his saber, spied it, and snatched it up.

"They're retreating," Annabelle informed him calmly. "The meat turned out to be a little too tough."

"Finnbogg heard, Annie!" the canine said, coming up behind them. His dark-stained jowls dripped blood. "We give them something to chew on."

She made a face. "Looks like you're the one who did the chewing, hacker."

Finnbogg turned away and wiped his face. Then, he wiped his hands on his fur. It was sometimes disconcerting how Finnbogg preferred using his teeth and powerful jaws in a fight to his equally powerful hands. But no one could argue with his effectiveness or his courage.

A loud crash made them turn. Chang Guafe or the Chang clone went hurtling through yet another stack of containers, smashed off its feet by a blow of incredible power from its opponent. Without hesitation the opponent dived after its prey. Empty cartons went flying. Full cartons burst open as the combatants rolled on the deck and grappled for advantage. Again, one flung the other off, and both rose to their feet. Arms and tentacle arrays reached out.

Suddenly, Sidi Bombay appeared between them. Annabelle gave a cry of warning, but the Indian ignored or didn't hear her. Instead, he pointed a small box at one of the cyborg warriors and it froze absolutely motionless, one foot advanced, one mighty fist caught in midswing. It resembled a horrible sculpture of some nameless god of war.

Clive had forgotten the stasis box that Sidi had stolen

from the Lords of Thunder, and he marveled as the Hindu dived and rolled out of the way with fluid grace.

The unaffected cyborg locked both its hands together, drew back, and smashed them into the face of its paralyzed foe. To Clive's horror flesh and bone and metal caved inward under the impact like so much melon pulp. The creature tottered for an instant and fell with limbs still locked in its last position.

The standing Chang Guafe turned slowly toward them as it retracted its tentacles into its body. Then, its shoulders drooped subtly as it advanced toward Sidi Bombay, extended a hand, and helped him up.

"How did you know which one?" Annabelle exclaimed. "I couldn't tell them apart!"

Shriek joined them, all six of her eyes agleam with excitement and cooling fury. She still held a handful of spikes, and her harsh breathing sounded like stones in a tumbler.

"I waited and watched," Sidi answered. He reached up and touched Chang Guafe on the arm in a gesture of friendship. "This one in the last moments risked a glance around to avoid falling on Tomàs. That's how I knew the difference. The wrong one would have had no such compunction."

"Tomàsfriend?" Finnbogg said in sudden concern. "Where is Tomàsfriend? Where is Samedifriend?"

"Right here, Jack," Samedi said, crawling out from one of the cartons where he had folded himself for hiding. "Hey, don' gimme that look. I got no weapons, an' these brittle bones break real easy. 'Sides, if anything happened to me, where would you survivors be without a guide?"

"Forget it," Clive said. "Where's Tomàs?"

Sidi Bombay led them to a far corner where the little sailor lay unconscious atop a mound of crushed containers. Clive recalled seeing him fall as his perch was knocked from under him. He must have been out since then. It was lucky the containers had hidden him from view.

Sidi Bombay dropped to his side, bent over him, and

began to massage his temples. Almost immediately, Tomàs's eyes snapped open. At first, a dull film covered the black pupils, but it quickly cleared as he came fully alert. "My gun!" he said, the first words from his mouth. He scrambled over on his knees and began feeling around for the missing weapon. He found it nearby under another carton and tucked it in his waistband as he looked around suspiciously. "Did we win, *amigos*?" Then, he backed a step and laid his hand on the gun butt. "*Christo!* Are you my *amigos*?"

Clive frowned. "What do you mean? Of course we're your friends!"

But Annabelle touched his shoulder. "I understand," she said, beckoning them to follow her. She pointed to the bodies of various clones as she walked. "Maybe you were too caught up in the fighting to notice. One of the advantages of this thing"—she tapped the controls of the Baalbec on her left forearm—"is that I don't have to fight, so my senses don't go all hyper. But look. Look at the faces. Almost everybody we've met in the Dungeon is here, several copies, sometimes. Almost every alien race, too. That jellyfish thing that attacked you, Clive. Remember the monster on the bridge at Q'oorna where you found Finnbogg? That might have been an early prototype."

Sidi Bombay cleared his throat. "Come to the forward door," he said, and they followed him. In the darkness to the side of the entrance stood a dozen or more clones all locked in stasis. Any of them would have made a fine addition to someone's sculpture garden. "I crouched here for a short time," Sidi explained. "Here are those who came through the door and turned my way. But look closely. Especially you, Missy Annabelle."

"Why, it's me!" Neville exclaimed, standing before his look-alike. He made a frame of his thumbs and index fingers and made a show of examining the face with his best artist's eye. "Technique's a bit rough, though. My jaw's much firmer, and my nose far more noble, don't you think? Those damned impressionists must be everywhere these days! Manet, you dog!"

Annabelle moved from face to face, peering closely. Then, she noted the two small doll-like clones deep in the darkness. She kneeled down and caught her breath sharply as she clapped a hand to her mouth. "Amanda!" she whispered in horror through her fingers.

"Not so, missy," Sidi assured her, going to her side and bending down. "Look closely. First this one"—he indicated the Amanda look-alike—"then this one over here." He drew her to the second clone.

It was hard to see in the gloom. Annabelle motioned Sidi back a little farther, then adjusted the Baalbec so that it gave off the faintest glow and lit up the tiny face. The hair was black like Amanda's, but straight and fine instead of curly. The eyes were subtly wrong, too, and the lips were too thin. "Why, it's me, sort of!" She looked to Sidi, then to the others as they all gathered around. "I don't understand!"

Chang Guafe bent closer as Annabelle scooted aside. The light of his ruby eyes put a blush on the doll face. Then, he straightened. "Microscopic scan reveals faint traceries of scar tissue at key facial points indicating surgical alteration." He looked directly at Annabelle as he continued. "Theory: Neither of these is a true clone of your child. They are clones of you, Annabelle Leigh, grown from or patterned on your genetic material. Your pattern would be similar, but not identical, to your daughter's. Cosmetic surgery, done with great skill and highly advanced techniques, corrects the differences."

"Then, it's possible the clones of my father are not made from him, either?" Clive interrupted excitedly as he sheathed his saber. "The tissue could have been taken from Neville. He looks enough like Father. And surgery did the rest!"

"Or even from you, Clive Folliot," Chang Guafe reminded him. "But I cannot be certain. I detected no scarring on the clone at the palace, nor will I expect to if I examine the one you fought." He waved a hand at the Amanda look-alikes. "These were made in great haste, obviously, perhaps as experiments toward the final model."

"It's not Amanda," Annabelle said with great relief. She closed her eyes and took a slow breath before she opened them again. "God, I was going quietly out of my mind for fear that they'd gotten hold of her somehow, that she was down here someplace in the Dungeon, too." She brushed a hand over her left forearm, shutting off the Baalbec. The light that surrounded her winked out.

"I know," Clive confided uncertainly in a muted half-whisper. "I keep wondering that same thing about my father." He bit his lip and glanced at his brother, feeling somehow that he'd confessed too much. But Neville's gaze betrayed nothing, no emotion that Clive could latch on to and share. How could he ever think of leaning on his twin's shoulder when it was cold stone? He might have gained a new respect for Neville, but he knew better than ever to look to his twin for that kind of support.

"Let's get out of here," he said.

· CHAPTER TWENTY-ONE ·

The Black Factory

As they pushed deeper into the underground complex, they found each chamber increasingly fantastical. The crystalline tubes now made a chemical-bearing webwork overhead. Fluids of vibrant color, mysterious in nature, raced toward some unknown destination, catching and scattering the light from the illumination panels, casting rainbows on the walls, spilling swaths and pools of blues, greens, reds, and golds on the floors and ceilings.

If the outer chambers were given over to storage, the ones they ventured through now were filled with machinery. The muted hum of powerful engines vibrated the air, and the steady *thrump-thrump* of pumps and compressors created a constant, monotonous rhythm. Automated conveyors carried familiar cartons from the outer chambers to other destinations. Robot arms at the junctures scanned the symbols on the boxes and transferred each to the appropriate belt for the next leg of its journey.

Alerted by a sudden high-pitched whine, Samedi spun around. "Get back, Jack!" he said suddenly, waving everyone back behind the base of what to Clive's limited experience appeared to be a huge electric generator. Once under cover he dared to peek over Samedi's shoulder and around the edge.

Four small tanklike vehicles rolled into sight. At first Clive thought they might be rat-catchers, but they were rather transport carts of some sort. Four slender metal grappling limbs rose up out of each tank body to hold securely in place a huge piece of equipment, the purpose of which Clive couldn't even guess. On smooth treads they trundled through the center of the chamber and out the far exit.

"Why did we hide?" Clive whispered to Samedi when the four vehicles were gone. "Can they sense us?"

"Think so, yeah," their guide answered. "They don't do nothin' 'cept let the rat-catchers know we're around, an' you can usually get away 'fore they show up. Still, who needs it?"

"Right," Clive agreed. "Who needs it?"

Samedi crept into the center of the chamber, looked both ways, then beckoned them out of hiding. They stole quietly out and into the next room.

A wall of flame shot up on the left side. Clive threw up an arm instinctively to protect his face and jumped away from it, slamming into a close wall as the fire quickly faded again.

Annabelle looked at him with concern, then stepped to the left, reached over some kind of equipment console, and rapped her knuckles against a transparent substance that formed the other wall. "Protective glass, I'll bet, hacker," she said. "Indestructible." She turned, leaned on the console, and looked outward. "Some view."

The others gathered closer and looked, too. They found themselves on an observation deck peering down from a dizzying height, but what they gazed upon Clive couldn't guess. The chamber below was vast if it was, indeed, another chamber at all. They couldn't see the other side for the foul smoke and smog that hung over everything, nor could they be sure of seeing the bottom. Hundreds of smokestacks thrust up through a hazy fog and belched flame and thick noxious vapor into the air. Bright, burning geysers spewed upward in flaring outbursts. Apparently, such a geyser stood right below the observation window, as every few moments the same eruption that had so startled Clive occurred again.

"It's like an industrial version of hell, Clive-o," Annabelle said, low-voiced. "There are cities a lot like this in my time, whole metropolises turned into factories."

"That can't be a city down there!" Neville scoffed, but the doubt in his voice betrayed him. "No one could live in that."

Annabelle backed off a bit and began examining the console that ran the length of the window and the room. Luminous dials and instrument monitors gave readings in symbols similar to those on the cartons. "Look," she said, pointing to a series of indicators spaced at intervals along the top of the console. "These needles quiver each time a geyser goes off."

"I saw a factory once," Sidi Bombay remarked softly as he continued to stare through the window.

Finnbogg went to Sidi and put an arm around the Indian's shoulder, and they watched together. "Reminds Finnbogg of nasty place Clivefriend called Dante's Gate, okay?"

Clive felt as if a sledge hammer had dropped on him, then realized it was not his surprise but Shriek's that shivered along the neural web linking them. Apparently, too, everyone but Neville shared it as they turned to stare at her. The arachnoid stood with all four hands pressed against the Plexiglas, and while some of her eyes remained focused on the dirty panorama below, the others focused on Clive.

Finnbogg being correctly speaks, she sent to them, unable to withhold her excitement or the sense of unease that accompanied it. *Could it be level seven the power plant for this Dungeon is? Entire world a great factory is?*

Clive scratched his chin. "I don't know, Shriek, that might be part of it. But that wouldn't explain the visions we saw at the Lake of Lamentations, would it? In fact, since you told me that someone is lifting images from our minds, I've been wondering whether we can trust any of our perceptions. What if they've been recreating those images?"

"Scrod me!" Annabelle exclaimed. "That would explain it. I meant to mention it sooner. Remember, Finnbogg jumped into the lake when he thought he saw his brother, and we had to pull him out. But he wasn't burned or hurt or anything. The water was boiling!"

"And our good friend Philo B. Goode pulled him right through one of those fire spumes when he tried to shake Finnbogg off his ankle," Neville added, his eyes narrowing with suspicion and anger. "Maybe the fire wasn't real, either. Maybe none of this is real."

"*Sim, stupido,*" Tomàs grumbled with bare civility. "Maybe we are home safe in our beds. Maybe this is all a dream." He held two fingers up before his eyes as he glared at Neville. "These are all I got, *senhor*. All I can trust is what I see. When the fire goes up, you stand still if you like. Tomàs is going to jump fast."

"A very practical approach to life, my friend," Sidi Bombay said as he shrugged off Finnbogg's arm and turned away from the window. "If you cannot distinguish between real and false, then react as if everything is real." He folded his hands and touched the tips of his index fingers to his lips as he looked at Tomàs. "Yet that puts you completely at the mercy of our Dungeonmasters. We must, instead, look through the illusion to find what is real, peel away the impossible to determine the possible."

Annabelle tapped a foot and frowned. "Yes, yes, that's very Zen, Sidi," she said impatiently. "All that 'sound of one hand' claptrap is great on a mountaintop back home. But down here, a strange world with strange aliens, it's hard to know just what is and isn't possible."

A soft shuffling in the rearward chamber silenced them. They heard the sound again more clearly—bare feet padding toward them. Clive made a motion with his finger and they scurried out of the observation deck and into the next chamber. It appeared to be much like the other. Huge banks of generators and great machines filled the immense space, and they crowded quickly into the nearest shadow to see what followed them.

Ever so quietly, Clive unsheathed his sword.

"Careful with that, Jack," Samedi whispered in the darkness beside him. "I got nothin' that needs ventilatin'."

"Relax." He heard Annabelle's gentle reassurance as she nudged Samedi. "With that sword we call him ol' Doc Longjohn. He thrills ya when he drills ya."

Samedi twisted around to look at her. Then he tapped Clive on the shoulder and asked with a curious expression, "Where you come from is she considered a defective?"

Clive glanced at Annabelle and glanced away quickly, afraid she might see his grin even in the gloom. He thought it wisest, not to mention the most gentlemanly, to say nothing at all. It didn't matter. When a few moments went by and he hadn't answered, she kicked him anyway.

"Lout," she muttered.

He waved his hand suddenly, cutting off any more talk. Footsteps echoed clearly from the observation deck. They pressed deeper into the shadow and waited.

Four demons wandered through the doorway, defectives whose wings had developed improperly. As they passed, Clive could plainly see the twisted nascent pinions folded against their backs, wings too small or too malformed to lift them. Still, sharp claws and fangs gleamed in the faint light, and the creatures rippled with bestial strength.

"Do you think they were looking for us?" Clive asked Samedi when the defectives had passed on.

"Hey, what am I, the answer man?" Samedi shrugged, and used his palm to carefully redirect Clive's blade, which had drifted a little too close for his comfort. "Seems to me everybody in the Dungeon's after you folks."

"Okay, it's nice to be popular," Finnbogg muttered unexpectedly from his crouched position in the shadow. He rapped his claws impatiently on the floor. "But while everybody looks for Finnbogg, Finnbogg should be looking for Smythefriend." He stood up and squeezed out into the chamber light. "Why do Finnboggfriends hide? Fight! Bite, chomp, and scratch to find Smythefriend! No more hiding!"

Annabelle edged out past Clive and patted Finnbogg sympathetically between the ears. The dwarflike canine frowned but suffered her touch with barely a growl. "Finnbogg," she said gently. "Why do you always call me Annie, not Anniefriend or Annabellefriend?"

Finnbogg shifted uncomfortably as the others came out of hiding. It made an almost comical sight the way his squat, powerfully muscled body slumped as Annabelle towered over him. He looked like a schoolboy about to get a scolding. "Annie is more than friend to Finnbogg," he answered weakly. "Annie is like little littermate. Not just friend, more than friend. Smell nice. Smell better than anything in the Dungeon." He looked up at her with big round fierce eyes.

"She really does smell, doesn't she, Finnbogg, old chap!" Neville leaned against the end of the generator with arms folded and one leg crossed, a big smirk upon his face. He pushed back a lock of blond hair that had fallen over his eyes. "What a piece of work is woman," he continued, grinning, "how noble in reason, how express and odoriferous." His grin widened. "I think that's right, yes. Always loved Shakespeare, you know."

" 'Oh, what may man within him hide, though angel on the outward side!' " Annabelle quoted, turning slowly toward Neville, bracing hands on her hips as she stared him down. " 'That island of England breeds very valiant creatures: their mastiffs are of unmatchable courage.' " She took another step closer to Neville, taunting him as she threw another insult. " 'I had as lief not to be,' " she said, " 'as live to be in awe of such a thing as I myself.' "

Neville stared, his back stiff against the generator, the grin vanishing from his face as his arms slowly slid out of their fold and to his sides.

"Hoist on your own petard, brother!" Clive laughed as he sheathed his saber. "She knows the Bard better than you do." Still grinning, he explained for the benefit of the others. "She called him a phony, a coward, and a vain bastard all in one breath." He made an appreciative bow to Annabelle. "That was poetry, indeed, granddaughter, if a bit harsh. He may bleed from such wounds."

Annabelle put on a big smile and patted Neville's cheek with much sweetness. "Perhaps I was too harsh," she agreed, "but one must teach a child its place, don't you agree?"

"Indeed, I do," Clive answered, bowing again, eyeing his brother with bemusement. Neville had, of course, recovered his composure. His brother always landed on his feet, like all tomcats. Still, it was fun to see him pushed off a limb sometimes. And to his credit, Neville was good-natured enough to accept a certain amount of teasing if it was done with any style at all. "And I think," Clive continued, pointing toward the far side of the chamber where the demons had exited, "that our place lies somewhere through there."

"No more hiding?" Finnbogg grumbled, rubbing the tips of his claws together, causing a wicked little rasp that lent meaning to his question.

Annabelle returned to Finnbogg's side and took his hand in hers. "We hide only when we have to," she assured him. "The important thing is to stay alive long enough to find our Smythefriend, right?"

Finnbogg's only answer was a low, unpleasant growl.

"Come," Samedi said, taking the lead.

The next chamber was dark, but their guide knew the way across. Annabelle moved slightly apart from the others and used the Baalbec to provide a bit of dim light. Clive worried that it made her too easy a target for any unseen attackers, but she had grown too intrigued by the contents of each successive room to turn it off.

This room proved no exception. Curiously, she peered from side to side as her glow touched rows upon rows of tall glass cylinders, all arranged according to some unknown order as if to make yet another mazework of their passage to the other side. Clive glanced upward and noted that the strange chemical-bearing tubes that hung from the ceilings of other chambers had apparently taken some other route.

"Someone comes!" Samedi whispered in a panic, stopping so abruptly that Clive bumped into him as the raggedy creature spun around. "Get back! Get down!"

"Get stuffed!" Finnbogg muttered rudely. With a bound he leaped atop one of the cylinders, caught his balance, and bounded to the next. Quickly, he disappeared from sight.

Clive grabbed Annabelle's arm as she snapped off the Baalbec and dragged her back into a narrow aisle formed by the arrangement of the cylinders where the others were already obediently huddled. "I've been meaning to talk to you about your language," he whispered in her ear. "Finnbogg's picking up some bad habits."

He looked over his shoulder and hastily counted noses. "Hey, where's Shriek?" he asked.

Tomàs pointed upward with the barrel of the beamer weapon. "She's went topside after the *cachorro*."

Annabelle glared. "Finnbogg's not a *dog*, you scrodhead. You mind your manners." She touched Clive's shoulder and pulled his ear close to her mouth. "Maybe we'd better help this time, hacker."

"Just keep your head down, Jack," Samedi advised as he removed his top hat and hugged it to his chest. "It's a busy neighborhood, all right, but they'll go by. We just gotta be careful."

Before Clive had to decide, a brief commotion sounded nearby, and out of it rose Finnbogg's growl and a choked yelp. That was enough for Clive, who jumped to his feet and moved into the passage, forgetting his own safety. He whipped out his saber again as he rounded a corner and glanced down another aisle. Nothing there. He moved faster, aware of his friends behind him now. The passage twisted, and he cursed whoever had stored the cylinders in such an unreasonable fashion. Finnbogg had taken the right course by going over the top.

Then, he stopped short as a sound like a glass lid settling into place rang in the darkness. He pressed his back up against one of the cylinders, drew a deep breath, and concentrated. *Shriek?* he called silently.

Her answer came almost immediately. *Ahead come, Being Clive. Safe it is.*

He looked at the others and indicated with a tilt of his head for them to follow.

"We heard," Annabelle advised him, touching her temple.

Finnbogg and Shriek waited for them just a few meters farther up the passage and down one of the side aisles. Finnbogg sat atop one of the cylinders, swinging his feet to and fro, banging his heels against the side of his perch, and looking pleased with himself. The aisle was too narrow for Annabelle to use the Baalbec, so at Shriek's suggestion Chang Guafe turned up his ruby lenses. The red light gleamed weirdly among the cylinders.

"Herkimer!" Sidi Bombay exclaimed, pressing his palms flat against the cylinder upon which Finnbogg sat.

Inside, looking thoroughly miserable and forlorn, squatted one of the froglike clones. His wide round eyes regarded them in abject fear, and he trembled visibly as he crouched back on his naked haunches and thrust half of his webbed fingers into his mouth. Sidi leaned closer and put his face against the outside to see better. Then, reflexively, he jerked back as a long, thin tongue shot out with amazing speed and power and smacked against the glass, leaving a smear of sticky saliva. Immediately, the Herkimer resumed its pose of pathetic dejection.

Finnbogg jumped down and held out his arm. Even in Chang Guafe's red light they could see the bloody welts on his wrist and bicep. "Nasty tongue," Finnbogg mumbled, "but Finnbogg choked Herkimerthing a little and put it in big jar. Okay?"

Clive nodded and shook Finnbogg's hand. "More than okay, my friend. You did well. Can it get out?"

Finnbogg showed all his teeth as he scowled at the creature in the jar. It cowered on the farthest side, hugged its knees to its mouth, and shivered. "Lid is very heavy and fits tight. Holes on top, though, so Herkimer won't die."

"Holes?" Chang Guafe inquired. The cyborg moved closer to the cylinder and touched it with his palm. He trained his gaze upward.

Holes and valves, Shriek answered. *Tubes inserted through top are, believe I. All cylinders such lids seem to have.*

"Theory," Chang Guafe responded. His lenses focused on Shriek's face, and four of her faceted eyes glittered in the bloody glow. "These are tanks for the breeding and development of clones."

"Let's get out of here," Clive snapped. He felt a sudden deep-seated loathing for the whole idea. Beings who bred other beings artifically and programed them for roles or tasks! It smacked of slavery and slavers, by damn! And he'd seen enough of that in places such as Zanzibar and India. He hated it!

When they finally reached the exit, Clive had worked himself into a quiet moral rage. "Give me that gun," he demanded of Tomàs, and when the little Portuguese handed it over, he grasped it in both hands, turned back into the chamber, and swept a continuous emerald beam back and forth. Cylinders melted or shattered in an orgy of destruction, and the room sparkled as silvery shards and splinters caught and reflected the beam's light. There was no hope that he could destroy them all. There were far too many. But he played the beam as far as it would reach.

An odd high-pitched note trilled suddenly, and the beam ceased. Clive pointed again, fired, and nothing happened. In the unreasoning heat of his anger, he cursed himself and the gun. His finger fluttered pointlessly on the trigger.

"¡Asno!" Tomàs cried in dismay. His hands curled into fists. "You broke my gun!"

Chang Guafe reached out and took the weapon from Clive and studied it as Tomàs spoke, lifting it up to his ruby lenses, passing it several times between his palms, running his fingertips over all its contours and angles. "The tone may have activated a safety feature to prevent an energy overload," he stated matter-of-factly. "Or it may have indicated the exhaustion of the energy source, in which case it is now useless. Without dismantling it I cannot make a determination."

"Keep it," Clive ordered, returning the gun to Tomàs and moving on. "If it's just a safety feature, or some kind of automatic shutoff, it might work again. If not . . ." He hesitated, then shrugged. "Beat somebody with it." He grabbed Samedi's arm. "No more delays," he said, ushering his guide ahead. "I want to know where Smythe is, and fast."

Samedi flapped his wrists. "Oooo, I just love an authority figure," he purred sarcastically, but he picked up the pace as ordered.

• CHAPTER TWENTY-TWO •

The Clone Banks

They moved through another series of chambers, each more complex and puzzling than the last, then down a long spiral ramp to another level of the complex. Crystalline tubes again made an elaborate lacework on the ceiling and along the sides of the walls. Some of the tubes radiated warmth. Others felt cold to the touch.

They followed a wide corridor for a short distance. At Samedi's direction they pressed close against the wall and went as fast as they could. "Rat-catchers," he told them. "They don't like defectives in this place." Halfway down the corridor he led them into yet another chamber.

Annabelle caught her breath. "Computers!" she gasped. Thousands of blue-screen monitors filled the room with a flickering light. Clive's jaw dropped. Never had he seen such machinery. He couldn't even guess the functions of most of the machinery he stared at. Words and numbers and graph lines composed themselves at a speed no human hand could equal. He watched it fascinated and horrified, feeling for the first time like some kind of ignorant, outdated primitive. It wasn't that he couldn't read the language, which he couldn't, or decipher the alien symbols, which, like those on the cartons, he assumed were numbers. He didn't understand how words could write themselves on the small screens, or how colored light could take the place of ink. He didn't understand where the information came from, and it frightened him that Annabelle seemed suddenly so comfortable and excited.

"These are life-function monitors," Chang Guafe announced suddenly as he stopped before one of the many consoles. "Electroencephalographic," he said, indicating a series of screens. "Cardiographic, galvanic response, respiration." He paused and bent closer until his red lenses reflected in the screens. "Unable to deduce the functions of remaining monitors."

Annabelle went to the cyborg's side and bent beside him. "Time," she said a few moments later. She tapped a line of symbols with a fingertip. "See how this last one changes so rapidly? Twenty-two characters before this one changes." She pointed to another line. "And exactly twenty-two of these before this line changes. If we stayed here long enough I think I could figure out the Dungeonmasters' clock."

She peered at the screens a moment longer, then straightened suddenly and covered her mouth with a hand. She turned wide eyes toward Clive. "My God, hackers!" she exclaimed softly. "I know where we are!" She moved to the next console. "Each station has exactly the same set of monitors. Temperature, pulse, EEG, they're all the same." She turned in a slow circle in obvious awe. "This is the nerve center. Like a hospital nurses' station. From here they can monitor a clone's growth and development." She turned back to Clive again. "But there are thousands of stations, Clive-o, and all of them activated. Do you understand? Thousands of clones growing somewhere at this very moment!"

Thousands of versions of his father. Maybe thousands of Nevilles or Chang Guafes or Amandas. It seemed obscene to Clive, and it filled him with anger. Maybe somewhere there was a clone of Clive Folliot, too, a perfect duplicate, but a duplicate whose mind had been twisted and changed, who moved to someone else's commands with little will of its own.

The Dungeonmasters were monsters. It didn't matter to

him how many factions there might be or what their purposes might be in bringing him here. Good guys or bad guys, he didn't care. Both sides used and manipulated these poor creatures. Someone had sent demons to attack him, and someone had sent Samedi to help. But even Samedi had been programed.

Was this the gift of scientific advancement? High-tech slavery? That word kept coming back to him. *Slavery*.

"Maybe we can find out where they are," Annabelle said with sudden excitement. She whirled around and bent over the console. "I know computers, and if I can just figure out these symbols . . ." She touched the keyboard experimentally.

"No!" cried Samedi, crowding forward to snatch her hand away. But he was too late. The screen flickered and went black. "Now you done it, babe. That's burned the dinner for sure." He turned to Clive in a panic. "Everythin' 's cruisin' on auto here, Jack. Now she's fooled around an' messed with things, the rat-catchers are gonna know someone's in here an' come runnin'."

Annabelle looked up guiltily. "But we can't leave here! Clive, this is a treasure mine! Anything we want to know about the Dungeon is probably buried in these computers!"

"The only thing I want to know, *amigos*," Tomàs snapped, edging toward the exit with Samedi, "is the way out."

More than anything Clive wanted time to smash this chamber, to destroy the equipment before him and put an end to this horrible place. His previous action had been a senseless gesture, a childish shattering of mere bottles to vent his outrage. But wrecking these machines might deal a real blow to the Dungeonmasters.

There wasn't time, though. He had to think of his friends and of rescuing Smythe. Without the beamer weapon it might not be so easy to defeat a rat-catcher.

"Out!" he told everyone.

Maneuvering around the consoles, they ran for the far side of the chamber. Before they'd gone halfway, though, they heard the smooth, soft whine of a rat-catcher's tread and looked back to see the metallic torso of one of the monsters as it sped into the room. A second came close after it.

"Run!" Samedi shouted. "They won't fire in here. Too much chance o' damagin' the computers!"

They ran, but before they could reach the exit another rat-catcher entered that way, blocking their escape. It raised its handless arms and pointed at them. Golden energy coruscated behind the focusing lenses as the creature waited for a clear shot.

Shriek screamed with a savage anger and ripped an entire console from the door. Smoking wires and broken circuits spit fiery-colored sparks everywhere as she lifted the mass high overhead and heaved it through the air. It crashed into the rat-catcher, knocking it over on its side, crushing it.

"Look out!" Neville cried, sweeping Tomàs and Sidi Bombay to the floor as a golden beam sizzled through the space where they'd stood instants before and struck another console. An explosion rocked the room, knocking everyone off their feet, filling the air with smoke and a terrible acrid odor. Debris showered down about them as a second explosion and a third followed.

Shriek's console had made a mess out of the rat-catcher, but half-buried in the rubble, one arm lay twisted at a crazy angle, and its force beam smashed a straight line of devastation from one side of the chamber to the other as console after console went up.

Coughing from a lungful of smoke, Clive scrambled to his feet and pulled Annabelle to hers. The two rat-catchers on the far side maneuvered toward them, still unwilling to fire and damage more of the precious monitoring equipment. Shriek pulled Neville, Sidi, and Tomàs up. With her fourth hand she grabbed a broken keyboard from the floor and sailed it toward one of their attackers. It bounced harmlessly off the torso without slowing the rat-catcher in the least.

They ran for the exit, but Clive paused beside the

wreckage of the ruined rat-catcher long enough to deal several hard kicks to the still-firing weapon arm, managing to move it just enough to redirect the beam into another row of consoles. The rapid series of explosions that followed filled him with grim satisfaction.

"The door at the end!" Samedi shouted hurriedly when they were out in the corridor again. "Through there!"

They tore down the hallway at a breakneck pace, mindful of the rat-catchers behind them. It wouldn't take those robot assassins long to plow through the rubble, and in this straight corridor there was no cover. If they got caught in the open, a single beam shot could get them all.

Suddenly a panel in the corridor wall slid back. Yet another rat-catcher whirred into their path. As its arms came up Finnbogg put on a burst of speed, leaped, caromed from one wall to the other, and went feet-first into the deadly machine. It teetered precariously, then fell over. Instantly, Finnbogg sank his teeth into its metal throat, growling with a wild ferocity. He gave a violent shake. Metal ripped, and blue-white electric fire crackled.

Every hair on Finnbogg's body stood straight on end, and his eyes shot wide with surprise. He tried to open his jaws and let go, but he couldn't.

A turbaned streak launched through the air, and a pair of arms circled Finnbogg's shivering body. Sidi Bombay's sheer momentum tore his canine friend free, and they both tumbled head over heels and lay flat on their backs.

A shimmering arc danced around the rat-catcher's throat. It spun its treads but made no effort to right itself, nor did the arms make any movement. Chang Guafe, though, took no chances. Bending low, he drew a deep breath and punched his left fist through the rat-catcher's chest plating. Almost immediately, the treads slowed and stopped.

At the end of the corridor, Samedi slapped his hand against a door, and it slid back in response. They rushed through, breathless, into a dimly lit chamber. Five surprised demons whirled to face them.

"Damn!" Clive cursed aloud, flinging himself at the

nearest of the defectives as it brought its claws up. He smashed his fist against its hard-edged jaw with all his strength, sending the creature reeling into one of its comrades. Too late, from the corner of his eye, he saw talons rake down toward his face. Then, the point of Neville's saber slid over Clive's shoulder. The talons hesitated, quivered, and Clive jumped away. Neville spared him a glance as he withdrew his blade from another demon's throat and looked quickly around for the remaining two.

He needn't have bothered. The pair lay senseless at Chang Guafe's metal-shod feet.

"Through there!" Samedi pointed to a door, which the five demons had apparently been guarding. He pushed his way between Annabelle and Finnbogg, stepped over the fallen defectives, and pressed it. The door opened at his touch, and they dashed inside.

Horace Hamilton Smythe hung stretched upon some kind of cross, held in place by no visible means. He was completely naked. His head had been shaved, and his beard. The veins in his body stood out in blue tension, and though his eyes were closed his face was screwed up in a soundless scream. Thin silver wires sprouted from his flesh, three from his forehead, two from just below his ears, one each from the bends of his elbows and knees. Two were taped to the sides of his groin, two from his belly, and one from just above his heart. His palms, too, sprouted wires.

The wires fed into a huge machine directly behind him and to smaller consoles on either side. Monitor screens reported his brain and heart functions as English-written data flashed in scroll function over another pair of screens.

"My God!" Clive gasped, horrified. "Get him down from there! What have they done to him?"

"His memories are being recorded and personality samples taken," Samedi explained.

Clive, Neville, and Tomàs pulled the taped wires from Smythe's chest and limbs while Shriek stripped away the higher. ones at his head. "I thought they couldn't record memories!" Clive muttered as he worked.

"Not deep memories, no," Samedi answered. All traces of his peculiar accent had once more disappeared. He moved to the console on Smythe's right side. "Not details. But the shallow memories. You know, habits, mannerisms, things you do without thinking about them. Speech patterns and the like. The machine probes those, records them, and feeds them into the central banks."

"To program other Smythe clones," Annabelle said.

"Any clone at all," Samedi corrected. "Once a record is made, his shallow memories can be impressed on any clone, whether it looks like Smythe or not. Or any part of his personality. Mix-and-match to suit."

"¡Auxilio!" Tomàs exclaimed. "Help! We can't get him down!" Try as they might, the little Portuguese, Sidi, and Shriek could not pull Sergeant Smythe from the strange cross.

"Oh, sorry," Samedi said, turning back to the console. "Have to throw this first." He moved a pair of switches, and the cross began to sink to the floor. "There's a specialized kind of presser field holding him to the platform," he added. "Be ready to catch him."

No sooner did the cross touch down than Smythe collapsed forward. Tomàs and Sidi caught him and eased him down to the floor. Smythe's eyelids fluttered briefly, then slowly opened. He looked up at Tomàs and let out a low groan.

"Are you in pain, amigo," the little sailor asked, "or don't you like my pretty face?"

Smythe rubbed his temples and gave another groan as he sat up with stiff effort. "What took you so long?" he asked, glancing around at his friends. Then, he saw Annabelle and shot a look at Shriek. "My God!" he cried suddenly, remembering his unclothed condition. He tried desperately to hide himself with his hands. "Ladies, please!"

"Please what?" Annabelle said sweetly as Clive, realiz-

ing the cause of Smythe's deep blush, quickly moved to
block her view.

"Turn around, for modesty's sake!" Horace Hamilton
Smythe pleaded. "I have no clothes!"

"But Shriek has six eyes arranged all around her head,"
Neville reminded him, grinning, leaning against one of
the consoles. He folded his arms and smirked, obviously
prepared to enjoy Smythe's embarrassment. "It won't matter if she turns around, she'll still see you."

"Well, close them, then!" Smythe snapped, staring at
the arachnoid as his bare cheeks grew redder still.

No lids have I, Shriek answered generally, and Annabelle giggled.

It was Samedi who came to the rescue. "Here, take
this, Jack," the clone said, removing his top hat and offering it to Smythe. "You just don't look right without a full
head of hair."

Smythe turned an even deeper shade of red, and the
color spread up past his eyebrows to darken even the top
of his scalp. He gave Samedi an I'll-get-you-for-this look,
but he snatched the hat and used it to cover his groin.

"Guess you better have this, too," Samedi continued,
his widening grin showing all his stained teeth. He slipped
out of his raggedy jacket, shook some of the dust out of it,
and tossed it to Smythe.

"My thanks!" Smythe uttered through clenched teeth as
he tied the sleeves around his waist and tried to adjust the
garment for the maximum amount of coverage. And it
wasn't much, Clive considered. Still, it would have to do.
They couldn't afford to linger.

Clive went to his former batman, put an arm around his
shoulders, and hugged him with relief. "You gave us a bit
of a scare, Horace, wandering off like that."

"Sorry, sah," Smythe answered sheepishly. "Only meant
to make a stroll of it, not a bloody holiday."

"Some holiday, eh?" Clive answered. He turned to
Samedi. "You said you could lead us to the Gateway. Is it
close?"

"Real close, Jack," Samedi answered as he hugged himself and rubbed his arms briskly. His thin translucent skin had a bluish cast in the dim light, and his ribs showed through unnaturally. Without his jacket he looked even more like a walking corpse, like the true Baron Samedi.

"Then let's go. But first," Clive added, turning to his friends, especially to Shriek and Finnbogg and Chang Guafe, "wreck this room."

It was pure, bitter joy for Clive to watch three such powerful beings go to work. And they so enjoyed their labor, too. In moments, they reduced the room to smoke and destruction.

In the outer room, two of the demons had regained consciousness and slipped away. They hadn't gotten far, however. Clive stepped out into the corridor in time to see the two rat-catchers he had eluded in the computer room. The mechanical killers moved back toward that room now, but behind them, by means of short retractable tentacles that grasped the demons' ankles, they dragged the ugly pair. A wide bloody smear that trailed along the floor proved the potential efficiency of the robots. Apparently, though, they were satisfied with any kill.

Clive ducked back until the monsters moved out of sight. Then he led the way into the hall. "Which way?" he asked Samedi, and the clone pointed and walked halfway up the corridor.

"Here," Samedi answered.

But Clive didn't see a door or any opening at all. He gave his guide a suspicious look and touched the wall where Samedi indicated. A section rotated outward a fraction.

"Remember my storage closet?" Samedi reminded him. "You couldn't see that door, either. The Dungeonmasters don't want defectives wanderin' around just anywhere, you know. So they hide some entrances. Most of us poor folks know about 'em anyhow." He pushed, and the door opened the rest of the way, wide enough to admit them two at a time. They crept inside.

Clive knew at once where they were. The vast chamber was dark, but thousands upon thousands of crystal tanks radiated a pale blue glow, and along the ceiling and descending into each vessel, crystalline pipes and tubes shimmered with vibrant chemical colors.

"It's beautiful!" Annabelle whispered in awe.

Clive shook his head. "It's monstrous," he answered.

They walked slowly, peering into the tanks at the lifeforms within. Some were mere embryos floating serenely in amniotic ambivalence. Yet even in that simple stage Clive could determine which were human or humanoid and which were the cloned offshoots of more alien species. Some of the tanks contained infant children. On the tops of these machines sat small, boxlike machines. Wires from these boxes passed down through the glass lids and into the beings' bodies.

At such an early age, Clive realized, the programing began. It made him sick.

At one of the tanks he passed closest to, his heart skipped a beat, and he jumped back into Annabelle. "What's wrong?" she asked, concerned, and he pointed.

An apelike creature floated within the tank, but its eyes were open, and it watched them. The eyes were disconcerting, indeed. The being glared at them sullenly with a palpable hatred that sent a shiver up Clive's spine. It didn't move, it didn't threaten or gesture. Its face remained utterly impassive. But those eyes!

"A defective," Samedi commented quietly.

"How can you tell?" asked Sidi Bombay.

Samedi looked at him impassively, then looked back at the creature in the tank. Flat-voiced, he answered, "You can tell, Jack."

Neville came to Clive's side as the company moved on. "I feel as though I'm walking through a zoo," he whispered as he glanced uneasily from side to side. Neville's hand never left the hilt of his saber now, and his tension was almost tangible.

"Not a zoo," Clive responded, barely able to find his

voice. He realized how long it had been since he'd had a drink of water. "A garden," he continued. "A garden." He stopped before a tank. It contained a perfect young boy of, perhaps, seventeen whose perfect British features were crowned with an unruly mop of blond hair. Clive closed his eyes and drew a deep breath and let it slowly out. He looked around. So many tanks as far as he could see. "A garden," he repeated once more, "and these are just waiting for harvest." He swallowed. "It's obscene."

He caught Annabelle's hand and gripped it tightly. Her flesh was warm, real, and a part of him. His blood coursed in her veins, his history beat in her heart and soul.

She glanced up and gave him a tenuous, uncertain little smile and continued to walk along. Annabelle was real, his child, his offspring, at least. He loved her, his great-great-granddaughter. He couldn't help it. He felt that bond and knew how strong it was, how unbreakable.

But that thing in the tank with its boyish body and blond hair. A clone, unarguably, but of his father or Neville? Or was it Clive Folliot? What if it was his? What did that make it? Son? Nephew? Cousin? How did a proper Englishman define such a relationship? What was his obligation to it? Was there an obligation? Was it even true life, or just a blob of cells with a familiar form, without a mind of its own until some machine gave it one?

He felt sick. He felt angry.

"I knew a pub like this once, sah," Smythe said suddenly, coming up behind him. "In Liverpool it was. You wouldn't believe the odd sorts floating around there, either, soaking up a little nutrient solution, if you get my meaning."

· CHAPTER TWENTY-THREE ·

Through the Looking Gate

"Audio sensors recording a disturbance," Chang Guafe reported suddenly, "approximately twenty meters to the left."

The company had gradually drifted into a tighter grouping as they passed among the clone tanks. Their faces glowed with the strange soft colors given off by the liquid coruscations of the chemicals, lending each of them a look as alien as any of the creatures in the vats. At Chang Guafe's warning they stopped and listened.

"Afraid I don't hear anything, old chap," Neville said, but he'd lowered his voice to a whisper.

Samedi tugged insistently at Clive's sleeve. "It don't matter, Jack," he said, shooting a furtive glance in the direction of the danger. "Our way's straight ahead. Nothin' over there for us."

Clive pushed Samedi's hand away gently, but firmly. He'd finally begun to note how his guide's accent thickened when he grew nervous, and there was no mistaking the look of fear in Samedi's gaze. Besides, Chang Guafe wouldn't have alerted them without good reason.

"What kind of disturbance, Chang?" Clive asked.

The cyborg hesitated as if listening again. "Weapons fire, shouting in many voices, pain cries, background sounds of destruction." He paused once more. "Analysis: violent confrontation on a considerable scale."

"If you don't mind my saying so, sah," Sergeant Smythe whispered at Clive's side, "if there's trouble that close, it wouldn't be wise to have it at our backs."

"But if it's that close, *amigo*," Tomàs interrupted, "why don't the rest of us hear it?"

"Apologies, human," the cyborg said to Tomàs. "My receptors are at maximum sensitivity. You are correct to point out the discrepancy. Nevertheless, the distance to the disturbance is as I stated." He looked from Tomàs to Clive. "It is an anomaly."

Clive sighed. All he wanted was to find the gate, but Smythe was right. He couldn't have trouble at his back without knowing its nature. "Let's check it out," he decided. "But keep down and out of sight. If they don't know we're around, let's keep it that way."

Chang Guafe led them through a maze of tanks using his sensors to choose the way. Clive kept his eyes on his cyborg friend and away from the tanks, themselves, having grown sickened by what they contained.

No one made a sound, not just to aid Chang Guafe, but for fear of being discovered by an unknown enemy. When they'd gone perhaps ten meters, Clive thought he detected a bare hint of sound from just ahead. Then came a solid *whomp* that vibrated the deck under their feet.

The company froze and looked at each other. Then, at Clive's direction they moved ahead. Everyone heard the sounds now, however faintly.

The southern wall of the immense clone chamber was made of clear thick Plexiglas that allowed a view of another chamber far below. Though the sound that reached them was greatly muffled, they could hear, as well as see, what Chang Guafe had warned them about as they pressed up against it.

"My God!" Annabelle murmured, leaning her forehead wearily on the glass as she stared outward.

No one else said anything.

There were light panels to see by on the lower walls, but no exits. Apparently, all doors had been sealed. Per-

haps a thousand defectives ran in helpless terror from the
ten rat-catchers that ringed the room. Beams of energy
ripped into flesh. Bodies literally exploded at the touch of
the golden light. There was no shelter, nothing to hide
under or behind except a wreckage of open cartons in the
very center of the chamber.

Raw organic compound, Clive recalled bitterly, and
with a sudden horrible insight, he turned to Samedi.
"What do they do with the bodies?"

"Recycle 'em, Jack," came the awful answer. "Waste
not, want not."

"The goop in the cartons?" Annabelle asked with a sick
look.

Samedi nodded. "Some of 'em."

Before Clive could ask another question a score of defectives turned and attacked the nearest rat-catcher. Some
grabbed its arms and tried to hold on. Someone climbed
onto its back and slammed fists against its metal head.
Hands locked on to its tread and sides. With a heave they
all lifted at once, and the machine teetered over on its
side with a crash, and a cry went up.

But the victory was short-lived, as their action attracted
the attention of the other rat-catchers. For an instant that
portion of the room became a small bright sun as all beams
trained on the group.

Annabelle spun away and covered her eyes.

Tomàs slowly drummed his fist against the glass. "I hate
this place," he muttered like a man balancing on the edge
of his sanity. "I hate this place."

Clive turned to Samedi again. The clone had slunk back
from the glass to lean heavily against the nearest tank.
Within it a tall, delicate creature with pointed ears floated
apparently in blissful sleep. But its hands seemed almost
to reach for Samedi's neck.

"What's going on down there!" Clive insisted, no longer
bothering to whisper.

Neville turned around, too. "It looks like a cattle roundup
I saw when I was Stateside."

"That's it, Jack," Samedi answered in a quavering voice. "That's jus' exactly what it is. You see, we're defectives, but some of us can think, an' all of us can hide. But they got to be sure of gettin' us so's we don' multiply too fast. So they put somethin' in the food cartons. The more you eat it, the more you want it until you got to have it an' you hurt real bad till you get it."

"Drugs?" Annabelle said incredulously.

Samedi nodded again. "They put a big supply of it in a big room like that one. Never the same room twice. An' everybody knows it's a trap, but you got to have the stuff. An' the first day the rat-catchers don't come, an' the second day they don't come, an' maybe they don't come for a bunch o' days, an' you think it's real safe, an' lots o' us finally come to get the food. O' course the rat-catchers show up 'cause they been waitin' the whole time jus' to get a whole lot of us at once."

Of a sudden, tears welled up in Samedi's eyes and streamed down his cheeks. He sank down to the floor with his back to the tank and cried. Then, the tears turned to soft sad laughter. He reached up and caught one tear on a fingertip and stared at it. "I'm free," he said without a trace of an accent. "I'm free of my programing. Just as they can't steal your deep memories, they can't give us the deeper emotions like love or grief or loyalty or compassion." He wiped away another tear and held it up. It sparkled in the pale blue luminescence from the tank behind him. "We have to find those on our own, and we can only do it when the programing no longer drives us." He looked up, and a hint of a smile flickered over his mouth. "I can cry now when I couldn't before."

He sat there for a moment more, his hands folded in his lap. At last he got up. "There's nothing you can do for those below, Clive Folliot, or for me, either. You see, I've eaten, too. But maybe you can find the Dungeonmasters, and when you do, think of us. Let's get you to the gate." He beckoned to the little Portuguese. "Come, Tomàs. I hate this place as much as you. Walk beside me." He put his arm around Tomàs's shoulder as he led the way.

"But Clive!" Annabelle cried as the company started to move away. "We can't leave them down there. It's a slaughter! We have to do something!"

"There's nothing we can do," Clive answered quietly. "Didn't you hear Samedi? It's the way of the world around here."

"If you want to stop it," said Sidi Bombay, pulling her gently from the glass wall, compelling her with his voice to look at him and away from the carnage below, "then you must stop the Dungeonmasters."

She looked at Sidi, at Clive, at them all. "I will," she said with a chilling fierceness. "Damn their souls, I will."

"We will," Clive amended, taking her hand in his, and with that contact he opened the neural link between them and let her glimpse just a portion of the pride he felt in her and the love he felt for her. In return, he tasted the flavor of her anger, which she had not yet mastered.

He backed out of Annabelle's mind as the company followed Samedi once more among the tanks. *Shriek*, Clive called silently, and the arachnoid's thoughts rushed open to embrace him.

Yes, Being Clive?

When things are calmer, he told her, *we must bring Neville into the web.*

Abruptly, Samedi stopped again. A huge metal cylinder stood on his right, and he looked at it thoughtfully. Familiar crystalline tubes rose out of its top and joined the lacework of pipes that supplied the chemical solutions that filled the clone tanks. There were symbols in black on its side, but if Samedi could read them, he said nothing.

He turned to Chang Guafe. "I have seen your strength," he said curiously. "Do you think you can punch through this?"

The cyborg stepped closer to the cylinder and touched it with his palm. A faint, high-pitched beep sounded, and there was a dim flicker of green light under his fingers.

Chang Guafe lowered his hand. "It is one-half centimeter in thickness," he reported. "I can breach it."

Samedi stepped back and made an inviting flourish with one hand. "Then please do so," he said.

But Clive interrupted. "Samedi, what is this?"

Samedi smiled, but Clive didn't like the look at all. There was something in the clone's eyes.

"I have served you well," Samedi said with the barest hint of a threat in his voice. "And if I, personally, have not, then my genetic material has. Three of me have died for you, Clive Folliot. If you cannot trust me now, then at least humor me in this. It means no harm to you."

Chang Guafe shrugged as he looked to Clive. "It is tensile metal of no great strength. I can breach it without damage to myself."

Clive frowned as he nodded. Everyone but the cyborg stepped back a pace. Chang's hand curled into a fist. With a single, sharp thrust he punctured the cylinder. A thin liquid spewed out around his arm, and when he withdrew it, a steady flow followed and spread quickly upon the floor.

"Yuck, nasty wet stuff!" Finnbogg yelped, leaping aside to avoid the flow. "Not okay!"

Samedi shrugged and turned to lead them away. "It's just a nutrient solution," he said over his shoulder.

"You mean, the clones in the tanks will starve without it?" Annabelle questioned.

Samedi didn't slow down to answer. "That's very unlikely. The monitors will record the damage and send repair machines. It will—how would you say it?—gum up the works. Possibly, they will even forget about the defectives below and dispatch the rat-catchers after us."

"Now there's a pleasant thought," Neville sneered.

"We'll be safely gone by the time they get here. You, through your gate, and me . . ." He shrugged. "By the way, Chang Guafe, here's another." He stopped before a cylinder identical to the first. "Would you mind?"

Four more times Chang Guafe punctured nutrient tanks

at Samedi's insistence. The floor became slick as the fluid seeped everywhere. A mildly unpleasant odor filled the air. Finnbogg held his nose and tried unsuccessfully to tiptoe from one dry spot to the next. "Yuck," he repeated with great distaste.

"It's not that bad," Annabelle chided, scratching him between the ears, but the look on her face said otherwise.

Finnbogg rolled big brown eyes up at her. "Annie have dead human nose," he told her defensively. "Finnbogg have very sensitive nose. All Finnboggs have sensitive noses." He pinched his nostrils again and said with finality, "Yuck."

Samedi stopped again before a panel of doors. They had reached the west wall. "This is the clone bank nerve center through these doors," he announced. "Lots of computers and machinery, but the gate to the next level is in here somewhere, too." He touched the panel with his palm. Nothing happened.

"It's locked!" he said with surprise.

"That's no problem," Clive answered resolutely. He was eager to leave this place, and no flimsy lock was going to prevent that. "Chang? Shriek?"

The door might as well have been made of tissue. The two aliens ripped it away with barely a pause, and the company rushed inside.

There were no computers, no machinery. In fact, the chamber was rather small and furnished like a Victorian drawing room with thick carpets and stuffed chairs, pictures that hung on the walls, and a fireplace with a crackling warm fire. A clock with a kindly old grandfather's face ticked loudly upon the mantel, and behind it, hung upon the chimney, was a large mirror, which reflected the entire room.

Before the fireplace two figures hunched over a table, a game of chess between them, and just behind them stood two more figures in heavy cloaks. The cloaked pair looked up at the same time and saw Clive.

"Drat and bother!" snapped the dark-haired female.

"Oh, shit!" said her brother.

"The Ransome twins!" Sergeant Smythe shouted, but before anyone could make a move, the pair shed their cloaks and with an astonishing leap, disappeared through the mirror.

Tomàs started forward. *"Pressa!* That must be the gate!"

But Clive caught his arm. "Wait," he said, approaching the two figures who had not yet looked up from their chess game. They seemed absorbed in their moves. One lifted a piece and carefully set it down on another square. The other had already prepared his counter and carried it through. Only then did they bother to acknowledge the intruders. Slowly, they looked up from the game.

Clive stopped as he stared at Philo B. Goode, once again in human form, and at his father, the Baron Tewkesbury.

"So, you've made it this far," Goode said appraisingly.

Annabelle tugged on Clive's arm. "Clones," she whispered.

"Are we, indeed?" Goode said with some amusement as he folded his arms over his barrel chest, grinning to his fellow player. The baron returned his gaze soberly. "So you can tell the real from the false now, can you? The illusion from the true? Have you learned that much?"

"Yes!" Annabelle snapped. "You're a clone, Philo Goode. You're both clones! And this room, it's fake, too, an illusion. You can take images from our minds. Shriek found that out. And this one's from mine. I've read *Through the Looking Glass.* The only thing missing are the kittens!"

Meow! Murffff!

They all looked toward the sound. Curled up on one of the overstuffed chairs sat a large white mother cat patiently cleaning the face of a smaller white kitten. At the foot of the chair a black kitten played mischievously with a ball of blue worsted yarn.

"You have learned," Philo B. Goode admitted grudgingly, "but you haven't learned enough."

Neville stepped forward, whipping out his sword in a

smooth threatening motion. "Then maybe we can carve some answers out of you, you bloody cob!"

"You, on the other hand, Major, haven't learned much at all." Goode reached into the pocket of his waistcoat and withdrew a stasis box like Sidi Bombay's. He pointed it at Neville and pressed the stud. Neville Folliot froze in midstep. "But then, that's why we gave up on you." He looked at Clive and grinned that hateful grin again. "Please don't reach for any of your weapons. You see, my friends, the game is far from over." He stared past them suddenly and his grin widened. "Aha. They're coming to take you away."

Clive spun about to see what Goode meant. Outside in the clone chamber three rat-catchers sped toward them, their arms leveled and glowing with a building golden fire. Then suddenly their treads began to spin uselessly as they encountered the slick fluid upon the floor.

"You're right, sir," Samedi said with mock civility as he leaned casually in the ruined doorway. "The game is not yet over." He opened a small box he held in his palm.

"Pickpocket!" Tomàs cried, patting himself. "He's got my matches!"

Samedi drew one of the flint-tips along the side of the box. A tiny flame flared, and a little puff of smoke purled upward about his face. He backed a step out into the clone chamber, and there was something in his eyes again that made Clive tremble.

"When at last you face the Dungeonmasters, Clive Folliot," Samedi said gravely, "then remember us. Remember me." He gazed again toward Philo B. Goode and hatred filled his dark, sunken eyes. "Checkmate," he said.

The match fell to the floor beside Samedi's feet. At once, the slick liquid caught the flame. With a rushing roar the outer chamber became an inferno. Samedi never even screamed as the fire rushed over him. He stood for a moment like a bright pillar, then just behind him, the nearest clone tank exploded in a ball of white-hot fury that knocked everyone to the floor.

Drops of burning liquid rained through the doorway. Smythe gave a shout as it touched his bare back. Frantically he rolled and beat himself. Finnbogg, too, gave a startled cry as a patch of hair on his rump began to smolder. Annabelle got to her feet, caught him, ripped off her blouse, and began to beat his backside with it.

More and more explosions rocked the outer chamber as tank after tank exploded. The heat raged through the doorway. The carpet began to burn where the liquid had touched it.

"I don't think that was a nutrient solution," Chang Guafe said.

"Are you trying to develop a sense of humor, cyborg?" Neville asked as he tried to pull Shriek to her feet.

"I have been analyzing the necessary elements," Chang Guafe answered dryly.

"Analyze them later," Clive urgently suggested. "Our friends have opted for the better part of valor. I think we should do the same."

It was true. In the confusion Philo B. Goode and the baron had made their escape, presumably through the mirror. Even the kittens were gone, if they had ever actually been there. As quickly as he could, Clive steered everyone toward the fireplace.

Then, as he dragged a chair from the table and set it before the mantel to use as a stepping stool to the mirror, he happened to glance at the chess game, and his heart skipped a beat. The fire and the danger vanished from his mind. He went cold inside.

It was not a normal chess set at all. Mingled among the white pieces he found small models of himself and all his friends. But among the red pieces there was a miniature of Sidi Bombay and one of Chang Guafe.

Suddenly, he remembered another chess set on an upper level—Green's set. That one had featured pieces modeled after Horace and Sidi. And—he remembered distinctly— his mother.

What did it mean? Could that set have any connection with this one?

The others, noting his strange reaction, bent closer beside him. With a cry of rage, he swept his arm across the board, sending the pieces flying in all directions. Had he acted fast enough? Had any of them seen? He whirled away from the table, breathing hard.

Without meaning to, he stared at Sidi Bombay, then at Chang Guafe.

Sidi noticed. "What is it, Englishman?" the Indian asked curiously.

Clive bit his lip. Then, the floor under his feet gave a strange menacing shudder. There were thousands of those clone tanks, he remembered, and vast stores of the chemicals that supplied them.

"Nothing!" Clive shouted over the growing chaos. He refused to believe the thought that crossed his mind. Maybe he couldn't tell real from false, but he knew his friends. He didn't give a damn about some pieces on a chess board. It was just another trick of Goode's meant to confuse him. Well, he wouldn't let it. *He knew his friends!*

"Through the gate!" he ordered, pulling himself together. "Let's get out of here!"

"Through the looking glass, you mean," Annabelle grumbled as she climbed up on the chair. "Come on, Finnbogg, let's go together."

Finnbogg climbed up on the chair beside her, and they each placed one foot on the mantel.

"That's a good idea," Clive agreed. "Everyone take a partner. That way, if we're separated, we'll at least have someone we can trust on the other side." He turned to his former batman and put a hand on his shoulder. "Would you go with Annabelle and Finnbogg? Keep an eye on them for me?"

"Of course, sah," Smythe agreed. "Though I'm sure we'll all be together on the other side."

"That sounds a little too much like a hymn, Sergeant," Neville said disdainfully. "Are you trying to be funny?"

Smythe sighed like a patient father with a petulant son. "The only thing I'm trying to do, sah, is pick up this cloak and cover my nakedness with it. If you'll kindly move your big foot?" Before Neville could move, he bent down and snatched a cloak one of the Ransome twins had dropped and jerked it out from under Neville's heel, nearly toppling Neville. Ignoring Neville's complaint, he fastened the cloak around his neck and hugged the folds of the garment around himself. "That's a little better," he said with a small, embarrassed grin.

Then, he climbed up on the chair and mantel with Annabelle and Finnbogg. Each with a hand out before them, the three leaned toward the glass and tumbled through.

Tomàs and Sidi Bombay went next, exchanging looks, then pushing off. Neville took one of Shriek's hands and stepped up on the chair. Gallantly, he tried to make room for the seven-foot-tall arachnoid. "She won't need it," Clive told his brother, and he felt Shriek's mirth over the neural web. She gave a jump and pulled a surprised Neville through.

"We go together, Clive Folliot," Chang Guafe said, stepping to the chair.

Clive eyed the cyborg, then took his hand. "That's right, Chang. There's nobody I'd rather have at my right side than you." *I don't give a damn about a chess board,* he added silently.

They climbed onto the chair and onto the mantel. The fire was halfway into the room now, the carpet nearest the door fiercely ablaze. Explosions continued to rock the complex, and smoke roiled everywhere.

"I'll remember, Samedi," he promised in a whisper. "I swear I will."

"We will," Chang Guafe corrected.

Clive looked up into the cyborg's face. Despite all the metal he found nothing frightening there. The ruby lenses were still windows to a soul, a soul he knew and trusted.

"You lose, this time, Philo B. Goode," he said aloud, "and every time."

"Is this an appropriate occasion for humor?" Chang Guafe inquired.

Clive rubbed a hand across his forehead to stop the sweat that threatened to run into his eyes. "Laughter is medicine for men and cyborgs," he admitted.

Chang's lenses glowed subtly brighter. "Then, 'There once was a cyborg named May, whose brother was certainly gay . . . ,' "

"Oh, no!" Clive groaned, and before Chang Guafe could utter another syllable, he pulled them into the mirror.

It was a long, long, long way down.

The following drawings are from Major Clive Folliot's private sketchbook, which was mysteriously left on the doorstep of *The London Illustrated Recorder and Dispatch*, the newspaper that provided financing for his expedition. There was no explanation accompanying the parcel, save for an enigmatic inscription in the hand of Major Folliot himself.

Our party united, we have traveled far from the terrifying chamber of the Lords of Thunder and tumbled onto yet another level of this blasted Dungeon! This level is most intriguing, filled with clones of ourselves and creatures we have encountered.

Now that I have found the real Neville, our major goal is a return to home and hearth. But before we can do that, there are two responsibilities yet to be discharged—finding Finnbogg's littermates, and vengeance against the masters of this hellish place!

abandon hope all who enter here

DANTE'S GATE,
THROUGH WHICH WE PASSED TO EXPLORE
ANOTHER LEVEL OF THIS INFERNAL DUNGEON

ONE OF THE WINGED DEMONS — THAT
SERVED OUR OLD ENEMY, PHILO GOUDE.

R MYSTERIOUS GUIDE
OUGH THIS HELL,
ARON SAMEDI.

THE VESSEL THAT CARRIED US
ACROSS THE BUBBLING WATERS.
NOTE OUR GUIDE HAS DOUBLED.

THE BRIDGE ACROSS THE CHASM;
THE ROPES ARE THREADBARE AND THE
BOARDS RIDDLED WITH WORMHOLES.

THE PALACE OF
THE MORNING STAR.

BARON TEWKESBURY, THE IMPOSTER!
LORD OF THE PALACE OF THE
MORNING STAR AND MY GREATEST BETRAYER

INSIDE THE PALACE, WE WERE SERVED BY THE FROG-CLONES, ALL NAMED HERKIMER.

THIS METAL MONSTER CALLED A RATCATCHER SHOOTS LETHAL RAYS AND CHASED US THROUGH THE CORRIDORS.

HERE, WE ARE BESIEGED BY CLONES OF EVERY CREATURE WE HAVE YET ENCOUNTERED. I BATTLED A CLONE OF THE MONSTER OF THE BRIDGE OF Q'OORNA...

...AND CHANE FIGHTS OWN CLONE.

IF THIS IS THE POWER PLANT FOR
THE DUNGEON, THEN WHAT MUST
THE DUNGEON BE?

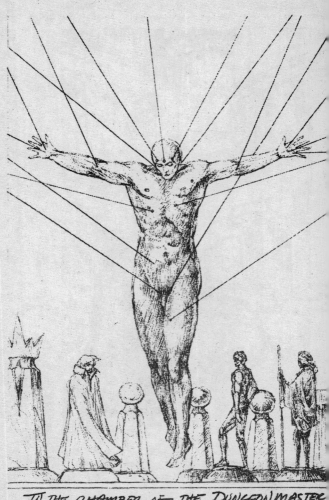

IN THE CHAMBER OF THE DUNGEON MASTER
SGT. SMYTHE'S MEMORY IS DRAINED AND RECORD

AND IN A VICTORIAN-STYLED ROOM, A CHESS GAM
WAS PLAYED WITH REPLICAS OF OURSELVES.

THE HALL WHERE THE CLONES ARE
PREPARED FOR THEIR UNNATURAL BIRTH.

EAPING THROUGH THE
IRROR IN PURSUIT
OUR CAPTORS.